D0789263

THE BRITANNIA OBSESSION

Richardson & Steirman
New York
1986

ISBN: 0-931933-01-3
Library of Congress Catalog Number: 86-061796

The Britannia Obsession
is published by
Richardson & Steirman
246 Fifth Avenue
New York, NY 10001

To Pat, Ivan, Cathy and those friends in London, Washington, and New York, for their support, input, and indulgence

ob-ses-sion: A compulsive idea or emotion associated with the subconscious and exerting a persistent influence upon behavior

Prologue

You start with one to reach a hundred, as the saying goes. So I would like the glory of being the first to start. It is not with words or paper that we shall change existing conditions. The last advice I have for true anarchists is to arm themselves according to my example with a good revolver, a good dagger and a box of matches.

Louis Chaves (French assassin)
1884

East Belfast, Northern Ireland, November, 1969.

The dawn arrived almost as an afterthought. A reluctant, swirling rainmist, drifting in silence from the West Irish Sea.

It was chilling, the man thought as he climbed the rotting stairs to the clapboard shack's littered second floor. Chilling with the air still laced with scents of smoldering rubber, diesel and the ever-present riot control gases deployed by the occupying British troops.

He smiled. To him, the smells were good.

Reaching the loft, he looked down at the sleeping child, allowing himself no particular sense of remorse.

Suddenly, outside, he heard the distinctive pulsing exhaust of an armored British lorry on patrol. He cursed under his breath. Had someone informed? Fingered him for arrest by the cowardly Irish Republican Army who questioned Provisional tactics as too extreme? Too violent? Too counterproductive? It would not have been the first occasion.

Moving quietly, he slid to the loft's single window and peered outside. At the corner to his left, the lorry sat idling, its soldiers training their weapons down North Queen Street, searching for violators of the curfew which remained in effect for another two hours. No, he had not been discovered. The vehicle lurched away, continuing its patrol up Old Crumin Road.

"Bastards," he hissed, stepping back from the window and turning to the still-sleeping child. "The day will come."

Walking over to the loft's sole bed, Peder Crandon looked down upon his son and shook his head disgustedly.

He was anything but a strong boy, he realized. At seven years of age, the child appeared almost sickly, with pasty porcelain skin and long, feminine-looking hair and limbs. His hands and feet were tiny. The child had obviously inherited his mother's long aristocratic nose and thin, bloodless lips.

Peder Crandon sighed heavily. The runtchild disappointed him. Had he supplied nothing to the boy's genetic bank? Surely not mindset, for the child continually cowered before the other Provo children. It was embarrassing. He was too weak to be nurtured, too spineless to be claimed. Better him raised by others, for he would never be of any value to the cause.

Reaching down, the man touched his son's cheek and watched the boy stir. For an instant, the eyelids fluttered and he caught a brief flash of color. No, he thought. As much as he wanted to, he could never deny the child was his. The eyes were the evidence. A pale, almost powdery blue, the irises were mirror images of his own. He cursed God. A cruel joke? A biological oversight? He dismissed the thought. In either case, it would soon make little difference.

"Time to get up," he whispered, gently shaking a frail arm.

Quite suddenly, the boy's eyes snapped opened. Wide with dilated pupils, they resembled some frightened animal's, darting nervously around the loft. "Father?" he asked, his voice trembling. "What is it? Why have *you* come?"

Crandon forced an indulgent smile. "You must be strong, my little one."

Craning his slender neck around, the child looked toward the window, then the stairs. "Where's mother?" he asked. "Why isn't mother here?"

With nothing more than tolerance, Peder Crandon reached over and gathered the child in his arms. "Your mother is dead," he told him, his voice carrying no more emotion than if he had been ordering a basket of kippers. "She was murdered by the British."

For a moment, the child did nothing, and this surprised his father. But then, through the thin flannel nightshirt, Peder Crandon felt the boy's bony rib cage begin to shiver, then heave as the sobs began.

For a brief instant, the man thought to say something to comfort the child, but he just as quickly decided against it. Better to let the shock wear itself off. To let the knowledge sink in. To treat the matter in a manly way.

For the next few minutes, they sat in silence. A father carefully ignoring the significance of the moment, and a son desparately needing solace, but finding none. The tears dried themselves and the boy stared up into his father's face.

"But what will happen to us?" he asked.

"You will be taken care of," the man answered, averting his eyes. "You will live with the vicar's family in Shaw's Bridge."

"Not with you?"

Peder Crandon shook his head. "It's not safe. The British want me dead also, but you will be fine. The vicar is a good man and will care for you as one of his own. It has already been arranged."

"But no, father . . . I can't . . . don't you see? I must live with you. Together we can punish the British."

The man shook his head. *Pathetic child,* he thought, rising and stepping back from the bed. "It's impossible," he lied. "This was the way your mother wanted it. Now gather your things. You must bury her this afternoon."

Walking to the top of the stairs, the man took one last look at his son. "The vicar's wife will come for you when the curfew lifts. After the funeral, you will go with her and do exactly as they say. Understand?"

The child nodded glumly. "But where will you be?"

"Close by."

"When will I see you again?"

Peder Crandon shrugged his shoulders. "I cannot tell you that. But do not worry; you will hear of me. I will avenge your mother's death, and each time a Brit dies, my thoughts will be of you. Never forget that, nor the memory of your mother's murder."

His pale eyes again filling with tears, the child swallowed and watched his father disappear down the stairs. "I will never forget," he whispered, his voice small in the cold, littered loft. "I love you, father."

But the man did not hear his son's words. He had already left the rotting house and was well on his way up Old Crumin Road.

For young Peder Crandon, the obsession had begun.

Manila, The Philippines, October, 1984.

In the gray light of dawn, Samuel Taylor shifted between the sticky hotel sheets and sighed. It would be a humid, oppressive morning. Another thick choking of polluted fog coating the city like some ugly cloak that forced the impression of quiet.

But it was an illusion. There was no quiet in Manila. By noon, the peace would again be shattered, ruptured by the Communist-led riots nipping doggedly at outrages committed by the Marcos government. Those murders, embezzlements, and political outrages were so central to the presidential power base, and, quite simultaneously, so naively endorsed by Taylor's superiors in Washington.

For them, Manila was but the latest round of dominoes, another addendum to yet another national security agenda. But for Taylor the assignment had been eleven months of compromise: three hundred and seven days of advising NISA, Marcos' secret police, on the finer points of interrogation, counterinsurgency networking, and, as in all the black arts, lying. It was a timewarp of forty-five weeks wherein he had moved to Manila, married a beautiful NISA translator, and then stood at the fringes of the funeral service while she was buried by a family who never had accepted him.

As a professional, a shattered Taylor had forced himself to endure after the funeral. But his reasoning was personal . . . he was simply trying to forget her murder, and, therein, his guilt.

But no, he corrected himself. Her death was political, so it was not murder. Assassination was the appropriate term. Yes, he thought, her death had been a political statement: an exercise of power to indicate nothing more than a Communist ability to penetrate NISA's inner circle and pluck an innocent life at will. She died because she was married to him. He should have been there to protect her rather than leaving her in the charge of another.

He had endured the previous seven months by forcing himself to slide deeper within himself, blurring his senses to ignore the subtle distinctions between right and wrong as defined by both Washington and Marcos. This, he knew, was the real test of professionalism. The valid means for him to preserve whatever measure of sanity remained lurking in his mind and allowed him to witness the tortures, beatings, or executions and remain, as they said on the circuit, "objective."

Careful not to disturb the girl sleeping at his side, Taylor eased from the bed and walked to the room's bamboo dresser. Reaching for a wooden kitchen match, he lit it with the flick of a thumbnail and held the flame to the tip of a Marlboro, sucking deeply at the smoke. It tasted good—a bit harsh, but still good, and he nodded appreciatively as the expected cough arrived on schedule.

As usual, Taylor ignored the irritation in his bronchial tubes and wrote it off to twenty-seven years in the business. He may have been an old gypsy war dancer, but he could still tango with the best of them. He had no time for lung disease.

Gypsy war dancer. He smiled at the phrase. It was almost as good as the first smoke of the day. *Gypsy-War-Dancer*. He repeated the phrase in mind, allowing the words to roll around in the back of his brain. Yes, it was appropriate considering that he had worked in the field during his entire career. But that was going to change. He was being given a section in Washington.

Questions, he thought, taking another deep pull on the Marlboro. It always seemed Washington had only questions, never answers. He smiled. Maybe he would change it. Surely he had enough experience, enough seniority, even enough snap to probably pull it off. But then again, he understood the circuit. He was and probably always would be essentially a field man, and the thought of rubbing elbows with the Washington school-tie crowd left him with a sense of dread. What the hell, he decided, the circuit was strictly C.O.D. They pay the freight, they get the package.

The girl shifted on the bed and Taylor glanced over as the covers slid down exposing her breasts. Small and richly dark, they began to rise and fall as she settled back into sleep. Just as well, Taylor thought, as he padded to the closet, retrieved his briefcase, and pulled out the teletype to recheck its information.

PAGE 01 BRAYDEN 050700 01 OF 01 292252K

S6 SI SPECIAL PROJECTS

ACTION SS-22 IMMEDIATE

S E N S I T I V E   I N T E L L I G E N C E

RE: NSC [292252K]

FM DAD SPECIAL PROJECTS

TO AMEMBASSY PHILIPPINES [PASS TO TAYLOR—MANILA]

INFO [PER REF] LIMITED DISTRIBUTION 1 THRU 8

SUBJECT: TAYLOR, SAMUEL ELOY

1. CONFIRM REASSIGNMENT SUBJECT THIS STATION. POSITION LEVEL CAREER 16 [SECTION CHIEF]. EFFECTIVE DATE 1 NOVEMBER 1984.
2. ACTION FACTOR LEVEL MANTEE-BISHOP THIS DATE. AUTHORITY OF UNDERSIGNED.

S6 SI DAD SPECIAL PROJECTS [BRAYDEN] 292252K

ENDCOMMUNICATION.....NOTHINGFOLLOWS....050700

Special Projects? Taylor thought, replacing the orders in his briefcase and locking its lid. He had never heard of it, at least in Defense. And who was Brayden, the man giving the orders? Where did he come from?

The questions again. He supposed it was not really that important anyway, at least at this late stage of the game. He'd seen it before . . . new projects. Berlin, Asia, Central America. Other clandestine charades. More spotty vignettes of frustration, of controlled confusion wet with liquid politics. Men seeking their own levels amid deceptions of the moment. The players. The planners. The targets. All savoring reality in spite of each other's efforts.

Taylor smiled. Yes, he could probably guess the future. But why? He enjoyed the unknown. The challenge. It was comfortably familiar . . . patterns of the haunt. That old black magic he conjured ever so well.

But that was then and this was now, and emotionally he was dry. Washington! He'd give it a whirl and just maybe he'd get Manila locked into the past.

Taylor dressed quietly and, as he opened the door to the hall, took one look back to the still-sleeping girl. Young, no more than sixteen, she had been a going-away gift from *Coronel* Umberto Rico, Taylor's counterpart in NISA. Of course she had tried to please him, and, quite honestly, Taylor had appreciated her efforts. But, as expected, he found himself again relegated to the helpless role of voyeur as she danced, and in the end, masturbated herself for him. If it had been different, Samuel Taylor would have been surprised. Since the funeral, he had found himself clinically impotent.

"Quae nocent, docent," he whispered, gently closing the door behind him and leaving for the airport.

We learn by what we suffer.

* * *

Washington, D.C., October 30, 1987.

Margaret Duncan was a happy woman as she stood in the foyer of the Smithsonian Institution, waiting for the rain to subside. At twenty-eight, she was the youngest and, according to rumor, the most attractive of the eleven female students who had received a one-year fellowship to attend the Woodrow Wilson International Center for Scholars. It had been time well spent.

After ten months, her dissertation was finally completed and in January, she would receive her Ph.D. in economics from the University of London. Good, perhaps, but even better and quite unexpected, she had also been approached by the McDonnell Foundation to use her thesis as the framework for a PBS documentary. The subject matter was surprisingly controversial; nonetheless her research was excellent and indicated clearly that the Irish-English problem was not altogether one of Protestants versus Catholics, but rather one of economics dating back to the potato famine when men had no work, and the entire Irish society became essentially matriarchal because women were forced to become the breadwinners of the families.

A short, feisty woman with dark, bobbed hair and mischievous blue eyes, Margaret Duncan clearly enjoyed defending her theory and had actually been on television twice the previous week, smiling demurely as she categorically debated whatever experts the producers had selected to challenge her.

Apparently, her genuine warmth had come through the debates intact, for she had been contacted by an agent who wanted to represent her in both the foundation negotiations as well as future television appearances. The man had even called her "the Carl Sagan of economics." It was an exciting turn of events for a girl who had worked her way through school and whose dreams had stretched only to the limit of becoming a full professor at the university.

She checked her watch; 6:30 P.M.

"Bloody rain," she whispered, looking out across the brick

quadrangle to the mist-shrouded Washington Monument. Her Toyota was parked two blocks away and she was supposed to have her initial meeting with the agent at 7:00. If she made a dash for the car now, she would no doubt end up looking like the proverbial drowned rat—not exactly the impression she wanted to make.

Deciding to make the most of the minutes until the rain stopped, she decided to freshen her makeup. Supposedly, she remembered, the mascara could be worn while swimming. If so, at least her eyes would be presentable. As for the hair? Well, there was a scarf in the Toyota. She could always wrap it up and run the risk of appearing a devotee of potato-famine fashion, as well as economics.

Chuckling at the image of herself hoeing around some peat bog, Margaret Duncan left the foyer and walked to the woman's lounge tucked into a far corner of the broad gothic lobby. The restroom was empty, and she was thankful for the small favor. She hated applying makeup, and the thought of having to carry on some inane conversation while applying mascara would only have made the tedium worse.

Pulling a paper towel from the white ceramic dispenser, she had just begun to dab at her face when the sounds of footsteps interrupted her thoughts. In the mirror, she saw a man standing less than ten feet from her. He did not speak.

"Wrong door," she teased, turning around to face the well-dressed intruder. "Yours is across the lobby behind the water fountains."

"I'm not looking for the restroom," he said, smiling warmly as he moved closer. "I'm looking for you, Margaret. It's about your being on television."

She laughed. "Television? Don't you think we can find some other place to talk about it?"

He laughed with her and she found herself staring into his eyes. They were blue, like her own—only much paler. Beautiful eyes, she thought. Beautiful eyes with an almost hypnotic pathos awash in the pigment. "If you give me a second, we can talk. But I have a meeting in twenty minutes, so it'll have to be fast."

"I understand," he said, his voice almost a whisper. "But you see, Margaret . . . I found your performance unacceptable."

She nodded. "Well I'm certainly no expert when it comes to television, but I'm sure with practice, my——"

Margaret Duncan was totally unprepared for the fist that shot to her left temple. Reeling from the blow, she slipped and felt the sharp corner of the sink gouge a deep cut across her chin. Collapsing to the floor, she fought to remain conscious.

The man followed her down.

Gradually, in slow veils of nausea, her mind began to clear and she became aware of pressures constricting her chest. Weights digging into her arms.

Forcing her eyes open, she found herself staring into the face of her attacker. Odd, but in an intense sort of way, she briefly thought of him as handsome. But the observation faded as rapidly as it developed. He was straddling her chest, his knees pinioning her arms. Pulling tendrils of her hair in his left hand, he forced her head closer to his chest. Then, quite suddenly, she realized that his lips were still parted in smile. Teeth white and straight. *No,* she thought, fighting an almost-uncontrolling urge to return the smile. *Twist. Fight. Make it hard for him.*

Pointless efforts as he pulled her even closer, shifted deftly, and pressed her into him. Her face touched his chest.

Crying now, Margaret Duncan forced herself to look up into his eyes, the pupils dilating as the smile faded from his lips. Then there was a pressure. A sharp point, not painful, seemingly growing from the base of the skull.

She could hear it now—not in her ears, but from within. Beckoning, it was the cadence of her pulse beginning to throb with the realization of the moment.

A thought. A momentary hope as from a long-repressed segment of her brain, the low, guttural scream began to evolve.

The man felt it, too, for at that precise moment, the mind of Margaret Duncan exploded.

As the convulsions stilled, the man placed the coin in her slackened mouth, closed the jaw, and kissed her tenderly on the lips. Then, almost reluctantly, he rose from her body and left the restroom, his footsteps echoing off marble floors. The ice pick remained in Margaret Duncan's brain.

It was 6:42 P.M. The rain continued.

Washington, D.C., November 4, 1987.

By 6:15 A.M., Patrick Callahan had already finished a substantial breakfast, ignored three telephone calls, and, for the second time, glanced through the morning news accounts of the defense-funding debates raging in the American Congress.

Excellent, he decided. The administration hardliners looked as if they had gathered enough strength to force a vote on the Senate floor. If so, he would make a point of visiting the opposition leaders later in the day for a bit of lobbying for Old Mother England. He smiled. If the funding increases were authorized, he would be able to claim discreetly a bit of credit for his input. Of course, he realized that this in itself would not assure a knighthood; nonetheless, many small feathers made a bonnet. But, if anything, he was a master at gathering small feathers from the Crown. It was a unique feat for a barrister's son from Dublin, even if his mother's family could be traced back to the Earl of Cardigan.

Draining the last of his coffee, he tossed the newspaper to the floor and pushed his ample girth back from the table, beginning mentally to enumerate the points he would cover with the ambassador later in the morning. Personally, he thought the Wednesday briefings an important ritual: not because of any business, of course, but rather because it gave him the opportunity of ingratiating himself further with the ambassador. Such were the benefits of his position.

Unfortunately, as British Consul General for Political Affairs, the majority of Patrick Callahan's time seemed to be consumed with the constant monitoring of the arguments for and against the expanded American defense budget. The budget was central to the Reagan administration's satisfaction of mutual-defense treaties and of obvious importance to Britain, which had come to rely upon American defense contracts to bolster her economy.

Granted, his analyses were probably important; nonetheless, Patrick Callahan did not relish the assignment. Defense matters were much too distasteful to his liking. A florid, squatty man of fifty-two, he was definitely no warmonger, privately preferring the cocktail parties to scenarios of war and destruction.

On the other hand, he had been able to gather a few feathers in spite of the subject matter. The *Washington Post* had quoted his observations twice in the previous week, and it looked as if he were going to be a guest on ''Meet the Press'' sometime before Christmas—events which dovetailed quite nicely with his admittedly inflated ego.

Yes, he decided, standing and walking to the foyer, he would issue another press release defining the British position before lunch. That would give the press ample time to meet their deadlines and ensure that he was again quoted in the evening papers.

As he picked up his briefcase and opened the door of his posh Georgetown town house, he made another mental note to include his clippings in the day's pouch for London. Musing that the Foreign Office might also enjoy seeing his name in print, the consul general allowed himself a soft chuckle. Indeed, he had become an expert in discreetly enhancing his political fortunes.

Stepping outside, he locked the front door and checked his watch: 6:21 A.M. As usual, he would walk the three blocks to Wisconsin Avenue, hail a taxi, and be at the embassy by 7:00. Fastidious, Patrick Callahan was a creature of habit—an accepted, yet lamentable, choice of attributes.

Pausing on the front steps, he breathed deeply of the crisp November morning and reflected upon the means to achieve even more personal exposure through clever handling of the American political debate. He did not notice the man approaching him.

"Callahan," the man whispered. It was not a question.

Turning, the consul general looked at the stranger. Handsome devil, he thought. And well dressed. But his face was not familiar. "I'm sorry. Have we met?"

"Yes, consul general," the man answered, his right hand tightening on the grip of the Ingram Model 11 machine pistol he wore concealed beneath a leather trenchcoat. "We have met each time an Irishman dies. And now is our final meeting."

Patrick Callahan saw the stubby thickness of the silencer being aimed at him and thought to scream. It remained a thought.

At precisely 6:24 A.M., the first 9 millimeter parabellum round turned the consul general's mouth into a mass of pulp. The second bullet tore a path into his forehead, through the brain, and exited just above to the rear of his left ear. It lodged intact in the door's wooden frame.

As he collapsed, Patrick Callahan's blood splashed onto his assassin's left shoe.

"Cow!" he hissed, savagely flicking the weapon's fire-selector mechanism to full automatic and watching as an additional thirteen rounds pumped into the lifeless body. The weapon empty, the man opened his trenchcoat and allowed it to sling back under his armpit as he stepped over to the corpse and wiped his shoe on Callahan's trouser leg.

The blemish removed, he reached into his coat pocket, selected the coin, and, bending over, inserted it into the wound which had been Patrick Callahan's mouth.

The violation now complete, he wiped his fingers on the ground, stood and slowly strolled away.

It was 6:26 A.M.

Peder Crandon felt exhilarated. Perhaps he would have biscuits for breakfast.

The First Day

We will not attack unless we are attacked; if we are attacked, we will certainly counterattack. That is to say, we must never attack others without provocation, but once attacked, we must never fail to return the blow.

Mao Tse-tung
1940

Chapter 1

IN THE DARKNESS a phone was ringing.

Taylor ignored the sound. It was an intrusion. A mistake. A pushing of reality into the confines of his dream. He willed the violation away.

But the ringing continued.

Taylor was awake instantly.

Chilled by the thin sheen of perspiration coating his body, Samuel Eloy Taylor reached for the phone.

"Taylor." He pressed the receiver to his lips.

"Sorry, Mr. Taylor. This is Lieutenant Ramsey, COMSEC two-five. The general requests your attendance at a briefing scheduled for zero-five-thirty."

Taylor was unimpressed. If there was anything he liked worse than being awakened in the middle of the night, it was the personality of General Thomas Brayden, his supervisor at Special Projects.

"I'm not in the mood for briefings, Ramsey. It's the middle of the night, and it's Sunday."

"Yes, sir," the officer agreed all too cheerfully. "I'm aware it's Sunday. But it's also zero-four-thirty, and a car has already been dispatched to your location."

Skeptical, Taylor glanced at the digital clock on his cluttered bedside table. It was 4:35 A.M. Smartass junior officers, he thought, deciding that Ramsey's youthful exuberance was also a bit much for the hour. "Any clues to where I'm going, Ramsey? I mean, I'd hate to overdress."

Taylor could hear the officer shuffling through some papers. "Uh, I'm sorry, Mr. Taylor. But I have no particular instructions as to uniform of the day. But the briefing is to be held at the general's residence, and you are to be ready by zero-five hundred."

Taylor chuckled in spite of the hour. *Uniform of the day?* He hadn't even thought of that term since the late fifties and his assignment to army intelligence in West Berlin. "Don't worry about it, Ramsey," he smiled, remembering his own tender apprenticeship in Cold War strategies. "Just send the car—I'll meet the driver downstairs. And tell him not to honk; no point in waking up the whole building."

"Yes, sir. Thank you sir." Ramsey sounded relieved. "Uh, shall I make a follow-up call?"

"Not today." Taylor was resigned to being forced to get out of bed. "I'll be ready with bells on."

"Yes, sir. Thank you, sir."

Taylor replaced the receiver without responding and flipped on the bedside table lamp. He evaluated the mess. A half-eaten Burger King double meat-double cheese, the clock, the phone, four wooden kitchen matches, one crushed pack of Marlboro Light 100s; and a plastic tumbler of Jack Daniel's, as empty as the ashtray was full.

Not too bad, he decided, poking in the ashtray and finding the longest butt. At least he hadn't eaten onion rings. Sticking the cigarette in his mouth, he grabbed one of the matches, lit it with a thumbnail, and, in order, fired the butt, coughed twice, and wondered why a used cigarette always tasted at least ten times stronger than a fresh one.

For Taylor, the question was rhetorical, and he dismissed it.

Holding the match vertically, Taylor sat on the edge of the bed and stared at the blue orange flame. Of course, he could have used any one of the dozen or so lighters he had stashed somewhere, but he still preferred kitchen matches. It was an avocation, he realized, which never ceased to annoy the general, who had personally given him at least three lighters; but then again, Samuel Taylor could never be called a man who rested on convention. He stayed with his matches.

"A *Sunday* briefing?" he whispered to himself, tossing the match into the ashtray as the flame burned down to his fingers. "Now what mysterious little intrigue has Brayden dreamed up now?"

Glancing at the clock, he knew it was time to get moving. The speculations would have to wait. "Once more into the breach," he sighed, tossing the butt into the ashtray and walking to the bathroom of the efficiency condominium he classified under the general heading of home.

Although he could have afforded something larger, by preference Taylor lived in a 900-square-foot flat on the eleventh floor of a contemporary high-rise in southern Alexandria, Virginia. Close to his office in the Pentagon, the unit possessed everything he considered necessary. A balcony offered a spectacular view of Old Town, the Potomac River, and the various Washington monuments. A small but seldom-used kitchen with serving bar. Bathroom, two closets, a single main living area, and a basement racquetball court, where he worked out at least five times a week, beating opponents half his age with surprising ease. It was an achievement the losers attributed not so much to his stocky athletic build, but rather the tenacious, almost bulldoggish way he played to win. Of course, when baited about his lack of finesse, Taylor would only smile, call it luck, and challenge the teasers to another game. If they accepted, he would promptly beat them again, and, on rare occasion, sometimes invite the loser to his apartment for a drink—Jack Daniel's. He would allow nothing else in his home.

Flicking on the bathroom light, Taylor glanced back into the condo's interior and nodded appreciatively. He had furnished it himself and was proud of the effect: a feeling somewhere between an exclusive men's club and an upscale department store furniture display.

The walls were covered in used brick and separated from the pressed tin ceiling by a thick band of dark mahogany-brown molding. In the center of the room, a brass ceiling fan spun lazily. Its single globe had been burned out for the better part of two years, but Taylor saw no reason to change it. He didn't like the light. In fact, he had changed every bulb in the room so none would have more than 40 watts.

It was a darkly peaceful place with matching Henredon bed, armoire, bookcases, and desk, all vaguely oriental, wedged tightly between two leather Chesterfield sofas, a black marble and steel cocktail table, and his most recent addition: a Fisher television-stereo home-entertainment system with an elaborate but unused remote control-device. Taylor had inadvertently thrown away its instruction manual with the original packaging material.

He looked to the bookcases. Two sets of encyclopedias, both in white pressed vinyl; a large collection of books on the Civil War; the circuit readings—Well's *Outline of History,* Sun Tzu's *Art of War*, Machiavelli, Mao, Guevara, Clausewitz, Marx, a few others. And on the bottom two shelves, his pride and joy; the complete sixty-volume set of *Great Literature*, all resplendent in their machine-tooled simulated-leather bindings, and all unread. Taylor had never mailed back the coupons, but the books kept arriving. Eventually he offered to return the books, but the company wanted only money. So, after six months of threats by some obscure collection agency in Chicago, he had gone to the Pentagon mailroom, filled out a postal form, and mailed the agency an official notification of his new address: the Christian Science Reading Room in Asunción, Paraguay. The badgering stopped immediately. Taylor called it "last tag."

Turning from his books, Taylor moved into the bathroom and twisted on the hot water.

"Bit shabby," he admitted to the puffy face in the mirror. The thirty years in the business had definitely taken their toll. His full head of once-dark unruly hair was almost half-gray, as were the bushy, challenging eyebrows. Deep worry lines ran laterally across his forehead. The nose, previously broken, had been misset, and the lips and jaw were set in a line which could be called determined.

Leaning closer to the mirror, Taylor wiped off the steam which was beginning to gather on the glass. Fortunately, his brown eyes were alert and still perceptive.

They were accusing eyes, Taylor knew. Skeptical eyes. Eyes whose intensity was surpassed only by the frequency with which they were forced to recall their observations. Eyes which demanded information. Answers.

Lonely eyes.

The body was holding up well, he thought, stepping back from the mirror and evaluating himself: 5'10', 180 pounds. With the exception of a slight bulge over the kidney and the scarred bullet wound just beneath the left nipple, it still resembled the physique of a younger man.

Well, not quite, he corrected himself. The shoulders were still wide, but of late had taken on a tired look. But all in all, he still possessed most of the prowess which had served him so well on the football field at Notre Dame. And, thanks to the racquetball, he remained a powerfully agile man.

But not a handsome man, he remembered as he began to shave. Never was, for that matter. An honest face, mostly. A laconic man, usually. Maybe even a Renaissance man, on rare occasion. But never handsome.

And as for the broken nose he had worried about so much in high school? He had learned to like it. He felt it made his face look lived-in. Kind of like a crusty old city editor who never understood the newsworthiness of food or fashion, yet allowed them reported for the simple reason they helped sell papers. The kind of face a man needed when working the circuit.

Taylor smiled at himself. No, he could not even recall a time when his vanity had ever been considered an issue—at least by him. There had always been the other concerns. More important. The wars, revolutions, and political infightings which had so rabidly consumed his youth, and now his middle years.

Still, with the exception of Manila, he could honestly admit to having absolutely no negative feelings toward his profession. He was not a priest; therefore he was spared the tedium of searching for petty ambiguities amid the even more obscure differences between legality and privilege. His work, he knew, was neither right nor wrong, appropriate nor inappropriate.

It was only the business. Only a narrow . . .

Suddenly he lurched over the sink. It was the pain again. Gnawing. Growing. Throbbing from his breastbone and burning its way slowly to his stomach.

Swallowing, he felt the nausea intensify and cursed his lifestyle. His time alone. The fried foods, the cigarettes, the Jack. The attempts to heal his impotence through the impersonal ministrations of prostitutes. The nightmares accusing him, teasing him, forcing him back to Manila.

Sweating, he dropped to one knee, splashing water on his face and sipping small tastes from the faucet until his stomach began to settle. Then the pain dissipated, becoming bearable again. He stood, reached for his toothbrush, and continued the morning ritual.

For Samuel Taylor, there was no reasonable alternative. The ulcer would again be forced into its appropriate category at the very bottom of his priorities, and attention to detail would take its place at the top.

The reason was pure curiosity. For in his three years of working for the man, this was the first time Thomas Brayden had ever summoned him on a weekend.

The general would expect nothing less.

Chapter 2

PREDAWN WASHINGTON WAS a coldly deserted place, an orderly matrix of salt and street ice winking suggestively between thick billowings of warm sewer gases.

"Enough room for you, sir?" the young driver asked as the Buick splashed across Pennsylvania Avenue.

There wasn't, but Taylor decided not to say anything. It wasn't the marine's fault anyway. "I'm fine, corporal," he lied, shifting in the cramped rear seat and vaguely remembering the pre-Carter days when all government limousines were Cadillacs.

"Let me know if you need anything, sir."

Cracking a window, Taylor lit a cigarette and looked outside. At least the rain had stopped, he observed: small consolation for the ungodly hour. "I will," he answered softly.

At precisely 5:28 A.M., the Buick turned off Foxhall Road and eased into the driveway of a modest Georgian manor house ringed by neat hedgerows of well-maintained boxwood—the general's residence. Understated elegance which, in Taylor's opinion, resembled a funeral parlor more than a private home. Indeed, it was a perfect reflection of its owner.

As the corporal steered to the circular parking area adjacent to the front doors, Taylor observed another vehicle parked discreetly under the porte cochere leading to the rear of the house. This one was a Cadillac. Engine idling. The profile of a driver slouched behind the wheel.

Odd, Taylor thought. Then, as the Buick wheeled to a stop, its headlights illuminated the license plate peeking from beneath the Cadillac's rear bumper.

British diplomat, Taylor realized, reading the letter prefix and number. Could the general be giving a tea party?

He dismissed the thought. Serious, he told himself. Stay on the serious side of that fine line separating absurdity and the trappings of government. But, in spite of the admonition, he chuckled to himself. What had they called it in Berlin? Then he remembered . . . the rhyme of the ancient bureaucrat: "*Who,* sir? But *why,* sir? Certainly not *I,* sir."

No, forget the word games, Taylor told himself. No time for self-amusement.

I'll be waiting, sir," the driver told him as he shoved the Buick into park.

Taylor leaned forward. "That's fine, corporal. But while I'm inside, I want you to do something for me."

"Yes, sir?"

Taylor nodded toward the Cadillac. "Wait about five minutes, then go over and start bullshitting with that other driver. See if you can get any information about his passenger."

The marine's face brightened. "What do you want to know, sir?"

"Nothing in particular. If you start bitching about the hour, he'll start. Don't worry. Just act interested and you'll find out everything he knows."

"I'll do my best, sir," the driver said, both pleased and serious about his assignment.

"You'll do fine, son. Just remember to listen."

"Yes, sir."

Taylor patted the young man on the shoulder, climbed out of the Buick, and walked rapidly to the main residence doors, where he took a deep breath, rang the bell, and waited.

If anything, Taylor had developed strong, but admittedly ambivalent feelings toward Thomas Brayden. On the positive side, the general was a brilliant man, inherently able to take the most complex national-security issue and simplify the problem intellectually so that each key consideration could be addressed in its exact order of importance. It was a talent Taylor genuinely admired and a gift which had made the general's trademark—the black Brooks Brothers suit—a familiar ensemble to both the National Security Council and the president. In this—his closeness to the power brokers—Taylor respected and trusted his superior.

Nevertheless, Taylor found Thomas Brayden's personality somewhat lacking.

Perhaps it was petty considering the greater scope of things; nonetheless, Taylor thought the general to be a condescending man spurred by an inflated ego and an almost insatiable desire to control others: a trait stemming from his years of military service as well as his diminished physical size—the second thing Taylor disliked about the man.

For some unshakable reason, Thomas Brayden reminded Taylor of a contemporary Heinrich Himmler. The resemblance was uncanny. Like the Nazi S.S. chief, the general was a sparse little man with thinning gray-blond hair and small nondescript eyes peering out from behind round wireless glasses; coupled with a ramrod posture and the cool impression of intellectual superiority.

Suddenly the door opened and Taylor found himself staring at the top of Thomas Brayden's head.

"Sam," the general said, stepping back to allow Taylor inside. "Good of you to come."

Taylor studied him quickly. The eyes seemed clouded, and even Brooks Brothers couldn't conceal his weariness. "It is a bit unusual, general."

"Unusual times, Sam," he nodded. "But come, I'll explain inside."

Following in step, Taylor trailed the general through a set of twin oak doors, down a richly carpeted foyer, toward the private study at the far end of a central hallway. Taylor knew the room well. He found it a bit too garish for his more plebian tastes.

About 20' x 40', with a 10' block-paneled ceiling, the walls were upholstered in deep green velvet. At one end of the study was a hand-carved white Italian marble fireplace with flanking french doors; and at the other, a huge 16th-century mauve-covered flemish tapestry which draped all the wall areas not covered by the velvet or the well-stocked floor-to-ceiling bookcases.

Taylor had not been impressed. He felt the room left one with the distinct feeling of having blundered into the boudoir of Catherine the Great, or the chambers of some aging pimp living out his years on the third floor of a well-heeled Parisian brothel.

Of course the props were resplendent: Baroque Florentine medallions; the teakwood and pewter *bureau buffet,* a mother-of-pearl gilded mirror, Persian rugs; Baccarat crystal; lots of pastel things. In short, everything which had led Taylor to believe that the general was color-blind.

"Sam," the general told him as they entered the study, "this is Elliot Prescott."

"*Sir* Elliot Prescott," the man corrected, turning from the pearled mirror and gliding toward Taylor. "Special Assistant to the Prime Minister's First Foreign Secretary."

Tra-la, Taylor thought, already sizing up the Englishman. Early fifties. Maybe six-foot. Thin with a paunch. Nothing special there.

But the hair. Greasy and combed back long. Even dyed unnaturally. But why the guano-looking brown?

Of course, to match the heavily lidded guano-colored eyes.

What about the mouth? Feral. Perhaps a hint of effeteness.

And those teeth. Dentures? No . . . capped. Sharp white teeth that sparkled like brilliant little razors when he spoke.

The shiteyes aside, Elliot Prescott struck Taylor as a man who practiced and mastered the subtle art of first impression. A smooth man. Polished in everything. From the expensive three-piece steel gray suit, to the way he slid around the room seemingly without moving his feet. Even to the manner in which he shook hands—more of a caress than a squeeze.

He was a dilettante, Taylor decided. A conceited man, replete with facelift, who obviously spent an inordinate amount of time and money pursuing his vanity and probably equal numbers polishing the illusion of aristocracy with carefully rehearsed understatement.

Yes, Taylor knew instinctively, this presumptuous little mink definitely belonged to the diplomatic plates. He was the type to demand them.

Quite suddenly there was silence in the room. Taylor realized he had been asked a question.

"I'm sorry, Mr. Prescott," he apologized. "But what did you ask?"

"Please, Taylor, call me *Sir* Elliot." The teeth winked, but the voice was cold. "I asked about your outfit . . . it's so, so . . ." He completed the comment with a graceful wave of the hand.

Taylor glanced down at his clothes. Dark blue parka, crewneck sweater, gray corduroy slacks, and lined chukka boots. "We aren't all diplomats, *Sir* Elliot," he answered, more pleasantly than intended. "So I generally dress comfortably."

"Sam refuses to shop in stores," the general added with an indulgent smile of his own. "He orders all his clothes through the mail."

"L. L. Bean," Taylor explained. "In Maine? If you'd like a catalog, I'll have them send you one care of the embassy."

The general's expression spread to Prescott. "Well, yes," he said. "I'd rather like that." More winking teeth. "As they say, clothes do make the man."

Asshole, Taylor thought.

"Well," the general said. "Now that that's out of the way, shall we get down to business?"

Prescott nodded and Taylor shrugged. Both men moved to the

pair of tapestried side chairs facing the general's black lacquer Chien Lung desk—the only piece in the room Taylor found even remotely attractive.

"I appreciate your help, Taylor," Prescott said as they sat down. "Particularly on short notice."

"No problem," Taylor lied, watching the general move behind the desk and sit down so heavily that Taylor wondered if he were in some kind of pain. "I'm an early riser anyway."

For a brief moment, there was a thick silence in the room. Then the general cleared his throat and began to explain. "Sir Elliot represents the British government."

Must have had a rich daddy, Taylor thought, nodding him on.

"He flew in from London yesterday to discuss with the president the recent murders here against the British. After their meeting, the president instructed me to look into the situation, track down those responsible, and eliminate the possibility of additional problems. Am I making myself clear?"

Taylor understood. "I assume you're referring to the murder of the consul general?"

"It was more than a simple murder," Prescott said coldly, sliding his chair even closer to Taylor's. "Consul General Callahan was assassinated."

Like Manila, Taylor thought. "Phony robbery details?"

The general nodded. "The British embassy leaked that as a cover story to buy us time. The man had a minimum of twelve bullet wounds from an automatic weapon and silencer. Nobody heard or saw anything."

"What about the body?" Taylor asked.

Prescott answered. "It was claimed immediately by the Foreign Office and will be taken back to London on my plane later this morning."

Nice touch, Taylor thought. "No autopsy report."

"None," Prescott said.

Leaning back in his chair, Taylor took out a match, flicked it,

lit a cigarette, and ignored the irritated glare from the general. "Press must have bought your story. I saw the news reports."

Prescott nodded. "Well, hopefully it will end there. The last thing the Foreign Office needs is a lingering inquiry on your television."

As a practical matter, Samuel Taylor saw nothing wrong with manipulating the press. And the degree of manipulation was merely a matter of perspective. There were no entirely objective newspapers or correspondents. All newspaper editors and TV producers possessed individual prejudices. It was human nature. Unfortunately, these same prejudices usually found their way into the news being jammed down the collective public throat.

Taylor smiled. It was always amusing to be able to use the press for a change. It gave him a warm feeling which, regrettably, he seemed to experience less and less lately.

"There is more, Sam," the general added. "Another murder two weeks ago."

Taylor sat up. "Before Callahan?"

Brayden nodded. "A British scholar at the Smithsonian. A woman."

Taylor could feel the tension in the study increasing. "How?"

"Ice pick," Prescott whispered. "Left in her brain."

Left in her brain? Taylor thought. Why would the killer leave evidence behind? Interrupted? Sloppy? Maybe making a statement? "Am I to assume the motive for the murders is political?"

"Assassinations," Prescott repeated, his voice still low. "But yes, they were political. Political and something a bit more human . . . revenge."

There was a minute of awkward silence as the general began shuffling through a neat stack of manila folders on his desk. "You recall the London Letter, don't you, Sam?"

Taylor nodded. "I read the memo. The counterterrorism first-strike agreement signed at the London Economic Summit."

Staring at Taylor, the general picked his words judiciously. "Sam, the president feels this situation fits into its frame-

work for a response outside of the more conventional channels."

Taylor's mind flashed a quick image of his dead wife. "Terrorists?"

The general nodded to Prescott and the Englishman began to explain. "It is the position of my government that the assassinations here in Washington are the responsibility of a radical splinter fraction of the Irish Republican Army—the Crandon Brigade." Prescott spit out the name.

Taylor crushed out his half-smoked Marlboro in the large brass ashtray on the corner of the desk. "I'm sorry, but I'm not familiar with that particular group."

"Of course. Let me give you a bit of background." Standing, Sir Elliot began to pace the room, clipping his words as he spoke. "Two years ago, a man named Peder Crandon was arrested in Belfast by Special Branch. He was a Provo intelligence officer whose responsibilities included procurement of weapons and explosives for the IRA to deploy against our people. He was also wanted for murder.

"Suffice it to say, it was a good catch because he had any number of sympathetic sources throughout Europe and had been traveling extensively, obtaining logistical support for the better part of a decade. In any case, during one of his earlier trips to Switzerland, I believe it was back in '77 or maybe '78, he became involved with a German girl. A girl named Ursula Brandt."

The general leaned across the desk. "Here's her latest." He passed Taylor an 8" x 10" color photograph. "It's about two years old."

Taylor studied the picture. Sensuous, late twenties, slender, with a flawless complexion, striking blue eyes, and provocative mouth set amid a wild mane of vibrant red hair. The impression of a wickedly beautiful woman. "Looks like a model for Tigress perfume," he said, placing the photograph back on the desk.

"She *was* a model," Prescott sighed. "One of the best in

Europe . . . at least in her late teens. Then she met Crandon. He turned the wench out."

"In what way?" Taylor asked.

"Brought her back to Ireland," Prescott shrugged. "Told her whatever a man tells a young, impressionable girl. Offered a chance to live on the edge . . . to run with death."

Almost dejectedly, Sir Elliot returned to his chair and sat down. "Evidently, Crandon fancied himself some political Svengali. But whatever he thought, it hadn't been six months before Ursula was living with him and learning how to kill upon his command."

Looking over, Prescott stared directly into Taylor's face. "She's an extremely dangerous woman," he said flatly. "Trained. Coldly efficient. And almost eager to use her beauty to—shall we say—gain a particular favor?"

Remembering the photograph with a new respect, Taylor nodded. "But now you feel she's somehow responsible for the deaths here?"

Prescott arched an eyebrow. "Not directly. Unfortunately, we have not as yet been able to ascertain her current whereabouts. Probably Libya."

"Probably?" Taylor accentuated the word.

The ploy worked. Taylor watched as Prescott's lips seemed to roll back and his lids dropped heavily over his eyes. *Like a shark,* Taylor thought. *A shark beginning to feed.* "You mean you can't find out?" he pressed, testing the Englishman's coolness.

To his credit, Sir Elliot recovered gracefully. The grimace smoothed itself into a diplomat's smile. "We have a saying, Taylor. *In the shadows all men seem friends.* Perhaps you've heard it?"

"No," Taylor admitted.

"No. I would suppose not. But perhaps in this context it could mean that one may never be certain of anything. As a professional, you should be aware of this—particularly when dealing with sources which are questionable, at best."

Prescott allowed himself a low chuckle. "Perhaps you are not aware of these things, Taylor. These considerations. These *shadowmen*. Could this be the case, Taylor? Could it be that you do not understand terrorists? Their rules? Their affinities? Their spurious little impulses?"

Leaning back in his chair, Sir Elliot crossed his legs and adjusted a well-tailored cuff. "Please, tell me, Taylor. Do you appreciate these factors? Do you have this understanding?"

Bastard, Taylor thought. Prescott had finessed him. Now he was the one being tested. "Of course I understand," he answered coldly, wishing he'd stayed objective in the first place. "But then I'm not the one asking for help—am I, *Sir* Elliot?"

Silent behind his desk, Thomas Brayden observed the psychological parrying with a cool, if critical eye. They were about equally matched, he decided. Prescott was more erudite, of course; nontheless, in his usual straightforward manner, Taylor was performing quite admirably. But unfortunately, Sir Elliot was not aware that Taylor's wife had been car-bombed by terrorists—nor, for that matter, his total lack of pretense when dealing with violence. If allowed, Prescott would continue to insult Taylor's intelligence. Knowing Taylor's propensity for holding grudges, those insults could only result in a permanent rift between them which would inevitably make things more difficult to control as the operation progressed.

"Gentlemen," the general interrupted matter-of-factly. "I think we would do well to get back on track." He looked to Prescott. "Perhaps you could define the parameters of the situation for us, Sir Elliot?"

Another flash of teeth. "Of course, general," he smiled, standing once again. "As I was saying, Ursula operated under Crandon's tutelage for a number of years. And our *sources*"—he stressed the word for Taylor's benefit—"have placed both her and Crandon at the planning of Lord Mountbatten's assassination as well as that of our ambassador to the Netherlands."

"Sam," the general added, "if you will remember, the

Provos—at least at that point in time—wanted to turn Northern Ireland into some kind of Third Worldish Democratic Socialist Republic along the lines of Allende's Chile."

"Allende," Prescott interjected, "with a liberal sprinkling of ramblings from Colonel Qaddafi's *Green Book*. Fortunately for us, the mainline Irish sympathizers backed off when the Provos went courting Qaddafi's bankroll to finance their new republic. In any case, with the usual sources of funding evaporating, the Provos readily accepted Muslim support. Ursula and Crandon became their logistical conduits with the Arabs."

Prescott shrugged his shoulders. "The bottom line, as you say, is that Ursula Brandt has contacts in every faction of the Muslim world. And this, Taylor, brings us to the point of her *indirect* responsibility for our current difficulties."

Deciding not to comment, Taylor nodded Prescott on.

"During the summer of 1984," he continued, sneaking a quick glimpse of his reflection in the mirror, "Special Branch was able to ascertain where and when a delivery of illegal weapons were to be smuggled into Northern Ireland. A surveillance was established at the designated point, and less than three hours later, Peder Crandon himself arrived to retrieve the cache.

"He was arrested, taken to Maze Prison, and held for about six weeks while awaiting trial for any number of charges. As things would have it, what we didn't know at the time was that Ursula had arranged the shipment in Libya and in fact was also in Ireland at the time of the seizure. How she evaded capture is anybody's guess; but she did, and Crandon refused to inform on her or any of the others involved."

Not surprising, Taylor thought. "So where is Crandon now?"

"Dead," Prescott answered, his voice emotionless. "Hanged himself in his cell."

Taylor twisted in the chair and looked over to Brayden. "You'll have to excuse me, general, but it seems I'm missing something somewhere. If Crandon is dead, who, then, is the Crandon Brigade? Ursula?"

There was silence in the room.

''Sir Elliot?'' the general prompted.

Gliding back to the desk, Prescott leaned almost casually against its corner and stared down at Taylor. ''This is the crux of our problem,'' he said softly. ''Evidently Ursula remained in Belfast after Crandon's none-too-timely demise, and during that time, converted a small number of young, extremely militant Irishmen to her beliefs.

''The few who have been taken alive all profess the same ideology: that human life has no real value. To them, nobody is an innocent, and they kill not for political reasons alone, but also for vengeance and the personal satisfaction and power they experience when taking human lives.''

''Psychopathic inferiority?'' Taylor speculated.

''To the nth degree,'' Prescott nodded, standing and beginning to pace the room. ''Of course there were the usual accusations that Crandon was murdered by Special Branch—that kind of thing is relatively normal. But after everyone else more or less forgot about him, Ursula and her little band of butchers surfaced. They called themselves the Crandon Brigade.''

Taylor could feel the hatred in Sir Elliot's voice. ''What's their pattern?''

''None,'' Prescott answered coldly. ''After they bombed an elementary school in southern London, they were publicly denounced by their own people. Even the Provos didn't condone the wanton slaughter of children. But that was merely to be their beginning.

''Two of the Brigade were killed when they attempted to machine-gun their way into a Provo safehouse in retaliation for the denunciation. Another was shot by Special Branch when he attempted to force his way into Buckingham Palace with explosives wired to his body.''

''So now they're operating in Washington,'' Taylor said. ''Or at least you believe they are.''

Prescott shook his head. "Not the Brigade per se," he corrected. "One man—Peder Crandon."

"Peder?"

The general answered the unasked question. "There was a son, Sam."

"Not unlike he's risen from his father's grave," Prescott added with a wave of his hand.

"Whatever," Brayden muttered, dismissing the comment as inappropriate melodrama as he spoke to Taylor. "Apparently Ursula also recruited him somewhere along the way," he said, reading from the file and paraphrasing as he went. "Young Peder hates the British for everything. His father's death. The violence in Northern Ireland. Even the death of his mother——"

"In 1969," Prescott nodded. "An accident, really . . . shot by the IRA when she was caught in a cross fire with a British curfew patrol."

Brayden continued, "Ursula cultivated the hatred, and after pressure increased against the Crandon Brigade in Europe, she led him to the Middle East." He flipped a page. "And from that point on, information concerning his activities becomes extremely sketchy until about two months ago, when a British vice-consul named Thomas Elrod was found dead in a bullet-riddled car at DeGaulle Airport outside of Paris."

"Still with Ursula?" Taylor asked.

Prescott nodded. "Witnesses stated there were two assassins. A man and a woman who generally fit Ursula and Peder's descriptions."

"Confirmation?"

"Pending," Prescott said. "But there was somewhat of a bizarre clue left in the vehicle: a British coin—a new *ten pence* piece."

"Probably symbolic of something," Taylor guessed.

Prescott held out his hands in a gesture of helplessness. "But of what? Nothing our people have been able to deduce."

Taylor made a mental note to see what could be bought for

ten pence. ''Probably not that important, but we'll look into it, too.''

''This is young Crandon,'' the general said, passing a file over to Taylor.

Opening the folder, in the left inside pocket was a color photograph of a frail but handsome man in his mid-twenties. Taylor committed it to memory. Stylishly long, but neat blond hair, an aristocrat's high cheekbones, thin nose, and slim straight lips, pale, almost colorless blue eyes, seemingly fixed upon some faraway place. He would have looked more at home on a polo field, Taylor decided. ''Stats?'' he asked the general.

''Five-nine, maybe one-sixty'', Brayden answered immediately.

Taylor nodded. ''Anything else?''

''These,'' Prescott said, passing him two glassine evidence envelopes. ''One was found on Callahan's body, the other at the Smithsonian.''

Taking the envelopes, Taylor evaluated their contents. Two coins a bit larger than a quarter; both silver, both bearing the raised bas-relief profile of Queen Elizabeth II on the obverse. He turned them over. The words *NEW PENCE* and the number *10* were inscribed in a circular pattern around the raised seal of the Crown. He handed the envelopes back to Prescott without comment and stood. His part of the meeting was finished.

''Anything else?'' he asked the general.

''I'll walk you out,'' Brayden answered. ''Sir Elliot?''

''Perhaps one final admonition,'' Prescott said, picking at an imaginary piece of lint on his lapel. ''Remember one thing, Taylor. Peder Crandon is totally without conscience. I cannot stress that enough. We assume he has received expert training because of the precision with which he carried out his activities. If not stopped, I shudder to think what the man may be capable of doing.''

Taylor managed a smile. ''I'll keep that in mind.''

Prescott nodded in approval. ''I don't envy your position, Taylor; nor am I privy to your techniques. Nonetheless, I can assure you this matter is well within the guidelines of our respective governments. The prime minister sincerely appreciates your discretion and cooperation. And I can assure you that our people are working on additional avenues of inquiry. Any information they may develop will be immediately passed to you."

Of course it would, Taylor realized, if only to guarantee that he was given enough information to assure his culpability if something went wrong with the operation. "I'll be expecting to hear from you, Sir Elliot." He turned to Brayden. "The dossiers?"

"Of course, Sam." Standing, the general stacked the files neatly and led Taylor down the hall to the front door, where he handed over the folders.

"Sam," he said, "I don't have to tell you how critical our time frame is. Query PCAC . . . activate a RAINDANCER contingency to stop Crandon. This is our first application of the London Letter domestically, so——"

"That's what bothering me, general—the domestic aspect."

Brayden held up his hand. "No discussions on that part of it, Sam. The president has sanctioned it personally, so no mistakes. We simply can't afford the political repercussions."

Taylor glanced briefly at the dossiers in his hands. "I'll begin immediately," he said softly.

"Good," Brayden smiled cautiously. "And one other thing."

"What's that?"

"I want Catlin in on this all the way."

"Why?"

"Three reasons," Brayden answered flatly. "She's your executive assistant. She's ready for it. And third, I believe I still call the shots around here!"

Taylor nodded. There would be no point in arguing. "Okay, general. I'll bring Catlin in. Now you must do something for me."

Always a trade, Brayden thought. "What this time?"

Taylor nodded back toward the study. "I want that prissy snob out of my hair and away from the section until this thing is resolved."

The general shrugged. "Fair enough," he whispered.

Turning, Taylor walked out the front door. "I'll be back when I have something tangible," he called back over his shoulder.

"I'll be here," Brayden said.

As he left the porch, Taylor looked up into the pale sky of dawn. It was overcast, and the clouds loomed cold and threatening. Pulling up his collar to ward off the chill, he glanced at his watch and headed eagerly to the waiting Buick.

It was 6:33 A.M. and the ulcer, the lack of sleep, and even Elliot Prescott's jibes were forgotten. They were replaced instinctively by a much stronger narcosis: the sweet, almost visceral anticipation of the hunt.

For Samuel Taylor, the sensation was pleasingly familiar.

Chapter 3

BERN IS THE seat of the Swiss federal government and nestled on the banks of the Aare River, the city remains a unique blend of antiquity tempered with the newness of the twentieth century.

Vaulted arcades basking in the shadow of Munster Church's Gothic spires continue to display furniture, wines and fine watches, tempting the crowds of well-dressed shoppers. And overhead, geraniums brighten the balconies of thick-walled stone houses which have lined the cobblestone streets for centuries.

With the yeasty flavor of fresh-baked bread floating in the air, it is a curious, yet beckoning place, a portal through which careful travelers may risk adventure and step back into the history of medieval times.

By design, strict building codes limit all structures of the Old Town to no more than four stories. In compliance, artists have gone two and three levels underground to pursue their pastimes, and several cellar theaters have opened beneath the streets. One, the Klein Theatre on Kramgasse Street, was presenting *Equus* in a former coal cellar furnished with antique church pews. And in another, a group of children was practicing for their Christmas performance of *The Nativity*. In Bern, such pastimes are encouraged. It is a city which prides itself on an appreciation of the arts.

But Hassim Saad was not interested in Bern's appreciations. Nor did he profess to be a patron of the arts. Sitting in a small outdoor café fronting the river promenade, he waited cautiously, his mind on business: weaponry and the veiled complexities of his chosen profession.

At fifty-two, Hassim Saad was a darkish man with small deep-set eyes, a large vein-laced nose, fleshy jowls, and long, wet-looking black hair combed back to reveal a distinct unpatterned baldness washing across his crown. He was a uniquely ugly specimen. A squatty, no-neck, even toadlike creature perhaps most closely resembling some diminished Mussolini. A Palestinian with the thick, moist lips of a spoiled child and a propensity to peer over a shoulder, not unlike a coyote on the run. Shrewd by reputation, a coward by choice.

Physically, he was diagnosed as terminal. His liver being consumed by carcinoma, the jaundice now seemed to ooze from his pores and weep openly from somewhere behind the ferretlike whites of his eyes. But being a pragmatic man, Hassim did not consider the disease a liability and accepted it in relative stride. It was a feigned bravery, really, drawn directly from the 500 milligrams of demerol he consumed every three hours.

To be sure, such frequency was unnecessary. Then again, to Hassim Saad, even the anticipation of pain could send him into a fit of cold sweats, followed by hyperventilation. It was an embarrassing state of affairs for a man of his calling.

At the moment, there was no pain. Leaning over the table he continued to pick at the steaming platter of lamb sweetbreads with short, chubby fingers.

Weaponry had become a science, he decided, popping a taste of the garlicky thymus into his mouth, chewing as he gazed at the pleasure boats gliding silently through the river's calm waters. It was far from the simpler times when the Old Man of the Mountains dispatched assassins to destroy enemies with long knives and stones.

He remembered Jael, the first freedom fighter, and the story of how he had effected the political assassination of Sisera by hammering a tent peg through the sleeping man's head. Hassim smiled. *Yes*, he thought. *Times would continue to change. But the three basic requirements of efficiency, simplicity and availability would always remain a constant.*

Now it was fashionable to kill any number of people from a distance. Consequently, firepower was an important consideration. Automatic weapons, but not those with *too* rapid a rate of fire. Guerrillas moved rapidly and were unable to carry large amounts of ammunition; nor were they predisposed to waste such a valuable commodity.

Then there was stopping power—perhaps in itself the prime consideration to the selection of weapons and ammunition. No guerrilla could afford the luxury of a target—or its bodyguards—to return fire. One fortuitous shot from an intended victim could destroy the timing of an entire incident.

Finally, there was size. To conduct urban warfare effectively, weapons had to be concealed. When these requirements were added to the characteristics of availability and ease of function, the perfect weapons of terror were defined.

Yes, he thought, leaning back in the chair, closing his eyes and breathing deeply of the yeasty afternoon air. *Perfect weapons*. Selections which over the years had led to the specialized applications so central to his lucrative business. The things that made his index of "availabilities" grow longer every day and therein only added to his reputation as keeper of the list.

To his clients, Hassim Saad was considered nothing less than a perfectionist who prided himself on an innate ability to determine the ideal weapon for any operation and then supply his selection to buyers virtually anywhere in the world. It was a talent which had made him a very rich man and also tended to let one overlook his pompousness and material indulgences. Those admittedly vain accouterments—cars, jewelry, lovers—Hassim coveted as luxuries afforded only wealthy men. His measure of aloofness, as he put it.

Glancing toward the cafe's street entrance, Hassim noticed the small Oriental enter the promenade dining area. No more than thirty years old, to the casual observer, the man appeared the typical Japanese tourist complete with camera, tennis shoes, and shoulder bag. It was a deceiving guise. Hassim knew the man as Kyoto, one of the captives released by Tel Aviv in exchange for Israeli soldiers captured during the occupation of Lebanon.

Hassim felt his insides twist slowly. Kyoto was an early member of the *Sekigun*, the radical faction of the old Japanese Red Army which had trained in Libya. A seasoned terrorist, Kyoto now held the distinction of being a bodyguard to senior members of the fundamentalist Islamic hierarchy based in Tripoli.

Taking another deep breath, Hassim forced his attentions back to the sweetbreads and attempted to appear nonchalant as he continued to wait for the client.

Actually, he realized, the Orientals were the perfect complement to Islam's rather *unfocused* efforts toward world domination, considering the *Sekigun* mindset—socialistic revolutionaries with strong mystical tendencies who felt that to die for their beliefs was the sole means of attaining a harmonious afterlife. To a man, they followed orders without question. Under Muslim control, the subtle transformation of this religious fervor into terroristic application became but another academic exercise for the fundamentalist leadership.

Tossing another morsel into his mouth, Hassim watched Kyoto with calculated respect. The reason was personal. Hassim Saad was a coward and understood that despite his relatively free access to what he euphemistically termed the "lesser statesmen," his knowledge of their activities left him in a pointedly unenviable and exposed position.

On the one hand, he was constantly forced to deny to the Swiss any association with arms sales. The authorities seemed to delight in hauling him in to "audit his banking relationships."

Fortunately, the audits were nothing more than an inconvenience; legally, Hassim was mindful not to violate any Swiss laws and absolutely refused to touch any type of weapon. When approached with a specific order, he would simply contact an associate in the country where the particular items were needed. The associate would supply the material and forward his commission.

For the client, this was an appreciated service. The munitions were always available where they were needed, thus eliminating the risk of transporting them across international borders.

Hassim's "referral compensation" was generally less—sometimes as much as 30 percent—because normally Hassim incurred no logistical costs in the actual handling of the items. Granted, Hassim knew he was probably cheated by his more enterprising associates. A simple manipulation of quantities, acquisition costs, whatever; but it was not really anything over which to risk destroying his networks. Indeed, a few dollars or francs was a small price to pay for the continuance of *la revolución*.

Hassim smiled at his personal interpretation of the phrase. If the Swiss could not actually document his funds as being obtained through some type of illegal activity, their own banking regulations prohibited them from disclosing his records to any investigative authority.

The rumors? The innuendos? The suggestions amused Hassim. He was merely a humble supplier of Persian artifacts to a fortunately active world market.

Aware of Hassim's none too discreet glances following him, Kyoto scanned the cafe and walked to a spot where he had an unobstructed view of both the promenade and the street. Then, leaning back against the railing overlooking the river, he glanced toward the arms dealer's table and shook his head in disgust as he raised the camera and snapped Hassim's picture. Through the telephoto lens, Kyoto could see the small beads of sweat lining Hassim's upper lip. He zoomed the lens in closer. Even the lip was now beginning to quiver. He was a weak man, this Hassim Saad. And any measure of weakness was repulsive to *Sekigun*.

Engaging the motorized film advance, Kyoto clicked off an

additional nine frames and wished the camera were an automatic weapon. Hopefully, he would be allowed to kill Saad later. He would remember to ask permission.

Hassim busied himself with his plate. Kyoto looked entirely too sullen and arrogant. His open hostility was like an inflamed nerve ending which only served to accentuate the involuntary shudder Hassim felt feathering along his spine.

It made the waiting interminable. Through no conceivable stretch of the imagination could Hassim bring himself to share a *Sekigunis* fascination with death. But why *this* meeting? Why now? Had they somehow discovered him out? Marked him for interrogation? Something painful?

No. Of course not. Not at this point surely. No . . . it was only his usual fears manifesting themselves. The other hand reaching out for its due. Repressed sensations indicative of his deceit. His tenuous position. Again interminable. Again seemingly a ritual since Munich. The Olympics. The assassination of the eleven Israeli athletes by the Palestinians and of Hassim's being caught in the midst of the aftermath. Trapped by an oversight.

It was an unnerving experience, even pathological in its agony.

Hassim Saad did not, nor had he ever, considered himself a terrorist. On the contrary he had been content to milk out a meager living peddling toiletries to oil crews working in the Middle East. Then Yassir Arafat entered the scene, and, for some reason, his ideas of a genuine Palestinian homeland appealed to Hassim.

Of course, at first, being anything but a political animal, Hassim had been reluctant to become involved; but gradually, over the course of some two years, his Palestinian birthright prevailed, and he came to realize that he owed Arafat something. Anything. Support, understanding, perhaps some small measure of financial consideration. Something benign. Something easy.

His decision made, Hassim requested and was allowed a meeting with the Palestinian leader in early 1972.

To Hassim's surprise, he found Arafat to be not quite a fatherly figure who directed the Palestinian Liberation Organization with a gentle, yet firm hand. He was the kind of man whose mere presence and manner made his followers want to do more without being asked directly.

Calling Hassim one of his lost children, Arafat decided to avail himself of the peddler's services. Obviously, the overweight, shapeless Saad had no place on any action team; but, as in all political affairs, there was definitely a slot for him. Arafat's commandos needed weapons and, if directed and nurtured correctly, Hassim Saad could provide this critical service. Arafat would give the peddler the opportunity to serve.

Hassim rose to the task. Following instructions, he traveled to Syria, purchased the required items, bribed the appropriate officials, and arranged to have the materials smuggled into Germany concealed in the tack trunks of the Egyptian equestrian team. As in the case of most successful operations, the Palestinian plan was simple by design. Owing to the quantities of sports-related equipment stacked at German customs and the general confusion attendant to thousands of athletes converging on the country, inspections were cursory, at best. Hassim, then posing as an Egyptian field judge, easily retrieved the weapons inside Germany and passed them to the Palestinian action team already in place outside of Munich.

For Yassir Arafat, the resulting attack was an unparalleled success. Satellite television beamed the details to over a half billion viewers, and the Palestinian cause was catapulted onto the world stage. For Hassim, it was another story entirely. He had made a novice's mistake—one small oversight which would alter his life forever.

He was caught with two passports . . . one Syrian, one Egyptian. Both counterfeit.

It happened at the Rome Airport in the week following the Munich massacre when he cleared customs. It was his own fault, really. Had he remained in the international transit lounge and waited for his flight to Algiers, he would never have been discovered. But he was hungry and wanted something a bit more substantial than snack bar fare. Like an idiot, he was heading for the main restaurant in the central terminal when he found himself in the customs line. Realizing that if he turned around, he would probably raise suspicions, Hassim tried to bluff his way through the checkpoint. His efforts resulted only in a closer inspection, the seizure of the passports, and his detention for additional investigation.

Hassim was a poor liar. After a two-minute flurry of questioning by an Italian functionary, he was left alone, locked in a tiny holding cell which smelled of disinfectant and had no windows.

Within the hour, Hassim had another visitor: an unusually large man with sharp, raw-boned features who possessed the bearing of a paratroop colonel, which Hassim later found out was exactly his background.

He introduced himself as Aaron. No last name—just Aaron. And as he tossed the forged passports onto a small table, Hassim knew he had just met his first Mossad agent.

Aaron questioned him for seven hours. Who was he? Why had he been in Syria? Germany? Italy? Why was he going to Algiers? Why two passports? Why? Who? When?

Hassim lied valiantly, but Aaron believed none of it. And finally, as they entered the eighth hour of the questioning, the Israeli told Hassim that due to his complicity in the athletes' deaths, he had been authorized to employ certain physical inducements in order to gain additional information.

At this Hassim had wet his pants and begun to cry.

Aaron was unimpressed and calmly detailed an abhorrent litany of various "motivational procedures" which could be adapted for Hassim's express enjoyment. All, unfortunately, would eventually lead to his untimely demise, of course. Would Hassim care to participate?

Was there any other way?

Aaron had considered the question as if not expecting it. "Yes," he had answered after a moment. "There could conceivably be *one* window of opportunity."

Hassim had cratered. After no more than four seconds of soul searching, he offered to provide Tel Aviv with inside information on terrorist activities in exchange for indulgence. Desperate for a source within the Palestinians, Aaron had agreed, at least until they could evaluate the accuracy of his intelligence.

Within six months, Hassim had proved himself. His information was valid. Soon thereafter, the Israelis kept their part of the bargain, and Hassim Saad slid into the murky world of intelligence barter as a paid Mossad agent. The price was the extension of his life.

''Damned Israelis!'' he cursed, glancing at Kyoto as he shifted in his chair. The bastards had kept him in place for over fifteen years now. Fifteen agonizing, increasingly hostile years as he picked his way through the various contingencies. Sifting details. Passing numbers, names, even targets to his ever-younger Israeli control agents. The line. That taut, ever-present pivot between keeping the Jews from killing him because he omitted some client trivia; and his clients from killing him because someone revealed he was owned by the Jews.

Then there had been the Crandon matter, he remembered bitterly. The Israelis had handled it entirely too loosely. Too brazenly. A fact, Hassim realized, which led to the undeniable conclusion that he was soon to be turned out. Offered up for the taking.

''Fucking Ursula!'' he whispered, unable to ignore Kyoto's glares burning into the side of his head. It it hadn't been for her seductive meddling, he wouldn't have been involved with the IRA in the first place. But no, she had smiled. Just *one* shipment. *One* small package for something special.

True, it was just *one* small package. Two point six pounds to be exact. The problem was that the *one* little package contained a Soviet RKG-3 antitank grenade which eventually found its merry way into the refrigerator of the British trade consul in Gibraltar. A package the consul no doubt wondered about for the two seconds prior to its detonation in his face.

Then again, it was probably his own fault, Hassim thought. *I probably shouldn't have mentioned the grenade to the Israelis*. How was he to know that the Israelis were going to fuck him? That the British were refusing to extradite an Israeli political criminal? That Tel Aviv had offered to trade the Gibraltar assassin in exchange for the political prisoner?

Fucking Crandon and his fucking bombs, he thought, picking at his fingernails with the corner of the table. The egotistical bastard had been sucked into the British-Israeli plan with virtually no effort at all. And even Ursula. For all her damned notoriety, she, too, fell easily in line.

Of course it *was* an excellent plan, Hassim remembered. Another case of brilliance in simplicity. He had contacted Ursula and explained that he had access to twenty-four Soviet AK-47 assault rifles and did she happen to know anyone who happened to want them? As expected, Peder Crandon was in Bern the following morning to handle the transaction. The meeting was recorded for posterity by a videotape crew from the Israeli embassy.

As expected, Crandon had been reluctant to actually take the weapons into his custody. For Hassim, this was only part of the plan. He explained to Crandon that the items would be drop-shipped from Libya via Lisbon, and all Crandon had to do was tell him where and when to have the weapons smuggled into Northern Ireland.

Enthusiastically, Crandon provided the instructions and Ursula was sent to Tripoli. Hassim would receive funding when she confirmed shipment.

From that point on, things progressed smoothly. The British set up a surveillance at the designated location, and, on schedule, the rifles were smuggled ashore by undercover British Royal Marines. When Crandon arrived to retrieve his booty, he was arrested and taken away in irons. Altogether, it was a quick, successful little plan.

It was also, quite concurrently, the reason for Hassim Saad's apprehensiveness as he waited in the promenade café.

In the three years since Peder Crandon's suicide, he had heard literally nothing from Ursula Brandt. No calls. No messages. Not even any intermediate communications. Of course, for obvious reasons, he had made a point of following her and young Crandon's escapades; but as far as any personal contact, there had been absolutely nothing.

Nothing, that is, until her call last evening.

Hassim sighed heavily. Ursula had all but ordered him to meet her at the café. But why? If—and it was entirely possible—in the previous three years she had somehow determined he was the one who had set Crandon up, then he would soon be dead.

On the other hand, if he had refused to show up, it would be out of character. As far as appearances went, he could only assume they were still friends. Knowing Ursula as he did, any uncharacteristic behavior on his part would undoubtedly raise her suspicions and conceivably prompt her inquiry into his current loyalties. Considering his conditional standing in the eyes of Tel Aviv, it gave the Israelis a relatively discreet way to rid themselves of a sick man's admittedly outdated services.

Suddenly Hassim stiffened.

Walking rapidly, purposefully, Ursula Brandt entered the café and headed directly toward his table.

Swallowing his fear, Hassim studied her. Even with her hair pulled back under a scarf and no makeup, she was still an incredibly wanton-looking woman.

For an instant, he thought to stand, then decided against it. It was not good. Her face was unsmiling. A cold mask of indifference.

Resigning himself for whatever was to come, Hassim slipped another demerol capsule between his lips.

"Oh, what a tangled web we weave," he thought, attempting a smile as she approached the table.

"Hello, Ursula," he said.

Chapter 4

THE ROOM WAS warm and humid. A squalid hovel illuminated by silent flickerings of a small television set splashing twisted images across peeling, broken walls. A small radio played softly, hushed renderings of a Mozart refrain which moved in concert with the light. And outside, the pale Washington dawn remained sequestered behind ragged pieces of aluminum foil hastily taped at right angles to the glass. Shadow upon shadow upon shadow. A safe place for the roach to forage.

Unconcerned with the lack of visibility, the insect scurried expertly across the wall inches from the man's head. Stalking toward the day-rent apartment's sink, it stopped to survey the piles of food-encrusted dishes and soggy cardboard containers. A smorgasbord to savor, then to sample in leisure.

Suddenly, from the bed, a bone cracked. A sharp, brittle sound that beat against the insect's antennae and prompted it to search for cover until the sound could be evaluated.

Perching itself astride a rotting eggroll, the roach turned to watch the man. Antennae twitching, its mandibles pulled at a particularly tasty segment of sour cabbage as it waited.

Peder Crandon inspected the chicken bone with the expertise of a hematologist. Impartial. Detached. The marrow remained a dark purple, and it pleased him.

Shifting on the bed, he looked to the roach and thought of Ireland. Of Shaw's Bridge. What was it the vicar had kept telling him? *No, Peder. Insects are God's creatures too. There is no reason to pluck their wings. To torture them. They have done nothing to you, have they, Peder? Have they harmed you in any manner? They have not, Peder. Now pray, Peder. Bury the insect with the others and pray God to forgive you.*

But in spite of the vicar, he remembered, the insects had become reptiles; the reptiles, birds; and the birds, mammals. He smiled at the orderly progression which somehow seemed to fill some youthful need. Some prepubescent calling. The logical development which, upon celebration of his fourteenth year, had found him achieving his first orgasm during the strangulation and dissection of Molly, the vicar's golden Labrador retriever.

Why have you done this, Peder? Molly loved you as I do. Molly trusted you. Why did you want to hurt her?

He had no answers.

Bury Molly, Peder. And after you have done so, I want you to pray. Pray to almighty God to have forgiveness upon your immortal soul.

Turning his affection from the roach, Peder Crandon looked at the girl's body. From the floor, she stared back with eyes sugared in death. He chuckled. Child, he thought, taking a bone particle between his lips and sucking at the porous interior membrane. He must remember to remove the wire garrot prior to disposing of the body.

He inspected the bone again. The marrow was gone, replaced by bits of partially chewed flesh suspended in milky saliva. Tossing the bone toward the sink, he examined his fingers. In the harsh light of the television, they glistened with a smooth film of grease.

Leaning down, he reached to the girl's face, caressing her swollen lips with soiled fingers. And as he slid a thumb into her mouth, his mind began to pray:

"There is a fountain filled with blood,
Drawn from Emmanuel's veins,
And sinners plunged beneath that flood
Lose all their guilty stains."

The roach watched the man for another moment. Then, realizing that the man was not a threat, returned to its foraging. The place was good, it decided.

It would lay eggs later in the day.

Chapter 5

"WORKED JUST LIKE you said it would, sir," the driver grinned as Taylor climbed into the Buick's rear seat.

Taylor nodded. "Good," he said, absently thumbing the dossiers in his lap. "Let's get over to the bunker. You can brief me on the way."

As they pulled out of the general's driveway for the twenty-minute run to the Pentagon, one phrase kept clicking in Taylor's mind: *One man's terrorist is another man's freedom fighter*.

He could not recall who had actually coined the expression, or for that matter where he had first heard it; nonetheless there was a certain amount of truth in the words. Every country had its skeletons.

Lighting a Marlboro, Taylor recalled when a member of the Baader-Meinhof gang, arrested in West Germany, made headlines during his trial by claiming that George Washington was a terrorist and that describing a man as such was nothing less than a term of honor.

Intellectually, Taylor disagreed with the defendant's self-serving definition. Perhaps, in the past, terrorism could be understood as some type of legitimate means of opposing national tyranny. But recently modern terrorist groups killed and kidnapped solely for public recognition . . . not for any realistic chance at international acceptance.

And now, evidently, Peder Crandon was attempting to add yet another dimension to the phenomenon . . . a political target for personal reasons.

Was he then a terrorist or a common murderer? Taylor thought about it. Crandon didn't claim any public recognition—calls to the newspapers, cryptic notes, demands, the normal criteria. But why leave the coins? Surely he was aware they would link him to the crimes. Maybe he was ordered to? Or maybe he simply did it to play with the Brits.

But still, Taylor speculated, without any public acclaim; without any public rationale for the targets, it would seem that Crandon had eased himself into—then immediately out of—the terrorist category. No, he decided. Peder Crandon was not a terrorist. He was a killer. Maybe a bit more sophisticated than others, but a killer all the same.

Fuck it, Taylor thought, dismissing the definitions from his mind. He was a circuit rider . . . not a politician. He would leave the subtle political analysis to people like Brayden and Prescott. His job was to stop Crandon—not theorize on the ramifications or motivations of international violence. Besides, he thought wryly, all the intellectual bullshit bored the hell out of him.

He glanced out the window. The driver had taken Rock Creek Parkway. On his left was the Watergate complex. Since the notoriety, Taylor had read where the waiting list for vacancies remained in excess of two thousand names. It was human nature to want some small bit of history in life, he supposed.

Then the Kennedy Center loomed into view. The sight of the building saddened him. It was one of the places he had brought his wife on their honeymoon trip to Washington. In spite of his good natured protests, she had wanted to see the capital of his country. He had finally agreed.

Taylor sucked deeply on the cigarette. The Kennedy Center. It was where they had spent their last evening before returning to Manila. He sighed. It was also human nature, he supposed, that he could not remember the name of the musical she had so enjoyed thoroughly. Perhaps it was better that way, but God, how he missed the woman.

Her memorial service had been an insult. Of course the people at the embassy did their best to appear concerned. The ambassador, his wife, the other women sweltering in the Filipino humidity. All expressing utterances of concern. Taylor had ignored them. He understood death.

The meditation room was patently State Department. A small alcove doleful in muted grays and black. A solitary bouquet of flowers. Drapes subduing the organ strains. America behind closed embassy walls.

Fighting an overpowering urge to flee, Taylor had walked to the altar displaying her photograph: a thin government-issue frame flanked by matching candles. The hollow pretense of authorized homage.

He had stood transfixed—perhaps by the flames, perhaps by his own thoughts. He could not remember. But then, as he watched her features being distorted by the candles, he had realized what was wrong with the scene. There was no evidence she had ever existed. The photographs were simply not enough. They would fade through the years, and, like memories, eventually wither and die.

Taylor wanted more. If there was to be death, he wanted it to be more tangible. Something he could keep. But it was not to be his, nor could it ever be.

Rolling down his window, Taylor tilted his face into the wind, in conscious effort to dry tears spawned from unspeakable emotion. He needed a drink. He needed to force her memories from his mind.

The Buick slowed through the turn at the Lincoln Memorial and crossed the Memorial Bridge to the western bank of the Potomac River. As they sloshed onto the Jefferson Davis Highway, Taylor looked up to the home of Robert E. Lee, stately on its perch observing the thousands of graves at Arlington National Cemetery. Here were more victims of other forgotten battles. Such was the legacy of Washington: the power of the present relying solely on the sacrifices of the past. To Taylor, the significance reeked with contempt. It was his city now and it was appropriate. With reluctance, he allowed the craving to pass. He would drink later. Peder Crandon came first.

"Tell me about the chauffeur, corporal."

The driver glanced back through the rearview mirror. "What part, sir?"

"All of it," Taylor answered.

For the next few minutes, the young marine relayed his conversation with the limousine driver and answered Taylor's questions. Yes, Prescott was some high-level diplomat. No, he was not assigned permanently to their embassy. Yes, both Prescott and Brayden had been at the White House—the driver whined about not having been allowed inside. And yes, as far as the chauffeur knew, he was supposed to drop Prescott off at Dulles Airport sometime later in the day.

"I kind of got the impression he didn't like Mr. Prescott," the driver added as he drove the Buick through the river entrance and onto the vacant concrete slab which served as the Pentagon's parking area.

"Why's that?" Taylor asked.

The corporal shrugged. "Just a feeling. He said he acted like some ruddy valentine running around in the middle of the night."

"A Ballantine? Like the scotch?"

"No, sir. A valentine . . . like the heart."

Taylor leaned forward. "You ask him what he meant by that?"

"No, sir. I just figured he was gay or something."

Taylor chuckled at the corporal's comment. "Never jump to conclusions, corporal," he smiled. "They have a way of slipping up on you and biting off your ass when you least expect it."

"Yes, sir," the driver answered, pulling to a stop next to the VIP checkpoint. "You want me to wait, sir?"

"No, that won't be necessary." Taylor saw no point in

keeping the young man tied up. He had no idea how long he would be and he could always request another driver from the duty officer. "And you did just fine talking to that chauffeur. If your C.O. agrees, tell him I think you should have administrative leave this afternoon."

Knowing that a word from Taylor would immediately give him the day off, the driver grinned broadly. "Yes, sir," he said. "Thank you, sir."

Gathering the dossiers, Taylor climbed out of the Buick and gazed up at the building. Four stories and ten city blocks around, the Pentagon was the world's largest office building, situated on the world's largest parking lot. It was a small city which housed some 40,000 workers operating around the clock, 365 days a year.

The Soviets were right, Taylor decided, recalling a recent *Pravda* article. The building *did* look like some huge medieval mausoleum dedicated to the gods of war, almost as if the architects had made no attempt to make its lines aesthetically pleasing.

Screw the Soviets, he thought, heading up the steps to the glass doors seemingly attached to the bunkerlike facade as an afterthought. What made them think they were such hot fashion plates anyway?

As he jerked open the doors and stepped inside, the word again flashed in his mind. *Valentine*. Again he searched his memory. Now he was almost sure he had heard the term before.

Valentine. No, he was positive it didn't mean anything gayish. Nor did it have anything to do with the holiday.

It wasn't an insult, but he couldn't remember it being a compliment, either.

Must be getting Alzheimer's disease, he thought. Maybe if he didn't try, it would come to him later.

Walking to the security checkpoint, Taylor produced a small leather wallet containing the laminated identification card bearing his name, photograph, job title, and signature to the guard.

"Thank you, Mr. Taylor," the army duty sergeant replied. "Have a good morning."

Taylor nodded absently, replaced the wallet in his pocket and walked around the checkpoint to a bank of elevators bearing the caveat *Restricted Access*.

Stepping inside number four, he pressed the selector sensor for the third floor, watched the door slide close and continued to think about *Valentine* while the elevator clicked upward. Still he could not place it.

As the door opened, Taylor stepped out and into the third floor's security holding foyer—a 12′ x 20′ room with one steel door.

"Access number please," a computerized female voice said softly.

"Zero-Four-Seven-Two-Niner," he responded, turning his face toward the closed circuit television camera.

"Thank you, Mr. Taylor," the voice immediately confirmed. "You are cleared for access at the sound of the tone."

The mellow electronic beeping began, and Taylor pushed open the door and entered the third floor. He was greeted by a crisp young navy ensign stepping out from behind a brace of television monitors. In uniform, the officer was wearing a holstered 9-millimeter Beretta automatic.

"Morning, Mr. Taylor. Could I get your signature?" The ensign indicated a ledger lying on the counter and handed Taylor a pen.

"You got it." As he scribbled his initials in the book, Taylor glanced up at the young officer. "Weekend duty, Kenny?"

"Yes, sir." The ensign was clearly bored.

Taylor returned the pen and the officer immediately leaned over and initialed his entry.

"Well, you know what they say," Taylor teased. "Something about seeing the world, isn't it?"

Smiling, the ensign returned to his post behind the monitors. "Two more months," he said. "I rotate to fleet at the first of the year."

"North Atlantic?" Taylor asked.

"Pacific."

Taylor was happy for him. "Well, you better watch out for those Soviet subs," he winked, moving around the desk and toward a second set of steel doors. "I understand there's some kind of bounty on hard-charging young ensigns."

"I'm ready for them, Mr. Taylor. I just hope they're ready for me."

With a wave of the hand, Taylor pushed through the doors and walked quickly down a deserted hall to a door identified by the notation *Special Projects Section*. Pressing the appropriate digits on a small keyboard lock to the left of the knob, the door popped open and he stepped inside, closing it behind him. It shut with an almost sighing resonance, and Taylor felt the usual twinge of discomfort. He supposed he would never get used to the hollow finality of the electronic locking mechanism which isolated his offices from the remainder of the Pentagon. He always had the distinct impression of being entombed alive, which in fact, was exactly the case.

Essentially, Taylor's operation was contained inside a huge vault with no windows. The floor, walls, and ceiling were comprised of one-inch steel plate with a 50,000 lb. per square inch tensile strength. And the door was cast from over two inches of tempered steel which in itself could probably resist a small nuclear explosion if put to the test.

Notwithstanding, Taylor was proud of his section. Walls were lined with large data-storage containers, and the desks supported individual keyboard terminals complete with video display screens and individual printers.

Looking toward the center of the room, Taylor began to smile. Isolated by a large Plexiglas inverted fish tank of a covering stood the pulse of his operation: the complex PCAC-980 computer, humming softly as it bathed itself in an eerie pale green light.

By design, the entire section was contemporary and functional. Chrome, glass, white enamel, and black leather combined to exude a first impression perhaps more suited to some sterile Soho art gallery. But the illusion did not concern Taylor. He felt that the preciseness of the room overpowered any type of human emotional response. And this was the exact image he had attempted and obviously succeeded in achieving.

Originally proposed in the early 1980s, the Personnel Command and Control Base, or PCAC system as it was generally identified, had been developed as a data bank of personnel qualifications. The system was available to various government agencies and several friendly nations who required a particularly qualified individual for a special assignment or position.

Upon request, PCAC would ferret through the millions of names in its banks and find the person most closely possessing the specific criteria set forth by the requesting agency. And to be sure, the requirements had proved to have been as varied as the individuals whose personal data were contained inside the system's memory banks.

As he walked over to the Plexiglas covering, Taylor recalled the fairly typical case when an official from the Department of Energy asked the section to locate an individual who spoke an obscure Central American Indian dialect. The kicker was that the individual also had to be a physician.

Within minutes, the requirements had been fed into the computer and the official had the name of a female flight surgeon assigned to NASA outside of Houston. The doctor's hobby had been linguistics.

By choice, Taylor never asked why a particular individual was needed, and the requesters seldom provided an explanation. As a practical matter, it was of little concern to him. The information developed by the requests was considered to be only an ancillary benefit, simply another means of gathering intelligence on those who requested PCAC's services.

Through an analysis of the particular requests, either from specific American agencies or the selected foreign governments, a pattern revealing any type of specialized activities involving the requesters could be easily discerned. This information, when evaluated with the volumes of data constantly pouring into PCAC from the various intelligence agencies, provided an incredibly broad base of raw information which could be retrieved and analyzed without the knowledge of the requesters involved.

In itself, this automated evaluation process represented a quantum leap forward in the continually evolving technology relative to intelligence assessment. However, when considered in comparison to PCAC's total capability, even this breakthrough emerged as only a minuscule part of its potential applications. Applications which had now introduced Peder Crandon into Samuel Taylor's world.

Since returning from Manila, Taylor had assumed direct responsibility as a conduit for "wet operations" conducted in the interest of the United States. It was a position he guarded jealously and one which had taken him to Austria, Italy, El Salvador, and, most recently, Belgium to—as he put it—"tidy up any loose ends": his euphemism for clandestine actions directed to punishing those who had somehow offended Washington.

What the public and most of the government failed to realize was that PCAC also indexed the names of hundreds of individuals, both government employees and outside specialists, whose talents had been catalogued carefully for future reference.

In the majority of cases, the specialists were needed for some unique covert project developed by one of the intelligence agencies or the military, and the necessary skills usually involved a proficiency with certain types of weapons or explosives as well as advanced training in skin diving, mountaineering, or similar esoterica. In these cases, Taylor *did* know the reasons for the requests; however he did not actually supervise the project. Except for one category; RAINDANCER. Under this umbrella, Taylor traveled, remaining on site while his operatives carried out their instructions.

Turning from PCAC's mainframe, Taylor walked slowly toward his office at the far corner of the section. As he had designed, the procedures for locating a RAINDANCER operative were essentially identical to any other random search. An access code was entered, and PCAC scanned its memories to determine the clearance of the operator. After verification, the operator entered a second code to initiate recall of the data and made a selection after reviewing the particular personnel abstracts generated.

RAINDANCER employed additional security procedures.

When selecting personnel to augment his "tidying" operations, Taylor had preprogrammed PCAC to automatically erase any queries the moment a search was completed. This precaution, in addition to an encrypted access control cipher, assured that *if* PCAC's integrity should be breached, there would be no electronic paper trail leading to any RAINDANCER personnel files—or, perhaps more important, any specific details of past deployments. Deployments which to date, were known only to himself, the general, Catlin, and those members of the National Security Council selected by the president.

"Morning, boss."

The throaty female voice startled him, and Taylor flinched with surprise. "Jesus, Cat!" He wheeled around and felt like an asshole for not noticing her name on the sign-in ledger. "You scared the hell out of me."

He nodded to a thick sheath of papers clutched to her breast. "What's going on? Stealing a few secrets for the Chinese?"

She smiled. "The Koreans pay better, Sam. You told me that."

He laughed at her response, again wishing things could be

different between them. Something less formal. Something more personal.

At thirty-four, Catlin Broussard had been his executive assistant for nearly a year. A bittersweet year, really. Eleven months during which he had been forced to the sidelines by the packs of junior officers who seemed to trail her like so many gerbils in heat.

He had learned to hate their self-confidence with a passion equaling the loathing of his own impotence.

Of course he could understand their interest. If anything, she was an exotic, if not exactly beautiful woman. When Taylor saw her type in public, he always wondered why her escort was some pencil neck whose idea of excitement was limited to opening a fresh package of soap-on-a-rope.

Cat was tall, maybe 5′9″, a perfectly proportioned 130 pounds, and chicly Creole with a smooth *café au lait* complexion, violent eyes, and a faint-but-discernible soft bayou drawl.

Her hair was short, not curly, and cut loosely in what Taylor considered a shag, left somewhat longer at the temples and nape. It was a lustrous deep brown frame which only served to accentuate her high cheekbones, wide but feminine nose, and sensuous lips.

Acknowledging his partiality, Taylor realized he had always been attracted to darker women—Oriental, Spanish, Mediterranean. But Catlin, with her mixed Negro-French ancestry, seemed to outdo all of them, and he never tired of watching her.

Like himself, Cat tended to shun formal wear and today, he noticed, was no exception. She was dressed down—tight faded jeans, a bulky ivory shetland wool turtleneck, cordovan-colored ostrich boots, and a paisley scarf draped casually around her neck. A man's gold Rolex hung loosely from her left wrist, matching two small loops piercing her ears as well as the thin bracelet Taylor knew she wore at her ankle.

But appearances were not the only thing that had attracted Taylor to Catlin. He had come to like her. Moreover, in a decision he reserved for few women, he genuinely respected her. She was both intelligent and eager to learn. Whether it came from the knowledge she possessed, a doctorate in computer science from Louisiana State University, or the fact she had been personally hired by the general, Taylor wasn't sure. But whatever the reason, he trusted her professionally. And as far as any personal relationship? Taylor forced himself to watch her from afar. It was a question of embarrassment.

"Seriously," he said. "What is all that junk?"

"Numbers," she shrugged, glancing at the papers. "I'm trying to project our budget for next year."

"We just did that!" Taylor vividly remembered the week of agony spent preparing the proposal.

"It was rejected."

"Rejected?" The petty bullshit infuriated him.

Catlin flashed a quick grin. "Get this—we didn't ask for enough money."

"Figures," he sighed.

She shrugged her shoulders. "Hey, don't blame me. You're the boss—I'm just a humble civil servant trying to spend the handouts from my elected representatives."

Taylor smiled at the sarcasm. "Well, if you can tear yourself away from the high finance, I need your help on something a little more critical."

"Critical?" She arched an eyebrow with the question.

"We have a RAINDANCER. The general wants you in on control."

"But——"

Taylor silenced her with a wave of his hand. "He *did* call you, *didn't* he?"

She nodded sheepishly. "Yes. But he didn't——"

"He wouldn't." Taylor continued to his office. "Look . . . I don't like end runs, Cat. But if that's what Brayden wants, so be it."

Although his tone held no animosity, Catlin knew he hurt.

They both knew Brayden had slotted her to take Taylor's place. But that wasn't supposed to be until Taylor retired—two more years, at the least.

Granted, she could pull it off. The actual operations were conducted by RAINDANCER selectees. Control was concerned only with planning, logistics, and liaison. But Taylor. She knew how he would react—personally.

In the past year, Catlin Broussard had come to realize one thing about Taylor. She understood the reason: work had become his escape, the vehicle through which he avoided any emotional commitment to others. Understandable, perhaps, given his history; but why with *her?* Had she been too pushy? Too eager? Did he find her unattractive? If he didn't, why did he continue to avoid her overtures of friendship?

And now he realized that the general was easing him out sooner, forcing him into the cold through events he couldn't control. She sighed heavily. It would only eat at him, drive him deeper into his shell, and probably devour him in the end.

Catlin knew it was wrong. Taylor was the most capable professional she knew.

If only the general had given her more time. Time to get closer to Taylor, time to understand him.

God knows she had tried; but just when she finally thought she had sliced through some layer of his psychological skin, Taylor had only proved her wrong by shedding that layer to reveal another, even thicker one beneath.

Nothing worked. Not the direct questions, nor the flirting, not even the subtle innuendos tossed out to expose the roots of his detachment.

As she turned and walked to the vault, the sounds of Taylor's whispering whistle drifted into the room. Coming from his office, it made her smile tenderly.

No doubt the toneless rendition would have been unrecognizable to Rodgers and Hammerstein; nevertheless, Catlin realized the significance. For Taylor, "Some Enchanted Evening" somehow made things a little clearer. Made the stress a little easier to manage.

He told her it was from *South Pacific,* and she had understood his interpretation. In a world of illusion, emotions were transitory. True, it was not a great thought, but it was the Samuel Taylor she knew and appreciated.

And this she thought, locking the vault and walking to join him, was the real reason for her decision. RAINDANCER or not, she would not stand idly by and allow the general to isolate Samuel Taylor further. He was her friend, and with friendship, some things were more important than others.

It was something they could work out together.

Chapter 6

"PLEASE," HASSIM SAID nervously as Ursula sat down across from him, "won't you join me in a sweetbread?"

She eyed the platter cynically. "I've never developed a taste for cooked lamb, Hassim. Its smell reminds me of burning human flesh."

Hassim thought of vomiting. "Well . . . of course," he mumbled. "I'll have it removed." Taking his napkin, he unfolded it and lay it over what remained of his lunch. "So, Ursula, how have you been?"

"Fine," she answered tersely, glancing over to Kyoto. "And you?"

"Business has been reasonably good," he said, flipping a pudgy hand back and forth. "Good months, bad months . . . normal."

Hassim waited for a response, but none came. "And how is my friend Yasif?" he asked, hoping that the reference to the former chief of Libyan intelligence would do *something* to ease the tension of the moment.

"Fine. I'm sure he would send his regards." Her voice was toneless.

A curious response, Hassim noted, deciding to probe. "I understand he is in the United States?"

Ignoring the question, Ursula stared coldly into his eyes, for the moment silencing any additional speculation on his part.

"Well," he said quickly, hoping to change the subject. "I

understand your business has also been good . . . DeGaulle Airport?''

''You understand too much, Hassim. And you talk too much.''

Hassim was aware of his palms beginning to sweat. ''But Ursula, I mean nothing. It is merely my work.''

''Perhaps,'' she said, her voice noticeably softer. ''But your work will cause your death, my friend. Maybe not today, nor even tomorrow. But one day . . .'' She let the sentence trail off.

Hassim looked over and noticed Kyoto moving along the promenade railing. The Oriental was glaring openly, and Hassim felt his pulse quicken in apprehension.

The conversation with Ursula was not progressing well at all. In less than a minute, he had somehow manipulated himself into a position where he was in danger of alienating the woman, and, through her, possibly Yasif. That would be an unthinkable scenario. For it would be impossible for him to do business without Yasif's tacit indulgence.

Then again, on the brighter side, it was obvious that she wasn't aware of his complicity in Crandon's arrest. So why the reason for her call? This incongruous little meeting?

Go slow, he reminded himself. *Follow suit. Let her direct the conversation.* Averting his eyes, Hassim forced himself to wait in silence until she decided to continue.

The ploy worked.

''I would like some tea,'' she said after two minutes of some kind of ridiculous meditation.

''Of course,'' he smiled. Signaling a sleepy-looking waiter, he placed the order, instructed that the sweetbreads be removed, and returned his attentions back to Ursula.

She was still an incredibly beautiful woman, he realized. But at the same time, different. Thinner maybe. More . . . was the word *fatalistic?* Almost as if her face were dissolving slowly into middle age. With no makeup, he could now detect spidery wrinkles at the corners of her eyes and others pulling deftly at the juncture of her lips. And her hair. Even pulled back under the scarf, he could see it was darker. Still red, only darker. He supposed she altered its color. Had there been gray?

But these were not the things that made her seem different. There was something else. Something more subtle about her general persona. Something missing, perhaps. He searched his memory and suddenly it hit him—her eyes.

He inspected them. Yes, he decided. Definitely her eyes. A startling difference, really. The sparkling deep blue of years before had somehow abandoned the reckless enthusiasm of their youth and faded into a powdery pale blue.

Had it really been three years since he had seen her? He counted back. Yes. Almost to the month. It must have been a difficult time, he mused as the man returned with her tea. Life was catching up with her rapidly.

Dismissing the waiter with a wave of his hand, Hassim leaned over the table and watched her take a sip of the tea.

"Ursula," he said softly. "Enough of this pointless talk of death. We are old friends. Tell me why you need to talk."

Carefully replacing her cup on its saucer, she looked into his eyes. "I'm sorry, Hassim," she whispered. "It's . . . it's just that things are so different now. Difficult." She sighed heavily.

So it appears, he thought, evaluating the woman across from him. Yes! A woman. Nothing more. If one did not know of the bombings, the killings. If one were to take her just this moment . . . she would be just another lonely person searching for something, needing something, unable to find where to look. Perhaps this was a clue of the puzzle. He would play her emotions.

"How may I help you?" he whispered, his voice a web of solace as he reached over and touched her hand.

"Times have changed."

"So it seems." He nodded toward Kyoto. "Bodyguards?"

Ursula shrugged absently. "Yasif's idea. I don't know whether he is to protect me . . . or merely watch."

Hassim understood. "It will pass, my friend," he reassured her. "In time, all things pass."

She pulled her hand away from his. "No, this will not pass, Hassim. I cannot allow it."

He said nothing and waited for her to take another sip of tea and explain.

"It's Yasif," she said. "He's become so . . . so . . ."

"You are lovers?" Knowing Yasif as he did, Hassim had already predicted her answer.

"Yes," she confirmed. "Now."

"But what of the Crandon boy?"

"Peder is in America," she sighed.

America? he thought, his interest stirred. "For what reason?"

"Yasif's idea," she answered sullenly. "To keep us apart."

"I'm not sure I understand." Hassim lied. Obviously Yasif wanted any competition out of the picture—Ursula *did* have that kind of effect on men, or so he had gathered from her somewhat prurient reputation. "But then again, who am I to know of such matters?"

Cupping her hands around the teacup, Ursula nodded knowingly. "I guess you knew we were forced out of Europe."

Hassim nodded. "Only rumors."

"It was probably just as well," she said. "Peder had learned as much as I could teach him, but I felt he needed more, so we went to Africa and lived together during his training."

"I remember now . . . Libya, wasn't it?" Hassim had visited the guerrilla training facilities on numerous occasions. They were hot, dusty, and completely lacking the niceties of civilized man. Constantly screamed at by Cuban and East German cadres, recruits were forced to live in threadbare tents, eat foods which were basically starch, seasoned with bits of goat or lamb, and share a large open-air latrine. Thinking about it, Hassim could almost smell the rancid stench that enveloped the entire compound.

"It must have been difficult."

Ursula nodded. ''When Peder finished the initial phase of his training, Yasif arranged for him to attend the Odessa Military Academy outside of Moscow.''

Hassim rested his elbows on the table. ''But that is not unusual. With Peder's background, Yasif probably felt he would make an excellent choice for the academy.''

''But in our case,'' she said glumly, ''it had nothing to do with training. By that time, Yasif had finally gotten around to expressing his romantic interests in me.''

''But he is a handsome man,'' Hassim remembered. ''You did not succumb?''

''Not while Peder was around. I didn't want to hurt him.''

Hassim supressed a chuckle. ''No doubt a blow to Yasif's ego.''

Ursula ignored the comment. ''Of course Peder knew nothing about any of this—only that the Russian training was to further prepare him for the retaliation against the British. He was so consumed with his personal vendetta that he couldn't see he was being manipulated.''

A typical strategy, Hassim thought. ''Yasif is a very resourceful man.''

Ursula nodded. ''Just after Peder left for Moscow, Yasif came to my quarters. He had just returned from the *Fatah* requiem where he had led prayers for those killed during the Rome-Vienna airport victories. He was crazed, Hassim. Almost giddy with power.''

Face indifferent, but loving the details, Hassim nodded her on.

''He called me his *property,* Hassim. No man has ever called me that.''

''It's only Yasif's way,'' he answered almost offhandedly. ''He feels he owns all of us.''

''I told him to leave and he laughed,'' she continued. ''He told me he had selected me for his whore. That if I didn't agree, he would arrange for Peder to die in Russia.''

Hassim twisted his face in sympathy. Yasif had used her, he thought, used her as he used everyone. It was unfortunate, perhaps; nonetheless, Yasif made the rules and controlled the board.

"So you had no options," he said softly.

"I love Peder, Hassim," she nodded, tears welling up in her eyes. "He was only fifteen when we met . . . I became the mother he never knew. I became his confidante. His ally. I gave him warmth. Compassion . . ."

Sex, Hassim thought briefly as she trailed on.

". . . Even understanding. Things he never knew."

Sure, Hassim thought sarcastically, as she tried to compose herself. Nothing at all wrong with a surrogate mother masturbating a sixteen-year-old boy as he chopped animals into little pieces. "You had a special relationship," he mumbled.

She glanced up. "He's never been with another woman, Hassim."

"I'm sure," he smiled.

Taking a deep breath, Ursula glanced toward the river and then continued, her voice little more than a whisper. "He's such a beautiful man. Considerate. When he returned from his year in Russia, he brought me a gift. Nothing expensive. Just a small music box . . . it played Mozart. Sometimes I think he's the only man who has ever really cared for me. The only one who—who——"

"Appreciates you," Hassim said carefully. He rather delighted in the confessor role and decided to play it to the hilt. "But Peder is not in Russia now. And you are away from Yasif. Surely you——"

"No," she interrupted. "Nothing is different, Hassim. When the Soviet training was completed, Peder and I executed the French operation. But when we returned to Libya, Yasif had left word that Peder was too well known in Europe."

Hassim nodded. "So Yasif sent him to America."

"Yes," she said. "Arranged to have him smuggled into the

United States and gave him a free hand to operate however he wanted as long as he continued to intimidate British interests.''

''And you, Ursula?''

''Me?'' she laughed at the word. ''I was ordered to stay away from all men and keep myself ready should Yasif ever decide he wanted me again.''

Her voice became a hiss. ''And if I didn't? Yasif said he would kill Peder. He called me a *proprietress of alternative.*''

Hassim leaned back in his chair. ''But Yasif is a diplomat . . . the Libyan U.N. Mission. He wouldn't kill Peder *now.* There would be too much potential for hurting the Libyan-Syrian axis if his teams were caught.''

Ursula shook her head. ''No . . . not Yasif's people. He told me he had contacts inside British and American intelligence and that it would be an easy matter to expose Peder and let the Americans do the killing for him.''

For the next few moments, Hassim considered carefully what he had just been told. It was a mess and he didn't like messes. Nonetheless, at least he now knew why Ursula had wanted to see him.

''I think I understand,'' he said affectionately, leaning over and cupping her hands in his. ''Now you and Peder need whatever little bit of help I can offer. Do not worry, Ursula. I will be pleased to speak with Yasif on your behalf.''

She pulled her hands away. ''I don't want you to speak with Yasif,'' she said flatly.

Hassim was confused. ''What would you have me do?''

''We need weapons, Hassim.'' Her voice was surgically precise.

''But——'' he stammered. ''You can get weapons . . . you, of all people, have sources.''

''Peder wants them in America.''

''But that is the easiest place in the world to get weapons.''

''Not special weapons.''

Special weapons? Hassim's mind raced with options. What?

Chemical? Biological? Nuclear? No. It was an impossible request. It was obvious that she was going around Yasif. And what of the Irishman? Was he no longer under Yasif's control? There was simply not enough information to support his treading on such dangerous ground.

"Hassim?"

He ignored her. No, he thought. He could not do it. Although, to many, Yasif's United Nations position gave at least the *illusion* of respectability to him, nothing was further from the the truth. In his eyes, Yasif would always be the ruthless Mephistophelian figure who retained responsibility for most Islamic-sponsored terror operations. No. He had feared the man for over a decade and would not allow himself to run the risk of alienation at this late stage.

"I want your answer, Hassim. I want it now."

He stared up at her. "Please don't ask me to do this, Ursula. Try Bouhler or Luedecke in Antwerp. You know them."

"I can't, Hassim." Her voice became a hiss. "I'm being watched."

"But Yasif . . . I cannot"—he searched for words—"he will kill me." Hassim looked into her eyes hoping to see some measure of understanding. There was none.

"Yasif trusts you," she said, nodding toward Kyoto. "He won't be suspicious of our meeting when Kyoto reports back to him."

Hassim shivered. "You are playing with my life, Ursula. If he finds out, he will kill me. He has no alternative. You know that."

Ursula nodded slowly. "And if you don't help us, *I* will kill you."

So it has come to this, he thought, her total lack of emotion echoing in his mind. But there had to be a way out. There was *always* a way out.

Pushing back from the table, Hassim stood and walked to the promenade railing overlooking the river. In the distance a young child was flying a bright red box kite, a small puppy darting circles around her as she ran to gain more altitude. Another world, he sighed. A simpler time.

Hassim felt smothered with regret. That was not his world. His was Ursula. Peder. Yasif. The Aarons of life. Unfortunate situations foaling desperate people. Violence breeding violence in a medium where all possessed an illusory sense of power and certainty thrived in a culture salted with commitment.

And Ursula? He shook his head. Her perverse morality, grandiose in its butchery, would allow him no quarter. If he refused, she would have Kyoto execute him. In that case, he would be dead within minutes. On the other hand, if he agreed to cooperate, he would be allowed to live and buy enough time to be able to find answers for Yasif. At least Yasif *could* be reasoned with.

So there really was no decision, Hassim realized. To prolong his life, cooperation was the only prudent choice.

He returned to the table and sat down.

"This is a beautiful place, Ursula," he said. "My favorite city."

"You will help us?"

He nodded almost imperceptibly. "What do you need?"

"The specifics are not important. Just a contact. A supply point."

Hassim expelled a deep breath of air. He was thankful that she did not request specific items. It would make his explanation to Yasif easier. "And where do you want these items?" he asked.

"In Washington . . . Washington, D.C." She glanced briefly at Kyoto. "I am joining Peder. He needs me."

"I understand," he lied, eager for the meeting to end. "There is a man named Montes," he breathed. "A Cuban. We have worked together, and he can be trusted."

"We need the material soon. Peder——"

He silenced her with a wave of his hand. "Not my concern,

Ursula. He will expect to hear from you. Other than that, I wash my hands of the whole business. As I said, Yasif is much too resourceful a man."

Ursula nodded. "How do we find this man Montes?"

"He is a professor at George Washington University. A teacher of art history."

"Thank you, Hassim." She rose. "Thank you for both of us."

Looking up at her, Hassim shrugged. "But what of your bodyguard?"

Ursula looked at the Oriental who was moving toward the table. "Kyoto?" she smiled. "He will not be a problem for long."

Hassim understood. "Take care, Ursula."

"And you, Hassim." Turning from the table, Ursula Brandt, followed by Kyoto, left the café through the street entrance. Only after she was gone did Hassim realize his hands were trembling. He wondered if she had noticed it, then realized she had. Ursula noticed everything.

Signaling the waiter, Hassim ordered a fresh cup of almond tea for himself, then looked out over the river. The wind was picking up and the boats were gone, now, replaced by soapy whitecaps licking methodically at the water's glassy surface. As he watched, the image began to jell in his brain. Haunting, it was Ursula's face, and then he knew why she had looked so different. It *was* her eyes. They were dead, he decided. Dead eyes impaled on a body racing in vain to overtake them.

The image was unnerving, and he twisted in his chair.

He welcomed the return of the waiter.

The two men watched in silence as Ursula, still trailed by Kyoto, left the river café and walked north, away from their dark blue Fiat. When she reached the corner, she turned left and began to stroll, almost coquettishly, down the ancient cobblestone walk which bordered the river and led back toward the Old Town section of Bern.

After a moment, the passenger climbed out of the vehicle and began to follow her as the driver took up the parallel on the street above. Both blended easily into the crowded streets of late afternoon shoppers and both went unnoticed by Ursula and Kyoto.

It was the fourth hour of their surveillance.

Chapter 7

WASHING HIS FINGERS, Peder Crandon continued to watch the girl's corpse. "Wench," he cursed. Swelling and soiled, he wanted her no more.

But what had it been? Desire? No—Ursula wouldn't allow it. The girl was like the times before Ursula. The Molly times. A throwback to the coal cellar. The choppings, the vicar, and the prayers. Only now it was different.

Nude, he walked over to the inert body and thought. But what? Should this now be a chopping? He considered it. No. Ursula would be angry. She had helped him stop the choppings, finally. No point in going back. If she found out, she would punish him for being bad.

He squatted down. But should he leave the sign? He thought about this, too. The girl *was* British. He knew. He had watched her come from the embassy. He had talked to her. Made sure. But somehow the whole thing was Mollyish. He wondered why. It was confusing. What would Ursula have him do? What would Yasif want? What would they tell him? He thought about it harder.

Pence or chopping? Chopping or pence? Chop-pence? Pencechop?

But wait—was that a smile from the girl's lips? He knelt over her body and leaned down, his face inches from hers. He would let her decide.

"Pence," he said.

She did nothing.

"Chopping."

Still the body did not react.

He snickered. Of course it did. The wench was dead. He knew. He had watched her die. He would make sure.

"Pence or chopping? Chopping or pence?"

He laughed out loud. The girl had given him the answer. Ursula would be pleased he had discovered it himself. He would remember to tell her.

Sitting cross-legged on the floor, he slid over so his knees were touching the dead girl's arm as Ursula had taught him. Then, reaching down, he grasped his penis and began to stroke it to erection.

Soon, he fantasized as his mind played thoughts of Ursula's arousing him.

No choppings, no pence. No choppings, no pence.

The phrase beat in his brain as he began his emission.

Curious, the roach thought. The human, that is. He appeared to be doing some strange dance for the amusement of his companion. But oddly enough, from what it could see, the companion was evidently ignorning his efforts. Even refusing to acknowledge the adulation. Strange, these humans. How they continued to tease each other.

Then again, it was not really a matter of concern. There was only the food, the warmth, and the nest. The humans could be left to their own peculiar recreations.

Moving to its spot—that place between the drain and the floorboards of the sink—the roach squatted and patiently began to lay its eggs.

The young would hatch in forty-eight hours.

Chapter 8

LOCATED IN A quiet corner just off the main computer room, Taylor's office was not large by executive standards. But it was cozy, functional, and perfectly suited to his personality.

Angled in one corner was the desk, an antique oak rolltop offset by Taylor's personal computer keyboard and large amber video-display screen. A printout monitor and shredder flanked the hardware modules.

The walls were covered in a rich bronzy walnut on which his souvenirs were hung: the old brass bell from Thailand, the antique Guatemalan temple rubbings, a Montagnard tribal crossbow from Laos, and the small carved plaque of his namesake, Saint Eloy.

Facing the desk were a well-worn leather sofa, an antique Chippendale coffee table, and two matching wingback chairs, all arranged neatly on a carpet whose color Taylor identified as "essence of dung."

Upon first impression, Taylor realized that his office appeared to be an extremely comfortable refuge, an eclectic blend of old and new. But like his home, Taylor cared only for a dark, peaceful environment in which to pursue his business. And as for his choice of furnishings? If asked, he would only shrug and explain interior design was something for rich people.

"Headache?" Catlin asked, entering the office and finding Taylor hunched over his desk, rubbing his temples in slow measured strokes.

"Just thinking." He looked up. "What does valentine mean to you?"

"Hearts," she said, handing Taylor a mug of steaming coffee, black with milk. "Why? Is it supposed to mean something else?"

"I'm not sure," he admitted. "It's something I think I should know. Can't put my finger on it."

Glancing at Catlin, Taylor realized she had no idea what he was talking about and decided to change the subject. "Like I said, we have a RAINDANCER, and the general has figured your time has come. Feel up to it?"

She took a sip of coffee. It was one of those questions with no good answer. "Like I said, you're the boss."

"No," Taylor corrected. "*Brayden's* the boss. I just follow instructions."

"That's not right, Sam. We both know you——"

"Don't patronize me, Cat," he interrupted her. "It's too early in the morning."

Irritated by Taylor's dog-in-the-manger attitude, Catlin walked to one of the chairs facing the desk and sat down. "I'm not patronizing anyone, Sam. And nothing's etched in stone. You and the general will work something out."

Flicking a match, he lit a cigarette. "Truce?" he asked, looking over at her.

Catlin smiled. "Truce," she repeated. "Now what's our time frame on this one?"

"Yesterday . . . as usual."

She arched an eyebrow. "So what's the problem? I'll query PCAC."

Standing, Taylor walked over to the sofa and sat down. "It's a shitty one," he told her.

"Who's the target?"

"An Irish terrorist."

"Where?"

"Here."

Catlin eye's narrowed. "The United States?"

"Washington."

Catlin gulped and shifted uncomfortably in her chair.

Taylor shrugged his shoulders. "We don't have much choice. The president let the sanction personally." He looked into her eyes. "Want out?"

"I want some details first," she said quickly.

"There really aren't many. Evidently he's some kind of *cause celebre* who's killing for personal reasons as opposed to political." Taylor took another deep drag on the cigarette. "His name is Crandon . . . Peder Crandon."

Catlin set her mug on the coffee table. "And whom has Mr. Crandon seen fit to offend?"

"Directly, the British. Indirectly, the president, I guess. Crandon's responsible for the killing of two Brits here."

"The consul general?" she guessed.

Taylor nodded. "And a female scholar at the Smithsonian."

"Who quashed the press?"

"Brits, I guess," Taylor said. "We really didn't go into that part of it. Why?"

"Just curious." She slumped back in the wingback. "You know, we're going to end up with our smiling faces in front of some Senate Investigating Committee one of these days, don't you?"

Wouldn't be my first time, Taylor thought recalling his testimony before a closed session of the Church Committee in the mid-seventies, where he had been forced to *explain* the 1970 assassination of Chilean General Rene Schneider. "In any case, the Brits have requested our cooperation under the terms of the London Letter."

Catlin stood and walked to Taylor's desk. "I thought our part was limited to actions outside the United States."

"I guess the president thought differently," he said matter-of-factly. "Whatever, the British have asked us to stop Crandon, and the president has agreed. Why don't we just let the politicians worry about the repercussions?"

Standing he walked over next to her. "So what'll it be? You in or out?"

Turning around, Catlin found herself staring at the small bas-relief wood carving on Taylor's wall. Saint Eloy. It had been a gift to Taylor from his childhood pastor back in Houston. Depicting a farrier at work, Catlin read the inscription at its base:

> "When horseshoeing a beast possessed by the devil, Saint Eloy chopped off its legs, completed his blacksmithing, and, with a miracle, put the legs back on the horse."

"What would *he* do?" she asked Taylor.

Following her gaze, Taylor smiled. "Saint Eloy? I'd expect he'd go for it."

"I'd expect he would, Sam." Moving to Taylor's desk, Catlin sat down in front of the computer keyboard. "I'll make the queries."

Taylor thought to say something; but then changed his mind as he continued to stare at the carving. Suddenly it hit him. *Valentine. Eloy.* It was a *saint.* Valentine was a name of a *person.*

Excited by the connection, he turned to Catlin. "Be back in a little bit, Cat."

She looked over her shoulder. "Where you going?"

"Joint Chiefs' library," he told her, already bulling his way out the door. "You just get the ball rolling on PCAC."

Library? she thought as she activated the keyboard. Strange time to check out a book. Then she began to smile. Expect the unexpected and then be surprised.

So it went when working with Taylor.

Chapter 9

"THERE *IS* NO other way." Hassim had already tired of the telephone conversation. "It is out of my control."

As he listened to the protests pecking in his ear, he wished he had never agreed to help Ursula. "Of course, I can appreciate your position, professor," he whispered. "Nonetheless, it is a situation which could be used to meet a certain indebtedness on your part. Do I make myself clear?"

Hassim glanced back toward the table. The waiter was in the process of changing the linen and silverware. Just as well, he thought. The air was becoming too cool for him to remain outside. "Certainly," he said into the receiver. "Normal commissions and routing instructions."

Hassim felt the release of tension from his chest. At last Montes was agreeing to cooperate. "Then it is settled," he said. "And I have your personal assurances the transaction will be concluded without any further participation on my part?"

A smile tugged at his fleshy jowls. "Fine, professor. It is always a pleasure. Good-bye."

Replacing the phone into its slot, Hassim climbed out of the booth and immediately left the promenade café.

Now it was settled. The next step was to simply advise Yasif of the details and he would have insulated himself from both the Libyans and Ursula.

Feeling quite pleased with himself, Hassim breathed deeply

for the crisp mountain air as he followed the cobblestone path to his Mercedes.

He chuckled. Why not treat himself to a late lunch? Something special to celebrate his duplicity.

But what? Surely not lamb; Ursula's comment had ruined his taste for *that*—at least for the remainder of the day. Perhaps veal. Yes, he thought. A thinly sliced veal dish enjoyed over a long, leisurely lunch.

And to drink? A carafe of chilled white wine. Allah was benevolent. He would understand the "medicinal" value of the beverage.

Hassim smiled. That was assuming, of course, that there was actually an Allah somewhere. Personally, Hassim doubted it, though he kept his reservations to himself.

But what to do after lunch? After he was suitably nourished? He knew, of course. He would pay a visit to the young Italian boy and spend the remainder of the evening sampling the pleasures of youthful exploitation.

His groin tightening in anticipation, Hassim picked up his pace and weaved expertly through the other pedestrians. It had been a good day, he decided.

But the evening would be even more rewarding.

Chapter 10

AFTER FIFTEEN MINUTES of cross-referencing, bibliographical indexing, and generally digging through the voluminous classified holdings of the Joint Chiefs of Staff library, Taylor finally found the abstract he had been hunting. Hopefully, it would resolve the *valentine* comment.

Entitled: *Allied Intelligence Matters [Great Britain] 1940–1960*, Taylor quickly thumbed to the index at the back of the three-inch-thick document, located the "Vs" and trailed his index finger down the page . . . Vidal, Vienna, Vietnam and the Vivian, Col. *Valentine,* 287–288.

He turned to page 287 and began to read. A few moments later, he knew the connection.

Colonel Vivian Valentine had been an old India hand who during World War II had served as the deputy chief of the British Secret Intelligence Service and later its security chief. His greatest claim to fame? Taylor smiled. He had unwittingly approved the hiring of Soviet agent Kim Philby by the British spy service.

Taylor flipped the page and read the definition set off in blocks:

Valentine: Slang term for British intelligence operatives who are authorized to cross between MI5 (counterintelligence) and MI6 (intelligence). Generally those persons of means with appropriate familial sociopolitical affiliations. [*Op. Cit.* Bryant Intercept, 6-9-71, Project JRATA-26G-301.624, page 2]

Interesting, Taylor thought, replacing the document on the shelf. So the good Sir Elliot was a spook. He wondered whether the general knew? He guessed not. Brayden was wired; but probably not that wired. At least he hoped not. If he was—then Prescott already knew everything about Special Projects. That, Taylor decided, was bullshit. Only another opportunity for a leak and an exposé in one of the Fleet Street rags.

As he turned and began the walk back to his section, Taylor had another thought. Could Prescott possibly be a Russian agent? He doubted it, and wrote off the thought to the reference to Philby in the document. Then again, at Prescott's age, he would have probably known Philby, if for no other reason than Philby had also been able to alternate between MI5 and MI6.

Lighting a cigarette and tossing the extinguished match to the floor, Taylor decided he would just play it safe. Spook or not, he didn't trust Elliot Prescott. What to do about it? Keep his suspicions to himself—knowledge was power. It was also, Taylor realized, the tool he would use to keep things under control.

British *or* Soviet, to Taylor it made no difference.

He wanted Prescott out of his life.

Chapter 11

PCAC PROGRAMMED FOR its run, Catlin sat patiently, waiting for Taylor to return and worried about her involvement in a domestic RAINDANCER operation.

It was illegal. Considering the tradition of American gunslinging, she realized it would eventually have been applied within the United States anyway.

It began as an idea, she remembered. A brief spark fanned from the ashes of the October 1983 bombing of the U.S. Marine barracks in Beirut and further fueled by the Department of Defense's investigative conclusion which stated tersely:

> "The U.S. Commander did not have effective U.S. human intelligence support; nor was there extant any substantive vehicle for requital proceedings."

President Reagan, outraged, had moved to create the "substantive vehicle" within two months.

The president, along with his national security adviser, Robert McFarland, developed a system wherein all "requital proceedings" would be consolidated inside a small subgroup of the National Security Council known simply as "the Caucus."

Comprised selectively of the president, McFarland, the chairman of the Joint Chiefs of Staff, and the directors of the FBI and CIA, the Caucus had no budget and no record of its inception. Reagan had commissioned it by verbal executive order.

Administratively, the Caucus's procedures were uniquely uncomplicated. If any one member received intelligence indicating that it could be in the *best interests* of the United States to have a particular individual "abdicated," a special meeting was called and the representatives reviewed the specific facts. If a quorum agreed to the necessity of such an action, a RAINDANCER was authorized and the operation planned.

Although the guidelines were in place, it was only after an initial simulation drill that the final administrative procedures were refined. To further streamline the process, the president made two changes. First, he expanded Caucus membership to include the director of the National Security Agency, thus widening the scope of operations to include targets identified through NSA's vast network of SIGINT and ELINT communications-eavesdropping facilities.

Secondly, to preclude power struggles between Caucus members, he decided that all RAINDANCER actions should be the responsibility of one *new* directorate which reported directly to the Oval Office and was buried under the umbrella of a much larger parent organization.

To the president, the appropriate parent agency was obvious: the sprawling Department of Defense. Reagan was shrewd. To give his new directorate even greater obscurity, he concealed it within the Defense Intelligence Agency, which itself was but a small segment of the total defense effort.

His selection was perfect, Catlin had to admit. Budgets could be hidden and personnel charged off to any one of thousands of subunits operating throughout the world. But for Reagan, this was still not enough. Consequently, for appropriations purposes, he established a third cover. The unit's "public" purpose: a high-tech federal recruitment service.

Pleased with his efforts, Reagan christened the RAINDANCER control directorate the Special Projects Section of the Defense Intelligence Agency. The "substantive vehicle" thus in place, he next went shopping for someone to run the section. His choice finalized in Thomas Brayden: Special Projects' first and only director.

Brayden had originally come to Reagan's attention through Robert McFarland and, by background, possessed all the necessary qualifications. The son of a wealthy Maryland customs broker and a West Point graduate, he was a childless widower who had served as the American military liaison in Madrid as well as both Korea and Vietnam, the latter where he was awarded his first star as William Westmoreland's Deputy Chief of Concepts Analysis.

Upon returning to the Pentagon, Brayden had been assigned to the Electronics Research Command, where he distinguished himself as the key tactician responsible for development of the Army's DC^3I intelligence distribution capability.

Awarded a second star, Brayden next moved to the White House, where he found himself working as Robert McFarland's personal adviser on Warsaw Pact forces.

McFarland immediately liked the new major general. He found him unassuming, intelligent, and not reluctant to offer his observations on foreign-policy decisions. Consequently, when Reagan asked McFarland for his input regarding the choice of an individual to head Special Projects, McFarland suggested Brayden and arranged a meeting.

President Reagan interviewed Brayden while vacationing in Santa Barbara. And, during a long walk through the isolated woods, explained the proposed function of Special Projects. Brayden agreed to the concept and asked for the position. With their pact sealed by a handshake, General Thomas Brayden returned to Washington and faded into the obscurity of the Department of Defense.

"A penny," Taylor said, interrupting Catlin's thoughts as he walked in his office.

Glancing up, she shrugged. "Oh I don't know. It just seems to me that the president is stretching the plausible-denial theory a bit much."

Taylor nodded at her reference to the tried-and-true doctrine which had governed covert operations since the Kennedy days. By interpretation, it protected the president by working on the assumption that if the White House was unaware of the exact details of an assassination, the president could plausibly deny responsibility of it. Moreover, if it was determined that the president had allowed an assassination to occur, that did not necessarily mean he had authorized it. The death would be interpreted as an assassination by omission, and the White House could not be held legally culpable.

"Like I asked," Taylor smiled. "Want out?"

"You know better than that. I'm just not wild about operating in *this* country. It negates all the safeguards."

Taylor held out his hands in a gesture of helplessness. "What can I say?"

Catlin shook her head. "Better think of something. Somebody screws up, and we're the ones answering questions. The Caucus will plausibly deny the whole thing."

"Can't argue with that." Taylor appreciated her comment. "But look at it this way, Cat. Just think how happy the Brits will be when we nail Crandon."

"One mark for our side?"

Taylor nodded. "A stroke for truth, justice, and the American way."

Catlin laughed at his cynicism. "Should have been a saleman, Sam. You definitely got the touch."

Taylor smiled with her. "Where we at?"

"Ready for recall," she answered, turning back to the rolltop and the keyboard. "Want to give me the subsystem reference?"

Picking up the dossiers, Taylor walked to the sofa and sat down. "Tarot," he answered, not looking up.

"Interface access?"

"Yankee-four-oh-six-Tango." Taylor listened as Catlin's fingers rapidly typed the entry-level designation for RAINDANCER personnel.

Pressing the entry key and activating the recall mode, Catlin turned back to Taylor, her eyes sparkling mischievously. "Ever been in a federal prison, Sam?"

He looked up sharply. Her face was set in a wide grin. "Don't worry," he laughed. "We can always defect."

Catlin chuckled. "Ah, yes, Christmas in Siberia . . . sounds enchanting."

Crandon's file in his lap, Taylor leaned back on the couch. "Better than Christmas in Leavenworth," he teased.

Before she could think of some clever response, Catlin's attention was drawn back to PCAC by a soft beeping tone. The computer had completed its search and was ready to print.

"By the way?" she asked, leaning over and pressing the hard-copy activation key.

"What's that?" Taylor answered, not looking up.

"What was the library all about?"

"Just covering the bases. Didn't turn up anything, though."

At that moment, the printer engaged. Its clatter engrossing them both for a long thirty seconds.

As it stopped, Catlin began to smile. Coming from the couch, Taylor was humming a different melody now, and mordant as it was, she really had grown to appreciate his sense of humor.

The tune was "Jingle Bells."

Chapter 12

PEDER CRANDON HAD moved the body from his room, and now he smelled the rotting newspaper and tasted the mildewed dust coating the back of his throat. It was cold in the abandoned storage shed just behind the old navy yard. But appropriate, he decided, as the musky dampness crept into his lungs. It had been a good choice.

Praying silently to himself, he ignored the hollow crunch of rodent droppings beneath his shoes and picked his way carefully to the small side door less than ten feet away. He licked his chapped lips and allowed himself a giggle.

It was the perfect stage. A masterpiece of the macabre. Surely they would know, but that would be playing directly into their hands. Teasing them. Forcing them to experience the helplessness. Living within the confines of their vulnerability.

No, he hadn't left one clue. But that, in itself, is what made it all the better. "Could there be two clues?" they would think. "Or more?" He giggled again. Yes, that was what he wanted them to think—maybe more. Three? Five? "We must do something," they would say. And to whom? He snickered, wishing he could be a flea in the British ambassador's ear.

Reaching the door, he paused and looked back toward the center of the shed. It was cloaked in darkness. He ignored the tickle of anticipation flicking at his scrotum. He reached over and snapped on the single overhead light. He left the shed and returned to the warmth of the car parked outside. Climbing in, he looked back.

Through the open door, the sixty-watt light bulb was beginning its vain attempt to warm the dead girl's corpse as it twisted slowly four feet above the fragments of rotting waste, directly underneath the light bulb. A mass of decaying flesh suspended by a thin nylon cord knotted tightly around its neck.

The wire garrote had been removed. It was simply too garish and, in his opinion, only detracted from the girl's image of unblemished innocence.

Chapter 13

PLACING HER ELBOWS on Taylor's desk Catlin studied the two printed readouts she had selected from the list of seventeen file references generated initially by PCAC.

Void of any personal information, the data sheets contained only an individual file number and the index codes of prior RAINDANCER projects the agent had either attempted or completed. If necessary, biographical histories could be retrieved by another query under the appropriate file number. But that would be later. Now she read the information on the first printout for what seemed like the hundredth time:

```
Y/406/T          RAINDANCER:TAROT
L-1781R213
P. CONSULOS:     CHILEAN   S-708R
H. PEREZ:        CHILEAN   S-988R
D.POSTAPOLUS:    CYPRIOT   S-654R
H. SCHMIDT:      E. GERMAN   S-543R
                 11010001001
```

Placing the readout on the desk, she took a sip of her coffee. Obviously this man had enough experience, as indicated by the four "R" designations following the assignment numbers. They indexed a successful project.

Catlin realized she could find out the details of a particular action by querying the "S" number back through PCAC, but in this case she wasn't curious. The man had traveled too much. It was conceivable he was known in terrorist circles—even to Crandon himself. If this were the case, the operation would be jeopardized before it began.

She turned her attenation to the second printout:

```
Y/406/T          RAINDANCER:TAROT
L-2397R879
J. LAMAULE:      BELGIAN      XS-091R
P. MOBATA:       SRI LANKAN   S-091R
                 11010001101
```

Instinctively, Catlin knew this was the person to hunt Crandon. Leaning over to the shredder, she destroyed the first readout.

Hearing the machine engage, Taylor looked up from the dossiers he was still studying. "Narrow it down?"

"Could be," she mumbled. "Need to check a few details."

Catlin entered the access code once again and queried the memory banks for both the biographical data on her selection as well as the details of the two previous projects.

In an instant, the desired digits appeared on the video monitor and, momentarily, she found herself transfixed by their softly pulsating amber images:

```
Y/406/T          RAINDANCER:TAROT
L-2397R879
MHY406T625L7     .......... XS-091R
                 ..........  S-091R
                 11Ø1ØØØ1111
```

The moment passed and, clearing her mind, Catlin activated both the memory search and printed readout keys. Shortly, she was aware of printed documents falling into the wire catcher next to the keyboard.

"*A bon rat, bon chat*," she whispered, thinking in Creole. *To a good rat, a good cat.*

As the printer disengaged, Catlin gathered the documents and stacked them on the desk next to the original readout. Then, taking another sip of her coffee, she turned back to Taylor who was now scribbling little notes in the margins of the dossiers.

"Interested?" she asked.

Taylor nodded. "Background?"

Catlin scanned the readout. "About the usual. ROTC Mississippi State . . . Special Forces Vietnam . . . Agency cross-border operations . . . oh, get this; he volunteered for Project Blue Light and went on the raid to free the hostages in Iran."

Taylor shook his head. "Dog fuck of the century."

"Evidently he thought so, too," she agreed. "Resigned a major's commission within the year and went to work for State." She looked up. "What's an RSO, Sam?"

He glanced down to the dossiers. "Regional Security Officer . . . they drag around our embassies, chase women, and write security surveys nobody bothers to read."

Par for the course, she thought. "Well, anyway, he was somewhere in Indonesia when——"

"Kelly Michaels," Taylor said flatly, looking up.

"Know him?"

"Taylor shrugged. "Uh-huh."

Curious response, Catlin thought, tossing the documents back to the desk. "So?" she probed. "Fill me in. Is he any good?"

"The general thought so," Taylor answered after a moment. "He recruited him. Then again, Brayden always was partial to the ex-army-agency paramilitary types."

"You should know," she suggested, with a direct reference to Taylor's own background.

"Too well." He closed his eyes and leaned back on the sofa. "You remember when our envoy to Sri Lanka was assassinated last year? It was right before Brayden brought you in."

"Sure," Catlin nodded. "But the file indicates two targets. I'm assuming there's more to the story?"

Taylor lit a cigarette. "Michaels was contracted to eliminate Pandesch Mobatua, the chief of the Sri Lankan national police."

''Mobatua had something to do with the death of our envoy?''

''Everything,'' Taylor confirmed. ''He was a communist, death-squad type, and under orders to foment a coup in the country.''

''Buy low, sell high,'' Catlin quipped.

Taylor smiled at the comment. ''Anyway, Jawardene, the Sri Lankan president, couldn't do anything about it, so he came to big brother.''

''Enter Uncle Sugar.''

''With the cash register,'' Taylor nodded. ''The State Department sent a man named Brandeis Falco to act as our special envoy to Sri Lanka. It was understood that Falco would offer Jawardene carte blanche American aid if Mobatua were replaced.''

''Military aid?'' Catlin asked.

''Hardly. Humanitarian bullshit. In any case, Jawardene lined his pockets, but still refused to get rid of Mobatua. The Sri Lankan people had no idea what was going on. They assumed Mobatua was killing on orders from Jawardene . . . the violence escalated . . . then there were a couple of riots . . . same old pattern.''

''I don't understand why Mobatua wasn't ousted.''

Taylor shrugged his shoulders. ''Everyone was scared of him. Everyone but Falco, and this really pissed Mobatua off.''

''So Michaels popped him?'' she asked.

''It came to that eventually. Mobatua was sick of Falco trying to undercut his authority, so he hired a man named Jacques LaMaule to kill him.''

''LaMaule?''

''Mercenary type,'' Taylor explained. ''Some ex-Belgian commando who'd been sucking up to the Cubans in Angola and was living in Sri Lanka peddling black market everything.''

Catlin nodded him on.

''As the story goes, Mobatua decided to invite Falco to Jawardene's country estate to set him up for LaMaule. Supposedly a conference on human rights.''

Catlin understood. "Falco couldn't very well turn down that kind of invitation."

"What self-respecting tea sipper would?" Taylor added. "The plan was for LaMaule to shoot Falco and then for Mobatua to arrest some innocent person to execute for the crime."

"The plan worked, I guess."

"The first part of it," Taylor nodded. "Falco was found dead about two miles from the estate. Somehow, Jawardene figured it out and passed the word to the in-country, CIA chief-of-station."

"Enter Mr. Michaels," Catlin said.

"The agency verified the story, and the director requested the Caucus sanction the assassination of both Mobatua and LaMaule."

"Exit the bad guys."

"Big-time exit," Taylor said, a slight smile crossing his face. "Two weeks after the sanction was ordered, Mobatua was found dead in his bathtub . . . his throat cut."

"Nice touch," Catlin said sarcastically.

Taylor missed it. "We thought so. But then the next morning it was LaMaule's turn. As he walked out of his warehouse, he promptly had his head exploded by a single rifle bullet."

"How come you're so familiar with the operation, Sam?"

"I was Michaels's control." His voice seemed detached. "I confirmed the hits and paid the money."

"Well," Catlin said after a moment. "I, for one, don't see anything wrong with his credentials—sounds like the typical all-American boy. What do you think?"

Ignoring her analogy, Taylor leaned forward and began to stack the dossiers on the coffee table. Time for hardball, he decided. "What do *you* think, Catlin?"

Damned Brayden, she thought. Now he had Taylor testing her. "Give me a break, Sam," she said wearily. "You know the man—is he good or not?"

Taylor wondered whether he should answer.

This, he knew, would be the pivot point of his relationship with Catlin. If he played the asshole, Brayden could use the ulcer to force him out on a medical. Bad plan. That would only leave Catlin trying to fill his shoes before she was actually prepared. Not fair to her, but more important, it could lead to a mistake and end up exposing the whole RAINDANCER contingency—not fair to the president.

He stared at her. Her eyes. Her breasts moving slowly as she breathed. Damn, she was beautiful. No, he couldn't leave her out there alone. He owed her more than that. She was smart enough. She would learn the circuit. She only needed time. Tutoring. Time to learn it *right*.

And him? What was the old phrase? He remembered: *Cooperate and graduate*. No, he decided. No percentage in acting the asshole. Everyone would lose.

"Sam?" she said. There was pain in her voice.

Taylor walked over to his rolltop. "Michaels is definitely ruthless enough," he said softly. "And he had no trouble whatsoever on the Sri Lankan assignment. A quick in . . . a quick hit . . . a quick out. A nice, tidy job for which he received fifty thousand dollars."

Taylor was acting cagy, she realized. "But what?"

"But nothing," he snapped, immediately regretting the tone of his voice. He turned and looked down at her. "I told you I didn't like this." His voice grew softer. "But Michaels?" He shrugged. "What do you think?"

"Can he stop Crandon?" she asked. "I need your input, Sam."

Taylor nodded. "Yes, he can stop Crandon."

"Then why the reservations?"

Not answering the question, Taylor reached down to the keyboard. "Well, now that that's settled, let's see where he is."

Catlin watched Taylor closely as he began to tap the keys activating RAINDANCER locator reference, but she said nothing. It was a question of respect—he was bringing her in and the reason had nothing to do with the general. Taylor had decided to tutor her.

It was almost sad, she thought. Taylor, like all of Thomas Brayden's recruits, herself included, were never allowed to know it all. Security reasons was the rationale. *Cellular cutout*, Brayden's term.

But with Taylor, she had reservations. She wanted Sam to know her whole story. From the general's recruiting her out of postdoctoral research, to her clandestine assignment in New York, to her being brought to Washington for the purpose of heading up the section.

Reluctantly, she followed orders.

Of course Taylor investigated her past. Even to checking her cover story which spanned her New York period. But, as Brayden designed, it passed inspection. Taylor learned nothing.

Last month she had asked the general for permission to tell Taylor the truth. He refused, explaining that Taylor didn't need to know of the *new* project because it wouldn't be activated until after Taylor's retirement.

Intellectually, Catlin could well appreciate Brayden's insistence on total security. Privately, she knew that if Taylor were aware she had spent time in the trenches, then relinquishing control would be easier for him to accept. The whole retirement issue became as painful to Taylor as *cellular cutout* had become for her.

"Where is he?" she asked, walking to Taylor's side.

"One minute," he answered, waiting as PCAC hummed softly in the background.

The RAINDANCER Locator System was basically designed along the lines of the army's DC^3I intelligence distribution capability, only in reverse. It was the general's creation, and he used it to keep track of his recruits.

Once Brayden approved a RAINDANCER operative, the individual was assigned the "L" number he would keep for identification purposes.

After completion of an assignment, or if the individual wanted to remain in contention for future consideration, they called the inward WATS number into the COMSEC-25, Defense Intelligence Agency switchboard. When the twenty-four-hour operator answered, the recruit gave the "L" number followed by a specific location and a telephone contact. COMSEC then programmed the information into PCAC's memory.

Once completed, the agent's locator file was updated and outdated information erased automatically. For security, as in all DC^{3}I functions, the COMSEC operators could feed only data *abstracts* into a particular PCAC subsystem; as the general designed, all COMSEC terminals were preprogrammed to shut down if any unauthorized retrieval of information was attempted: an event witnessed by a piercing alarm in the COMSEC command office as well as in Special Projects. To date there had been no attempts to penetrate the system.

"I guess he's moved," Taylor mumbled, staring at the video monitor as he leaned over and activated an additional key. Instantly, the printer engaged.

A second later, it stopped and the printed sheet fell into the wire catcher. Picking up the document, he glanced at it briefly, then passed it to Catlin.

Taking the paper, she found herself staring at the concise entry:

```
Y/406/T            RAINDANCER:TAROT
L-2397R879
LQL406T625L7...BOTTLE KEY,  FL
                   11Ø1Ø1Ø111Ø
```

"Where is Bottle Key, Florida?" she asked after a moment.

"I'm not sure," Taylor answered, already typing another query into the computer as he disengaged the printer. "But I guess we have to know . . . there's no phone contact listed."

In an instant, the video screen splashed a jumble of abbreviations and acronyms across its glass face. Taylor interrupted the data. "It's a small island in Florida Bay. Ten miles east of Key Largo."

Without waiting for a response from Catlin, he turned and reached for his telephone, punching digits from memory.

"Andrews, Special Air Wing," a young voice answered. "May I help you, sir?"

"Patch me through to the duty officer," Taylor ordered.

"One moment, sir." Taylor was placed on hold.

"Major Hudgins," the officer answered. "What can I do for you?"

Taylor spoke rapidly. "This is Taylor, Special Projects, I need a manifest. We have a RAINDANCER in effect as of zero-six-hundred."

"Wait one, sir." The officer placed Taylor on hold again.

As he waited, Taylor realized that the major was verifying the RAINDANCER authorization code; and although he would be unable to discern any particular details, Taylor also knew the RAINDANCER designation would start a burst of activity at Andrews Air Force Base.

Located just outside Washington, Andrews served as the home of the Special Air Missions Wing. Those responsibilities included support for the fleet of presidential aircraft as well as those used by hundreds of other government officials and members of Congress. In the majority of cases, manifests were supposed to be requested at least forty-eight hours in advance; but due to the RAINDANCER authorization, Taylor was able to procure an aircraft at any time.

The officer came back on the line. "You're cleared a RAINDANCER."

Taylor gave his requirements in short, clipped sentences. "Thank you, major. I have two for transport to Homestead. Upon arrival, two rotary to Bottle Key. Manifest three return Homestead. And three Homestead to Andrews. Wheels up in approximately two-zero minutes. Any questions?"

"No, sir," the officer answered. "We're standing by."

Disconnecting Andrews, Taylor punched another set of numbers on the telephone. His call was answered in mid-ring. "COMSEC."

"This is Taylor, I need a chopper to Andrews. Pad three, five minutes."

Without waiting for confirmation, Taylor hung up the phone and turned to Catlin. "Pack up the beads and blankets," he told her, nodding to the dossiers on the coffee table. "We're heading south."

"But——"

"We'll be back tonight," he added.

"It's not that, Sam."

Picking up his briefcase, Taylor looked at her. "What then?"

"I want to know what happened between you and Michaels on the Sri Lankan assignment."

A pained expression crossed his face. "It's not important," he said, walking to the office door. "Consider it a personality conflict . . . a failure to communicate . . . Hell, Cat, consider it anything. Probably my fault anyway. Now grab those files and let's get moving."

Catlin knew any more probing would be pointless. Obviously, Taylor was not going to explain. Making a mental note to study the details of the Sri Lankan action, she picked up the dossiers and followed him out.

And so it repeats, she thought, glancing up at the digital wall clock in the main computer room.

It was 11:55 A.M., and the meek had yet to inherit the earth.

Chapter 14

HASSIM SAAD LEANED forward in the overstuffed chair, put his elbows on the table, and picked absently at the remainder of his meal. On any other occasion, he would have enjoyed the *escalopes de veau,* which were the speciality of Le Gaulois, but today his appetite failed him. It was through no fault of the chef.

With its stone floors, wood-beamed ceilings and walls, the restaurant prided itself on serving the best French food in Bern—perhaps in all of Switzerland. But it was becoming late, and the murmur of Sunday dinner conversations, punctuated with occasional bursts of laughter, went unheard as Hassim's thoughts returned to the telephone conversation with Eduardo Montes.

In retrospect, he realized, something wasn't right. And although he couldn't but his finger on the reason, he felt an odd sense of "exposure." It wasn't anything Montes had said, nor was it anything different. But there was *something*.

It was almost the same feeling he had just before meeting Aaron in the Rome airport. But not as strong. Not as visceral. Just—*odd*.

Popping a Demerol in his mouth, he thought of the professor as he swallowed the capsule dry.

Like himself, Eduardo Montes was more than an arms dealer. But where Hassim also worked for the Israelis, the professor functioned as an operative for the *Dirección de Intelligencia,* the Cuban intelligence service. Hassim wondered whether the professor's cross was as heavy as his.

He suspected not.

The *Dirección de Intelligencia*, or DGI, had been under the command of a Soviet KGB general since 1968. From that humble beginning, it had become the major link with various international terrorist movements.

The DGI sent representatives to every corner of the Third World. Their assignments were straightforward: to initiate or provide assistance in the furtherance of political unrest. It was a broad-based strategy. Cuban advisers, trained terrorists on every continent, built up vast arsenals, much of it supplied by both Hassim and Montes, to support their operations. In Hassim's opinion, the Cubans had no equals. History had proved him right.

In Libya alone, equipment sufficient to outfit five Soviet motorized rifle divisions stood ready to maintain terrorist strategies. Within hours, the material could be shipped to such countries as Lebanon, Colombia, and Nicaragua for large-scale operations, or to meet the more modest requirements of terrorist factions laboring in Western Europe, Africa, or Scandinavia.

Poking listlessly at a slice of onion, Hassim leaned back in the chair. As of course a professional, he could only admire the simplicity of the Soviet plans. With the Cubans as surrogates, the Kremlin could actually supply the equipment, the training, and the targets, but remain detached from the violence by proclaiming Cuban intervention as an outgrowth of Castro's own brand of foreign policy. So far, the approach had worked.

The Russians' commitment to furtherance of international terrorism was a position no Western government could prove. In fact, Soviet policy dictated that propaganda efforts criticize terrorist acts while its diplomats pointed out there was no terrorism in Russia.

It was ironic that, in spite of the Kremlin's disinformation efforts, Moscow continued to provide safe havens for terrorists in East Germany, Bulgaria, and Czechoslovakia.

Montes was lucky because for the Cubans, the Soviets—for

that matter, even the British—were infinitely more civilized and indulgent than Yasif and his whole host of Islamic power brokers. Hassim also knew that they paid better.

Hassim walked into the restroom and began to wash his hands in an antique brass sink. Perhaps the reason Montes did not want to become involved with Crandon was Crandon's connection with Yasif.

Hassim could understand *that*. In the symbiotic relationship between arms dealers, Hassim understood that there were times when one was forced to ignore certain "reservations" about clients. Montes owed him a favor. Once he had pressured Hassim into providing explosives to a particularly nasty band of Puerto Ricans for one of their silly little *liberación* bombings in Europe.

On any other occasion, Hassim would have refused the men if for no other reason than their asinine rhetoric. But, Montes had insisted, so he had complied. If politics made strange bedfellows, terrorism made whores of everyone.

Hassim shook his head. Perhaps Montes was tiring of the duplicity. That would be unfortunate. Hassim knew fatigue was a precarious frame of reference in which to operate.

Surely the professor knew that once in, you could never walk away. Hassim knew it. There were too many debts. Too many people. Too many secrets.

Twisting off the faucet, Hassim sighed. It was a never-ending exercise and really none of his business. The professor would find it out for himself. In the end, everybody did.

Flicking the water from his fingers, Hassim moved to a neat stack of paper towels. Then, as he inspected his fingernails, a vision of the young Italian boy flashed in his mind. Nude and hard, the child would be waiting.

A man entering the restroom ignored the Arab primping in the mirror and walked to the sink, turning on the water.

Hassim glanced at him—late twenties, heavy, looked like a beetle in a ski parka. Not even attractive, he decided, taking one last check of his teeth in the mirror before walking toward the door.

As Hassim reached for the knob, the door opened and a second man stepped inside. A bit older, dressed in dungarees and parka, his smile displayed crooked tobacco-stained teeth. He closed the door and moved his back against it.

''Excuse me,'' Hassim said politely.

The man did not speak, the smile fading behind thin, compressing lips as he blocked the door.

Suddenly, Hassim felt the unyielding pressure of a pistol rammed into his left kidney area. Hassim gasped.

''Quiet, faggot!'' Beetle hissed. The man began to probe Hassim's soft back with the muzzle with measured jabs. ''Be quiet,'' he threatened. ''If you resist . . . I'll sever your spinal cord.''

Hassim squealed in pain as the muzzle scraped the cord.

''Understand now?'' Beetle said.

Hassim managed a nod.

''Fine,'' the man whispered. ''Now follow him,'' he ordered as Yellow Teeth turned and led the way out of the restroom.

The kidnappers led Hassim through the restaurant quickly and efficiently. At the late hour, the time between lunch and the evening meal, the dining room was all but deserted as waiters placed chairs on their tables to clear the floor. The employees paid no attention to Hassim nor his companions.

As they neared the front door, Hassim wanted to scream, to run, anything to get away.

As if anticipating an outburst, Beetle leaned over. ''Your spine, faggot. Remember your spine.''

An involuntary contraction gripped his bowels, and Hassim decided to do nothing. There was no doubt that Beetle would like to carry out his threat.

The late afternoon was cold as the three men left Le Gaulois, passing within inches of Hassim's Mercedes, then walking fifty yards to the kidnappers' Fiat.

Shoving Hassim into the cramped rear seat, Beetle slid in beside him. Yellow Teeth climbed in and started the vehicle.

As they pulled from the curb, Hassim began to shake. "What do you want?" he asked. "What have I done?"

The driver glanced at Hassim in the rearview mirror. "In due time, Hassim. In due time."

Hassim slumped in the seat. Depression tempered with morbidity.

Who were they? He had any number of enemies, but who were Beetle and Yellow Teeth working for? The Israelis? Swiss? Yasif? He couldn't tell from their accents or their clothes.

He looked down at the man's pistol against his ribs.

Identifying the weapon as a Czech M-52 automatic with silencer, Hassim shuddered. He was familiar with the pistol. It fired a 7.62mm bottleneck cartridge at more than 1,600 feet per second and was one he had sold to factions across the Middle East. It was the handgun of choice for Islamic terror actions.

The infamous guerrilla Carlos had employed one to kill Michael Moukharbel, the friend who had betrayed him. He had also used one to kill two French agents who, acting upon Moukharbel's information, attempted to arrest him in a dingy Paris apartment.

A uniquely powerful weapon, one of the shots which killed Moukharbel passed through his body, then the apartment floor, the ceiling of the room below, a molded plastic table and still retained enough velocity to bury itself so deeply in the lower apartment's floor that it was impossible to dig out.

It was an assassin's weapon.

It was also the type of pistol issued to Yasif's personal bodyguard. Hassim cursed his stupidity.

He should not have helped Ursula without Yasif's permission.

Now he would pay for his oversight.

Chapter 15

A NUDE KELLY Michaels swam effortlessly through the clear waters of Florida Bay. He was at peace. It was his private sanctum where he could be alone with his thoughts.

He moved underwater and savored the exhilarating sense of buoyancy. The sensation never ceased to fascinate him. Dipping and soaring with no other effort than the lazy thrusts of his powerful legs and smooth paddlings of his flippered feet.

Prolonging the moment, he watched as a pair of jellyfish pumped past him. Like living parachutes, they, too, floated gracefully through the blue green waters heading for the smooth mirror of the surface.

Michaels approved. Their freedom pleased him.

Diving deeper, the blurred tapestry of the bottom rapidly assumed dimension and color. Through his mask he could see deep winding gullies carpeted with sandy shells and jagged outcroppings of pastel corals. It was a seductive vision. Descending deeper to a place so primitive, he felt as if he were trespassing into solitude.

The silence was acute, broken only by the sound of his regulator bubbles gently violating the perception of isolation. It was a place detached.

Flashing gold and blues, three queen angelfish approached him out of curiosity. A moment of inspection, then they darted away, secure in their mutual commitment. Next, a silvery school of spadefish shimmered into view, hanging next to him as he dropped down, approaching a forest of staghorn coral whose raised, arched branches resembled uplifted human arms suspended in time.

Beside him, a red squirrelfish, dorsal fin wide, peered cautiously from its rocky hiding place. And below, several large black groupers waited in ambush for passing prey. It was the cycle of life in the waterworld and Michaels respected the hierarchies defined long before man's tentative return to his source. He would do nothing to alter it.

Suddenly he noticed a flicker of gray cutting through the water just at the limits of his vision. Holding motionless, both frightened and fascinated, he watched closely as a seven-foot tiger shark rocketed toward him.

Diving at the last moment, the beast swept within five feet, its barnacled caudal fin clearly visible as it propelled the fish through the water. Speeding down, the predator devoured one of the less fortunate groupers, then paused to consider another.

A moment later, it was gone, leaving as abruptly as it arrived.

Checking his watch, Michaels knew it was time to leave. His air was low, and he was more than 200 yards from the beach.

It was late afternoon by the time he finally climbed the stairs to the wooden deck which served as the front porch of his home, a structure which was actually nothing more than an old weathered A-frame cabin used previously by marine biologists from the University of Florida as a support base for field research activities. Nonetheless, it was dry and comfortable, and Michaels considered himself fortunate that the property had become available after the federal grant money for research projects was curtailed.

On university records, Kelly Michaels was designated the caretaker for the Bottle Key Facility; however, as both he and the university realized, he did little more than relax because the cabin was the sole structure on the island. The arrangement worked well for all concerned. Michaels, being content to be left alone, wanted no reimbursement for his services. And the university, self-serving as always, readily applied his quarterly stipend to increase the earnings of selected scientists in the biology department.

Dumping his equipment on the pitted sun-bleached boards, Michaels turned and gazed out over the sand to the water beyond.

"You were gone a long time," a voice called to him.

Not looking back, he nodded. "Worried?"

"I always worry. You should know that by now."

Turning around, he walked toward the woman sunning herself at the far end of the deck.

"You shouldn't," he told her. "Never does any good."

Twisting onto her back, the woman closed her eyes and stretched. "Rather I stopped?"

Smiling, Michaels sat down on the woven bamboo mat which served as her pallet. "No, Mai Lei," he said softly, allowing his eyes to travel down her lithe nude body. "Just can't get used to it, that's all."

"You've no choice," she teased. "It comes with the package."

"I guess it does."

Born in Bangkok, Mai Lei had been his lover for almost three years. Three good years. The daughter of an expatriate French banker and his Thai wife, Mai Lei had inherited the best of both the Oriental and Caucasian features. She was a classic Eurasian beauty, and at twenty-seven, still possessed the high cheekbones and wide mouth which had attracted him to her in the first place.

Reaching over, he caressed her hair. It fanned out behind her head, but when standing, it reached to the small of her back, shining with an inky luster which intensified the blueness of her almond-shaped eyes. By any man's standards, Mai Lei was both an exotic and sensual-looking woman. And this, he supposed, is what made the monogamy so much the better.

Sliding closer, he began to explore her body, letting his figures trail the valley between her small, firm breasts, across the amber tautness of her stomach and finally resting his palm on the smooth, hairless mound of her pubis. She responded immediately.

Almost imperceptibly, her breathing quickened and the cocoa membrane of her nipples began to harden. Under his fingers, he soon felt the soft beginnings of her undulations as she slightly arched her back to increase the pressure of her womanhood. Then, quite unexpectedly, she began to giggle.

"Kelly Michaels," she baited him. "Have you no shame?"

He looked into her eyes, the blue darker now, even more of a contrast to the tawniness of her skin.

"Hey, lady," he laughed, lying back on the pallet and lacing his fingers behind his head. "It has nothing to do with shame. I'm just a trained love slave trying to get by."

Sitting up, Mai Lei twisted around cross-legged, facing him. "From the way you're sprawled out, it seems *I'm* the love slave."

As usual, Michaels was enjoying the banter. "Make you a deal?"

"What?"

He smiled. "You give me five minutes of love slaving now, and I'll give you two hours later."

"I've heard that story before."

"I'll cook dinner," he added.

"And clean up?"

"Hard bargain, lady," he sighed. "But what the hell . . . deal."

"Good," she whispered, easing over next to him.

Closing his eyes, Michaels felt her hair fall over his chest as her hand began the slow, intimate custom. After a moment, she shifted her position ever so slightly and he was aware of her swollen nipples tracing invisible lines across his chest and her breath upon his thighs as her tongue probed. He arched his hips.

She responded. Soon her mouth and hands were moving together. Twisting, his mind oblivious to anything but the sensations inspired by the woman, he reached down, gripping her hair as she urged his release.

The conclusion came rapidly.

For a second, his body recoiled, then shuddered with the reflexive spasms of his climax. Holding him tightly, she pulled at him harder until his passion was spent.

Later, they lay entwined in each other's arms. Eyes closed, but not sleeping. Neither spoke. Neither moved. The simple sharing of touch sufficed for the moment.

Then, Mai Lei raised herself up on one elbow, studying his body. She was pleased. The time on the island had been well spent. His skin was deeply tanned and muscles hardened from countless hours of diving the reefs.

Physically, Kelly Michaels was a ruggedly handsome man, a bit over six feet, with large hands and feet. His hair was long and his full beard short and sun-streaked, as were the thick eyebrows which lay low over solemn, cunning dark eyes.

Turning on his side, he looked up at her warmly.

"What?" he asked, realizing she had been staring at him.

"Just looking." She reached over and touched the small half-moon scar just beneath his left eye. It was white, now, in contrast to the tan, and she wondered how much the wound had hurt. He would never tell her.

She touched his lips with her fingertips and he smiled. It was a boyish smile. A bit crooked. One-sided, even. A smile that, when he allowed it, made him look at least five years younger than his thirty-eight years. She wished he'd try it more often but knew he never would. Kelly Michaels was a hard man. To those who didn't know him, he would appear more like some itinerant rock star, but she knew the real Kelly: a cold, self-sufficient hunter of men who, outside of his personal commitment to her, cared nothing for the rest of the world or its people.

To Mai Lei, this was fine. She loved him as he was.

"I don't like it when you stare at me," he said after a moment.

"I like to look at you," she whispered, tracing the scar again with a fingertip. "Kelly?"

"What?"

"I want you to quit."

Not again, he thought. She'd been harping on that ever since he'd returned from Sri Lanka.

"And do what?" he asked. "Enroll in McDonald's management-trainee program? Hey, that'd be great. I could design a new burger—a claymore mine with bacon and cheese—a McMichaels."

Mai Lei refused to laugh.

"I'm serious, Kelly," she said softly. "You've already had so much pain . . . so much hurt. It has to stop somewhere."

With his hand, he reached up and smoothed the hair falling loosely over her shoulder. "It will," he said, meaning it. "I want to grow old with you, lady. Two more runs and we'll have enough stashed away to be able to pull it off in style."

"We already have enough. You know that."

"That's *your* money," he said flatly. "I won't live off it. Our deal was for me to add to the pot. Remember?"

She shrugged and Michaels sat up on the pallet.

He knew she hated the violence of his work, of what he had become. Of course they never really discussed it except in generalities; nonetheless, her concern always seemed to lurk just beneath the surface. He left it there.

She was right. They did have enough money. But he was a soldier. He had been one since high school and knew no other profession. And he was always looking for new wars, fresh opportunities to test himself, more chances to meet the pawns in the latest round of political deaths. No, he realized, it was something more than money.

The bottom line was the killing. It had become an addiction.

Deciding that he didn't feel like talking, he kissed Mai Lei on the shoulder and hopped up.

"I'm going to grab a shower," he said. "Don't run off."

She laughed, Michaels noticed that the tension of the previous minutes was replaced by a brilliant white smile.

"And where am I to go?" she asked, waving an arm around. "I haven't seen a boat in two days."

"That's because you're *my* lady," he teased.

"Humph," she breathed, sitting up cross-legged on the pallet. "Well just don't forget *your* lady has two hours of attention coming later."

"In for a nickel . . . in for a dollar," Michaels said, turning and disappearing into the A-frame.

Mai Lei watched him walk away. Then she stood and leaned against the rusted metal railing surrounding the deck. Staring into the darkening waters of the bay, she tried once again to make some sense of their relationship.

She knew she loved him. She had since they met at the embassy reception in Bangkok. But, regardless of her efforts, she could not get him to communicate his feelings. Of course he loved her—at least to the extent any man could love a woman. But, for some inexplicable reason, he still refused to acknowledge it—almost as if he were unable to say the words.

Perhaps he would change when he finally quit. She moved back from the railing and walked to the cabin door. And as long as there was some glimmer of hope, she would wait. For her there was no real alternative.

Despite his moodiness, despite the craziness, Kelly Michaels was a worthy mate.

Besides, she smiled, he made her laugh.

Chapter 16

As the Fiat lurched through the darkness, Hassim swallowed and continued fighting the impulse to vomit. Forty minutes out of Bern, Yellow Teeth had left the hard, well-maintained surface of the Steffisburg Highway and headed west, climbing into the Alps on a forgotten road. And now, shivering as they bounced along the rutted, twisting trail, Hassim put his hand against the window glass. It was getting even colder. The chill of fear was eating into him.

It was a demanding exercise for the driver. Any lapse of attention would plunge the car off the steep embankment and into the valley. But Yellow Teeth managed to avoid the sink-holes and furrows caused by untold years of melting snow and rain.

As they inched higher, the car suspension gave way to a barrage of teeth-shattering jolts as it fought its way up the incline. Leaning forward, Hassim took the opportunity to peer out the front windshield. With the headlights on high beam, he could distinguish the faint silhouette of a farmhouse situated at the far end of a long, winding driveway. It looked deserted.

The rock house stood straight and imposing. Despite its modest size, it was ringed by a low granite wall crumbling in spots. Even its roofs was constructed of shingles, sliced thinly from larger hunks of the stone which had been carried from the nearby quarries.

It was like a crypt. Cold. Impersonal. Reeking with malice.

"Out!" Yellow Teeth ordered as he pulled the Fiat to a stop adjacent to the front door.

Hassim managed a meek nod and climbed out. He felt detached, mentally asunder—not unlike some stringed marionette dancing across a Kafkaesque landscape. Swallowing again, he looked around in a vain attempt to stave off nausea by focusing on his desolate surroundings.

Behind the cottage was a waterfall. Its mist reflected slivers of moonlight which bathed the entire landscape in a surrealistic vapor.

To the right of the house was a trail which quickly became a path as it climbed higher. Despite the cold, Hassim's hands began to sweat. For hundreds of years, nothing had changed in this sparsely populated area of secluded farms and hamlets—the most remote region of the Swiss Alps where living was hard, and only the rich could avail themselves of life's amenities.

One hundred yards away, behind the cottage, the silent outline of a helicopter propelled the scenario directly into the twentieth century.

Hassim looked over to the driver.

Yellow Teeth smiled slightly. "This way."

With Beetle and the pistol behind him, Hassim followed the driver across a flagstone path to a rotted door hanging loosely on the front steps of the cottage.

It smelled like potting soil.

The interior of the stone cottage was as Hassim expected: a few pieces of broken furniture, dirt, and bits of jagged ceiling stone littering the granite floor. He glanced around. With the exception of a small fire crackling in the the fireplace, the inside appeared empty, and, for the most part, hidden in darkness. He wondered about the helicopter but said nothing as he waited for instructions.

"Strip," said Yellow Teeth, walking to the fireplace and warming his hands.

"What——" Hassim was stopped in mid-thought by the pressure of the Czech automatic at the base of his skull.

"Your clothes, faggot," Beetle whispered, poking the weapon deeper into Hassim's neck. "Take them off. I want to see your naked ass."

The trembling began again. Hassim could not make his hands function correctly. "Please!" he begged as his fingers fumbled with the buttons of his shirt. "Let me explain. Let me work with you."

The driver stood as Beetle moved next to him. Together, backlit by the fire, they waited silently for Hassim to finish undressing. Hassim avoided their amused eyes.

When Hassim stood before them in underpants and socks, Yellow Teeth ordered, "The rest of it."

"Wait!" Hassim pleaded. "Let me talk to Yasif. Let me tell him——"

Stepping over, Beetle pointed the pistol directly into Hassim's left eye. "Naked, faggot," he hissed. "I want you naked. I want to look at your naked ass."

Paralyzed by the black hole of the muzzle inches from his face, Hassim retreated into a curious dreamlike state and removed the remainder of his clothes.

Trying to hide his shriveling manhood behind his hands, he stood before the two strangers, shivering as the night's cold sniffed at his scrotum. He began to sob openly. The kidnappers grinned.

"Sit down," Yellow Teeth said softly.

"Please," Hassim whimpered.

The muzzle touched Hassim's forehead. "Sit, faggot."

Hassim dropped to the floor, gasping audibly as the fallen ceiling stones tore at his buttocks, puncturing the soft masses of exposed flesh.

Satisfied, Yellow Teeth turned and disappeared into the shadows.

A moment later, the walls echoed with a heavy metallic scraping followed by the sound of sloshing liquid. Turning in the direction of the noise, for a brief instant Hassim's nostrils were assaulted by the oily stench of diesel fuel. A second later, the odor filled every pore of his body as the driver splashed him with the fuel. Hassim's screams shattered the silence of the night. Frantic, blinded by the vapors, Hassim clawed to his knees and tried to run.

Yellow Teeth anticipated the response. Moving in close, he waited until Hassim gained his balance, then rammed the fuel can into his temple. Dazed by the blow, Hassim fought to remain conscious as he collapsed to the floor, gasping for breath.

In that alien place, somewhere between dream and reality, Hassim Saad soared freely. Mindwings expanding. His body completely oblivious to the cold and pain.

He was suddenly aware of the slight tugging in his right hand, but considered it more of a nuisance than anything else. No, he would ignore it and continue to experience the floating sensation of semiconsciousness.

Ten minutes later, Hassim's detachment ended as he became aware of a voice pulling at his consciousness.

''Mr. Saad?'' it inquired.

He tried to respond but the result was unintelligible.

''Please, Mr. Saad,'' the voice repeated.

It was a courtly voice, Hassim thought. A deeply melodic voice that reminded him of something. But what? He couldn't place the memory.

Wait. He was beginning to recognize the voice. But from where?

''Mr. Saad.''

Of course, Hassim decided. It was the voice of a wine steward. Yes, that was it. The voice of a discriminating wine steward suggesting a bottle of rare Bordeaux. ''Yes,'' he mumbled.

''Please, Mr. Saad.'' The voice continued to guide Hassim back to the present. ''We really don't have much time.''

The waves of euphoria were replaced by fresh washes of

nausea, and Hassim began to vomit. The wretching cleared his head and his vision returned slowly.

"I'm sorry, Mr. Saad. But we do have a few simple questions."

Opening his eyes painfully, Hassim focused on a tall, slender, hawkish-looking man with close-cut gray hair and bushy eyebrows, wearing a dark turtleneck sweater. Hassim estimated him to be close to sixty. It was impossible to make out any other details due to the glare from the fireplace.

"Ah, Mr. Saad," the man whispered soothingly. "You are back with us."

Staring up, Hassim decided hawkish was the wrong term. If anything, the man loomed over him more like some vulture inspecting a slab of carrion. "Who are you?" Hassim slurred, trembling with shock.

The man smiled, a brief flash of long white teeth. "Chatsworth," he said pleasantly. "Basil Chatsworth."

Hassim was immediately aware of the stranger's clipped British accent. "I don't understand," he moaned, still fighting unconsciousness.

"No. Of course you don't. And I must apologize for any inconvenience on your part." Chatsworth's voice oozed with politeness. "But please, indulge me for a moment. We do not have much time, and I have questions for you. But first, some ground rules."

Unable to comprehend, Hassim stared in silence as Chatsworth turned to Yellow Teeth and nodded. Smiling, the driver handed Chatsworth a small ceramic dish. Something on it was burning, but Hassim was unable to identify it.

Taking the dish, Chatsworth knelt down and placed it on a stone inches from Hassim's eyes.

Curious, Hassim attempted to focus on the fatty matter that was slowly twisting, withering in the heat of the flames.

Oddly enough, it looked and smelled like lamb sweetbreads.

Then, simultaneous with the scream building in his soul, he identified the object. It was a human finger—his!

As his anguished howl filled the room, Hassim became aware of the coolness licking at his right hand. Bringing it up to his face, he found a tidy bandage covering the severed area. Slowly, his scream faded into a low, guttural moan as he closed his eyes and writhed on his stomach.

"Please, Mr. Saad." Chatsworth's voice radiated understanding. "May I have your attention for another moment?"

His face streaked with tears and diesel fuel, Hassim glared and said, "What?"

"To put you at ease, perhaps it would be prudent to explain a few points. I am attached to the British government. I understand you were under the impression that my men were employees of Yasif?"

Hassim said nothing, and Chatsworth leaned over even closer to his face. "Nothing could be farther from the truth," he said. "Yasif is nothing more than a common terrorist, and no amount of diplomatic acceptance will change that face. Do I make myself clear?"

"Why my hand?" Hassim asked, turning over to face the man.

"Yes," he nodded. "Of course. Your index finger has been removed surgically, the wound sutured, disinfected, and anesthetized. Should you choose to cooperate, you can be back in Bern by the time the anesthesia wears off."

"Bastard!" Hassim spit the word.

Chatsworth ignored the insult. "Of course, if you decline to cooperate, I will respect your decision. Unfortunately, I will also be forced to simply continue removing parts of your anatomy until we are able to arrive at a mutual understanding." He paused to let the threat sink in.

"In either case, Mr. Saad, the option remains yours. I think you understand."

Hassim understood completely. He had seen this very approach employed any number of times, and the result was always the same. It never failed.

The procedure was a blend of primitive torture which, despite the loss of body parts, was a painless exercise while devastating the victim psychologically.

Many individuals would gladly give their lives for a particular cause, no matter how bizarre, but few could endure the systematic dismemberment of their own bodies before their very eyes.

"Are we in agreement, Mr. Saad?"

Feeling the intensity of Chatsworth's stare, Hassim sat up and nodded. "May I cover myself?"

"No, Mr. Saad. You may not."

Shivering uncontrollably, Hassim stared into the Englishman's stony face. "What do you want to know?"

The smile flashed again. "Excellent, Mr. Saad. I knew we could negotiate an arrangement."

Standing, Chatsworth began to circle Hassim in slow, measured strides. "With whom did you speak this afternoon?"

Hassim closed his eyes. The question cut deep. After so many years in the business, he had come to pride himself on being able to pick out those who could be watching him. It was an unforgivable mistake. He had become too complacent.

"No one," he answered.

Chatsworth expected the lie and disregarded the statement. "You were talking with Ursula Brandt."

"We are old friends."

"I realize that, Mr. Saad. Where is she now?"

"I have no idea."

"Bern?"

"I don't know."

"Zurich? Paris? Where, Mr. Saad."

"I don't *know.*"

Chatsworth shook his head. "The wrong answers, Mr. Saad. Have you forgotten our understanding so soon?" Retching again, Hassim looked up. Chatsworth glared back.

"I told you," Hassim said, "I have no idea."

Chatsworth allowed himself a disgusted glance toward his associates. Beetle did nothing. Yellow Teeth shrugged non-comittally. He turned his attention back to Hassim. "What did you discuss with Ursula Brandt, Mr. Saad? Surely I would find the details of interest."

"I'd be a fool to help you—you know that."

Chatsworth nodded knowingly. "Yasif again, Mr. Saad?" He began to smile. "Or could it be the Israelis?"

He leaned over, lowering his voice as he spoke. "Your Jews cannot help you here, Mr. Saad. They have proven themselves untrustworthy. Brokers of half-information. Half-truths. Always wanting more than they are prepared to give. No, Mr. Saad. It is different this time. This time we do not play Israeli trading games. Why do you think we are here? I will tell you, Mr. Saad. We are here to enable you and me to conclude our business on, shall I say, a one-to-one basis? Yes, one-to-one—free from Israeli meddling."

Placing his hands over his ears, Hassim tried to shut out Chatsworth's voice. It was a pointless effort as the Englishman continued.

"It occurs to me that it would be prudent to talk, Mr. Saad. Muslim-Jew. Jew-Muslim. They are interchangeable. Different motivations, of course, but interchangeable. I'm sure you see my point?"

Hassim said nothing.

"Of course you do," Chatsworth smiled. "So that brings us to now, Mr. Saad. And to me. You see, I am neither religious nor political. I allow myself no such indulgences. I have only needs, Mr. Saad. Information needs." He held out his hands in an exaggerated gesture of helplessness. "And to fill these needs, I have only you."

Again Hassim declined to comment.

Chatsworth laughed out loud. "Of course, I could be wrong.

Perhaps you like wallowing around nude as your extremities are amputated.''

He squatted down, his face inches from Hassim's. ''Do you, Mr. Saad? Do you enjoy uncivilized pastimes? Does the thought of pain tempt you? Are you a masochist? Tell me, Mr. Saad.''

Hassim's mind reeled with the singsong taunts from Chatsworth's leering mouth. Maybe the British were simply looking for Ursula? If he helped them . . . they would let him live. He doubted the Israelis would care one way the other.

But Yasif? If his possessiveness was as intense as Ursula said—then Yasif would order his death if he informed on her.

His position was desperate. A way out? Chatsworth had suggested it—worry about Yasif later. Now survival was the primary concern. Anything was better that sitting naked on a granite slab watching sadists dissect his body.

''Where would you like to experience pain, Mr. Saad? Fingers? Toes? Penis? Testicles? What's your pleasure, Mr. Saad?''

''She owed me money,'' Hassim blurted.

''For what?''

''Explosives.''

Nodding indulgently, a mirthless smile on his lips, Chatsworth seized Hassim's left breast. ''I do not believe you, Mr. Saad,'' he said twisting the sagging flesh with powerful fingers. ''Your impudence offends me.''

Hassim squirmed in agony. ''Weapons,'' he whimpered. ''She wanted a contact for weapons.''

Chatsworth twisted harder. ''Why?''

''I don't *know!*'' Hassim screamed.

''Why, Mr. Saad?''

Hassim began to sob. ''For her friend.''

Chatsworth released him. ''What friend?''

''I don't know.''

Reaching down, Chatsworth grabbed Hassim's thigh. ''Who, Mr. Saad?''

''Please . . . not there,'' Hassim begged.

"Who, Mr. Saad?" The hand slid higher.

"An Irishman—she didn't tell me his name."

"You are lying," Chatsworth said. "I have no time for lies, Mr. Saad. Nor do I indulge in hollow threats." He nodded to the kidnappers.

The two men pounced on Hassim, pulling at his arms and legs. After a brief struggle, they had him spread-eagled on his back.

"You are a sow, Mr. Saad," Chatsworth commented, as he stepped between Hassim's open legs. "An obese, insolent sow whom I will enjoy converting into a eunuch."

Like some spectator in a slaughterhouse, Hassim watched in horror as Chatsworth knelt between his legs and pulled his flacid penis away from the groin. The fingers were cold. Rough.

Panting, Hassim looked up at the driver. Raising a syringe, the Englishman tapped its side. Then he pressed the plunger, watching as a few drops of a colorless fluid squirted onto Hassim's quivering stomach. "I leave you your memories, Mr. Saad."

Chatsworth cupped the frail scrotum and inspected it. Like some light-sensitive creature, it withered at his touch.

"I will save it for you, Mr. Saad," he whispered. "I understand that in Sumatra they're sold as coin purses."

As he felt the needle pierce the tissue at the base of his penis, Hassim screamed. Immediately, the sensations began. The numbing spread through the juncture of his thighs and across his entire groin. He became aware of another terrifying effect: the impression of warm liquid dripping between his legs. He began sobbing anew.

"What is the Irishman's name, Mr. Saad?"

Raising his head, Hassim forced himself to look. He cried with relief. The liquid was urine, not blood.

"The name, Mr. Saad," Chatsworth repeated.

Looking up, Hassim retched. Poised in Chatsworth's right hand was a surgical scalpel.

"Please, Mr. Saad," Chatsworth said, poising the blade an inch above the penis. "Some things can never be undone."

"Crandon," Hassim panted between sobs. "Peder Crandon."

Chatsworth nodded. "And where is Peder Crandon?"

"United States." His throat filling with mucus, Hassim allowed his head to fall back, trying to ward off the tremors jerking at his spine.

Chatsworth squeezed the penis. "And Ursula Brandt?"

"I don't *know!*" Hassim spit between clenched teeth. "She's going to meet Crandon."

Chatsworth began twisting the penis. "When, Mr. Saad?"

"I don't know," Hassim screamed. "Soon . . . tommorrow . . . today. . . ."

"Who is their weapons contact, Mr. Saad?"

The tremors passed. "I don't know," he cried openly. "I gave her nothing."

"Look at me, Mr. Saad," Chatsworth ordered.

Forcing himself, Hassim raised his head. In spite of the medication, he could feel the pressure constricting his manhood.

"You are close, Mr. Saad. So very close." Chatsworth scratched the scalpel blade on the purplish tip of Hassim's flesh. Nothing more than a pinprick, but blood oozed out before Hassim's eyes.

"The contact, Mr. Saad?"

"*Eduardo Montes.*" The scream was almost unintelligible.

Careful not to harm the membrane, Chatsworth raised the scalpel and released the penis. "Eduardo Montes?" he repeated calmly.

"Yes," Hassim sobbed.

"Where can I find him?"

Hassim's sobs faded into sporadic whimperings. "Professor . . . Cuban . . . George Washington University . . . "

"Thank you, Mr. Saad," Chatsworth said softly. He stood up and nodded as the two men released their prisoner.

Instinctively, Hassim curled into a fetal position, rubbing his bruised penis frantically.

"You see, Mr. Saad," Chatsworth said politely, "cooperation wasn't all that difficult."

Hassim did not answer. He allowed himself the luxury of slipping into unconsciousness.

"What now?" Yellow Teeth asked. "Acid bath?"

"I don't think so," Chatsworth said. "We'll use him again. Give him another injection and let him sleep. Then take him back to his car."

The driver nodded. "Where will you be?"

"London." Chatsworth checked his watch. "My plane leaves Zurich in two hours."

Chatsworth turned back to Hassim. "A pleasure meeting you, Mr. Saad. The prime minister appreciates your timely assistance in this matter."

The business with Hassim finished, Basil Chatsworth turned and left the farmhouse, heading to the helicopter. It was going to be an incredibly long night.

Chapter 17

HOPPING FROM THE cold shower, Kelly Michaels dried himself briskly, then stepped over to the tape deck next to the bed. Fumbling through the cassettes, he selected one, inserted it into the player, flipped on the power, and turned up the volume.

The four oversized speakers began to throb with the heavy bass of The Beach Boys launching into "California Girls." Some things would always be right, he thought.

Singing along, he shuffle-danced back into the bathroom and affected a number of "intent male model poses," flexing his muscles before the mirrored wall.

"Can't wait till tomorrow morning," he said to his reflection.

"Why's that, Kelly?" he answered in a falsetto, trying to mimic a would-be female admirer.

"Cause I get better-looking every day." He uttered a sharp yelp and spun around on the punch line. Granted, it was a silly little routine, but if there was anything he liked better than the "dogs of war" crap—it was amusing himself. It hadn't always been so easy.

"Fucking gooks," he whispered as he leaned close to the glass to examine the scar under his eye. He hated the scar. Not that it was so ugly. On the contrary, most women liked it—considered it a dueling scar. He hated it for a strictly personal reason.

It stood as mute testimony to the one time in his career when he had goofed. No excuses. No way to rationalize it. His attention to detail had cost the lives of three innocent people and nearly his own. If the shrapnel had hit one inch higher, it would have cost him an eye. The doctor had called him lucky.

Privately, Kelly Michaels would have given both eyes for the chance to alter history; but realizing that was impossible, he had vowed he would never cut corners again.

From the bedroom, the tape played on and after a moment of transition, "Sloop John B." blasted throughout the A-frame. The song took his mind off the past. He again sang along as he picked up Mai Lei's brush.

He began to chuckle. What to *do* about his hair? When wet and combed back, it reached his shoulders.

And the beard? Originally he had grown it to alter his appearance after the Sri Lankan assignment. He never thought Mai Lei would like it. But she had and now called him her "lord of the reefs."

What the hell, he thought. He wasn't running for office. The hair and beard could continue to grow until *they* got tired. Now it was Beach Boys time.

As "Sloop John B." segued into "Help Me Rhonda," Michaels strutted back to the bedroom. From the wicker dresser, he picked up the carved ivory miniature Buddha Mai Lei had bought and set into an gold ear stud. His ear wasn't pierced, then, so she did it herself. It was her gift to him, in celebration of their first year together. Michaels liked the effect and wore it except when diving. Somehow it kept things in perspective.

Still shuffling in time with the music, he inserted the post in the lobe of his left ear and wondered what the cadre back at Fort Bragg would think of it.

Probably shit in their pants, he thought. *Probably think he'd——*

Suddenly Kelly Michaels froze. It was that sound again, throbbing under the driving Beach Boy bass, a deep, pulsating echo in his brain. A hallucination?

Listening intently, the vibrations grew more intense. It was no illusion. The rotor blades of a helicopter cut the air for lift. One felt it as much as heard it. Remembering, he thought vaguely of Asia as he identified the type of aircraft approaching the island: 1,800 horsepower Pratt and Whitney. Military configuration.

"Shitheads!" he said, not bothering to dress as he walked quickly to the outside deck.

Mai Lei was already there, dressed in a loose flowered cloth wrapped low on her hips, her breasts bare, the nipples peeking discreetly between the two long pigtails draped over her shoulders. Michaels recognized her Tahiti look and stood next to her.

"Expecting company?" she asked.

He didn't answer. Looking west, he could see the helicopter approaching at about 200 feet and closing fast, the orange glow of the setting sun a dramatic backdrop.

"Probably looking for dopers again," he told her. "They keep screwing with us, and one of these days I'm going to blow that slick out from under their fat DEA asses."

Dropping to 50 feet, the pilot banked over the cabin. Michaels could read the *U.S. Air Force* stencil on the tail boom. "Bastard!" he yelled, raising a finger in the international gesture of contempt. "Get the fuck away from my house."

Completing his initial pass, the pilot banked again, adjusted his turn and flared to a landing on the beach in front of the A-frame. Once down, Michaels glanced at Mai Lei. She was staring up at him.

"Don't leave me again, Kelly," she said softly. "I don't know how many times I can go through it."

Aware of her eyes misting with tears, Michaels reached down and cupped her chin in his hands. "Hey, it's probably narcs, like I said. I'm not planning any trips."

But as he looked back to the helicopter's opening door, Michaels knew he was wrong.

"Ready, Catlin?" Taylor asked, disengaging the double-locking mechanism and sliding the hatch panel open.

"Right behind you," she answered, releasing her seat belt.

Taylor jumped out onto the sand and, waiting for Cat, helped her out. Together they covered the forty yards to the A-frame, both attempting, to ignore The Beach Boys' "Wouldn't It Be Nice" blaring from the cabin as well as from a dozen speakers concealed in the shadows.

"Hello, Kelly," Taylor said to the naked man standing at the top of the stairs.

"Taylor," Michaels replied curtly, looking at Catlin. "Who's brown sugar?" he asked good-naturedly.

"Catlin Broussard," Taylor answered. "My exec."

Michaels eyed her professionally. "Broussard," he nodded. "Cajun lady?"

Cocky bastard, Catlin thought. "Creole." She headed up the stairs, her right hand outstretched. "Any chance of you putting on some pants, nature boy?"

Shaking her hand, Michaels smiled at the term. "Only for you."

Catlin returned the smile. "Thank you, Kelly." She took a furtive look at Mai Lei.

"Mai Lei," Michaels explained.

"Hello, Mai Lei," Catlin offered.

The Eurasian woman walked toward the stairs. "Excuse me," she said softly, squeezing past Catlin and Taylor as she stepped down onto the beach and walked away.

"I'm sorry," Cat told Michaels. "Did we——"

"Not your fault," he interrupted, turning to Taylor. "RAINDANCER?"

Taylor nodded. "We didn't come for dinner."

"You weren't invited," Michaels shot back, crossing his arms as he leaned onto the railing. No point in wasting time. It would be better for Mai Lei if he left with a minimum of conversation.

"Who's the bad guy?" he asked.

"An Irishman," Taylor answered.

"He's a terrorist," Catlin added.

Michaels shrugged. "Makes no difference, Creole lady," he told her as he looked down the beach toward Mai Lei. "Where is he?"

"Washington." Catlin was unable to shake the impression that Michaels considered the contract just some minor irritation interrupting his personal life.

"Dinero?" he asked, turning his attention back to Taylor.

"The usual," Taylor said. "Fifty in the currency of your choice."

Michaels glanced back to Mai Lei. "Hundred. Then I'm quitting, Taylor."

Taylor paused for a moment. In or out, that was Michaels's decision, and he couldn't care less. The problem was that time was running short. Despite his personal feelings toward the man, Catlin's selection was appropriate. Michaels could stop Crandon.

"Cayman?" he asked.

Michaels nodded. "Mai Lei's account."

Taylor understood. "It'll be credited by noon tomorrow."

"I'll get my gear," Michaels said, turning and padding toward the cabin. "You can brief me later."

After he had left them, Catlin leaned over to Taylor. "Jesus," she whispered. "I don't know what I was expecting, but it definitely wasn't anything like *this*. Hell, Sam, I feel like I'm in some 1960s California artist's colony." She shook her head in disbelief. "I mean, really . . . pierced ears, beards, sarong-wrapped topless women, The Beach Boys? I'm surprised he didn't offer us herbal tea and cup of brown rice."

"We weren't invited for dinner, remember?" Taylor said, turning around and facing the water.

"But he's a flake."

"You're only a flake if you're poor," Taylor sat down on the steps. "If you have money, you're eccentric. Kelly's eccentric. He's also a pro."

"I thought you didn't like him." Catlin sat down on the wooden steps next to him. "Why make excuses for him?"

Taylor turned and looked into her face. "I *don't* like him, Catlin. I told you we have a personality conflict. I'm not making excuses for anyone."

Catlin said nothing. After a moment, Taylor turned back to the water and continued. "Kelly's a byproduct of the system," he said, his voice sounding sad even to him. "He's no different than you or I."

"But he doesn't care who the target is," Catlin reminded him.

"No," Taylor agreed. "But does it make any difference to us either?"

"Of course it does. If Crandon had been——"

"Been what?" Taylor interrupted. "Something other than a terrorist?" He nodded slowly, choosing his words carefully. "What if he had been a priest killing for religious reasons? Or a lawyer killing for legal reasons? Or even the president of a country killing to protect his people?"

He shook his head. "No, Catlin. It really didn't make any difference to us either. We're running it simply because the Caucus authorized it. Nothing more, nothing less. Like I said, Kelly's no different than we are. If you can accept that one thing—remember that one thing—you'll understand something that took me twenty years to learn."

He turned and looked at her. "It'll serve you well, Cat. It'll keep you from thinking you're something you're not."

She stared into his eyes. "Is that what I'm doing now, Sam? Thinking I'm something I'm not?" She watched his eyes cloud with the question as he looked away.

"I don't know, Catlin," he answered. "You have to judge that for yourself. I know only what I'm *allowed* to know."

Deciding to drop the subject, Catlin said nothing. For the next few minutes, both she and Taylor stood in silence, each staring toward the water.

So he *still* suspected there was more to her story, she thought. Perhaps that was the reason he continued to remain aloof. It was ego. Taylor's pride was hurt. Feeling uncomfortably deceitful, Catlin decided just as soon as the Crandon matter was resolved, she would explain it all to him. As for the general . . . . she would cross that bridge when the time came.

Taylor was not really thinking about anything, just staring at the helicopter crouched low on the sand at the water's edge. In the gathering darkness, its red strobe lights were growing in intensity, their rhythmic pulsations lulling him with a hypnotic fixation.

"Mai Lei is a beautiful woman." Catlin broke into his reverie.

"Very beautiful," Taylor agreed, looking in the direction of the slender silhouette wading in the shallow surf. "She worked for the agency in Bangkok for almost five years before Kelly came along."

Catlin was surprised. "Doing what?"

"Playing social butterfly with the Soviets."

"Good?"

Taylor nodded. "Very. She's an excellent listener and has total recall."

"Why'd she get out?" Catlin asked.

"To go with nature boy, I guess. Maybe she's a Beach Boys fan."

"She's in love with him. That's fairly obvious."

Taylor shook his head. "I doubt he'd recognize the feeling. I don't think he's the type."

"Whatever." Catlin brushed the sand off her jeans.

"Where you going?" Taylor asked.

Catlin shrugged. "Just for a walk. I'm feeling kinda antsy."

"You'll get used to it," Taylor said as she turned and headed for the water.

"I'm not sure I want to," she called back over her shoulder.

But you will, Taylor thought, watching her swaying hips as she walked away. It was all part of the process.

Chapter 18

SIR ELLIOT PRESCOTT was exhausted by the time he reached the ornate apartment building just off Shaftesbury Avenue in London's venerable theater district. The flight from Washington had left him irritable, and all he really wanted was to be able to spend the last few hours before Monday morning quietly sampling the pleasures of his mistress.

Nicole Dubois had occupied the third-floor flat for almost a year, and Sir Elliot was more than just a familiar face to the discreet but courteous staff.

Curtly acknowledging a liveried valet, Sir Elliot strode across the deserted lobby, entered an elevator and went to the third floor, where he walked even faster down the thick oriental carpet and rang the bell to 3-C.

After a brief wait, the door opened. "Elliot," the girl squealed, "you said you were going to be in America!"

"I was," he answered, stepping inside and closing the door behind him. "I've just returned from Heathrow."

"A good trip?" She managed adroitly to keep her breasts peeping through the faint wisp of lacy camisole which hung loosely from her shoulders and ended, appropriately enough, just above the thick path of exposed pubic hair.

A voyeur at heart, Prescott did not immediately answer. Rather, he allowed his senses to indulge themselves in a particularly delicate evaluation of the girl's innate provocativeness.

A dark, even wicked-looking French nymphet, Nicole Dubois

was the perfect accouterment to Sir Elliot's admittedly meticulous brand of debauchery. At eighteen, her figure remained almost childlike; but with high, firmly pointed breasts and hips just beginning to flower into womanhood. She was an aspiring actress, and Prescott had yet to accept the fact she was all his.

Reaching over, he touched her exposed left nipple and felt it stiffen under his fingertips. Nicol was the same age as his youngest daughter. Perhaps that was what made the liaison so carnal, so prohibitive.

"Did you miss me?" she smiled coyly.

He nodded. "The best part of any trip is returning to you," he told her as she began to kiss the fingers holding the nipple.

Nicole made a purring noise. "Does your wife know you're back?" She looked up at him with wide hazel eyes.

He sighed, began to undress as he turned toward the bedroom. He glanced around the flat. He had spent considerable time and money educating Nicole on the finer things of life, and now his tastes were well reflected in the paintings and objets d'art she proudly displayed.

"No, Nicole," he said softly. "She is in Surrey with her parents and doesn't expect me until tomorrow."

Her eyes dancing, she dropped the camisole to the floor, walking nude to the bedroom door. "Good," she breathed, beckoning him to follow. "I have you all to myself."

Eyes fixed on the taut roundness of her buttocks, Sir Elliot followed without reservation.

Nicole was already in bed when he entered the room. Twisting seductively on the cool linen sheets, she began to rub herself as Prescott undressed, prissily folding his clothes and draping them over the back of a chair.

"Hurry, Elliot," she whispered, her voice vaporous. "I need to feel you."

Slipping out of a pair of silk shorts, Prescott could feel his own passion as he moved toward the bed. "God, you're incredible,'' he groaned, sliding in next to her. ''I can't believe you're really mine.''

Nicol smiled. ''Let me please you,'' she hissed, arching her hips into him as her tongue snaked into his mouth.

Sir Elliot pulled away, rolling onto his back and spreading his legs to allow the girl to kneel between them.

Nicole moved quickly. Leaning forward, her breasts touched his chest as she kissed him fully on the mouth, letting her tongue dart briefly, teasingly across his perfect teeth.

Prescott shifted and with exquisite slowness, she began to move downward, leaving behind a chilled ribbon of moisture as she licked his chest. His stomach. His loins.

Prescott moaned openly as he became aware of her hair trailing behind the ribbon, caressing his body with a spidery fullness as he suddenly conjured up a vision of his daughter. It was a splendidly obscene image of incestuous abandon. Wantonly sinful. He prolonged the thought.

Panting, Prescott felt his penis extend as her tongue continued to probe, urging him to even more lurid depths of debauchery. His daughter. Nicole. His daughter and Nicol together. His wife watching.

''Please,'' he begged.

Nicole did not speak as she crawled up his body and poised herself. Squatting above him, she took his hand and placed his fingers to her womanhood. Greedy now, Prescott was acutely aware of its wetness. His desire was accentuated by the musky release of lust.

He attempted to penetrate her. Nicole moved. Twisting deftly, she smiled and took his hand from between her legs. Then, slowly, leisurely, she impaled herself upon him. She took his fingers into her mouth, sucking flagrantly, audibly, as they began to sway together.

Grimacing with pleasure, Prescott looked up at his mistress as she rocked against him, moving in increasingly tighter circles.

Suddenly Nicole trembled, and he was aware of taut contractions spawned from deep within her vaginal walls. The clawing sensation became stronger. Too intense. Too palatable. Releasing himself to the pleasure of his thoughts, Elliot Prescott joined the girl in a long, purging orgasm.

Then he slept a deep, refreshing sleep.

He was a world away from the affairs of England. Affairs which were of considerable interest to Nicole Dubois as she watched him.

Fool, she thought, staring down at the man sharing her bed. *They had been right.*

Elliot Prescott was nothing more than a star-crossed amateur.

Chapter 19

REACHING INTO THE bottom dresser drawer, Michaels touched the cool metal of the tiny Czech machine pistol. *Excellent weapon,* he thought. Light—less than five pounds—and short—only ten inches—it offered both efficiency as well as concealability.

Clearing the breech, he squeezed the trigger on an empty chamber. He smiled. With its flat black finish, the Skorpion looked more like a child's toy than a deadly machine capable of spitting out over 800 steel-jacketed .32 caliber rounds per minute. ''Sweetness,'' he whispered.

For low-intensity warfare, Michaels knew there was nothing better on the marketplace. The weapon had proved that on all too many occasions.

A Skorpion was used to kill Italian Prime Minister Aldo Moro. Another was used in the assassination of Francisco Coco, the chief prosecutor of Genoa. In South Africa, Skorpions were repeatedly employed in the open gun battles between the various factions arguing the apartheid issue. And in El Salvador, four American marines had been murdered when their restaurant table was riddled by guerrillas firing Skorpions.

Again clearing the breech, assuring himself it was safe for travel, he placed it on top of his clothes, shoving it into the corner of his kit bag next to a Sionics D-7 silencer. Machined to fit the Skorpion, he knew that the silencer reduced the effective range of the machine pistol to less than 100 yards. This was acceptable only because, at the same time, it also greatly enhanced the efficiency of the Skorpion's full automatic shot pattern by compressing the bullets into a much tighter kill zone. The funneling effect increasing the odds of controlled target penetration.

After zipping the bag he reached behind him and caressed the hard rubber grips of the Soviet Marakov pistol he wore concealed at the small of his back. Snugly fitted into a custom-designed pancake holster, the automatic held a special significance. Its previous owner, a Chinese Communist major, had been the first man Kelly Michaels had killed on behalf of the United States Government.

Closing his eyes, he could still remember the darkness of the Laotian jungle and the heavy smell of rot which had sucked hungrily at his pores. The major had been advising a group of North Vietnamese regulars when the PRAIRIE FIRE spike team caught them in a small clearing. Having just been assigned to cross-border operations, it was Michaels's first ambush.

The firefight was brief and intense. In less than thirty seconds, sixteen Communists were dead. Picking through the bodies, he had taken the Marakov off the dead officer's body. To Michaels, the pistol was a constant reminder of just how temporary life could be.

"Fucking gook!" he whispered, picking up the kit bag and leaving the bedroom. "He should have had a man on the parallel."

"Got everything?" Taylor asked, looking at Michaels dressed in jeans, western boots, and a safari jacket.

"Everything I need," he shrugged. "Where's Brown Sugar?"

"Catlin's in the chopper," Taylor answered. "You need a few minutes with Mai Lei?"

Michaels glanced toward the shadow of the woman walking at the far end of the island. "We don't do that anymore. She's burning out. No point in fanning the flames."

He turned back to Taylor. "Let's just get moving. The sooner I can get back, the sooner I can get out of these pants."

Taylor wasn't amused. "I want you to do something for me, Kelly," he said, as they began to walk across the sand to the helicopter."

"You're still calling the shots. What?"

"Play it close," Taylor told him. "No more screw-ups—I'm not sure I'll be able to fade the administrative heat."

"Isn't that what old spooks are for? We do the job—you cover up!"

Taylor allowed the slur to pass.

"Don't worry, Taylor." Michaels continued to taunt him. "You'll land on your feet. Don't forget you've been there before, right?"

Glancing over, Taylor studied the younger man's profile for a moment. "We both have, Kelly." His voice was flat. "Some things just don't go away."

Michaels arched an eyebrow. "Still with the *noche del bestia?"*

Taylor said nothing.

Reaching the helicopter, Michaels tossed his kit bag through the hatch. "There's something I want you to do for me," he said, turning to Taylor.

"What's that?"

"If I get jammed up on this deal—make sure Mai Lei gets it all worked out. I don't want the beast eating at her, too."

Taylor didn't trust himself to answer and only managed a nod. *Noche del bestia*. The phrase cut deep. Climbing aboard the helicopter, he avoided both Michaels's eyes and Catlin's greeting. *Night of the beast,* he thought.

God, how he wanted a drink.

As Michaels climbed inside, the turbines immediately began to whine with an earsplitting pitch as they powered up. Conversation was impossible. Taylor, thankful for the respite, stared at Catlin as the torque increased.

A moment later, the helicopter shuddered violently and lifted up to a height of twenty feet, hovering while the pilot made a last-minute check of the instruments. Satisfied that all systems were functioning, he dropped the nose and the helicopter shot forward, heading for the Florida mainland.

As they crossed the west tip of Bottle Key, Taylor glanced out the small bubble window next to his shoulder.

Standing at the water's edge was Mai Lei. She did not look up as they passed over, and Taylor knew instinctively that she was probably weeping in that stoic manner women do when their men leave for war.

The tears, the prayers, the waiting. Taylor had seen it a thousand times and wondered if Michaels had ever allowed himself to think how agonizing living alone could be. *Noche del bestia*—the soul razor.

Taylor wished that experience on no man. *That* beast was much too cutting a nightmare.

Especially when deserved.

Chapter 20

"ELLIOT?" NICOLE SHOOK his shoulder gently.

"What?" Prescott mumbled, his mind dulled with sleep.

"It's for you."

"Me?" Groggy, Sir Elliot did not understand.

"The telephone." She handed him the receiver. "I told them you weren't here, but they insisted."

Instantly, Prescott was awake. Who could possibly know he was with his mistress? Surely not his wife!

Rubbing his eyes, he reached reluctantly for the instrument. "May I help you?"

"So sorry to disturb you, Sir Elliot. But it seems we've inadvertently acquired some information on the Crandon matter."

The voice on the other hand was entirely too cheerful for Prescott's sour mood. "Who the devil is this?"

"Oh, yes. So sorry, Sir Elliot. This is Basil Chatsworth, THIMBLE Zurich?"

The surgeon, Prescott thought, remembering the MI5 agent's *nom de guerre*. "Of course, Chatsworth. Please go on."

"It's a Mr. Saad, Sir Elliot. An arms dealer? We interviewed him in Bern. I'm pleased to report he was eager to cooperate in our inquiry."

Prescott sat up in bed. Unable to conceal the excitement in his voice, he said "Yes, yes, Chatsworth. Please go on."

Listening intently, Prescott allowed Chatsworth to relate the facts without interruption, merely grunting replies to the information the counterintelligence people had obtained. After several minutes, he'd heard enough.

"Excellent, Chatsworth," he interrupted. "I shall leave for Washington within the hour. Prepare a full memorandum of the interview for my files."

"Of course, Sir Elliot," Chatsworth replied. "And on a more personal note, sir?"

"Yes?"

"You may be assured of my absolute discretion."

Bastard, Prescott thought. *They always want you to know they have something on you.* He glanced at Nicole. Eyes closed, she was lying back on the bed. "A point well taken, Chatsworth. Thank you."

"Thank you, Sir Elliot."

And go to hell, Prescott thought, handing the receiver to Nicole.

"Something important?" she asked, hanging up the phone.

"Just business," he sighed, climbing out of bed and beginning to dress. "Nothing to bore you with. Now go back to sleep. I'll ring you later."

"But Elliot," she pouted, stretching provocatively. "You've only just arrived."

Half-dressed, he leaned over the bed and gave her a quick fatherly kiss on the forehead. "I know, and I don't like it any better than you do. Unfortunately, we have little choice in the matter."

"Please call, Elliot. I miss you already."

Walking toward the bedroom door, Prescott looked back toward the bed. "I know you do, Nicole. And I promise I will—in the morning."

Lying back on the sheets, Nicol watched him leave. A moment later, the sound of the apartment door closing filtered into the bedroom.

"Fool," she laughed, climbing out of bed.

Walking to the bedroom closet, she slid open the door and

reached up to the rear of the top shelf. Disconnecting its wires, she pulled out the small Sony tape recorder and returned to the bed.

Sitting on its edge, she flipped the recorder's selector switch to *battery* and rewound the tape. It took twelve seconds.

Then, taking a deep breath, she pressed the *play* button and listened carefully to the telephone conversation she had secretly recorded.

After listening to the tape once, she replayed it, this time making notes. Satisfied the facts were straight, Nicole Dubois lit a cigarette and reached for the telephone.

Dialing the number, she rewound the tape for a third time.

"International operator," a bored woman's voice answered.

Nicole pressed another button on the recorder. The conversation was erased immediately. "Yes. I wish to call New York."

"What is the number?" the operator asked.

Nicole gave it from memory.

Chapter 21

IT WOULD MAKE an excellent bomb, Peder Crandon predicted, swallowing the last of the smoked sardines and tossing the empty tin in the general direction of the room's cluttered sink. A fitting application for the only explosives he head been able to smuggle into the country from Mexico.

Wiping his oily fingers on the sheets, he lay on his side and began methodically to unload the contents of the small olive canvas sack, carefully spreading the material across a blanket at the foot of the bed.

Working with practiced fingers, he deftly extracted the eight blocks of tetrytol, carefully removed their asphalt-impregnated wrappers, and tossed the waxy packaging material to the floor. It was unnecessary.

By design, each two-and-a-half-pound block of the explosive was cast into a single line of detonating cord which passed lengthwise through them, not unlike floats on a fishing net. When activated, the resulting chain of explosions would ignite with almost twice the velocity of the 21,000 feet per second offered by TNT—an equation that, considering the target's size, was necessary to assure total destruction.

Tetrytol could be ignited by either an electrical or nonelectrical triggering device with a time-delay override. He had used this procedure before and it provided sufficient time for him to get away from the fireball, yet remain close enough to be able to observe the annihilation. This was the true beauty of military technology.

Attaching the time-delay mechanism to the last block of tetrytol, he cautiously inspected the mating of the charge with the thin platinum wire bridge which would be heated by the electrical current. Satisfied the coupling was secure, he then attached the two lead wires protruding from the delay's metal shell to the nine-volt battery-powered timing device. With the current now completed, the liquid display of the digital timer began winking in slow pinkish pulsations. The bomb was operational. All that was left was to actually set the timer when he was ready to plant the device.

Inspecting the connections once again, he slid the explosives gently back into the canvas sack. Only the timing device remained exposed.

Glancing at his watch, he reached in his pocket and extracted a shiny "10 NEW PENCE" coin and added it to the contents of the bag. Then, snapping the sack shut, he climbed off the bed and began to strip.

When he reached the site, he would have less than a half hour to penetrate the target, arm the bomb, and make good his escape. After thirty minutes, tetrytol's chemical composition had a tendency to become waterlogged. Then the odds of a successful detonation dropped considerably.

But it would not be a problem, he decided, as he donned the black rubber wet suit. The cold and the darkness would cover his approach.

He began to snicker.

The Brits, he thought. *Tonight they would pay even more.*

Chapter 22

REPLACING THE RECEIVER on its cradle, Yasif leaned back on the leather settee and closed his eyes—a calculated effort to control his growing rage.

For a diplomat, it was a difficult task.

For a Bedouin, it was all but impossible, both emotionally as well as physically. Yasif remained the classic Bedouin warrior despite his forty-eight years.

An inch under six feet, he was a darkly handsome man. Rugged with thick, smooth hair and a neatly trimmed moustache and goatee. The hair was black but glossy, appearing almost navy when contrasted with his even white teeth, thin lips, and swarthy olive complexion.

He was a powerful man. A severe man. An athlete with the inherited strength of a horseman with powerful arms, legs, and shoulders. Intelligence coupled with a proud arrogance concealed beneath his clothing, enhanced by the traditional Bedouin *kheffiyah* he wore on his head.

Yasif was a man used to controlling events. It was a passion he savored, one which allowed him little tolerance for oversight. And this, since the phone call from London, was the reason for his indignation. It had been *his* oversight which had caused the problem. Now he was furious.

Of course, Nicole had performed well—little consolation considering her news. But Ursula's actions? Unexpected. A *personal* affront. She was deliberately ignoring his instructions.

And what of that Crandon lunatic? Because of Ursula's impulsive little meeting with Hassim, the British now possessed enough information to conceivably arrange his capture. Everything would be ruined if he were pressured to talk.

Standing, Yasif removed the *kheffiyah,* folding the cloth carefully as he walked to the window of his forty-sixth floor suite in the New York Hilton at Rockefeller Center. The view was breathtaking, the city awash in lights.

Below him lay Manhattan, the financial center of America and most of the free world. The island appeared suspended, he thought, looking toward the horizon. Its golden towers floating between the darkness of the Hudson and East rivers. An oasis of diversity. Of international brotherhood symbolized by the United Nations' thirty-nine stories, poised gracefully on the East River's banks.

Yasif thought the irony incredible. A few years ago, he would have been refused entry into the country or arrested on some obscure criminal charge. But those days were over. Now he carried a diplomatic passport and was exempt from the regulations governing the masses.

Due to his status in the Libyan Mission, Yasif paid no taxes and was free to buy cars, jewelry, even expensive foods without paying any sales taxes whatsoever. Even his limousine could be left anywhere, for he was immune from parking tickets. It was a far cry from the dusty refugee camps of his youth and his forty years of devotion to Islam. Fortunately, unlike some others, he had been able to keep his faith.

It had been a rewarding life, he thought, resting his forehead on the cool, damp glass. A good, exhilarating life with many successes and few setbacks. An era in which he had been given the divine honor to rewrite history and had done so with a bold stroke. The will of Allah. That weighty responsibility offered to few and hardly ever to a nameless orphan from the Sinai Peninsula. To Yasif, it was holy regard he had fought to acquire and retain. It was the sole purpose of existence.

Leaving the window, Yasif returned to the settee. Again closing his eyes, he sat down, clearing his mind to concentrate on Nicole's call.

Actually, the issues were twofold. First, there was the situation with Hassim and the British agents. That could be cleared up easily. The second problem was more complex. This would be the one to test him. Ursula's involvment made it *his* decision alone.

He had knowingly violated one of his own cardinal rules. He had allowed himself to become emotionally attached to one of his subordinates. Since this was personal, he would be forced to resolve it personally. Arab pride would not allow him to dole it out to some underling. But first, Hassim Saad. Yasif picked up the receiver for the direct telephone line to the Secretariat's Libyan Mission.

Instantly, a deep male voice answered. "Excellency?"

"Send a card to Hassim Saad in Bern. He should be at Le Gaulois within the hour." Yasif paused for a moment, then continued. "I want him contacted by dawn."

Yasif hung up the phone without waiting for a response. The fact that his orders would roust some lower-level functionary out of bed was of no concern whatsoever. Yasif was certain that his instructions would be followed to the letter. He gave no quarter when it came to mistakes or excuses.

Putting Hassim out of his mind, he leaned back on the settee and directed his attentions to the larger picture: the problem of Peder Crandon.

As de facto chief of the Tripoli-based Islamic Liaison Office, Yasif supervised the great majority of Muslim-sponsored terrorist operations. It was an amorphous title, really, not unlike the *Hezbelluh* of Lebanese bombing fame. There was no real organization, no offices, and absolutely no paper trail which could be traced back to the Islamic Triad of Syria, Libya, and Iran. It was only a name. The internal control designation under which terrorism operated was authorized and directed by the Triad representatives living in Tripoli. Men who, despite his frequent trips to New York, still considered Yasif the real organizational power and from whom he drew the authority to recruit anyone in order to further Islamic destiny. He was an authority, witnessed by his retaining of numerous action teams. Depending upon operational complexities, these might be German, Cuban, or, if open Islamic ties were desired, the less sophisticated Muslim splinter factions—those suicidal zealots who drifted between the Mideast resettlement camps. It was a deadly strategy which continued to work for the sole benefit of the Triad.

From the humble beginnings of the PLO, the evolution had moved toward cooperation between the militant Islamic states. To Syrian collusion. To Libyan participation and the signing of the Libyan-Syrian Axis. To finally, within the last three weeks, with the Ayatollah Khomeini pledging Iranian support. It was in place now. The Triad would alter the balance of world power—the United Kingdom of Islam.

A unified Muslim nation. Powerful. Rich. Controlling 40 percent of the globe's known hydrocarbon reserves and composed of 75 million devoted followers. People sharing Yasif's fiery Bedouin blood, who would gladly sacrifice their lives to support the will of Allah and the teachings of Mohammed. It would be the acceptance of Mecca as the world center and the Koran as all men's Bible. The dream reached. The hope fulfilled.

But the call from London could well alter the scenario entirely. If Crandon were captured by British or American authorities, the repercussions would be felt throughout the Arab world.

Yasif cursed his one weakness. Had it not been for Ursula, he never would have allowed the Irishman to operate independently. Crandon was too irrational. But Ursula . . . the ultimate courtesan. She was like a drug. He needed to possess her. To experience her lust . . . her animal beauty. To feel her flesh against his.

"Damn the woman!" The mere thought of her long red hair and white skin provoked a hollow, twisting sensation in his loins. He stood up and forced the thoughts from his mind. Yes! He would stop Peder Crandon *personally*. There was no other alternative. There must be no mistakes. If it leaked out that he was Crandon's mentor—the one who arranged his terrorist training, the one who ordered him into the United States, the one who arranged for him to be smuggled in through Texas, the one who . . . who . . .

Yasif's mind raced with disjointed thoughts. Embassy attacks . . . car bombings . . . diplomatic murders . . . It was all so foreign to Americans. All just brief news highlights.

But if the American public discovered that a senior member of an Islamic diplomatic mission had sanctioned the assassination of a British consul general a few blocks from the White House, the results could be fatal to all Muslims, particularly the still-embryonic Islamic Kingdom.

The cagy Ayatollah would immediately dissociate himself from Syria and Libya. Then, with President Assad denying any knowledge of Libyan activities, the Syrians would quickly withdraw support. The splintering would begin anew. The dream would be shattered.

No, he could not allow it. It would set back Islamic destiny by centuries.

He glanced at the slim Piaget watch on his left wrist: 8:30 P.M. He would take the 10:00 shuttle to Washington, find Crandon, and kill him.

Walking to the telephone, he picked up the direct line.

"Excellency?" the voice answered.

"Outside line."

"Immediately, excellency."

When the dial tone sounded, Yasif punched the Washington telephone number from memory.

Moments later, the connection was made, and a phone began ringing in the darkened room just off Logan Circle.

"Thank you for calling," a curt metallic voice answered. "If you leave a brief message, I will——"

"Bastards!" Yasif cursed, slamming down the receiver.

Irritated by the answering machine, he stalked over to the window and placed his hand on the glass. It was getting colder, he noticed. He would take a topcoat to Washington.

Chapter 23

ONE THOUSAND MILES to the south, at the exact moment of Yasif's decision, the pilot of the Learjet 24D slammed the throttles forward beginning his acceleration down runway QUEBEC 9 of Homestead Air Force Base.

As the engines screamed with 6,000 pounds of thrust, the small jet shuddered and then lifted up, climbing steeply in the hazy Florida night banking north over the Atlantic.

Reaching a cruise altitude of 46,000 feet, the pilot reduced power to the engines and poured himself a cup of coffee from a large silver thermos. "Anyone else?" he asked, turning to the three passengers in the compartment behind him.

In turn, Catlin and Taylor declined.

"No, thanks," Michaels added, shifting uncomfortably in the hard upholstered seat. Coffee would not soften the memories brought back by the helicopter ride. The first step to overcome was fear.

Savor it, he remembered. It was the awareness part of the fear matrix. It was always the same at the start of a mission. He guessed it came with being a soldier which, despite any civilian status, was precisely what he still considered himself.

The fear matrix, he thought. *Reaction. The ritual every man endured in his own unique way.*

He swallowed. This was the difficulty in leading men to war. Some folded under the pressure. Others ripened with the challenge. It was the unknown quantity, the guess how one would respond when survival depended upon a split-second decision. It was all so fragile.

Since time eternal, fear of death had been a pervasive fixation in the soldier's mind. Certainly he was no exception. Realistically, not to respect its possibility was the attitude of a fool. Conversely, to let fear rule was equally foolish.

Selectively, Michaels had trained himself to straddle the middle ground. The approach had worked. He knew it would continue to do so.

Others were not as perceptive. Regretfully, there were throngs of men whose preoccupation with fear had ruined them; they lived each hour as if it were their last, some writing their own epitaphs. Their petty little idiosyncracies—insomnia, phobia, an endless list as each person attempted to find normalcy in the confusion of unchecked anxiety. A normalcy achieved only in death.

Then there was that smaller group, the ones full of individual bravado. These were the dangerous ones. Unable to admit their apprehensions, even a brief reference to the word *fear* could set them off on a tangent of unwarranted brutality. In a drunken stupor, a Laotian mercenary had once explained this phenomenon by proudly proclaiming, "To admit my fear would be equal to my death."

Michaels turned back to Taylor. "I'll look at the material now."

Taylor nodded. "Catlin?"

Reaching under her seat, Catlin extracted Taylor's briefcase. Placing it on her lap, she snapped it open, removing the file folders with Crandon's background information.

Taking the dossiers, Michaels opened the top one without pausing. Staring first at the man's photograph, then at the stack of papers, he realized it would take at least an hour to digest the information.

Reaching up, he snapped on the overhead reading light and settled back to study the man he was going to kill.

Catlin glanced at the small digital clock in the Lear's forward bulkhead. They would be in Washington by midnight. Sliding her own seat back, she leaned over to Michaels. "If you need anything else, let me know."

He didn't look up. "No problem, Creole lady," he lied. "You'll be the first one I call."

Chapter 24

THE DRIVE FROM Washington had taken Peder Crandon the better part of an hour. But now, as he lay on the jetty overlooking the Baltimore Harbor, he knew it had been well worth the effort.

Despite a cool rainmist hanging low over the murky water, he could still distinguish the silhouette of his prey. A wisp of shadow floating silently on a choppy charcoal basin.

He thrilled at the sight.

The *H.M.S. Repose* was a 140-foot research trawler assigned to the International Commission on Ocean Pollutants. Stuffed with electronic sensing equipment, it was powered by four General Motors diesels and carried a crew of twenty. It was also, if Crandon were to believe yesterday's television coverage, the sole British contribution to the NATO member project studying the effect of toxic waste dumping in the Atlantic Ocean.

Anchored some 200 yards from shore, the *Repose* was dark. And, with the exception of a periodic flashing of its stern light, the area immediately surrounding the ship appeared deserted. Still, Peder Crandon waited. From experience, he knew to continue the surveillance for at least another seven minutes if surprise were to remain his ally.

He listened. There were no sounds indicating his discovery—only the quiet splashings of the tidal surge gurgling against the rocks.

Moving quickly, he removed the outer layer of clothes and sprinted to the water's edge—the black wet-suit blending perfectly into the jetty's jagged crannies. Pausing, he breathed deeply of the fuel-stained, brackish water; then, looping the canvas bag around his neck, he slid slowly into the ocean.

For the first few yards, the depths were surprisingly shallow and he was aware of a thick ooze of bottom mud sucking at his SCUBA socks. He ignored the sensation and when the surface reached his chest, he shoved off, and began to breaststroke into deeper water.

A strong swimmer, Crandon covered the distance to the trawler within minutes. Closing to 15 yards, he paused. Treading water. Watching. Listening.

He heard nothing. With the exception of the stern light, the ship remained veiled in darkness. *Fools,* he thought, kicking the last few feet to a boarding ladder on the trawler's starboard side. The presumptuous morons didn't even have a deck watch.

Gripping the ladder, he paused again. Now he could hear the soft muffled growls of bilge pumps and the exhausts hissing from an onboard generator. He smiled. There were no human sounds. His progress had gone undetected.

Moving quietly, Crandon heaved himself to the scarred deck, paddled quickly to the aft of the trawler, and down into the passageway leading to the main engine room. He was eager to plant the tetrytol and leave the ship. Eager for the explosion. Locating the diesels, he wedged the sack between two large fuel lines twisting up from within the bowels of the ship. Certain this placement would cause the most damage, he activated the timer, pressed the small blue button, and watched as the pinkish digits danced before his eyes. When the numbers read "10:00," he released the button. The device was now armed. The mellow pulsations indicating ten minutes until detonation.

He felt a surge of excitement. "Soon, my friend," he whispered, heading up the main passageway to the main deck. "Soon your arrogance will be rewarded."

Stepping into the night air, Peder Crandon was suddenly aware he was not alone. Spinning around, he found himself staring into the white face of a man wearing a British naval uniform.

Obviously scared, the young sailor was making no attempt to draw the pistol from the holster hanging at his waist. His lack of presence would cost him his life.

Ramming rigid fingers into the sailor's throat, he allowed the man to choke and fall back. Before he could recover, Crandon stepped in close, spinning the man around.

The rest was efficient and silent.

Reaching around the sailor's head with his left arm, Peder Crandon squeezed, incapacitating the man's upper body. With his right forearm, he began to apply a steadily increasing pressure at the base of the man's skull. Two second later, he felt, more than heard, the distinctive pop of the spinal cord being severed.

He let the body drop to the deck and, without further delay, sprinted to the aft of the trawler and dove into the water.

As the time read 00:32, Peder Crandon, ignoring the jagged rocks slicing at his feet, scrambled to the top of the jetty and looked back toward the *H.M.S. Repose*.

He checked his watch. Detonation in thirty seconds.

00:17. He began to rock in concert with the stern light.

00:03. He began to snicker. Close now.

00:00. Baltimore Harbor errupted into a brilliant flash of orange followed by the deafening thunder of the trawler's obliteration echoing across the open water.

Teeth grinding, Peder Crandon watched in awe, surrendering himself to the magnificence of the concussion spheres lapping at his body.

Then the sensations faded into the night and he began to dress for the drive back to Washington.

He had received her cable at noon. Ursula would be arriving in less than twelve hours.

There was still much to do, he reminded himself. New living accommodations. New plans. Selecting larger British targets. Ursula would understand, he smiled. She would help. Together they could begin anew.

The Second Day

The errors that are made in other things may sometimes be corrected; but those things that are done in war, the pain coming straight on, cannot be amended.

Machiavelli
1520

Chapter 25

VAGUELY AWARE OF voices whispering in the darkness, Hassim Saad slowly regained consciousness.

Forcing his eyes to focus, he coughed twice as he checked his surroundings. Apparently he was still in the old farmhouse. Somehow, someone had managed to dress him.

Twisting, he tried to move, groaning audibly as a gnawing pain burned its way from his mutilated hand.

"You're awake," Yellow Teeth said from the shadows.

Hassim did not respond. Still fighting nausea, he was unable to make his limbs function. As he tried to drag himself to a standing position, he collapsed on the stone floor, exhausted by the attempt.

"Where's Chatsworth?" he asked.

"Gone," Yellow Teeth answered. Grabbing Hassim's armpits he jerked him upright. "Get to the car, faggot. You're going back to the restaurant."

Sluggishly, Hassim allowed himself to be led outside. It was still dark as the kidnappers shoved him onto the rear seat and slammed the door.

Leaving him alone in the rear, Yellow Teeth climbed behind the wheel and started the vehicle as Beetle jumped into the right front seat. Seconds later, they were proceeding cautiously down the rutted incline toward the main highway. For Hassim, bumping and jarring was painful. He fell into a fretful sleep, whimpering as he relived the pain and trauma suffered at the hands of Basil Chatsworth.

Fifty minutes later, Hassim awoke. He raised his head and looked out the front windshield. They were back on the Steffisburg, speeding toward Bern.

He glanced at his watch. The crystal was shattered. "What time is it?" he asked, leaning forward.

The kidnappers ignored the question. Slumping back in the seat, Hassim sat in silence. Looking at his bandaged hand, he began to think about his position and the story he would tell Yasif.

He would deny any cooperation with the British. There was no reason for Chatsworth to tell Yasif he had cooperated—he would only be exposing himself. Yellow Teeth and Beetle? Functionaries—no problem. They would follow Chatsworth's orders.

He felt somewhat better. Yes, get in contact with Yasif quickly and tell him about Ursula, Crandon, and Montes. How Ursula forced a meeting using Yasif's name. Yes, that was the story. As for the missing finger, how could he explain that? Of course. It had been removed surgically. He could say that the loss had something to do with his cancer.

The lie began to coalesce in his mind as the driver slowed at the city limits. A pinkish gray light began to glow on the horizon.

As Hassim watched, dawn slowly ripened in intensity until the sun rose in a brilliant splash, bathing the mist-shrouded city in a pure white light that reflected off the Aare River and freed Bern from its crypt of darkness.

Fifteen minutes later, Yellow Teeth pulled the Fiat to a stop just across from Le Gaulois, the restaurant from which Hassim had been kinapped.

"Out!" he ordered.

As Hassim climbed out of the rear seat and closed the door behind him, Yellow Teeth rolled down his window. "The surgeon has some news, faggot."

"What?" Hassim asked.

"You are a British agent now," Yellow Teeth smiled. "You are to add us to your list."

Hassim saw no reason for the conversation to continue. He nodded, watching the Fiat speed away. British, Israeli, he thought. It was all too suffocating.

It was still too early for the townspeople to be out, and the streets were deserted. At the end of the block, his Mercedes waited where he had left it. He fumbled in his pocket for the keys as he walked the 25 yards to the car.

Opening the door and sitting down in the soft leather seat, Hassim began to shake with relief, knowing he was lucky to be alive. He would go to his penthouse, take a shower, then call his doctor. His hand needed attention and he felt fortunate to be in Switzerland, where doctors were as discreet as bankers.

Starting the Mercedes, Hassim noticed a small white envelope on the passenger's seat next to him. It had not been there before. Curious, he picked it up, gave it a cursory examination, and opened it.

Inside, the envelope was a small white business card. In Arabic script it bore only a name:

YASIF

For a moment, Hassim was puzzled. Then the significance of the card shocked him. A scream was building in the corner of his mind. He flailed at the door, scratching to escape, when the pressure sensitive timing device was activated by his weight on the driver's seat. An irreversible sequence of events was initiated. After a fifteen-second delay, the timer engaged an electric blasting cap which, in turn, detonated the two pounds of amatol situated beneath his buttocks.

The resulting explosion ripped the Mercedes to bits and scattered debris over a two-block radius. The sound of the bomb awakened the city and echoed off the distant mountains, finally dissipating some six minutes later.

Yasif would have been pleased. The Islamic action squad had followed his instructions perfectly.

Later, the manager of Le Gaulois surveyed the destruction to his restaurant. He had been fortunate. Except for the broken windows, the building had suffered no structural damage.

He had already contacted his insurance carrier and the glass company. The windows would be installed before dark. Good, he thought. He would be open for the evening meal and business would be excellent. The Swiss were an inquisitive people, and he expected a large crowd to visit the site of the bombing.

Smiling, the manager curtly saluted the hole that was Hassim's grave and wondered how he was going to jam the additional tables into the already-packed dining area. That was the problem with the restaurant business, he decided.

There were always too many decisions.

Chapter 26

CATLIN'S ESTIMATION HAD been correct. It was after midnight by the time their black sedan pulled to a stop under the portico of the Crystal City Marriot in Arlington, Virginia.

Located just across the expressway from the Pentagon, the hotel held a government contract to house transient workers. Kelly Michaels would be staying there while in Washington.

Michaels looked out the window. The building depressed him. He had probably even stayed there before. After a while, all hotels tended to look identical: cigarette-burned carpets, the obligatory pool area, and, lest he forget, the whirlpool and sauna. He looked over to Taylor. "What's the plan?"

"Grab some sack time," Taylor answered. "We'll get back to you in the morning."

"Any particular time?"

"I'll call first," Catlin added.

"Mind if I keep these?" Michaels held up the dossiers.

"Just don't lose them," Catlin said, smiling slightly.

Michaels returned her smile. "Not to worry."

From behind the driver's seat, Taylor watched the two of them closely. They were becoming too chummy. He knew why: Catlin's inexperience. He'd talk to her about it. RAINDANCER was not running for prom queen.

"Just check in and stick close to the room," Taylor said, making it sound like an order. "And Kelly?"

"What?" Michaels answered sullenly.

"No big productions, no screw-ups."

Asshole, Michaels thought, climbing out of the car. "No problem, chief. I'm only a walk-on. You're the big producer."

"Just don't forget it," Taylor snapped, putting the car in gear as Michaels slammed the door and stormed toward the lobby.

"Was that really necessary?" Catlin asked as they drove out onto the expressway feeder.

"What? The baiting him?"

She nodded.

Taylor glanced over at her, then back to the road. "Yes," he said softly. "He's been vegetating for almost a year. I'm trying to get his mind sharp again."

"But he'll just end up——"

"Hating me." Taylor completed the sentence. "And that's exactly where I want him—hating me. It won't hurt my feelings whatsoever, and it'll force him to take it out on someone else."

Catlin understood. "Crandon?"

Taylor nodded. "Exactly."

"I guess I never thought about it that way," Catlin admitted.

Saying nothing, Taylor decided to give her time to do so.

"Thank you, Mr. Kinkaid," the Oriental desk clerk said after reviewing Michaels's registration form. "Do you need a porter?"

"No," Michaels answered, "I'll be able to find it."

"Fine, Sir. Room 1012." The Oriental offered a toothy smile that exposed two gold-capped front teeth. "And I'm sure you will enjoy your stay with us." He slid a key across the counter.

Michaels took the key and began walking toward the bank of elevators at the far end of the lobby.

Pressing a button, the door opened immediately and Michaels stepped inside. He pressed number ten and waited for the doors to close. He directed his attention to a large poster bolted in lucite to the elevator wall.

The advertisement proclaimed the superb cuisine and dancing offered by the View Top club on the Marriot's roof. *You expect nothing less*, the title boasted, depicting, as apparent proof, a young couple feasting on no less than thirty pounds of beef and staring lovingly into each other's eyes.

"Bet they really pack 'em in," he chuckled, envisioning a herd of drunken businessmen buying rum and Cokes for giggling teen-aged hookers. No, he thought. He'd better pass on *L'affaire* View Top. Life was too short.

As the doors began to slide closed, a tall black man jumped inside.

Bearded, he sported a flashy synthetic silk jacket, black shirt, and white shoes. His hat, a matching white fedora, was cocked rakishly to the side of a tight, well-oiled Afro.

Truth in advertising, Michaels thought, moving to one side of the elevator. *You expect nothing less.*

As the car jerked into motion, Michaels heard the distinctive click of a switchblade knife opening. He glanced toward the man.

The black returned the glance with a broad grin as he began to pick at his fingertails with the knife's point.

Michaels looked back at the selector panel. The man had not pressed another button. The only floor illuminated was the tenth.

Shit, he thought. The last thing he wanted was to fuck around with some black D.C. Caesar who was planning to mug him. He sighed with digust. Perhaps he should take the knife away and spank him. No, that wouldn't do any good. Caesar would probably cry, or, more likely, file a civil rights suit with the ACLU.

Of course, Michaels realized, he could simply kill him. But the body would certainly cause someone, somewhere to care. Definitely out. Taylor had talked about big productions, and besides, a hotel murder wasn't exactly the most sophisticated way to begin a covert operation.

Suddenly Michaels had a flash of inspiration.

Remembering the Marakov tucked at the small of his back,

he thanked his sixth sense as he dropped the kit bag to the floor and reached back to withdraw the pistol.

Careful not to look at the pimp directly, he brought the weapon up in his right hand and began to clean the fingernails on his left hand with the Marakov's front sight.

The point made, Michaels glanced over to the black and grinned openly. "Wanna wrestle? Let's go two out of three falls."

Caesar did not speak; instead, he peeked furtively at the floor indicator. Noticing that the car was between the sixth and seventh floors, he reached over and pressed the button for number eight.

A long four seconds later, the elevator stopped on the eighth floor and the pimp, folding the knife, scurried out, heading silently down the deserted corridor.

Michaels laughed as the door closed. *Perhaps Indians really did breed the buffalo,* he thought, remembering the old insult. In any case, Caesar definitely possessed the genes of both species.

Fuck it, he thought finishing the ride to the tenth floor. *Into every life a little rain must fall.* Finding his room, Kelly Michaels went directly to bed. Washington would never change. Nor would he expect anything else. After all, it was his nation's capital.

Chapter 27

URSULA BRANDT, LIKE most other guests in the fashionable Valois Hotel, had been shaken awake by the explosion of Hassim Saad's Mercedes. But she had no idea as to the identity of the unfortunate victim.

As she lay in bed staring at the intricately handpainted ceiling, she thought about Peder Crandon and the cable she had sent care of the apartment house in Washington. The message was addressed to John O'Mahoney.

After running with the Irish for most her adult life, Ursula found Peder's new alias particularly insightful, one stemming back to the roots of Ireland's civil wars. Ursula appreciated its significance.

In the mid-nineteenth century, the potato famine, typhus epidemics, and emigration restrictions reduced the population of Ireland by one-third. But while nearby one million Irish were dying of famine, England continued to import the bulk of Irish foods while Anglo landlords only added to the outrage by evicting the poverty-stricken farmers and razing their villages. In 1848 the Irish rebelled. The rebels were decimated by the British, and thousands of Irishmen were killed. A handful escaped, fleeing the country to continue the fight from abroad.

Ten years later, one of the escapees surfaced in the United States and founded a secret society dedicated to the cause of Irish independence. The clandestine organization, drawing support from the Irish-American *Clan na Gael,* soon spread back to

Ireland. Its leader, a man who had lost his family at British hands, became one of the first Irish republican legends. His name was John O'Mahoney.

Ursula warmed with the realization. Peder was moving toward his destiny, and she wanted to share it with him.

Suddenly her thoughts were interrupted. Outside, in the sitting area of her suite, she heard the door unlock, followed by the soft patter of footsteps. She relaxed. The footsteps were familiar.

Kyoto, she thought. It must be 6:30. The Japanese bodyguard amazed her, for he never seemed to sleep. Every time she opened a door, Kyoto was there, waiting—almost as if he possessed some uncanny ability to read her thoughts, to predict her movements.

She stretched. On the other hand, like all men, he, too, had weaknesses, and she was a master at manipulation.

Slipping silently from the bed, Ursula drew the drapes closed. The sunlight which had filled the room gave way to a more sensual backdrop which bathed the walls in melancholy promise. Returning to the bed, Ursula pulled her nightgown over her head and tossed it to the floor. Then, after pulling the sheets down to the bottom of the bed, she crawled onto the mattress, turned onto her stomach, and stretched out nude, arms apart, legs spred wide.

"Kyoto?" she called.

A moment later, the bedroom was illuminated briefly as he entered the room. "You slept well?" he asked, closing the door behind him.

"Within reason. Come to me, Kyoto."

Instantly, Ursula was aware of the man walking to the edge of the bed and sitting down.

"What shall we do today?" she asked.

"More shopping?" he suggested as he began to massage her shoulders in a slow circular motion.

"No," she sighed, enjoying the muscular pressure of his fingers. "Perhaps we should go to Rome?"

"If that is what you wish." His hands moved lower.

Ursula could feel her body responding to his touch as he continued downward, probing her flesh with his fingertips. His hands moved deftly, compressing her buttocks, lingering at the juncture of her thighs and touching the wetness she could neither control nor suppress.

Almost tenderly, Ursula allowed Kyoto to urge her onto her back as was their habit. Twisting seductively, she followed the tradition once again and rolled over, thoroughly aware of her own muskiness. She raised her arms beckoningly over her head and spread her legs, exposing herself to him, shuddering as the moistness of his breath brushed the petals of her mound.

The relationship between Ursula and Kyoto was something few would understand. Thrown together by events not entirely under their control, their interdependence was one drawn from mutual need. It was seldom planned in advance and was not discussed afterwards.

Kyoto never actually made love to her, at least in the more traditional sense. Rather, he took her with his mouth, reaching his climax at the moment of her orgasm. It was a unique arrangement which soothed them both, a primitive satisfaction of isolated wants, each consumed with personal fantasies and solitary releases.

Jerking mechanically, Ursula felt the beginnings of gratification. Kyoto felt it also. He worked faster. He could not allow his own release until the woman flooded his senses with her emission. Unable to restrain the contractions, Ursula melted into his face. At the exact moment of her release, she reached the bedside table and retrieved the weapon. Feeling the iciness of its grips in her fingers, she released a low, guttural moan to coincide with the arching of her hips.

Savoring her climax, Kyoto pulled away, rising up on his elbows so he could watch her eyes in the pleasure of their fantasy. Lips coated with her dew, he looked into her face.

The silenced Spanish 9 millimeter gun coughed twice as its bullets found the Oriental's face, destroying his skull. Kyoto's brain burst into a remarkable splash of orgasm and death at one and the same time. He collapsed quietly, choking on his own blood.

For a few minutes, Ursula Brandt did nothing. She was aware of the man's warm blood pooling beneath her, but the sensation was not unpleasant. Delighting in the newfound feeling, she looked up into the fresco of the ceiling and savored the experience.

Finally the moment passed, and Ursula regained her composure. Tossing the pistol to the floor, she hopped from the blood-soaked bed and walked into the bathroom.

She would shower, call a taxi, and be at the airport within the hour.

"Tonight I will be with Peder," she whispered to her reflection in the mirror.

"Tonight I will share his world to come."

Chapter 28

THE SUN HAD been up for almost two hours by the time Basil Chatsworth reached Shaftesbury Avenue and the London apartment of Elliot Prescott's mistress.

He was exhausted. Between the flight from Switzerland and being awake all night, all he really wanted was to finish and go home to bed. He would endure no nonsense, he decided, as he picked the lock to 3-C and entered Nicole Dubois' darkened flat quietly. He simply wasn't in the mood.

Shattering her sleep, Chatsworth tore back the covers, jerked the nude girl from her bed, and threw her to the floor.

"Good day, Miss Dubois," he said politely. "Would you be good enough to answer some questions?"

Frightened, Nicole stared up at the man hovering over her. "How did you get in here?"

"Whom do you work for Miss Dubois?" Chatsworth asked, his eyes studying her naked body.

Attempting to cover herself, Nicole squirmed under the clinical glare as fear gave way to outrage. "Who are you?"

Chatsworth offered a benign smile. "Please do not be alarmed, Miss Dubois. My name is Chatsworth, an associate of Sir Elliot's. I believe we spoke on the telephone earlier?"

Nicole remembered. Pulling a blanket around her, she climbed back on the bed. "Elliot will kill you for this," she threatened. "You have no right to be here."

"Of course not," Chatsworth agreed. "And I must apologize

for any inconvenience. However, as I've indicated, there are several questions to which I must have answers."

Nicole screamed, "Questions? I'll answer none of your questions. Get out of here or I'll call the police."

Chatsworth ignored the threat. "Whom do you work for, Miss Dubois?" He sat on the edge of the bed.

Glancing around the room, Nicole decided that he was alone. Briefly, she thought of escape.

"Please do not attempt any foolishness, Miss Dubois," Chatsworth admonished, watching her eyes. "Just answer my questions. I can promise it will be easier for both of us if you cooperate."

Nicole stared into Chatsworth's face and, as she attempted to size him up, the faint wisp of a smile flickered across her lips. "I am an actress," she pouted, allowing the blanket to fall away from her breasts. "Do you find me pretty?"

Chatsworth shook his head. There was no way she could even begin to understand the importance of the situation. Nor did she know of the two years of problems uncovered by MI5 since they had initiated limited surveillance into the various *affaires du coeur* indulged by key members of the prime minister's policy-making staff.

Due to the ever-increasing incidence of foreign infiltration, double agents, and the proliferation of both hetero and homosexual sex scandals, the prime minister had ordered the measures personally, under the Official Secrets Act. Their purpose was straightforward: to uncover and plug potential security leaks before they became an embarrassment to the Crown or affected British policy.

Prescott was a perfect case in point. Serving as the prime minister's special adviser on political violence, he was allowed access to intelligence gathered by both MI5 and MI6—an acutely sensitive position. Nonetheless, Chatsworth had accepted responsibility for Prescott grudgingly. His reasons were personal. Primarily, Chatsworth hated arrogant, wealthy aristocrats and

Prescott was that and more. But perhaps more important, Chatsworth found the entire matter distasteful. The very idea of spying into the boudoirs of Britain's leaders was loathsome. Notwithstanding his feelings he recognized the necessity for such procedures. He swallowed his personal reservations and served the Crown as ordered.

Now, it seemed, his efforts had been rewarded. A pen register on Nicole Dubois's telephone had broken a pattern. Unfortunately, it had not provided sufficient information to preclude a personal interview with the woman.

Able to determine a number dialed and the length of a particular call, pen registers did not actually record the conversation per se. What they did do, was provide a standard as to normal telephone use so that anything unusual could be detected easily.

In Nicole's case, the report of her call to the international operator was indeed irregular. So much so that Chatsworth considered it blatant.

In the seven months since the pen register's installation, Nicole Dubois had made no international calls. This fact, in addition to its time frame, less than fifteen minutes after his talk with Sir Elliot, had triggered Chatsworth's suspicions.

He could investigate the phone company records, but that would take twelve hours. And even then, he would know only the number called, but not the details of the conversation.

To Basil Chatsworth, coincidence must not be disregarded. And now the interrogator was back in his element. He had to identify the person Nicole had called and evaluate the damage.

If his hunch was wrong, Sir Elliot would have him brought up on charges. Chatsworth hoped she would cooperate.

"Whom do you work for, Miss Dubois?"

Nicole twisted her half-nude body to face him. She smiled coyly. "I am an actress. Do you wish to touch me?"

"No, Miss Dubois." He lowered his voice as he leaned

closer to her. "I do not want to touch you. I want to know who you called last night."

"What call?"

"The international call . . . duration one minute and forty-three seconds?"

Nicole's eyes narrowed to slits. Her cover was unraveling, but that had always been a possibility. She must not talk. It would only hurt the cause and anger Yasif. "I made no international calls," she answered defiantly, already planning her escape from London. "Now get out of here."

Chatsworth sighed heavily. She was forcing him to extract the information. People were stupid, he decided. Why couldn't they see he would always get what he wanted. Everyone talked in the end. Hassim Saad was a prime example. And now there was this childtramp. She, too, would cooperate.

Basil Chatsworth slammed his cupped palm against her left ear. First her eyes rolled upward, fluttering briefly; then she pitched forward lapsing into unconsciousness. Satisfied that she would offer no further resistance, Chatsworth rose. It was time for *the surgeon* to begin his work.

Ten minutes later, Nicole awoke and found herself tied securely on top of the sheets. She was on her back, still nude. Chatsworth was looming over her holding a small metal box the size of a pack of cigarettes.

It was an invention of his own design, a sophisticated type of transistorized voltage regulator, which he patterned along the lines of a normal household rheostat. It could raise or lower the intensity of electrical current, but that was where the similarity ended. At one end of the box there was a seven-foot power cord which could be inserted into any electrical outlet.

The box itself offered two retractable copper wires which could be extended to a maximum of six feet. The ends were attached to matching alligator clips. Power was regulated by a small thumb wheel protruding from the center of the control box. When rotated back, the power was turned off. When rotated forward toward the copper wires, the instrument could deliver a maximum of 900 volts through its alligator clips.

"Will you cooperate?" Chatsworth asked calmly.

Eyes wide with fear, Nicole stared at the sinister-looking box in his hands. "But I am only an actress," she whispered, her voice trembling.

"Very well, Miss Dubois," Chatsworth said once more sitting at the edge of the bed.

Nicole watched as he leaned over and gently touched her left breast, rubbing its nipple until it stood erect. Then Chatsworth attached one of the clips to the nipple. The pain of metal teeth biting into her flesh caused her to whimper.

"If you scream, I shall electrocute you," Chatsworth explained.

The tone of his voice—its evenness—sent a wave of fear through her. Suppressing an urge to cry out, she began to pant. "Let me suck you," she breathed. "Let me up. Let me show you what . . ."

Taking the second clip, Chatsworth leaned across her chest. "Whom do you work for, Miss Dubois?" he asked holding the second clip poised above her other nipple.

"I will work for you," she hissed. "Use me. Use my body. Untie me . . . let me show you how to use me . . ."

Attaching the clip to the her right nipple, Chatsworth then leaned back and engaged the thumbwheel, watching as Nicole Dubois's body twisted in agony. Eyes snapping open, she arched her back in protest. In some dark part of her brain, she tried to scream. No sound emerged. The current was paralyzing her vocal cords.

"Whom did you call, Miss Dubois?" Chatsworth repeated as he turned off the currently momentarily.

Her heart beating wildly, Nicole's body had broken out in sweat. She could feel perspiration running down her body.

"Fuck you, bastard!" she screamed between gritted teeth.

Considering the insult, Chatsworth thumbed the wheel calmly, this time a bit stronger.

Nicole began to buck in an obscene dance as she strained against the bindings. Every muscle in her body rippled under the smoothness of her skin, undulating away from her breasts.

Cutting the power, Chatsworth removed the second clip and watched her body relax. He waited for her to regain some semblance of composure.

"Whom did you call last night, Miss Dubois?" he asked softly.

Nicole had never experienced such pain before. Her muscles were screaming in protest. She was suddenly aware of the bitter stench of urine mixed with the sickly sweet scent of burned flesh from her nipples. Panting to ward off spasms of nausea, she spit the words. "New York . . . Yasif."

"Yasif?" *Again the Libyan,* Chatsworth thought. First with Hassim, understandable. But with Sir Elliot's tart? Perhaps with Sir Elliot himself? Indeed.

"Why did you call him?" he asked her, placing his hand on her abdomen, rubbing in slow circles, moving lower until his fingers touched her sweat-soaked pubic hair. "Tell me, Miss Dubois. Tell me why you called Yasif."

Fighting the urge to vomit, Nicole squeezed her eyes shut. "It was my instructions."

"Whose instructions?" Chatsworth asked, his fingers now probing between her thighs.

Aware of his fingers, there was no doubt where Chatsworth would burn her next. "It was a few months ago." She paused to let her breathing slow down. "Yasif contacted me and told me to tell him if Elliot ever mentioned someone called Crandon. Last night was the first time . . . the first telephone call. I just had a number . . . I don't know why . . . I don't know . . . . " Realizing that she had been forced to talk, Nicole began to sob uncontrollably.

Chatsworth nodded in understanding. *Reasonable,* he thought. Evidently Prescott wasn't involved, and of course he would have had no way of knowing his trollop was a Libyan plant.

Now there would be the hard part. He would have to contact Sir Elliot and advise him of the results of the interview. Naturally, Prescott would express all kinds of shock and disbelief, the normal response of a man when exposed as a witless dupe.

The really interesting bit of intelligence was Yasif's concern about Crandon. It didn't fit into the normal Libyan scheme of things. Too close to the flames, as it were. Too potentially telling.

Another problem, he decided, was that Sir Elliot was handling the Crandon matter. It would be up to Chatsworth to explain the connections to the Foreign Office and the prime minister.

Watching the whimpering girl, Basil Chatsworth experienced a flood of ambivalent thoughts. Nicole would be just another unfortunate casualty. Another cross-reference in another forgotten file.

But life was like that sometimes.

Reaching down, he quickly spread the lips of Nicole Dubois's womanhood with medical precision. Holding them apart, he reached over with his other hand and attached the second alligator clip to the moist skin of her inner membrane and moved away from the bed.

Feeling the second clip cutting into her labia brought Nicole back to reality. The realization of what was going to happen gouged at her mind. She realized it would be useless to cry out.

Staring into the young girl's eyes, Chatsworth felt the presence of a long-forgotten emotion: pity. He forced it back before it caused him to make a mistake and rationalize another alternative.

With their eyes locked together, Chatsworth rolled the thumbwheel to full power and, for the final time, the body of Elliot Prescott's mistress performed its lurid ballet as the voltage tracked throughout her nervous system. She danced against the bindings as the stench of blistering flesh permeated the bedroom.

Disconnecting the wires, Chatsworth placed the instrument in his coat pocket. Then he untied her and stuffed the bindings into his other pocket. The evidence removed, he leaned over and arranged the corpse of Nicole Dubois tenderly in her bed, straightening the sheets and fluffing the pillows. His work completed, he was gone minutes later.

Chapter 29

THE PREFLIGHT PASSENGER screening at Zurich's Kloten airport was a long, involved affair, due to the recent spate of attacks involving international air carriers: KLM, Air-India, TWA, Egypt Air, the others. Her Lufthansa flight stopped in Munich before continuing on directly from Germany to Washington.

Actually, she could have selected an airline with a more relaxed attitude toward security, but time was of the essence and her choices were limited. The Lufthansa offered the fastest, most direct service to America. It was only fitting that she fly her Fatherland's national carrier.

After purchasing her ticket, a stooped, elderly porter directed her to the end of the line to await a security check prior to boarding. Ursula complied without comment. Then, after waiting patiently for the better part of an hour, she was motioned toward a makeshift metal counter and instructed to open her bag.

She moved forward cheerfully, hoping that the bulky sweater and well-worn jeans gave her the appropriate image: that of artist—perhaps a sculptress—traveling between exhibitions.

The inspection officer was a balding, obese, middle-aged man. He was also German. Lufthansa trusted only their own.

Unzipping the bag, Ursula stepped back from the counter and surveyed the Lufthansa holding area as the man poked through her belongings. She detected three other security men dressed in plainclothes. Young, tanned, and hard-looking, they stared at the passengers with cool, undisguised suspicion.

Facists, she thought. From experience, Ursula knew the guards to be members of the elite West German Border Patrol Unit, GSG-9. Considered to be Germany's first line of defense against terrorism, they had a reputation of carrying out actions with deadly efficiency.

Ursula studied their bodies. Under their three-quarter-length black leather coats, she could make out the faint outlines of the 19'' Heckler and Koch MP5 submachine guns slung loosely at their sides. Carrying diplomatic passports, the men were exempt from Swiss laws against carrying weapons.

Finishing his inspection, the man stepped back from her bag, gesturing for her to close it up and wait.

Ursula obeyed in silence. He grabbed the bag and tossed in on the conveyer belt. Then he turned back to Ursula.

''Your luggage is checked through to Washington. You may claim it after you arrive.'' The inspector spoke English with a thick Bavarian accent.

''Thank you,'' she answered.

''Ticket?'' He held out an ink-stained, fleshy hand.

Ursula passed over the packet containing her ticket and waited. She knew what he was looking for. Outdated statistics suggested terrorists purchased only one-way fares. Hers was a round-trip passage and that indicated she would return to Switzerland in two weeks.

''Passport?'' he asked, returning the ticket folder.

Ursula gave him her passport. It was stolen. It stated she was a Swiss citizen living in Fribourg, just southeast of Bern. Her occupation was listed as ''artisan.''

Taking the passport, the inspector thumbed through the pages, read the biographical information, and turned to the photograph. He checked the stamped embossing over the likeness, then compared it to Ursula. Satisfied that it was the passenger, he then considered the passport in general: cut of the paper, printer's marks, preciseness of the punch holes, the inks. It was all in order. Not counterfeit. All visas obtained.

"Thank you, Frau Rundle," he said, passing the document back to her. "You may proceed to the blue area." With a finger, he pointed vaguely to a dark turquiose door at the far end.

Ursula tensed. Standing adjacent to the door was a fourth member of the German counter-terror squad. "Thank you," she said, turning and walking toward the blue area.

As she approached, the man from GSG-9 eyed her professionally. Ursula knew he was looking for any suspicious bulges which would possibly be weapons or bombs. Thankful that she was unarmed, she walked straight up to the young security guard.

"Is this where I go?" she smiled, consciously adopting a Swiss accent for the question asked in fluent German.

The officer's expression did not change. After a cursory glance, he merely nodded and opened the door for her. Ursula stepped through the doorway and into a small anteroom.

"This way, please," a harsh female voice called to her.

Moving around a corner, Ursula found herself in an even smaller booth. "What is this?" she asked the German matron who greeted her.

"You must submit to a body search before boarding the aircraft." The woman voice sounded almost mechanical.

"But——" Ursula protested.

"It's routine. Due to the problems, you know." The matron turned to close the drapes to the tiny cubicle. Ursula pulled her sweater over her head and slipped her jeans down to just below her knees. She wore nothing underneath.

Turning around to face Ursula, the matron was unable to disguise her shock at finding Ursula naked. "That wasn't really necessary," she stammered. "I was only going to pat you down."

"I don't mind," Ursula smiled, sensing the older woman's

interest in her lithe, muscular body. "I have nothing to be ashamed of."

The matron regained her composure. "Turn around, please," she told Ursula coldly.

Holding her arms away from her body, Ursula performed a tight, yet sensual pirouette for the woman. "Is everything satisfactory?" she taunted.

Averting her eyes, the German woman pulled back the curtain and shuffled away. "Yes. You may board now."

Pleased with her own impertinence, Ursula dressed quickly, left the cubicle, and proceeded to the entrance ramp. Minutes later, she was strapped securely in her tourist-class seat over the left wing. By the time the Lufthansa 747 cleared the end of the runway, Ursula Brandt had already decided on her course of action. She would remain on the aircraft during the Munich stopover and sleep until the plane was on final approach to Dulles Airport.

Knowing Peder as she did, it was conceivable that any future opportunities for rest would be few and far between. Squeezing her thighs together, Ursula allowed herself to drift into a languid, erotic drowsiness. Then, as the pilot began to chase the sun to America, she slipped into a dreamless sleep.

Chapter 30

THE TAXI WHEELED into the covered parking area at the Washington Hyatt Regency and stopped. Yasif paid the driver and climbed out of the vehicle.

Standing next to the cab, he checked his watch: 1:10 A.M. ''Bastards.'' His plane had been delayed by air traffic over New York's La Guardia Airport and again upon arrival in Washington. Seething with anger, he charged into the lobby.

Entering the hotel, Yasif paid no attention to the five-story glass atrium, its ornate fountain, or the large numbers of live trees growing out of the polished marble floors. Consumed only with the Crandon mess, he walked directly to the registration desk.

He gave the night clerk an assumed name and paid cash for three days' lodging, ignoring the clerk's pleasantries he rode the glass outside elevators to his suite on the ninth floor.

After a quick search for listening devices, Yasif dialed the Washington number again, waiting impatiently for the connection to be completed.

After a moment, the ringing began. Yasif held his breath, hoping he wouldn't again be forced to endure the recorded message.

''Yes?'' a voice answered on the third ring.

''Yasif,'' he whispered. Yasif could hear only low breathing on the other end of the line. ''We must meet,'' he added.

''When?''

"Tonight."

"Impossible."

"Tonight," he repeated a bit louder.

"But it's after midnight."

He made it an order. "You *will* come."

"But . . . where?"

"The Dubliner."

"Where?"

"The Dubliner . . . in the Old Commodore Hotel."

"When?"

Yasif glanced at his watch. "Thirty minutes."

"Very well."

Yasif replaced the receiver without additional explanation. There was no purpose in discussing the situation on the telephone. It was too personal. Besides, he had to meet his informant face-to-face to make sure of things.

Fingering his worry beads absently, Yasif stared through the glass. Below, the whole of Washington stood twinkling in the night. *A powerful city,* he thought, turning away from the panorama and walking toward the door. *It was unfortunate its leaders were his enemies.*

The Dubliner remained one of the few Irish bars in Washington. Originally part of the hotel's old dining salon, the entire building had been remodeled and during the seventies, the bar had emerged as one of Washington's most popular night spots, due to a liquor permit which allowed alcohol to be served until 3:00 A.M.

Selecting a booth in a dimly lit section of the bar, Yasif sat down, ordered coffee, and studied the furnishings in detail. He enjoyed the antiques in the room. Since childhood, Yasif had always marveled at old things. Traditions of the past. It was an observation no less anguishing than its pointed truth.

His world of Islam had no tangible past: only the nomadic violence and tragedies which seemed to shadow it regardless of the time or place in history. "To the will of God," he prayed softly.

The Dubliner was a snug place. Its carved cabinetry had been imported from Belgium. The years of polished care now reflected light from the milk-glass wall lamps which bathed the leather booths. Even the mosaic brick floors mirrored the patterns of the lamps.

The bar was a work of art, a place to meet friends and enjoy a few moments stolen from routine. Yasif could not recall a time when he could afford the luxury of relaxation. There was always too much work to be done.

"Hello, Yasif."

He looked up. The woman had approached his booth in silence. She was still very beautiful, he decided. He stood up and leaned over, kissing her on both cheeks. "Hello, my pretty one."

"It's been a long time," she whispered, detecting the sadness in his dark, soulful eyes.

"Yes, it has." They both sat down, squeezing together on one side of the booth. "I was afraid things may have changed between us."

"Of course not, Yasif. It was just late. I didn't mean to be rude. I wasn't expecting your call." He stared into his coffee cup and said nothing. "What is it?" she asked. She reached up and touched his cheek.

"I have played the fool." He turned and looked into her eyes. "Now I must ask your help, Catlin."

Catlin Broussard was obliged to help Yasif. First, under agency orders, they had once been lovers in New York. More important, Yasif had to be reassured she was still one of his "assets." Privately, she hoped she wouldn't have to sleep with him again.

"You know I'm always here for you," she whispered, reaching over and taking his hands in hers. "What do you want?"

Yasif was pleased. ''But first I must warn you. It may be compromising.''

Catlin shook her head. ''Such is the nature of our business,'' she smiled, hoping to cheer him up. ''Tell me what you need.''

Yasif began to explain the Crandon problem as they left the Dubliner and took a taxi to her Logan Circle apartment.

Their conversation would last until dawn.

Chapter 31

"SIR ELLIOT?" THE Royal Air Force sergeant gently touched Elliot Prescott's shoulder, waking him up.

Prescott refused to open his eyes. The modified British B2 Vulcan bomber was cold and cramped. Sleep had been his only escape.

"Sir Elliot?" the sergeant persisted, shaking harder.

"What?" Prescott snapped, his eyes flashing his irritation.

"Sorry, sir," the sergeant responded sincerely. "We are on final approach."

"Of course," Prescott replied tersely, looking around to get his bearings. In front of him, the navigator was reading a map, hunched shoulders washed in filtered amber light. Farther ahead were the pilot and copilot, both locked in a warm compartment which insulated them from the rest of the crew. And then there was the sergeant crew chief, uncultured enough to disturb him.

Twisting to his left, Prescott peered out the small Plexiglas window just at his shoulder. He couldn't believe he was completing his second trip across the Atlantic in less than twelve hours. "Blasted Irishmen!" he cursed under his breath. "May they all rot in Gaelic hell."

The first call from Chatsworth had been bad enough. At least they were now positive that it was Peder Crandon who was operating in the United States. And, if Hassim Saad could be believed, they now had the name of the weapons contact in Washington. The gaps are beginning to fill.

Unfortunately, that was not the *real* problem, as far as he was concerned. It was Chatsworth's second call which had been very unnerving. Elliot Prescott could simply not accept the evidence against Nicole, or believe that she had used him, or that she was a Libyan agent.

Rationally, he had to accept the information from MI5 as factual. Chatsworth had no reason to fabricate a conspiracy. He had nothing to gain. Consequently, the information must be valid. Aside from the Libyan connection in the Crandon matter, the *real* issue was the personal blow to his own ego. That and the knowledge that he was being snickered at in the halls of Number 10 Downing Street. His career might be destroyed unless he found some way to twist it into a different perspective. Perhaps some story that Nicole was a double agent? Or that he knew of her Islamic connections? No one would believe him.

Damn Libyans, he thought. *Damn Nicole. Damn Chatsworth. Damn the whole damned coven of Conservatives now laughing behind his back.*

Sulking in his seat, Sir Elliot considered switching to the Labour party. At this point, it was well worth the speculation.

As the Vulcan circled and began its sloping, measured descent, Elliot Prescott watched the Washington morning. Storm clouds rolling in from the north, he listened as the pulsating turbojet engines beat at his ears. "Damn machines!" he cursed, deciding the noise had given him a headache. His thoughts turned back to Nicole and how to salvage his political future.

What in hell were the Libyans doing mixed up in all of this? Why would Crandon be working for *them?* He thought about it. There were no logical answers—only more questions. Was it some measure of revenge for expelling the Libyan embassy staff from London? Or something drawn from the economic sanctions to embarrass the Americans?

There had to be Libyan interests involved. If not, then why Nicole's direct connection to Yasif? And why Yasif and not one of his underlings? It was all as nebulous as it was critical. Perhaps he was just too close to it? Too involved to be able to function impartially.

Rubbing his eyes, Elliot Prescott suddenly felt old. For most of his political life he had been hearing about Libyan madmen and Libyan intrigues. In some way he still failed to understand the bastards, and they had touched him personally. Nicole's death was a personal affront. If not for Yasif, Nicole would still be waiting. Now she would wait no more. Conscious of his simmering rage, Elliot Prescott decided to press the Americans harder. And when the time came, he would also find a way to include Yasif in the bargain—the man had to die!

He looked down and observed the red and yellow lights marking the runway at Andrews Air Force Base. Seconds later, the Vulcan's tires screeched in protest as the large jet glided onto the tarmac.

The pilot reversed the thrust of the engines and Prescott was propelled forward, straining at his shoulder harness. Outside, screaming wildly, the four Olympus turbines gradually slowed the bomber's momentum until the parachute drag brakes were activated and the plane jerked to a halt.

Stepping from the Vulcan's access ladder, Prescott grabbed his bag and looked around. They had stopped at the extreme outside perimeter of the air base. No tower. No hangers. Only a tall chain-link fence separating the base from the surrounding marshy countryside. Desolate and openly flat, it reminded him of Scotland's moors.

The sound of an approaching vehicle caught his attention. Speeding up from behind the bomber, a black Lincoln limousine wheeled around the edge of the Vulcan's wingtip and stopped less than ten feet from him. Walking to the car, he opened the door and was greeted by Samuel Taylor and Thomas Brayden.

"Quick trip, Sir Elliot?" Brayden smiled.

"Entirely too quick, general," Prescott agreed. "What time is it here?"

Taylor checked his watch. "Eight-fifteen, Monday morning."

Prescott began to set his watch. "Well, I see you received my dispatch."

"White House Signal patched it through at zero-four-hundred," Brayden explained as the limousine began to pull out.

"We figured we could save time if——" Taylor's words were drown out by the sound of the Vulcan's engines as the pilot began to roll. A few moments later, the bomber had taxied far enough away from conversation to resume.

"Your boys don't waste much time," Brayden observed.

Prescott shrugged indulgently. "No doubt I interrupted whatever they were doing. It was rather short notice for them, and I'm reasonably sure their priorities don't extend as far as taxi services."

The three men watched the Vulcan through the Lincoln's rear window. Upon reaching the end of the runway, the military jet turned and launched immediately into the wind. Within seconds, it was gone.

Prescott turned to Taylor. "You were saying?"

"That we could probably save time by talking in the car."

"Excellent idea." Prescott glanced to the open space between the rear seat and the driver and arched an eyebrow.

"I'll get it," Taylor said. He reached over and activated the glass partition to separate the driver from the rear of the limousine.

With the privacy shield slid into place, Prescott took a deep breath and began. "Gentlemen, it seems we have a new twist in the Crandon situation. The Libyans might be directly involved."

"Libyans?" Brayden sat back in the seat. "Reliable information?"

"Yes, general," Prescott nodded. "Developed through a Libyan informant in London." There was no trace of emotion in Prescott's clipped tone. "Considering the source, I find it to be much more than merely reliable."

"Who is Crandon's control?" Taylor said.

"An Arab named Yasif, the number-three man at the Libyan U.N. mission."

"I know the man," Brayden said. "He was one of Arafat's top advisers in the early PLO days. He's been in an out of New York under Libyan cover for two years."

"Bad actor?" Taylor asked.

Brayden nodded. "From what I remember. Terror broker. The FBI tried to get an agent next to him once, and he disappeared. They never found the body and never developed enough information to enable State to jerk his diplomatic status."

"What about the local source?" Taylor asked Prescott. "Your Telex indicated a Washington contact?"

"Precisely," Sir Elliot answered. "Crandon's looking for additional weapons. He's going to use a man named Eduardo Montes. Evidently he's some kind of professor at George Washington University."

"How old is this information?" Taylor asked.

"Six . . . eight hours. Chances are Montes has not yet been contacted. Ursula Brandt is the one with his name as a contact, and fortunately, the Royal Air Force does not fly at her convenience."

The general leaned forward in the seat. "Ursula en route here?"

"Yes," the Englishman answered. "My people estimate that she will arrive in Washington sometime this afternoon."

Brayden turned to Taylor. "Alert Liaison Section, Sam. Maybe Immigration can pick her up before she clears customs."

Fat chance, Taylor thought. Liaison would be lucky to find customs' telephone number. "Just as soon as I get back to the office."

"One other problem," Prescott added.

"What's that?" Brayden asked.

"The prime minister is arriving tomorrow morning to make a joint announcement with your president."

Taylor couldn't believe it. "With all this going on? I don't know how you people breathe with your heads so far up your asses."

"Sam!" Brayden shouted.

Taylor did not regret what he considered to be a valid, if inappropriate comment. "Sorry, Sir Elliot," he said. "Nothing personal. Can't the visit be postponed . . . at least until we have Crandon under wraps?" Taylor already knew the answer.

"No," Prescott confirmed. "Unfortunately, it cannot. It is a full state visit to celebrate the joint development of the STEALTH bomber."

Joint development? Taylor was taken aback. "But STEALTH is American technology."

Prescott gave him a tolerant smile. "No, Taylor. It is not only American by any means. Your president has granted an exclusive license for Britain to build an additional fifty of the bombers for sale to our NATO allies."

As Prescott talked, Taylor's mind raced over the aircraft's specifications. Constructed of a new graphite-epoxy compound, the STEALTH bomber was essentially a flying wing that was stronger than steel, yet possessed half the weight. This structural break with tradition, coupled with the aircraft's four on-board computers, allowed the pilot to control some forty adjustments per second required to keep the bomber tactically efficient.

Actually, Taylor realized, the supercritical wing offered ideal maneuverability and virtually spinproof handling. A feat accomplished by the additional of gill-like projections termed *canards* which allowed the bomber to make radical supersonic turns while at the same time increasing handling and lowering stall speeds. STEALTH was capable of flying at Mach 3 while climbing to over 110,000 feet, one Air Force officer had told Taylor, "That dude can turn on a dime." Taylor believed that and more about the plane.

Not only could it fly at high altitudes, but it could also drop down to hug earth contours, suppressing enemy electronic countermeasure systems and pinpointing hostile radar-directed weapons. It was a uniquely ambitious application of technology which allowed STEALTH to neutralize enemy systems while hiding itself electronically from enemy strike aircraft. In effect, the bomber was invisible to enemy radar and at least fifteen years in advance of anything in the Soviet arsenal. He couldn't believe the United States was sharing the breakthrough with the British.

"I had no idea," he admitted.

"No," Prescott said. "Not many people did."

Taylor looked at Brayden. "You?"

The general nodded. "If you stop and think about it, a joint American-British project was the perfect answer to getting more bombers in the air. At a billion dollars apiece, we're funded for only one hundred. If the British can build fifty, that will ensure allied tactical air supremacy well into the next century."

Taylor nodded. The Americans and British had shared development of military hardware before. The British invention of radar in World War II and most recently, in 1985, when Great Britain was awarded a multibillion-dollar contract to supply the U.S. Army with its new battlefield communications system.

"Lots of dollars involved," he said to no one in particular.

"Fifty billion to be exact," Brayden added. "But in addition to the obvious cash injection into the British economy, it seems the bombers are also a way around strategic arms reduction quotas."

Taylor understood. "Because they're not included in the delivery system quotas."

The general smiled coldly. "It was a Russian point—they didn't want their BLACKJACK or BACKFIRES included, so . . ." He let the sentence trail off.

"It will work for both our countries," Prescott said. "The actual building of the aircraft will put people to work in England. With elections just around the corner and the Socialists nipping at her heels, the P.M. feels this is the perfect approach to shoring up our defense industries and strengthening her political bargaining position. The blasted Socialists have been harping on her economic policies for nearly three years now. With the STEALTH project, she can poke them back in their cages with little more than words."

"And we get strategic oneupmanship in the process."

"Correct, Mr. Taylor," Prescott nodded. "But the point of the matter remains that we do *not* live with our heads up our arses. It is impossible to postpone the prime minister's visit. Timing for the announcement is critical. Too much political propaganda value would be lost if we do not allow sufficient time to capitalize on the media impact gained by the joint declaration with your president."

"I guess," Taylor said. So the Brits were getting STEALTH. He couldn't believe it. For ten years, it had been the hottest hi-tech secret in Washington. Even the bomber's main contractor, Northrop Corporation, had jumped on the sneaky pete bandwagon by offering up one of their own. A Northrop engineer, Thomas Cavanagh, had been recruited by the Soviets to steal the STEALTH's avionics. Unbeknownst to him, the FBI found out and arranged for Northrop to switch the microfiche before Cavanagh could make his drop. They did, and the Soviets found themselves the proud owners of the avionics design for the Northrop T-38A Talon. Made in 1961, the details were totally worthless. As for Cavanagh? Taylor remembered reading that he had been arrested, entered a conditional plea of guilty and was languishing in some federal prison while his case was on appeal.

Well, Taylor decided, the Soviets wouldn't have much longer to wait. With the Brits getting their fingers on the plans, the Russian embassy could probably add its name to the design distribution list and nobody would notice. What was it the Russians called the British? Taylor remembered. *Shavki*. Amateurs.

Lighting a cigarette, Taylor cracked a window and stared at nothing as the smoke filtered outside. *Media impact?* he thought. What the fuck kind of priority was that supposed to be? Why not just invite Crandon to their little garden party. He'd give them enough *media impact* to pass around.

And Prescott. What a consummate asshole. No, check that. What an *arse*hole. A vision from *Alice in Wonderland* came to mind. It was hard to take Prescott seriously. For that matter, it was hard to take anyone seriously if, when you put his skinny *arse* in the right costume, he'd be a ringer for the Mad Hatter. But the rabbit? Every Hatter needed a White Rabbit. So where was it?

Taylor smiled to himself. He wondered how many carrots the general could eat.

Probably a lot, he decided.

Chapter 32

SLOUCHED IN THE passenger-waiting area at Dulles International Airport, Peder Crandon watched the people. Ursula's flight had been on the ground for almost thirty minutes, and she was still somewhere between customs and immigration.

"Nine o'clock," he mumbled, watching the minute hand on his watch ease onto the number twelve. The waiting had been difficult. Time passed slowly.

He considered the others in the terminal. He loathed them. They were fools. Cattle to be led. Fodder to be consumed. Weakness displayed in their dependence upon others.

His left eye began to twitch.

He was the exception. Unique. One of a kind who thirsted for the caramel nectar of revenge. The others were his personal pawns. He could give them life by not ending it. Conversely, he could end their lives by merely taking it. Subtle choices.

He began to chew at a cuticle.

Few people knew him. If others knew his secrets, he would end up someone's pawn. Unacceptable. The only people totally trustworthy were himself and Ursula.

Their relationship was founded upon a mutual respect, commitment to each other. A rational give-and-take. They were not out to receive something from each other without offering something equally valuable in return.

At least that was the way it started. But now? He wondered about it. In retrospect, perhaps things were not as they first appeared. Odd. Why hadn't he thought to question her motives before?

In the beginning she had helped him. Taught him. Made introductions for him. But things were beyond that *now*. *He* was the one with the power . . . *now*. *His* operations were propelling them into *now*.

Ursula was doing nothing in her own right *now*.

Now. Now. Now. He snickered again. Louder.

Perhaps she was trying to subvert his power base? Or steal some notoriety from him? This, too, would be unacceptable. He decided to watch her closely. To see if she tried to distort things, by telling him what to do. Those little suggestions. Unacceptable overtones. He could not have one of his pawns doing *that*. Her place was to follow. To wait. To obey. He and only he was the leader.

He glanced at his watch again—the hand was over the one. He cursed. Only five minutes has passed. The target for his paranoia continued to be Ursula Brandt.

They're all whores, he thought. Even Ursula, the woman who was attempting to direct his life. He should have expected it.

He had never even heard of a relationship where a woman did not end up being used sexually by a man. Even his mother. His father had done it to her. And Ursula? She had done it with him and his father. He knew. He had watched them once—poke-suck, suck-poke. Pence or chopping. Chopping or pence.

All women were all whores. It was inconceivable that they were good for anything else but sex. Not for comfort, surely. He could not remember ever feeling starved for the warmth of human contact or companionship. He was secure in his own right and felt that Ursula was an intrusion he would be forced to suffer for the pleasure of her body.

His mind filled with contempt toward his own mother. He thought about the two women together and wished he had had the occasion to poke-suck his mother before her death. He had told Ursula his thoughts and she understood.

The feeling of excitement overcame him when taking advantage of Ursula. It was more intense than any sensation or pleasure. But shouldn't it be? What was Ursula? What were all women? Just breasts, thighs, buttocks, and moist dark holes lined with spurious little licking cells.

Yes, he giggled. That was precisely it. Nothing more. He had been correct. The true essence of gratification was in the domination.

Sex was merely another operation. Just a matter of control with him possessing full rights of ownership. That was the way it would be. Copulation occurring only when he wanted it, at the place he desired, and in the manner he ordained. He alone was the master.

Sitting upright, he studied the other passengers. He squirmed. The cattle were staring at him. Some accusing him with their eyes. He should destroy the eyes. Blind the questions with them.

He walked to the large window overlooking the outside taxiways. The airport was busy. He allowed himself to become transfixed by the numbers of aircraft, service vehicles and shuttle trams crisscrossing the tarmac. Watching, but not seeing, his mind began to run again. To another time, another airport, another country. To the most devastating operation ever launched at a civilian airport in a time of peace: the Israeli counterattack against the Palestinians for the hijacking of two unarmed El Al flights. The Israeli response was perhaps the most perfect counterterror operation ever witnessed. It was also the one he had been assigned to examine for his final thesis at the Odessa Military Academy.

After determining that the hijackings originated in Beirut, the Israelis responded by inserting forty commandos in a late-evening attack on the main runaway of Beirut International Airport. After exiting their aircraft, the commandos dispersed into three groups. One entered the passenger lobby and, barking orders in Arabic, quelled the panic and successfully suppressed any opposition.

The second group inspected the Arab-owned aircraft on the ground. Any passengers or crew members found on board were escorted safely back to the terminal area, where they could be watched by the first commando team.

The third group secured the perimeter of the airport. Since the facility was located less than three miles from Beirut itself, the Lebanese responded to try to repel the attackers. They never made it. The Israelis set up a roadblock on the road to the airport, and the Lebanese were intercepted. The Lebanese forces retreated after the commandos released smoke canisters in a successful attempt to confuse the rescue force.

After all was secure and all passengers safe, the second commando team planted explosive charges on all Arab planes. The final tally was thirteen aircraft, including nine jetliners, totally destroyed. Their mission completed, the Israelis reboarded their transport planes and returned home. The raid—done with textbook precision—had taken less than one hour.

Like the Soviets, Peder Crandon appreciated perfection. As he continued to observe the activity on the tarmac, he visualized himself leading the attack against the facility. He selected the spots where he would place his fire teams and explosives would be most effective.

But he would not be as discriminating as the Israelis. He would destroy all of the aircraft with the exception of the lumbering Pan Am 747 refueling at the southern end of the main runway. The Pan Am's colors pleased him. Yes. He would use the blue-and-white 747 to fly him away.

He envisioned himself the victor. His name on the lips of all the world's people. He would possess the immortality of Che Guevara, of Adolf Hilter, of . . . yes, even of Jesus. All of them. All, at one and the same time. All of civilization would be at his feet. Feeling a cool shiver of excitement, Peder Crandon laughed out loud, totally oblivious of the others in the terminal.

It was an eerie laugh. A low, wicked utterance. The noise

ushered in a more acute significance. It was the sole overt indication that the gentle fabric of Peder Crandon's mind, that elusive tendril of whatever sanity remained, had finally torn itself asunder. And, like priceless crystal smashed into shards of glass, his obsession splintered into insanity.

Ursula wouldn't notice immediately. Outwardly he still retained the same intelligence, the same objectivity—even the same charm. But deeper, somewhere in the quicksand of abstract thought, Peder Crandon had drifted into madness.

His parents' deaths were no longer motivating factors for murder. Now, Peder Crandon saw only his new self-image, that of some invincible god. He began laughing.

Ursula heard the laugh. Then she saw him. She walked quickly to his side and touched his arm. "Peder?"

He looked at her and smiled. "Hello, mother, did you bring me a gift?"

She leaned over and kissed him on the cheek. "I always do," she said warmly. "Have you been saying your prayers?"

"Yes, mother," he nodded. "Twice a day, just like you told me to."

"You're a fine boy, Peder. Your father would be proud of you."

"I want that more than anything, mother."

"I know you do, Peder," she said softly. "It's something we both want."

Chapter 33

"WHERE'S OUR RAINDANCER now?" the general asked as the Lincoln pulled up to the Pentagon.

"Close," Taylor answered, climbing out. "Our Sri Lankan boy. He's just waiting for instructions."

"Good," Brayden said. "Keep your fingers on him, we may have to move fast. After you alert Liaison on Ursula, get me the file on Yasif and anything we have on Montes. Sir Elliot and I will be at Foxhall Center."

Foxhall Center? Taylor thought. *Fancy term for home. Must be for Prescott's benefit.* He let it pass.

"I'll have it there within the hour," he said. "Anything else, general?"

Prescott answered. "Perhaps finding Crandon would be nice."

Shithead, Taylor thought, wishing he could slap the smirk off the Mad Hatter's face. "I will, *Sir* Elliot," he told him. "Just consider it my valentine gift to you. I realize it's a bit early, but I'm sure you appreciate my meaning."

Eyes narrowing, Prescott looked at the general, then back to Taylor. "It seems to me you——"

"Excuse me, Sir Elliot," Brayden interrupted. "But our time is limited."

"Of course," Prescott agreed.

The general glanced up at Taylor. "See you in an hour, Sam."

Taylor knew he was being dismissed. "I'll be there," he

said, closing the car door and heading up the steps to the Pentagon.

After watching Taylor disappear inside, Prescott turned back to Brayden. "Your Mr. Taylor is a very perceptive man, general."

Brayden nodded. "You seem to have a leak in your organization," he said matter-of-factly.

"So it seems," Prescott agreed, his voice a whisper. "I suppose I shall have to take steps to identify the oversight."

"Taylor deals with *our* oversights," Brayden added, his tone a blend of pride laced with an unmistakable measure of diplomatic taunting.

Prescott did not let it bother him. "I'm sure he does, general," he said softly, looking back to the Pentagon as the Lincoln pulled out. "I'm sure he does."

"Sam," Catlin called as Taylor hurried into the Special Projects Section. "Where the hell have you been? I've got something to run by you."

Taylor ignored the question. "Contact Liaison," he told her. "The Brits think Ursula will be arriving here this afternoon. I want coverage on all points of entry here and in Canada." He glanced at the digital wall clock: 9:28 A.M. "Michaels still at the Marriott?"

Catlin nodded. "I talked to him earlier."

"Well, keep your fingers on him. He has a tendency to showboat if you give him a chance." Wheeling around, Taylor stalked toward his office.

"Will you wait a goddamned second!" she yelled after him. "I've got something to show you."

"Later, Cat. I've got to pull up a couple of files for the general. He's waiting for them at Foxhall."

She grabbed his arm. "Read this!" she ordered, shoving a sheaf of papers toward him.

"What the hell . . . "

"Just read the damned thing. It'll only take a couple of minutes."

"Pausing, Taylor took the documents. The inscription at the top of the first page immediately caught his attention.

OFFICE OF THE MEDICAL EXAMINER
DISTRICT OF COLUMBIA
WASHINGTON, D.C. 20202

Medical Examiner's Report of Autopsy

"What's this supposed to be?" Taylor asked.

"Just read it," Catlin told him.

"Where did it come from?"

"British embassy."

"Any coins?"

Catlin shook her head.

"Then why——"

"Just a gut feeling. I want to know what you think."

Taylor had learned to respect gut feelings. "Okay," he told her. "While I'm looking this over, I want you to pull two files for me. One on an Arab called Yasif. He's the number-three man in the Libyan U.N. Mission. The other, a Cuban named Eduardo Montes. He's an academic at George Washington University. I want a complete run, including photos of both of them."

Before she could say anything, Taylor started walking back to his office. Reluctantly, Catlin turned, sat down at the closest PCAC keyboard, and initiated a national agency check on the two names. It was painfully difficult to type Yasif's name. She programmed it anyway.

Reaching his office, Taylor switched on the light and flopped onto the sofa. Then, lighting a cigarette, he began to read. The report's date was yesterday's, he noted.

BISHOP, JENNIFER LEA
3451 M STREET NW
WASHINGTON, D.C. 20210

Reference: ME-29872

The postmortem examination was performed by Kenneth D. O'Quinn, M.D., F.A.C.S., Chief Medical Examiner, District of Columbia, beginning at 3:45 P.M., at the District of Columbia morgue.

HISTORY:
The decedent had been missing for about six days. At 11:47 A.M. this date, her body was found hanging in an abandoned warehouse.

EXTERNAL EXAMINATION:
The body was that of a well-developed, well-nourished 14-year-old Caucausian female appearing older than the stated age, in a moderate to advanced degree of bloating decomposition, weighing 110 pounds and measuring 65 inches in length.

She was clad in a black T-shirt, on the back of which there was inscription "Tour of the Americas." On the front of the T-shirt there was a posterlike imprint with the inscription "U-2." In the T-shirt was a label with the inscription "medium 38-40." Underneath the black T-shirt there was a white brassiere. She was also wearing a pair of faded blue denim jeans, on the right back pocket of which was the label "LEVI'S." Underneath the jeans there were a pair of white panties. The panties were soiled with urine and postmortem fluid. She wore no shoes or socks.

The head was symmetrical and covered with reddish blonde hair measuring up to 14 inches in length.

The facial features were markedly distorted due to bloated decomposition with greenish black discoloration. There were marked exophthalmus with the eyes being extruded through the eyelids. The color of the eyes could not be ascertained. The nose was intact. The lips thick and pouting with the tip of the tongue protruding between them. There was a 2mm space between the middle upper incisor teeth. There were neither cavities, restorations, nor extractions. The wisdom teeth were unerupted.

The pinnae of the ears were intact. Both earlobes were pierced twice with a gold earring with a dangling small heart. The chest and the well-developed breasts were markedly distended with postmortem tissue gas. There was marked red greenish postmortem discoloration of the skin of the trunk and upper extremities. There were also extensive areas of skin slippage. The abdomen was markedly distended and tympanitic. The external genitalia were those of an adolescent female. The pubic hair was female in distribution. The labia majora and minora were intact. The vaginal opening was intact. The hymen was narrow, semilunar in shape, and intact. No abnormalities were present in the vagina.

The anus and the rectum were also intact and free of traumatic abnormalities. The lower extremities were symmetrical, intact, and better preserved than the rest of the body. The toenails were covered with a light pinkish nail polish. The upper extremities were symmetrical and intact except for rather advanced postmortem autolytic changes and extensive areas of skin slippage. The fingernails were short and also covered with a light pink nail polish. Smears from the mouth, vulva, cervix, and rectum were negative for spermatozoa.

"PCAC's running," Catlin said, as she entered Taylor's office.

"Good," he nodded, placing a finger on the page to mark his spot. "What's this thing——"

"U-2?" she guessed.

He nodded again.

"I ran it through the system," she told him. "International rock group—Irish."

"North or south?"

"North."

"Humph," Taylor said. "How come this came from the embassy?"

"Her father was a British economist attached to the World Monetary Fund," Catlin explained.

Taylor said nothing.

"So what do you think?" she asked. "Crandon?"

"I don't know yet," Taylor admitted. "I'm no forensics expert, and the no-coins deal kinda throws me off."

"But it could be him, right?"

Turning back to the document, Taylor hoped she was wrong. He decided to finish reading, and to mark certain points for rereading.

INTERNAL EXAMINATION:

A midline incision was made from the chin to the pubis releasing an abundant amount of gas from the body cavity. The skin and subcutaneous tissue at the level of the umbilicus measured 1 inch in thickness. The breast tissue was mainly of the adipose type. The rib cage was intact. The thoracic and abdominal cavities contained several ounces of postmortem serohemorrhagic fluid. The thoracic and abdominal viscera were intact and in their usual anatomic relationships. The vermiform appendix was present at the tip of the cecum.

HEART:

The heart weighed 260 grams. The epicardium was smooth and glistening.

The rest was normal, so Taylor skipped it.

THYMUS:

The thymus weighed 20 grams. It was fibro-fatty and mildly autolyzed.

LUNGS:

The lungs together weighed 650 grams. They were normal in size, shape, and configuration. The pleural surfaces were smooth and glistening. There was no petechia. The tracheo-bronchial tree contained a moderate amount of serohemorrhagic fluid. On sectioning the lungs, the cut surfaces were congested and brownish-red with mild autolytic changes. There was an increase in crepitance due to decomposition.

LIVER:

The liver was normal.

SPLEEN:

The spleen weighed 120 grams. The capsule was smooth and intact. On sectioning, the red pulp was completely diffluent with advanced decomposition.

GENITOURINARY TRACT:

The kidneys together weighed 220 grams. They were symmetrical and normal in size and shape. The capsules stripped easily, disclosing a smooth, congested cortical surface. On sectioning, there was a mild autolysis of the tissues and congestion; but there was still a clear cortico-medullary demarcation. The ureter were intact. The urinary bladder empty. The genitalia were those of a nonparous adolescent girl and unremarkable. The vagina was intact.

PANCREAS AND ADRENAL GLANDS:
Moderate autolytic changes.

GASTROINTESTINAL TRACT:
This appeared normal.

NECK:
The organs of the neck were examined through a midline incision. There was a remarkable crushing of the tissue in relation to an external ligature mark which ran parallel to the angle of the jaw. To a lesser degree, there was also an unremarkable hemmorage of additional subcutaneous tissue which traversed the neck on a somewhat lesser plane with no upward angle. The strap muscles were intact. The upper trachea and larynx contained a scanty amount of brownish red mucoid fluid. There was no hemorrhage in the larnyx. The laryngeal cartilages and specifically, the thyroid cartilage was intact. The epiglottis, tongue and cervical column were intact.

HEAD:
The scalp was reflected in the usual coronal fashion revealing an abundant amount of subgaleal postmortem infiltration of serohemorrhagic fluid. The calvarium was intact. At the base of the skull, there was hemorrhage into the postmastoid bones. The

dura mater was intact. The brain was advancedly autolyzed and had to be scooped from the cranial cavity. No other pathological abnormalities were evident.

DIAGNOSIS:

1. Asphyxia do to ligature strangulation.
2. Decomposing body.

MANNER OF DEATH:

It is my opinion, based upon the fact that the body was discovered hanging by the neck in the aforementioned warehouse, physical evidence at the scene, investigative circumstances surrounding the death and the autopsy findings, that the decedent, Jennifer Lea Bishop, came to her death as a result of asphyxia due to ligature strangulation. The undersigned reserves a determination of either suicide or homicide pending additional investigation by appropriate agencies and notification of the undersigned as the subsequent investigative data develops therein. It is noted that examination findings support either contention.

For a moment, Taylor stared at the scrawled signature of the medical examiner. Then, he handed the report back to Catlin, who had been waiting for him to finish reading.

"So?" she asked.

He lit another cigarette. "With what you told me, I'd bet he killed her."

"You sure?"

He nodded. "Reasonably."

She looked down to the document in her hands. "How do you figure it?"

"Look at the section on neck examination." Standing, he

waited for her to open the report and find the paragraph. "See where the M.E. said there was some lesser crushing of the tissue with no upward angle?"

She found the sentence. "Yes."

"It's a wire track—a garrote. Probably steel or nylon."

Walking to his wall, Taylor stared at the carving of Saint Eloy as he continued. "When a person is hanged, the rope travels upward until it is finally stopped by the jawbone. That leaves the marks the M.E. found with an upward angle. When someone is garrotted, the track runs in a straight line—the lesser crushing."

He turned and looked at Catlin. "It's the sign of a pro. Someone who would know that the bruises caused by the rope would obscure any tracks left by the wire. Someone like Crandon."

"But why would he just leave her hanging there? And why no coins?"

Taylor shrugged and thought of Jennifer Bishop. He knew why. He had seen it before in Chile and in the Philippines. The coins weren't really symbolic of anything *critical,* they meant something personal to Crandon. Something the girl didn't. In Manila, one of the Communist "sparrow team" assassins had displayed a similar pattern. On some victims, he left his sign—a bleached mollusk shell—but on others there was nothing. In Chile, it had been a dead *tuco-tuco,* a small rodent.

After capture, Taylor had been present at both men's interrogations. Both, he realized immediately, were insane. And both, evidently as Peder Crandon was now doing, killed on two completely unrelated levels.

The sign meant the victim had been targeted for some political reason, yet the assassin killed them for whatever reason he had become a killer in the first place. In Chile, a *tuco-tuco* had been used by the *carabineros*—the national police—to feed political prisoners. The assassin, it turned out, had previously been jailed and forced to eat the rodent. The jailing and its attendant torture eventually became the reason he was able to be recruited as a leftist assassin: to strike back against the *carabineros*. In Manila, the scenario was identical. The prison food had been raw mollusks.

When the sign was absent but the killer was the same, it indicated a murder for a much baser reason: pleasure. As it was called on the circuit, the assassin had become a *perdidisto:* a man whose predisposition to political killing had twisted itself to the point where nonpolitical targets were necessary to feed his addiction for death. Of course, the targets were always of the same genre, Taylor remembered. In Chile, the *carabineros*. Here, the British. But always—*always*—the sign was missing. Yes, Taylor decided. Peder Crandon had become a *perdidisto*. It was not a good thought, for in his thirty years on the circuit, he had seen the phenomenon only on the two previous occasions. And both times, the men's actions had been impossible to predict until after they had been captured and eliminated.

"You didn't answer my question." Catlin interrupted his thoughts.

He was a world away. "What question?"

"Why no coins?"

Briefly, and probably not very successfully, Taylor attempted to explain his *perdidisto* theory.

"But the coins aren't food, like the rats and shells."

"No," Taylor agreed. "But I'm sure they are symbolic of something. Coins or no coins, this whole thing is taking on a whole new light."

"What do you mean?"

Taylor turned back to Saint Eloy. "The girl was killed at least two days before the consul general."

"Jesus," Catlin said. "I didn't even think of that. If you're right about the *perdidisto* thing, then there could be any number of bodies out there just waiting to be found."

Nodding, Taylor glanced over to Catlin. His eyes were cold, his voice almost threatening. "I'll tell you one other thing, Cat."

"What?"

"That little girl really suffered. It took her at least ten minutes to die. I'm going to wipe Crandon off the face of the earth."

Catlin was not sure what to say. She had never seen Taylor enraged. He was handling it with a tensile strength. It was another side of him, the side the general had hired.

Thinking he probably wanted to be alone, she turned to leave the office. She got as far as the door.

"You get Liaison alerted?" he called after her.

"Just like you said."

"What about the files on Yasif and Montes? They ready yet?"

"Should be."

"Well, pack 'em up. I've got to get them to the general."

As Taylor started walking toward the door, Catlin reached out and grabbed his arm. "There's something I have to tell you, Sam." Her voice sounded small even to her.

"What?"

"It's about Yasif—I was with him last night."

Taylor blanched. He knew he had heard her correctly. He wished he hadn't. He felt like odd man out again. "The General know?"

She nodded.

Bastard, he thought. "Will you tell me about it?"

Catlin nodded. "I'm not supposed to," she whispered, looking at the floor. "He says you're cut out, Sam."

Taylor understood. Reaching over, he touched Catlin's chin gently and lifted it up so he could watch her eyes. It was the closest they had ever been, and Taylor knew her next answer would be indicative of all that was to come.

Le dessous des cartes, she thought feeling like some criminal for not telling him before. *From the bottom of the deck.*

"Yes, Sam," she whispered. "I will tell you the truth."

"Will you?" he asked. "I need you, Catlin."

Chapter 34

ARM-IN-ARM, THEY WALKED the few hundred yards to his room. To the casual observer they could have been any young couple searching for privacy.

Peder Crandon spoke only of the upcoming mission. Ursula listened, responding to his questions about Hassim Saad and the Washington weapons connection now in place.

Personally, Ursula thought his plan too ambitious. A noonday rocket attack on the British embassy? It was too brazen. Too complex. They would need at least three more men to ensure success, but Peder was positive they could do it alone. He refused to think about any escape plans. It was not like him. Something was wrong.

Peder had registered at a hotel close to the airport. It was a neutral ground. An impartial shelter belonging to neither him, nor her, the *room* was the way Peder always celebrated their reunions. An immediate, almost perfunctory lovemaking in a place alien to them both—the surroundings forcing them closer, helping them forget their separation.

But Peder Crandon had changed. As Ursula lay in the darkened room, she knew something was wrong. His frequent mood swings left her uneasy. Though he looked forward to his touching her, she could not ignore a sense of apprehension she felt as he moved around.

He stopped at the edge of the bed and knelt down. Then, as Ursula rubbed the back of his head, he buried his face into the mattress and began to pray, as was their ritual.

"There is a fountain filled with blood,
Drawn from Emmanuel's veins,
And sinners plunged beneath that flood
Lose all their guilty stains."

"That was beautiful, Peder," she whispered. His fingers grasped hers, and he allowed himself to be pulled into the bed and into her arms, their mouths locking together in mutual want.

Slowly, he broke the kiss, watching her face as his hand stroked her hard, flat stomach, her mound, and along the insides of her legs. Marveling at the symmetry of her body, he thought about the other men who had possessed her.

Reaching under her buttocks, he spread her legs wide. Slowly, then with increasing fervor, he began to caress her womanhood.

Crandon watched her face intently, his mind a chorus of distemper.

Whore, he thought. How many cocks had she consumed since they were last together? The questions made his grow harder. More intense. Licking his lips, he reached to the back of her neck and slowly forced her down upon him.

Ursula needed no urging. Instantly, she slid lower and eel-like, took the smooth penis between her lips. He tasted like toffee, she thought. It was so good with Peder. So very good. She slid her tongue back and forth. She loved him. Would do anything for him. Give him her body. Her soul.

Whorebitch, he thought, pulling himself from her mouth and rolling out from under.

Barely able to conceal his building rage, Crandon stumbled from the bed and twisted her around to a kneeling position. He held her face down on the rumpled sheets with her buttocks up, rocking with anticipation. Standing behind her, he began to spank the smooth flesh.

Her mind swirling with pleasure, Ursula crouched before her lover, backing against him. She felt him violate her.

Back up to it, whore. That's all you're good for. Pig, his mind screamed. *You foul sweating pig. You have soiled me, whore. You will be punished.*

Totally abandoning herself to the waves of ecstasy, Ursula reacted violently. She was a puppet. As the contractions began, she arched her spine upward, backing even harder into him.

Grabbing her hair, Peder Crandon slid the tip of the slim Afghan boning knife into the side of Ursula's neck three inches beneath her right ear. As the ten-inch blade poked through the opposite side, he jerked it forward in a smooth upward angle.

"You will rule me no more, mother. For now I am invincible."

Dropping the knife to the floor, Peder Crandon pushed back from the body and watched her crumple, raglike, face down on the bed.

No, he decided. He could not allow himself an orgasm. He had been bad. He had chopped again. *No chopping, no pence. No chopping, no pence.*

Dropping to his knees, he lay down across the body of Ursula Brandt and began to whimper as he recited his prayers. Ten minutes later, he was finished.

Within the hour, Peder Crandon had already forgotten Ursula Brandt. As he sped back toward Washington, his mind was filled with one thought: the planning of his strike.

There was only one more detail to be addressed. Eduardo Montes. The rest would take care of itself. He knew he could not be stopped.

He was far above such worldly concerns.

The concerns of lesser men.

His calling had become divine.

Chapter 35

LEANING ON A small table in his Washington Hyatt suite, Yasif wished he had not bothered to check with his agents in New York. The news had been discouraging.

Kyoto had been neutralized by Ursula, who was now missing—more problems in an increasingly complex situation.

At first he allowed himself the luxury of hoping she had been kidnapped by the British or the Israelis.

But now he realized this could not be the case. No, Ursula had executed her bodyguard and fled Switzerland. She was probably in the United States.

"Ingrate," he cursed, pushing back from the table and vowing once again to kill the Irishman. No, he corrected himself. Not just kill, exterminate.

Walking to the window, Yasif gazed through the glass as if searching for some clue. A large bank of blue black clouds was approaching the city from the west. Already advance droplets of water were tapping at the glass.

Staccato bursts of lightning heralded the storm's arrival. *The majesty of nature's violence,* he thought, turning his attention to the street below where pedestrians were scurrying for cover.

The sight of people made him feel lonely, somehow wishing that all he had to worry about was protection from the weather. For the old days were gone, and the problems of Islam increased as the elders managed the faith like some huge corporation—a corporation with no central office.

The Islamic movement had been expanded to allow special-interest splinter groups as well as new converts to join. But in reality, the growth had reached the point of being unmanageable.

Islam per se, had no gross national product, no industry, and little technology. Its sole asset was the dream of a united statehood by people willing to sacrifice themselves to realize the dream. Yasif shared the nationalistic fervor of Islamic autonomy, but he was also a realist. He knew he would not see the unification of Islam in his lifetime.

The problem, Yasif realized, was that there was not yet any mutual trust binding Iran, Syria, and Libya. It was a shortcoming which could only be hampered by the burden of Peder Crandon and the obvious treachery of Ursula.

Yasif turned from the window. Eduardo Montes would be at the university by now. He would pay the Cuban a personal call. Of course the professor would be intimidated by the *direct* contact; nonetheless, there was little alternative. He would have to forgo the usual Cuban intelligence intermediary.

Yasif did not consider this an issue. Montes was merely another tool—cast from the same mold as Hassim Saad, only *español*. Besides, the very last thing he wanted was to ask the Cubans or the Soviets for help. It would only make it appear as another example of Arab blundering.

If the professor declined to cooperate, Yasif could have Montes killed within twelve hours. The choice would be left to the Cuban, Yasif decided. And should he be killed? In that case, there was always Catlin. Dear, well-meaning Catlin. What with the Americans well into their own efforts to stop Crandon, having her was like sitting in on their planning sessions.

Two completely different approaches to finding Crandon—inside and outside. Either way, Crandon could be located and eliminated.

As he walked to the door of his suite, Yasif pulled on his black cashmere topcoat and made another decision. Despite his feelings and despite her potential value to Islam, Ursula Brandt would have to be made an example for others.

Regretfully, it would be such a waste. She had proved herself the ultimate courtesan. Wicked and beautiful, with a simple flick of a tongue she had turned boys into men and men into stallions. Yet he would have to order her death to save face.

Yasif took the outdoor glass elevator to the hotel lobby. As he descended, his thoughts returned to Catlin. He had offered to let her make love to him and she had wanted to. But it was her time, she said. If he didn't mind, she didn't.

The very thought was repugnant. He had explained that to her once before. Evidently she had forgotten his reservations, and she had pouted. Once again he was amazed at how much women desired him. It seemed as if he were the only *real* man left in the world.

Stepping out of the elevator, Yasif walked quickly across the lobby to the main doors of the Hyatt's New Jersey Avenue entrance. Catlin. She had told him her problems. Simple ones, he remembered thinking. He supposed they were important to her.

He had skillfully skirted the specifics of what he wanted with half-answers. They had sipped chicory coffee until dawn, when he was finally convinced she was still his agent. He began to talk more openly, to tell her more—his fears that the United Kingdom of Islam was being destroyed by the erratic Peder Crandon.

Wide-eyed, Catlin had listened to everything. Then she offered whatever measure of support she could. Yes, she would keep him advised of American efforts to stop Crandon. If the Americans located him first, she was prepared to advise Yasif.

"What if American lives were to be lost in the process?"

Catlin told him it was unimportant.

"Why are you doing this?" he asked.

She had smiled and kissed him fully on the mouth.

He didn't press the subject. All that remained was to devise a test to see if the Americans had turned her against him. If they had, then the Pentagon would also lose her services.

Chapter 36

SAMUEL TAYLOR DIDN'T bother to knock before yanking open the general's front door, slamming it as he charged towards the study at the rear of the Foxhall residence. He hoped they had heard him coming.

As he stalked into the room, he found Brayden behind his lacquered desk and Prescott perched demurely in the chair Taylor had occupied during their previous meeting. Both men were drinking coffee and eating doughnuts from a silver platter. Prim and proper, Taylor thought of two old queens looking through a kiddie-porn magazine.

"You play it close, don't you?" he said sharply, glaring at Brayden as he tossed the Montes-Yasif dossiers on the desk. "How about I just let you run this little dog-and-pony show yourself?"

"Bit tense aren't we, Taylor?" Prescott remarked.

Fuck off, Taylor thought, ignoring the Englishman and continuing to stare at Brayden.

"Would you care to explain?" the general asked.

"Privately," Taylor said, nodding toward Sir Elliot. "That is, unless your lordship here is also part of your circus?"

Indignant, Prescott sat upright. "Your lordship? For your information, my government has given me——"

"I don't give a damn what *they've* given you, Prescott," Taylor interrupted. "*You're* giving me a pain in the ass."

Prescott began to say something, but the general spoke first.

''Just a moment, Elliot,'' he said softly. Then he turned to Taylor. ''What's going on here, Sam?''

Again Taylor nodded toward Prescott.

''It's not a problem,'' the general reassured him. ''But your attitude and rudeness are. What's biting you?''

''Catlin Broussard.'' Taylor did little to hide the contempt in his voice. ''She spent the evening with our friend Yasif.''

Leaning back in his seat, the general's eyes narrowed as he placed his fingertips to his lips and studied Taylor.

After a moment of silence, Prescott spoke. ''Catlin Broussard? Will someone kindly tell me what you're talking about? And what about Yasif?''

Reaching up, the general removed his glasses and placed his elbows on the desk, staring at Taylor as he answered the question. ''Catlin Broussard is Taylor's executive assistant.''

Prescott shrugged his shoulders. ''And?''

''And she's also an intelligence agent,'' Taylor added.

Prescott thought about Taylor's explanation. ''So,'' he said after a moment. ''Who else staffs intelligence agencies?''

''You're missing the point,'' Taylor said, leaning over the desk. ''I'm sure the good general here would be happy to let you in on his private little network. Correct, general?''

Brayden had enough. Anger was one thing, insubordination another. ''Sit down, Taylor,'' he ordered. ''And stop acting like a first grader who found out somebody's been playing in his sandbox.''

Taylor returned to his chair and folded his arms, wondering whether he really wanted to hear the explanations. The bullshit.

''First things first,'' Brayden began. ''Sam, you've obviously talked to Catlin this morning?''

''Obviously,'' Taylor said.

''Where is she now?''

''Heading to the Marriott to keep tabs on our RAINDANCER.''

Prescott felt as if they were purposely leaving him out of the conversation. ''Gentlemen, I'm not used to having my questions unanswered. I'm losing patience. If I don't get answers, I'll be forced to have the president clear this up for me."

Realizing things were getting away from him, Brayden felt obliged to explain.

"Catlin Broussard is a double agent," he said softly. "She works directly for me." As he spoke, the general stared directly at Taylor. "I recruited her a number of years ago, when she was still in Louisiana. After she received her doctorate, I sent her to New York under deep cover. At the time, the whole Middle Eastern community was looking for technicians to either design or update their computer capabilities. Catlin was perfect for the job. Single, intelligent, attractive, and qualified. They trusted her. Then, she met Yasif. He was traveling with Arafat in New York. This was prior to his assignment to the Libyan mission." Brayden paused. "Any problems so far, Sam?"

Taylor shook his head.

"Good," Brayden continued. "They dated when Yasif came to New York." He turned to Prescott. "Actually, her relationship with Yasif was a byproduct of her initial assignment."

"Which was?" Sir Elliot asked.

"To program her client's computer with a random access code—a back window, if you will—to allow us clandestine surveillance of everything entering or leaving the system."

"Interactive processing," Taylor mumbled.

"Exactly," the general confirmed. "Each transaction recorded by us as it occurred."

"Why wasn't I told?" Taylor asked.

"No need," Brayden said. "With your ulcer, you'll be retired within ninety to a hundred and twenty days on a medical. Besides, the new project won't be activated until Catlin takes over the section."

Taylor was suddenly stunned by the cold, hard facts.

Brayden put on his glasses. "You've had your day in the sun, Sam. The business is too automated for you old Terry-and-the-Pirates types. It's nobody's fault. It's just the way it is."

Before Taylor could respond, the general turned back to Prescott. "When Catlin lived in New York, we didn't realize how important Yasif would become. Nonetheless, they became friends and eventually lovers."

Taylor experienced an unexpected pang of jealously upon hearing the word *lovers*. "You encouraged it?"

"Of course I encouraged it," Brayden said. "We suspected that Yasif was involved in the Islamic terror networks, but we never had anyone close enough to confirm his level of participation. That is, until Catlin."

The general took a sip of coffee. "A lot can be learned from pillow talk, gentlemen. Catlin got information which led to the capture of four terrorists just by being in the room and listening. She also prevented the bombing of a TWA 747 by Muslim extremists working out of Rome."

"Your assistant is a brave woman," Prescott told Taylor.

The general nodded in agreement. "I think the facts speak for themselves."

"And Yasif knows she is working for you?" Prescott asked, looking to Brayden for the answer.

A slight smile creased the corners of the general's mouth. "He knows only what I wanted him to know. Catlin's here in Washington to get the agency's career leader. Yasif would have been suspicions of any elaborate cover stories, so she simply told him the truth: that she'd been offered a job at the Pentagon."

Taylor added, "You wanted Yasif to believe that if she went to work for us, he would have access to our information."

The general grinned. "Couldn't wait for her to start."

Prescott understood. "A bit of disinformation?"

"A bit," Brayden answered. "After six weeks, she told him how well she was doing at the agency. He decided not to risk exposing her. Consequently, he made no requests for nearly a year."

"Until now," Taylor pointed out, "and he's the connection to Crandon."

Strutting in front of Prescott, the general said, "Now, Elliot, we have a special contract employee standing by. His name is Kelly Michaels. It's his responsibility to deal with Crandon. Am I making myself clear?"

Prescott nodded thoughtfully. All governments had their "special employees." Men like Chatsworth, like Michaels. "Yes," he told Brayden. "Perfectly clear."

"Good," the general replied. He looked at Taylor. "It's your turn, Sam. Tell us about Catlin and Yasif."

He did.

Chapter 37

KELLY MICHAELS AWAKENED early to Catlin's telephone call. She ordered him to remain in the hotel until she called at 10:00. Hopping out of bed, he went for a quick swim in the heated pool and ate a large breakfast. He returned to his room to await instructions.

He could still remember a time when the thought of sitting around would have driven him crazy. He was used to it now; besides, they were paying for the trip and the kill. Finding the target was their responsibility.

Until Taylor gave him some idea where Crandon could be found, there was nothing else for him to do but wait. It was nothing new. He had learned to follow instructions—the hard way.

From his window, Michaels could see the Pentagon in the distance. The building brought back memories. Bad memories. His last official act in the army had taken place within its walls; the inquiry regarding the failed raid into Iran to free the hostages at the American embassy. It was witch-hunting in the best American military tradition.

Personally, Michaels thought the mission failed because of excessive secrecy during its plannings. For obvious reasons, it was necessary for President Carter to direct the joint chiefs to maintain a high level of security. He really had no choice. He could little afford the political and diplomatic repercussions of sending an armed force into another country. But, as Michaels told the investigation panel, keeping the presidential image intact caused problems for the troops.

The officers in the raid were not told the reasons nor the location of the action. Consequently, they could not prepare their men without terrain maps, no aerial photographs, no building mock-ups, or, for that matter, no simulations.

As a result, the assault force was dropped into the middle of a desert with no order of battle to tell them what they were supposed to accomplish. Their only clue was a timetable that was supposed to be followed to the minute.

Michaels shook his head. The Iran operation was the most absurd mission of his military career. He was assigned to fly in the lead Hercules C-130 Blackbird from secret airfields in Egypt to an obscure point in the Iranian desert near Tabas. From the initial insertion zone, his team was to be picked up by one of the eight Sea Stallion helicopters from the aircraft carrier *U.S.S. Nimitz* and ferried to another point closer to Teheran.

From the second landing zone, his team was to split from the main force, proceed to the Iranian Foreign Ministry and free the American *chargé d' Áffaires,* Bruce Laingen, who was being held separately from the other hostages.

With the diplomat in custody, the team was to make its way back to the embassy compound, join the liberated hostages and the main assault force, and wait for pickup by the helicopters. On paper, the mission looked fairly good.

Unfortunately, the actual operation bore little resemblance to the plan approved by President Carter. The proposed timetable wasn't even close.

The C-130s landed the main attack force on schedule, smack in the middle of a bank of smugglers and a busload of tourists. The chase was on. Eventually, no doubt due to Operation Eagle's Claw superior firepower, the unfortunate Iranians were finally captured and subdued. The problem was that nobody knew what to do with them.

Things went downhill from there. One of the helicopters and

a C-130 were refueling when they collided and exploded. The resulting fireball did little to enhance the secret operation. At 3:00 A.M., the flames were the brightest thing in a thousand miles of desert.

In the middle of the confusion, sat Colonel Charles Beckwith. At the inquiry, Michaels had listened to his testimony in amazement. As mission commander, the ground operation was his responsibility. It was also his ticket to a general's star.

The good colonel had always been a quick-to-think, quick-to-act soldier and was pleased to testify before the board of inquiry. He told the panel of general officers that he knew things weren't going as planned when only five of the expected eight helicopters showed up. The generals all nodded soberly at this revelation. The colonel was obviously Joint Chiefs of Staff material due to his uncanny ability to arrive at such astute observations. They begged him to continue.

The colonel explained that the only thought running through his mind was that the operation was going to fail. Finally, Beckwith told them, he sat down in the middle of the desert and cried tears of frustration. That was the truth, Michaels remembered. The colonel realized that the failure of the raid was not his fault, that he was just a soldier following the orders of his commander-in-chief.

President Carter was running a close race for reelection and could not publicly accept responsibility for the failure. Consequently, Charles Beckwith became the scapegoat for the entire mess. It cost the United States military one of the best guerrilla-warfare officers it had ever produced and it had cost the colonel his career. Michaels sighed. The last time he'd heard, the colonel was living in Texas and lecturing.

"Round the jack to a queen," Michaels sighed softly, watching his breath fog the glass, then evaporate slowly. On a brighter side, at least *he* had found work out of the hearings. It was where he had first met Thomas Brayden. He had been one of the generals on the board of inquiry.

Turning away from the window, Michaels walked to the bed. Glancing at the clock radio bolted to an end table, he stretched out on the mattress. 11:02 A.M.

His employers were already an hour overdue.

Chapter 38

"NO OTHER VARIABLES?" Prescott asked as Taylor concluded his summation of the facts.

"There could be," Taylor answered. "I'm just repeating what Catlin said without trying to read anything into it." He looked at Brayden, toying with a pencil on his desk. "How do you want to handle it, general? We can squeeze Montes and hope Crandon pops out. Or we can let Yasif do it for us and pick up the brass and ammo afterward."

"What do you think?" Brayden asked.

"Gut feeling?"

The general nodded.

"Run it both ways," Taylor told him. "Let Catlin stay tight with Yasif while Michaels works the weapons deal. If one approach craters, then we've still got the second to fall back on."

Prescott cleared his throat. "Well, I think the sanction by your man Michaels is perhaps the most expedient. After all, that contingency is already initiated."

Eat another doughnut, pinhead, Taylor thought. Aloud he said, "We've told you *three times* he's standing by. You get a fourth and they can all play bridge together. You ought to learn to listen sometime, *Sir* Elliot. It'd open up a whole new world for you."

"Enough of that, Sam," the general said. "I think we all want the same thing here, correct?"

Prescott glowered. Taylor shrugged.

"Let's try to work this out." The general began to pace his study. "From what you've told us, Elliot, and from what Taylor said, there may be some esoteric options we could consider."

Esoteric? Taylor hated that word almost as much as he did *serendipity*. To him it meant the speaker didn't know *what* he wanted, much less how to get it. "Like what?" he asked.

Choosing his words carefully, Brayden spoke slowly. "First, let's review what we do know . . ."

Great, Taylor thought. *Now Brayden was going to play Sherlock Holmes and waste some more time.*

". . . first, we now know who Crandon's weapon's contact is."

"Montes," Prescott blurted out.

Nice guess, Taylor thought.

"Exactly," Brayden confirmed. "And we know Montes is here in Washington."

"At the university."

Taylor couldn't believe it. Prescott was grinning as though he'd just won the New York lottery.

Pulling off his glasses, the general pointed them at Taylor as he spoke. "What do you think, Sam? Has Crandon contacted Montes?"

"Can we assume he hasn't? Suppose Ursula slipped past our people and passed him the word. Or maybe he already had contact and the whole business with Hassim Saad was a smoke screen?"

"I doubt that," Prescott said. "My information is——"

"I'm sure it is," Taylor interrupted. "But we have to cover all the bases. And as far as I'm concerned, the only two games in town are Montes and the weapons, and Yasif hunting for Crandon himself. One or the other is going to meet up with Crandon, and we have to be there when he does."

"And we will, Sam," the general said. "We will. But

Yasif.'' He began to smile. ''Yes, Yasif has given us an even more viable approach to solving two problems at once.''

Elliot Prescott understood immediately. ''That *is* an interesting possibility. But could we actually do it?''

Taylor studied the two men. He had no idea to what they were referring, but it was obviously something they had considered before. ''Do what?'' he said.

''Sir Elliot?'' Brayden offered the Englishman the floor.

Taking the cue, Prescott sat upright in his chair. ''Consider this, Taylor. Wouldn't it be amusing if we could eliminate Crandon and somehow implicate Yasif and the Libyans at the same time?''

Why not? Taylor thought. *The Libyans were assholes anyway.* ''What do you have in mind?'' he asked Prescott. Allowing himself a quiet, almost intimidating chuckle, Sir Elliot leaned back and began to outline his thoughts.

''Homicide'' is a general term used to describe the killing of one human being by another. But not all homicides were considered criminal. Elliot justifed *excusable* homicide as a definition relevant to both Yasif and Peder Crandon.

In effect, the strategy proposed by the Englishman was pointedly straightforward, and its long-term consequences made it politically important.

Since the mid-1970s, support for terrorist groups, including the provision of camps and training facilities, had been the central element of Libyan foreign policy under Colonel Muammar Qaddafi. With the exception of American oil embargos, pulling U.S. personnel out of Libya, and one air strike against Libya, few Western governments had actually done anything to punish the colonel for his activities.

Now it seemed that Yasif had provided the link and the vehicle to finally strike back at the Libyan despot. Provision 5.51(b)(6) of the London Letter codified the authorization for a strike against any world leader who could be linked *directly* to a terrorist act. And, in this case, Yasif appeared to be that particular link. It was the evidence for which both Washington and London had been waiting for well over a decade.

After Sir Elliot completed his proposal, the general spoke. "If we arrange to have Yasif killed in connection with Crandon, then the collective Western governments will have the key to censure the Libyans economically and diplomatically."

"Precisely," Prescott nodded. "With no official diplomatic standing, we can initiate offensive actions against Qaddafi."

Taylor was uncomfortable. He had the distinct impression that stopping Crandon was just a minor cog in a much larger political propaganda exercise. "And how are we supposed to tie up all the loose ends?" he asked.

"A simultaneous news leak from Washington and London," Brayden answered.

"Stating what?"

"Stating"—the general paused and took a deep breath—"that . . . a Libyan-backed terrorist has been identified in the United States. That under the direction of Yasif—a U.N. diplomat—he is responsible for all the acts of violence against British interests in the Washington area."

"And what do we use as proof?" Taylor asked. "Yasif won't talk, and with diplomatic status, we won't even be able to hold him while we build our case."

"It's not Yasif we need, Sam," Brayden said softly. "We'll use something even better. A living, breathing Peder Crandon."

"But Yasif will deny the whole thing."

"No he won't, Sam," the general said, "Yasif will be dead."

"Yasif will be the nail in the Libyan coffin," Prescott added, "an extremely large nail. And if *you* take the time to listen to what *we're* saying, you'll agree we cannot afford to pass up an opportunity to rid ourselves of the Libyan annoyance once and for all."

"So what happens to Crandon?" Taylor asked.

"Suicide," Prescott said, chuckling softly. "Just like his father, he will be found hanging in his cell."

"After he's been suitably used."

"Suitably used *publicly,*" Sir Elliot corrected.

Taylor nodded. "What's next?"

"Two things," the general said. "Get Catlin to entice Yasif into a situation where Michaels can get to him. After he's dead, squeeze Montes and find those weapons—kill him if you have to. I want Crandon stopped before he does anything else."

"And capture him alive."

"If you can," Brayden said. "Get moving on this at once. The prime minister arrives here tomorrow. I want the president to be able to brief her on our plans. Any questions?"

"What about Ursula?" Taylor asked.

"What about her?" Brayden shot back. "She's not part of the equation anymore. If she shows up, capture her. Kill her." He looked at Prescott. "Will Great Britain ask to extradite Crandon?"

"No," Prescott answered.

The general looked back at Taylor. "Kill her," he ordered.

"I understand." Taylor rose. "By the way . . ."

"What, Sam?" Brayden said.

"How do you know the president will approve all of this?"

The general glared back with obvious contempt. "I believe that's something *I* have to worry about, isn't it, Sam? You just follow orders."

Taylor realized that additional conversation would be pointless. "I'll get on it." He walked to the door of the general's study.

As he reached the hall, he turned back to them. "Incidentally, we may have come up with two more victims: a girl and a British sailor on deck watch."

Neither man seemed too surprised. "Any coins?" Prescott asked.

"No!"

Prescott dismissed the information with the wave of a hand. "Forget them. Without the coins, there is no proof it was Crandon."

Taylor stepped back into the hall, and walked to the front door. But he knew he couldn't forget Jennifer Bishop. It was Crandon, all right. The girl's death was going to be avenged.

Chapter 39

"LIES," EDUARDO MONTES said, carefully folding the editorial page and setting it at the corner of his cluttered university office desk. If one were to believe *The New York Times* story, it would appear that the Americans were winning their covert war in Cambodia.

Closed budget hearings must be in session, he decided, or the CIA would never have allowed such details into print. In any case, he knew the story was factually incorrect. The CIA *was* using chemical weapons. Their deployment had again become fashionable for both sides.

As for the Cambodians? Well, nobody really cared about them anyway. Their country was the perfect laboratory for the Americans and Soviets to test each other's binary expertise without any meddling in the region. Such was the price of poverty.

Chemwars, he thought. He must remember to locate some binaries. With the superpowers setting the trends, the rest of the Third World would demand some, too—and soon. Yes. His clients would expect him to be able to deliver. As always, he would be prepared.

At fifty-three, Eduardo Montes was a wiry, spidery man who looked and played the part of a respected, wealthy, professor of art: decked in tweeds, linens, and soft Gucci loafers. Chicly acceptable, he was almost pretty and moved easily in the circle of rich university benefactors which comprised Washington's social and power elite.

It was a good life, eons away from the open pre-Castro days of Havana. He smiled. Education was marvelous; it covered a multitude of sins.

With short white hair, dark skin, and a mouthful of even, polished teeth, women were still drawn to him. He could discuss art, the old Masters, the subtle interpretations in a deft brush stroke, while their husbands were concerned only with affairs of state. The neglected wives loved the attention of the charming bachelor, and he slept with many of them.

Eduardo Montes was not discriminating. Matron or debutante, obese or emaciated, he would smile, call them *mujer,* and make each one feel like the most beautiful in his kingdom. Giggling like schoolgirls, they shared him willingly, calling him their little *mariposa*—the little butterfly, as he fluttered between their silk-sheeted beds.

He was a charming man. A courtier of women. A man who used the wives to talk about their husbands, to uncover the facts behind the rumors. His purpose was simple: with conflict came killing, and with killing came the need for guns.

For Eduardo Montes, the social life was an investment in his financial future: knowing where to sell his weapons.

Of course the husbands—much less the wives—suspected nothing. In their rather myopic eyes, he was merely another early refugee from Castro's government. His money? He had been one of the fortunate ones, the son of a successful Cuban planter and former agricultural minister who had funneled the family money to Miami prior to Batista's fall at the hands of the Communists.

And now he was above approach. For almost three decades he had been able to live the life of the rich Latin expatriate, far from suspicion, even accepting American citizenship in 1974.

In addition to serving as an arms dealer to selected Kremlin-backed political factions, Eduardo Montes was also considered an agent of influence by his superiors who occupied the old seven-story building housing KGB Headquarters in Moscow's Dzerzhinsky Square.

Extremely low-echelon, he was not a spy in the purest sense of the term. On the contrary, he realized he was lumped into that broad category comprising journalists, politicians, and academics who occupied influential positions within a foreign country, yet demonstrated an ideological commitment to Soviet policy.

A strong relationship had developed between him and Moscow. He would pass along a bit of juicy gossip to one of the District's "rezidents" and within months he would be contracted to broker an arms deal somewhere in Central or South America. It proved to be an arrangement which worked well for all concerned, and the deals were very profitable.

"Professor?" He glanced at the intercom. "Professor?" it repeated. "Are you in?"

"Yes."

"I'm sorry, professor, but there is someone here to see you," his secretary said. "No appointment."

He hoped it wasn't one of the damned graduate students. The last thing he felt like doing was discussing the finer points of Paul Klee's color experimentations. "Who is it?" he asked.

"A Mr. Yasif."

Yasif? His coming to the university was *very* out of the ordinary, perhaps even dangerous. It was three years since they last met for dinner at New York's Four Seasons restaurant. Why was he here? He leaned over to the intercom. "Send him in, please."

Seconds later, the Arab was ushered into the professor's private chambers. Rising to greet him, Montes immediately noticed the deep circles under Yasif's eyes. The man was exhausted, Montes noted. He decided to adopt the air of an old friend as he offered his hand. "Yasif, the years have been kind to you."

"Hello, Eduardo," Yasif said, shaking the outstretched palm "Good of you to see me on such short notice."

"Nonsense. Please sit down. Would you like a coffee?"

"No." Yasif took a seat in the worn leather chair next to the professor's desk. "I've been drinking coffee all night. My kidneys couldn't take any more."

Laughing politely, the professor scurried behind his desk and sat down with a smile still fixed on his face. "Well," he began somewhat nervously. "So how many years has it been? Two?"

"Three, Eduardo," Yasif said. "It's not like you to forget."

"No . . . of course not," Montes said, beginning to fidget with some papers on the desk. "It just seems the older I get, the more time seems to——"

"You know about Peder Crandon," Yasif interrupted, doing nothing to disguise the accusatory tone of the statement.

The smile faded from his lips. "The name. I've heard the name."

"Has he contacted you?"

"No. Is there some reason he would?"

"Weapons."

"Weapons? What makes you think that?" Montes asked, hoping his voice reflected an acceptable amount of surprise tempered with shock.

"We all have our sources, Eduardo," Yasif said.

"But——"

"Hassim is dead. Unfortunate; nevertheless, such are the risks when one deals with this Peder Crandon. Do you understand my meaning, Eduardo?"

"There is a problem?"

Yasif nodded. "A slight miscalculation, but nothing which cannot be resolved. Assuming, of course, we can work together on the solution."

We? Montes thought. The word hung in his mind like a tumor as he considered Hassim's fate.

"But Yasif," he said. "You know you can always rely on my cooperation. Of course, if I'm to be of assistance, perhaps I should be told a bit more about . . . " The professor let the words trail off, hoping it would prompt Yasif to explain.

Briefly, Yasif touched on the high points of the Peder Crandon saga. Eduardo Montes listened in silence.

"Miscalculation is a bit of an understatement," he said, when Yasif finished his explanation.

"Words," Yasif said coldly. "Regardless, Peder Crandon must be eliminated. I want you to——"

The professor completed the sentence. "Make him available to your associates."

"No," Yasif said, staring directly into the Cuban's eyes. "Make him available to *me*."

"Aren't you getting a little long in the tooth for that sort of thing, Yasif? With your status, wouldn't it be more prudent to dissociate yourself from the entire matter?"

Yasif shook his head. "It's not open to discussion."

The professor nodded in sympathy. Yasif had placed himself in an untenable situation. Financially, it was a situation which begged to be exploited. "May I ask another question?"

Yasif nodded sullenly.

"With our friend Hassim now deceased, who is heir apparent to his business?"

In spite of everything, Yasif had to smile. "You amaze me, Eduardo," he said. "You have become the ultimate capitalist."

"I am a businessman," Montes shrugged. "Besides, what you are asking is something I've always taken great pains to avoid."

"I know," Yasif admitted. "Because of our friendship, I can persuade Hassim's clients to deal with you."

Eduardo Montes thought about it for a moment. Cooperate and become rich? Or decline and die? There was no choice. He preferred the carrot to the stick anytime. "You realize, of course, that I will have to clear my participation. It may take two or three days."

"We do not have that time, Eduardo. His attacks have become too brazen. I need your assurance now."

"But what if he doesn't contact me?"

"I know the boy too well. He will contact you. He knows your name is safe. That's the way he was trained."

The professor nodded slowly. "Whatever your rationale, I am still obliged to report my cooperation."

"No!" Yasif said angrily, reaching into his breast pocket and extracting a white envelope. "I assure you that what I'm asking is in no way counter to Soviet intentions."

He passed the envelope across the desk. "This was distributed to us by the KGB rezident in Tripoli just last week. I would ask you to be good enough to read it while I avail myself of the facilities. The information should save us the two or three days you mentioned."

As Yasif left his office, Eduardo Montes opened the envelope and extracted a slim sheath of papers. Essentially, it was a directive, accompanied by a cover letter.

COMRADES,

Annual Directive Number 72 laid down certain variations within our constant strategic framework. Comrade General Zukov has informed me of the successful manner in which you have implemented this approach. In this regard, the following Directive is a continuation of your instructions, yet with a brief alteration of plans due to different developments in different parts of the world. You will note the variations carefully.

The strategic objectives of the Central Committee and the essential role of the *Komitet Gosudarstvennoe Bezopasnosti* in the achievement of these objectives remain constant.

We have enjoyed some outstanding successes. Progress has been substantial in South Africa, Guatemala, and Peru. In addition, the steadily increasing influence of the militant left in Great Britain, in Parliament, in educational circles and, most importantly, the trade unions, has been increasingly undermining the will of the British people and therein, support of the Conservative party. But there are now new problems connected with the ideological policies of Eurocommunism, particularly with respect to detente and the projected development of a huge additional NATO strategic weapons systems in Great Britain.

You have recovered well from the discovery of the *Hezbulluh* cell in Brixton and are commended for your handling of this matter. But due to anticipated hostile dialogue between the United States and Moscow, with the British being central ground for the weapons question, your instructions are to avoid any action which may affect world opinion against the Central Committee.

In this respect, we wish to regard Great Britain and the United States as areas where any *overt* activity would reflect negatively on the Party. It is imperative that sufficient time be given our comrades in Britain to preclude construction and deployment of additional tactical weapons in that location through more subtle means.

The changes in this policy may well involve potential complexities. If additional discussions are necessary, you should be prepared to travel to Bucharest for further consultation. As stated in Annual Directive Number 54, you should continue to suggest additional projects regardless of geographical location.

Comradely greetings,
Petrov Yefimov
DIRECTOR, MIDDLE EAST OPERATIONS
KGB HQ MOSCOW

Finishing the letter, Eduardo Montes felt his pulse quicken. Indeed, Yasif had no choice. Peder Crandon's actions were diametrically opposed to current Soviet policy.

"So?" Yasif asked, returning from the restroom.

"I've just read the letter," Montes answered, looking up. "Should I read the rest?"

"Items four and five."

Quickly flipping through the document, the professor located the indicated sections:

> [4] The election in Britain must take place within the next few months. When it does, your instructions are to take every step to support broad-based strikes which are to be initiated in protest of Conservative economic policies in the weeks preceding the election. It is the intent of the Central Committee that business in Great Britain be brought to a standstill.
>
> It is further directed that you are to discourage attempts to divide the Labour party in order to create an independent Socialist Party. Control of union stewardship is currently extant and these dedicated comrades will carry the banner of the revolution for the millions of their subordinates. Great Britain will be reduced to the bare soil from which the working man will emerge as the new collective spirit of the future.
>
> [5] Any development that weakens the national sense and purpose of Tory Britain is something which must be encouraged. But only in the strictest sense of discretion, as has been indicated in all previous Directives. The situation in Northern Ireland remains of vital importance. It is a festering lesion and a permanent threat on Britain's exposed flank. Consequently, we will assist Irish operations, but discourage pointless violence against British concerns *outside* of Northern Ireland.
>
> The increasing number of immigrants in Britain, particularly those with Socialistic leanings, create an untapped resource for the revolution. Race hatred, like class hatred, should always be encouraged. But you will neither condone,

nor support any activity which could jeopardize strike contingencies without specific authority from *Moscow Centre* or the appropriate *Referentura* within your respective countries.

Looking up from the document, Eduardo Montes realized that his hands were trembling. "I—I had no idea," he stammered. "My position—it is so functionary."

"Now you realize how explosive the situation has become? How far-reaching its effects?"

"Yes."

"It's the STEALTH technology," Yasif added.

"What is?"

"In the Yefimov letter," Yasif said, "the new weapons development? The British are going to manufacture the American STEALTH bomber. That's the reason for the Kremlin's shift in policy toward Great Britain."

Twisting uncomfortably, Eduardo Montes felt like a small child who had inadvertently stumbled onto a private family secret. It was too important. Too complex. Too far removed from his *mariposan* lifestyle and the petty responsibilities of a low-level agent of influence.

No, he thought, it was not worth the risk. Not even for Hassim Saad's clients and the money. "I'm sorry, Yasif," he mumbled. "But I have to report it."

"You silly fool!" Yasif hissed, lunging over the desk and jerking the papers from the professor's fingers. Then he slapped the documents against the Cuban's face. "Don't you realize the significance of these documents?"

Cringing, Eduardo Montes was unable to make his brain function. "I—I—" The words would not come. He wanted to flee.

Yasif was incredulous. "You really don't know, do you?" he said, regaining his composure.

Not trusting his voice, Montes could only manage a shrug.

Shaking his head in disgust, Yasif flopped back in his chair.

The coward, he thought, watching the professor squirm. *If there was any other way. Any other contact . . .*

But there wasn't. He would have to make the best out of Montes. "I'm sorry, Eduardo," he said, his voice soothingly soft.

The professor looked at him. "I have no knowledge of these things, Yasif. Mine is the Latin world—small deliveries to even smaller groups. Your letter, your Directive—those are things I have no right to read."

"But you have read them, Eduardo. And the words are not mine. They are from your people."

"I know," the professor nodded glumly. "But——"

"Think of it, Eduardo," Yasif whispered. "Think of how beautiful the Soviet plan could be. England, weeks before the election, a national strike, the streets amass with people. Socialists. Labour. Raising their voices against the Conservative establishment. England. No trains. No newspapers. No television. No taxis. No industry. Think of it, Eduardo. The country paralyzed by strikes. Fires with no firemen."

"The Conservative government can do nothing to stop the strike. A week. Two. Then the elections. Whom does a young mother vote for? A young father? Their children are hungry—there is no food. Their children are sick—there are no doctors. They will vote in the tens of millions. But they will vote *against* someone. They will vote against the Conservatives who brought the blight upon their land."

Enthralled by the plan, Eduardo Montes nodded approvingly, as Yasif continued slowly, his voice now a euphony of encouragement.

"But you see, Eduardo. All of this. All of these things. It is more than mere social revolution. It is plan. In Yefimov's letter. The weapon systems. The STEALTH. It will become a moot point. Once in control, your comrades in the Social Labour movements will simply vote them away. They will become nothing less than a footnote in history. Can you appreciate these things, Eduardo? Can you understand the strategic implications?"

"Yes," Montes answered, his voice small and detached. "It will change everything."

Yasif nodded. "But one thing could stop it."

The professor said nothing.

"Peder Crandon," Yasif explained. "He could change it. His actions could be the catalyst to keep the English people together. Think of the Falklands. The assassination of Lord Mountbatten. The Battle of Britain."

Yasif waved a hand in the air. "These things, Eduardo. These things give the British people a rallying point. Something to keep them together and endure. If Crandon's actions are associated even remotely with Moscow, your people's plan could be destroyed."

As he stopped talking, Yasif realized that his argument was rather weak. But the professor also knew he would be killed if he didn't cooperate. Yasif also realized that the rationale was general enough to allow Montes to save face by appealing to his sense of Socialistic commitment, rather than complying simply because of his fear of death. Men—especially Latins—needed their pride.

"Plans must be followed," Montes said.

"And it is a good plan," Yasif agreed. "So there must be no deviation."

"I will still have to report it," Montes told him.

"It would be better if you didn't. If the Irish ever found out we stopped Crandon, they could hurt Soviet plans by not supporting the British strike. The results could be as dangerous as the Americans finding out we supported him in the first place."

"Very well, Yasif. I agree. What do I do?"

"Four things," Yasif said. "Two different caches, a promise, and——"

"What promise?"

"That you don't tell the Soviets until *after* Crandon is dead."

"You have my word on that," the professor lied. "What will be in the caches?"

Standing, Yasif began to pace the room. "That will depend on what the Irishman tells you he needs."

"Do I give him what he asks for?"

"In part."

"You said there were four things. What's the fourth?"

"A device. Small. Effective. Instant detonation."

"I don't understand?"

"But you will, Eduardo," Yasif told him. "Perhaps you should take the remainder of the day off."

For the next thirty minutes, Eduardo Montes listened intently as Yasif told him exactly what to do. Believing that he was helping Moscow, he agreed to everything. Of course, he was mistaken. For, like many others, he was only being used by Yasif.

Chapter 40

"CREOLE LADY," KELLY Michaels said, opening the door to his hotel room for Catlin. "I guess two hours late is better than not coming at all?"

"I guess." Catlin walked inside.

Sensing her mood, Michaels became serious. "What's the matter? New problems?"

"No," she told him. "I'm supposed to wait here until the powers that be decide on our next move."

"Mi casa, su casa," Michaels shrugged, sitting on the edge of the bed. "Anything new on Crandon?"

Before she could answer the question, they were interrupted by the telephone. Michaels leaned back to the beside table.

He answered on the second ring, "Ten-Twelve. Just a minute." He handed the receiver to Catlin. "Taylor."

"Yes," she said, taking the phone.

Michaels watched her for another second. Still listening to her side of the conversation, he walked to the closet to gather his things. It was time to earn his money.

"What's the drill?" he asked as Catlin replaced the receiver.

"Just capture him."

"That's not my contract, lady," he said coldly. "Alive is a whole new set of problems."

"Not my idea," Catlin admitted. "It's Taylor's orders."

"Sounds like a typical Taylor plan," Michaels quipped. "Brings us back to square one."

"Taylor's coming here," she said. "Somebody got a line on Crandon's weapons supplier, a man named Montes. He'll be able to tell you where he is."

"A weapons contact?" Michaels laughed. "Yeh, I'll bet he'll jump at the chance to snitch. Maybe we can all take a lunch together? A little white wine and quiche."

Catlin was not in the mood for Kelly Michaels. "I'm afraid I won't be there," she told him, walking to the door.

"I don't get it. You told Taylor you'd wait for him."

Stepping into the hall, Catlin stuck her head back inside the room. "Tell Sam I'll be in touch. Tell him Saint Eloy is calling."

Chapter 41

"LINE TWO, PROFESSOR. A Mr. Saad," his secretary said on the intercom.

"Thank you."

Lifting the receiver, he took a deep breath. "Yes?"

"You are expecting me?" the voice asked.

"Yes," Montes answered. "What is your number? I'll call you right back. I don't want to talk on this line."

"I'll wait no longer than one minute," Peder Crandon said.

"There's a pay phone just outside my office."

"Fine," Crandon said, giving him the number of the public booth in the foyer of the Freer Gallery of Art on Jefferson Avenue at 12th Street.

Forty seconds later, the phone rang. Crandon picked it up in mid-ring. "Yes."

"Mr. Saad?"

"Yes."

"Montes."

"You can talk now?"

"Yes."

"You are prepared to supply me?"

"What is required?"

In brief, choppy sentences, Crandon sketched his plan for the attack on the British embassy. Then he asked for Montes's recommendations.

The professor considered the factors which would need to be

addressed: portability, power, and, of course, some type of communications device with which to monitor embassy security personnel.

Yes, he told Crandon. The necessary equipment was available immediately. Cost? Twenty thousand American. They would meet at 6:00 sharp. When the funds were paid, Crandon would be told the location of the materials. The meet? A restaurant called The Broker—in the 700 block of Pennsylvania Avenue.

"Until later, professor," Crandon said.

"Good-bye, Mr. Saad."

Disconnecting Peder Crandon, Montes deposited another quarter into the telephone and punched in the number. The call was answered on the third ring.

"Santana." The voice was Latin and thickly accented.

"Montes," the professor said softly. Then he hung up the phone.

It rang back almost immediately. "Yes," he said.

"Problemas?" Santana asked.

"I'm not sure," Montes admitted. "But it is something I think you should know."

"Diga me," the voice instructed.

Speaking in quick Spanish, Eduardo Montes tried to explain what he knew.

After he had finished, Santana suggested a personal contact: 1:00 P.M. at the Lincoln Memorial.

"But what should I do until then?" the professor asked.

"Exactly as Yasif instructed you," Santana told him. "I will have further orders at one."

The telephone went dead in Montes hands. *A personal contact?* He had met Santana only on two occasions. The first time, he thought Santana was an alias. Later, his suspicions had proved correct when at a university reception for King Juan Carlos of Spain, Eduardo Montes met Santana again. He was reintroduced to his current Soviet liaison agent under his real name: Antonio de las Marias. His position? Chief of protocol for the embassy of Spain. They had avoided all open contact since the reception.

The professor deposited a third quarter into the telephone, pushing the numbers from memory. The line to the garage apartment behind his Maryland country house was busy. He was mildly irritated. No doubt Sylvio was talking to one of the other young *Ton-ton Macoute* lieutenants living in hiding since the fall of Baby Doc Duvalier's Haitian dictatorship. Hated by the Haitian people, twenty former secret policemen had fled illegally to the Washington area after being targeted for death by the government which had replaced Duvalier. Sylvio was their technician.

Trained in violence, Sylvio was the perfect addition to his small, tight arms network. He was ruthless, trustworthy and of course, a communist. As for taking care of Yasif's instructions? Sylvio would enjoy it—he hadn't designed a device in nearly a year.

Hanging up the phone, the professor decided to try again in ten minutes. Buried on the estate, Sylvio would have to dig up the equipment, clean it, then get it to the locations Yasif had indicated.

The professor checked his watch: 12:20 P.M.

If he started by 1:00, Sylvio could have everything in place by 4:00.

Plenty of time, Montes decided, walking back to his office.

Instant detonation.

He wondered what kind of explosive Sylvio would select.

He would watch the news to find out.

Chapter 42

"TEN-TWELVE," MICHAELS answered.

"I'm downstairs," Taylor told him from the house phone in the lobby.

"You want me to check out?"

"I've already handled it," Taylor said. "Don't leave anything in the room."

"On my way." Hanging up the receiver, Michaels grabbed his kit bag and headed downstairs. As he walked out the Marriott's front doors, the horn of a dirty silver and black four-wheel-drive Chevrolet Blazer honked. *At least he's driving the big one,* Michaels thought, walking toward the truck.

"Where's Catlin?" Taylor asked.

"Not with me," Michaels said as he slammed the door. "You don't know?"

"What'd she say?"

"She'd be in touch, then something about some Saint Eloy calling her." Michaels eyed Taylor suspiciously. "She was supposed to wait for you, wasn't she?"

Nodding, Taylor pulled the Blazer into gear and drove out of the hotel parking area. "She mention anything about a man named Yasif?" he asked as they pulled onto the street.

"No," Michaels answered. "Just a Montes. Gun peddler."

"Yes," Taylor said. "Montes." *Damn,* he thought again. He had told her the general's plan on the phone: *Yasif sanction and Crandon capture.*

"Who's Yasif?" Michaels probed, sensing something else was going on, something related to his contract. "We got another player?"

"Later. When did Catlin leave?"

"Thirty seconds after she spoke to you? Why?"

Taylor didn't comment.

"Tell me what's going on," Michaels said. "I mean, I don't like this 'capture Crandon' thing in the first place. So if there's something else, I want to know about it. You owe me that much, Taylor."

Taylor knew he was right, but before he could answer, a soft beeping tone began to pulse from the dashboard. Reaching over, Taylor popped open the glove compartment and pulled out a telephone.

"Taylor," he said, hoping the call was from Catlin.

It wasn't.

"Taylor, COMSEC two-five. Metro has located the vehicle."

"Location?" Taylor asked.

"Twenty-first and F. Southwest corner."

Right at the university, Taylor thought. "They give a description?"

"Wait one," COMSEC advised.

"Montes?" Michaels asked.

Taylor nodded. "He works at George Washington University. DMV has him driving a BMW L-7, but it was a new purchase, so the license tags weren't in the box yet. I asked the locals to poke around the school. We got lucky."

"How'd you develop Montes?"

"Brits pegged him," Taylor answered.

"Taylor, COMSEC two-five."

"Go ahead, COMSEC," Taylor answered.

"Metro advises it's a silver blue with a white pinstripe."

"Tell 'em we appreciate it, COMSEC," Taylor said.

"You need them to stand by?"

"That's affirmative, COMSEC. Tell 'em we'll be the ones in

the black over silver Blazer. We should be there in about one-zero."

"COMSEC clear."

Taylor handed the handset to Michaels. "What if Montes has already powwowed with Crandon?" Michaels asked, returning the handset to the glove compartment.

Taylor looked at him sharply. "No bullshit?"

Michaels shook his head.

"Then we're fucked—at least this time around."

"No fallback plan?"

"No," Taylor admitted. "You want out?"

Looking out his window, Kelly Michaels thought about Mai Lei. "No. Like I told you, this is my last time in the saddle. I just want to make it right with you, that's all."

Taylor's mind flashed a memory of the Filipino car bomb. He knew what could happen if things weren't right—innocents got caught in the middle.

"I'll figure something out," Michaels added.

"We'll see," Taylor muttered. Privately, he didn't share Michaels's optimism. Catlin was the difference. Her actions looked anything but encouraging. Leaving unexpectedly and not telling Michaels seemed to indicate one thing: she had been turned and was a Libyan agent. When push came to shove, she'd decided to run with them. Swallowing, Taylor felt his ulcer act up. Until he learned otherwise, the entire PCAC system—RAINDANCER included—would have to be considered compromised. The security implications were devastating.

Crossing the Arlington Bridge, Taylor shot up 23rd Street past the State Department, then ran a red light against traffic as he wheeled the Blazer onto F. A block later, he pulled into the loading area behind the American Red Cross building and eased to a stop next to an unmarked District of Columbia police car.

"I owe you a drink," he told the young, freckle-faced detective driving the Ford.

"I'll take you up on that sometime," the officer grinned.

"Your BMW is parked right over there. Haven't seen anyone around it yet."

Twisting around, Taylor looked over his shoulder. "You do good work," he smiled politely. "I'll buy you two."

"Anytime," the detective said, starting his car and driving out onto the street.

Taylor moved the Blazer to the right of an overflowing trash dumper and backed it in so it would appear that they were moving cargo. Then, with Eduardo Montes's BMW less than a half block away, he turned off the motor and began to wait.

"Yasif?" Michaels reminded him.

Taylor looked at him levelly. "He's Libyan," he said softly. "Catlin was supposed to tell you that in addition to capturing Crandon, you were supposed to kill Yasif."

"But she didn't."

"No, Kelly. She didn't."

Michaels thought about it for a second. He realized why Taylor was worried. "You don't know where she is, do you?"

Taylor sucked deeply on the Marlboro. "No," he said, letting the smoke drift between his lips. "No idea."

For the next minute or so, both men sat in silence, staring blankly at the silver BMW.

Michaels finally spoke. "The serpent sheds her skin?"

There was no response from the driver's side of the truck.

"I don't like it, Taylor."

"Neither do I."

Shifting in the seat, Kelly Michaels looked over to Taylor. "I think you ought to tell me about the Creole lady."

Taylor did.

Spoken out loud, the facts sounded even worse.

Chapter 43

ENTERING HIS HOTEL, Yasif saw Catlin Broussard immediately. She was sitting on one of the overstuffed sofas next to the deserted lobby-bar area.

She looks nervous, he thought. It was a good sign. Walking to the sofa, he sat down next to her. "Surely it cannot be that bad," he said.

"I feel it is. They've marked you."

"Me?" He was surprised. "Why?"

"I wasn't told. But they have. Crandon's to be taken alive and you're to be . . ." She let the words trail off.

"Do not worry my little one," he smiled, reaching over and patting her hand. "The mirror is sometimes parallax."

Catlin stared into his eyes. "I don't understand."

"There is no need. Are you going back?"

She shook her head. "I don't want to."

Any final decision at this point would be premature, Yasif decided. It would be better to wait and see how the next few hours unfolded.

"Here," he said, giving her his room key. "Wait in my suite. I shall join you shortly."

Taking the key, Catlin stood. "I want to go with you," she told him. "I'm tired of the pretense."

"It will be difficult. After this, I shall return to Libya for good."

"Then take me with you."

"Perhaps I shall," he whispered. "Now go upstairs. I will be there in few minutes."

Leaning over, Catlin kissed him tenderly on the cheek, then she turned and walked slowly toward the elevators. As she got on one, Yasif headed to the men's restroom just behind the hotel gift shop.

Shoving the door open, he surveyed the inside quickly. With the exception of one occupied stall, it was empty. He decided the other man was not a problem. Stepping to the wall phone, he deposited the coins and punched the WATS number to the Libyan switchboard in New York.

"American Mission," a voice answered in accented English.

"I need a vehicle and a hardpack at my hotel," he ordered. "One hour." Hanging up the phone, he left the restroom and headed for the elevators.

The hardpack was a weapon: a Browning High Power 9 millimeter pistol, complete with two fourteen-round magazines. It would be untraceable. Yassif was an expert with the semiautomatic and respected its firepower. The maximum effective range was only 50 yards, but considering its intended use, this was not a liability.

He wanted to watch Peder Crandon's face just before he killed him. He wanted to watch the Irishman beg for his life.

Stepping in the glass elevator, Yasif rode to his floor in silence. But Crandon would come later, he told himself. Now it was time for Catlin. Time for the questions. Time for the answers.

When he was sure about her loyalties, then there was time to get her to Tripoli. After a hysterectomy, she would make an excellent whore.

Chapter 44

TAYLOR WAS LIGHTING his fourth Marlboro of the surveillance when he saw Eduardo Montes. "Bingo," he said softly.

"Short dude in the trenchcoat?" Michaels asked, sitting up in his seat.

Taylor nodded. "Looks just like his driver's-license picture."

"They never look the part, do they?" Michaels commented.

"Not from what I've seen," Taylor agreed, watching carefully as the Cuban jaywalked across F Street, headed directly to the BMW, unlocked the door, and climbed inside.

Taylor turned the ignition on the Blazer. "What are you carrying?"

"Skorpion," Michaels answered.

"What else?"

"The Marakov."

Grunting approval, Taylor shifted the truck into gear as the BMW inched from the curb, turned right, and passed within 20 feet.

Driving with one foot on the brake, Taylor rolled slowly onto the street, picked the BMW out of traffic, careful to maintain a four-car buffer between them.

"What about you?" Michaels asked, as they trailed Montes through a left-hand turn onto 23rd Street. "You still lugging around the old Colt automatic?"

"Still," Taylor nodded. He knew the .45 caliber pistol was generally considered passé since the military had gone to 9 millimeters, but the Colt had served him well and putting it on the shelf would have been like abandoning an old friend. "The same one I was first issued in Berlin," he said, immediately embarrassed by the pride in his voice. "Nineteen and sixty."

"It's a relic," Michaels said cynically as they splashed across Virginia Avenue heading toward C Street. "Give me a nine mike-mike anytime."

He was babbling, Taylor realized. Nervous. Taylor understood; he felt it, too.

Suddenly Taylor saw the BMW swerve to the right lane, its brake lights flashing as Montes entered the traffic circle around the Lincoln Memorial. "What the hell is he doing now?" Taylor asked.

"Parking," Michaels said flatly as the BMW pulled to the curb and stopped.

"Great!" Taylor sighed. "Fine time to go sightseeing. Well, we just can't stop in the middle of the street. Keep an eye on him, Kelly. There's a bus stop on the reflection pool side. I'll pull in there."

As Taylor accelerated toward the bus area, Michaels turned and watched Eduardo Montes climb out of the BMW, sprint across the traffic circle, and walk up the steps to the Lincoln Memorial.

"He's on the ground," he told Taylor. "Got any binoculars?"

"There's a C-90 in the console," Taylor said, pulling the Blazer to a stop between two yellow school buses.

Reaching between the front seats, Michaels popped the console lid. Inside, he found a 33-power Celeston spotting scope. "Nice," he smiled, lifting the 4-pound, 12″ instrument and twisting off the protective lens covers. "I'll bet Mai Lei would get a real kick out of one of these back on the island."

"If this works out, you can have it." Taylor said. "Here, let me look."

Since the Lincoln Memorial was on Taylor's side of the

truck, Michaels passed the scope and waited while Taylor crouched low in the seat and focused.

"See anything?" he asked after a moment.

"Just a bunch of kids," Taylor answered, scanning the milling crowd rapidly. "Kids and a . . . wait . . . yes. I see him. It's a meet."

"Crandon?"

"No," Taylor said. "Latin-type. They've moved behind a column . . . shit!"

"Let me see."

Taylor ignored the request. "Okay. They're coming out now. It's another Latin for sure. Five-ten. One-forty. Well-dressed. Early sixties. Looks kinda like a thin Mario Lanza."

"Who?" Michaels asked.

"Before your time," Taylor said, giving Michaels the scope. "Focus on Lincoln's left knee, then drop it down a little to the left."

"I got 'em," Michaels told him. "Looks like the other guy is doing all the talking. You read lips?"

"No," Taylor said. "You?"

"No." Michaels passed the scope back to Taylor. "Third column from the left."

Taylor focused the scope, this time extremely tight on the face of the other man. "You know something, Kelly?"

"What?"

"This second guy looks kinda familiar to me."

"Spook?"

"No," Taylor said softly.

"Cuban?"

"No. Not that either."

"Maybe he's another gun peddler?" Michaels suggested.

"Maybe. But I'm thinking . . . okay, wait a second. Montes is walking away. Whatever they were talking about, they're finished. You still see the BMW?"

"Yeh," Michaels answered. "Just hang loose . . . he'll have to drive right past us to get out of the traffic circle."

"Well, let me know," Taylor said, putting the lens covers back on the scope and returning it to the console. Lighting a cigarette, he began to think about the other man. He couldn't place the face. Not just yet. But just like *valentine* had, he knew it would eventually come. He just hoped it came in time.

"Okay," Michaels said. "Let's roll."

A moment later, the BMW slid past on the Blazer's left. As it shot by, Taylor pulled in behind, again taking the trail, again leaving the buffer.

As they drove past the Federal Reserve Building, Michaels looked over at Taylor. "You never told me."

"What?" Taylor asked.

"Who's Mario Lanza?"

Taylor smiled. "He played Caruso in the movie."

"A singer, huh?"

"Yeah," Taylor nodded. "Something like that."

From that point, their surveillance continued in silence as they sped across the District, then deep into the Maryland countryside. As they passed Rockville, Taylor glanced at his watch. It was 2:10 P.M. and still no word from Catlin.

He was not a happy man.

Chapter 45

"I THINK YOU'D better look at this," Catlin said as Yasif entered his suite.

Curiously, she was sitting cross-legged on the carpet directly in front of the television set. "What?" he asked. "Something about Crandon?"

"Something about Ursula," she corrected. "She's dead."

"Dead?" He walked behind Catlin and sat on the edge of the bed. "Where?"

"Dulles Airport," Catlin told him, as she turned up the volume. "Listen."

". . . FBI sources confirm that the body discovered just forty minutes ago has been positively identified as Ursula Brandt, a thirty-year-old, self-avowed West German terrorist . . ."

Yasif watched as a photograph of Ursula was displayed on the screen. She looked beautiful.

". . . Brandt, a former fashion model, has been linked with numerous bombings and assassinations throughout Europe and was wanted by both British and French authorities in connection with two unrelated homicides . . . "

The anchorman came back on camera.

". . . We are now going live to our reporter on the scene, Cindy Ward, who is standing by at the Dulles Airport Marriott. Cindy, are you there?"

Mesmerized, Yasif watched as the scene shifted to a young black woman standing outside the hotel. In the background, he could clearly see swarms of emergency vehicles, lights flashing, as they darted between a thin line of uniformed police officers who were attempting to control a crowd of onlookers.

"Yes, Bob," she answered. "I am here at the Dulles Marriott, where authorities are attempting to piece together the scence of a bizzare and violent murder."

"Cindy, what do we know at this time?" the anchorman asked. "Well, Bob," she began. "I've just finished speaking to Jim Bounty, the special agent in charge of the Washington FBI, and frankly, they don't seem to know much more than we do."

She consulted her notes as she continued. "Apparently, the body of Ms. Brandt was discovered by a maid at approximately one-twenty. Local police alerted the FBI after an initial investigation determined Ursula Brandt's background."

"And she was definitely a terrorist?"

"Yes, Bob, so it appears. Authorities are making no statement as to why she was in the United States. She arrived in Washington this morning on a Lufthansa flight direct from Munich, but beyond that, the FBI is declining to comment on any other aspect of this case, including motives or suspects."

The camera cut back to the studio and the anchorman looked directly into the lens. "Thank you, Cindy. We will get back to you later. Of course, for our viewers, we will keep you posted on any new developments in this baffling case. Now a word from our local sponsors."

Catlin turned off the sound. Yasif felt cheated. It was not Ursula's death that bothered him, it was the fact that only one person could have known when and where she was entering the country: Peder Crandon. "Sorrow is a two edged sword," he sighed. "One side sharper than the other."

Pulling himself wearily to his feet, Yasif walked around Catlin and into the bathroom to wash his face. *Bastard*, he thought, splashing the cool water into his eyes. Crandon had now added yet another insult to his long list of outrages. "Until your death, my Irish friend,'' he vowed to his reflection in the mirror. ''Until your death.''

Drying his face, he walked back to the bed and lay down. ''I am tired, Catlin,'' he said softly. ''I must nap for a few minutes.''

Standing, Catlin moved to the edge of the bed and sat down ''I *am* sorry,'' she whispered, touching his face with her fingertips. ''I know this is difficult for you.''

Reaching up, Yasif caressed her fingers with his. ''You will be my queen,'' he told her, pulling her closer. ''And I shall be your king.''

Leaning over, Catlin kissed him fully, gently on the mouth. Then, as his hands began to slide down her body, she pulled away.

''Please,'' she said. ''I want to be clean for you. We must wait until tomorrow.''

''Very well,'' he smiled, closing his eyes and allowing sleep to come as Catlin stroked his cheek tenderly.

Chapter 46

EDUARDO MONTES SHIFTED the BMW into fourth gear and admired the BMW's surge of horsepower as he drove deep into the Maryland countryside. He felt good, much more sure of himself since his meeting with Santana.

Snapping in a cassette, the tape deck began to emit the upbeat big-band sound of Glenn Miller as he relaxed, humming along in time with the music. Ahead, a little-used highway resembled a slender ribbon of platinum, a flashing reflection of diffused sunlight slicing through the columns of maple trees lining the asphalt.

"Pennsylvania-six-five-thousand," he sang, turning up the volume.

Slowing for a curve, he pressed a button on the console and the BMW's sunroof slid back, as cold, scrubbed air whipped around his head. He breathed deeply of its scent.

Only in America, he thought, squeezing the soft leather of the seat. In Havana, or even Moscow, such a lifestyle would not be permitted.

But this was his reward. Luxury not even reserved for the heads of Socialist states. He would change nothing. Indeed, he loved Western decadence almost as much as he enjoyed the place he called home. *Que lindo!* What a magnificent waste of space and money. It was so very befitting of his indulgence.

Braking hard, he wheeled between the large stone pillars defining his driveway; then, accelerating again, watched excitedly as the spectacle of the estate unfolded as he sped toward the main house.

Situated on seventy-eight acres, it was a residence of baronial grandeur. Designed in colonial fieldstone, the twenty-two room interior was nothing less than a showcase in the classic country-manse tradition.

A raised central entry hall overlooked any number of the lower areas; the expansive living room with massive stone fireplace, the formal dining room opening onto a stone terrace. Even his private library, with its breath of gentlemanly intimacy replete with fireplace, paneling, and display cases stuffed with dozens of antique blackpowder handguns.

Formal landscaped gardens surrounded the main residential area from the remainder of the estate. The country house, as he called it, contained six bedrooms, each with a private bath, in addition to the professor's own suite of rooms.

Pulling the BMW behind the house and into the five-car garage, he parked next to his vintage Aston-Martin grand tourer coupe and climbed out. The Jeep Wagoneer was gone, he noticed, so Sylvio was using it to shuffle the equipment.

As he entered through the rear door, Eduardo Montes considered his instructions from Santana. They were ambitious, but who was he to question the plan? Santana had told him to pass along the order, and he would do just that. Santana had promised a lucrative arrangement with the *Tupamaros* movement, which had again reared its head in Uruguay.

Stopping in the kitchen, he called to Inez, his Honduran cook of fifteen years. "Sylvio has called yet?"

An ancient Miskito Indian woman looked up from the sink. "He call back," she said, nodding.

"When?"

The woman turned back to the sink. "Don't know."

He shook his head as he left the kitchen and walked to his study. One would think she would have learned to tell. She never had. But it was a small price to pay for her culinary expertise. Her *olla podrida* casserole was an art form in itself.

Squatting in front of the study's fireplace, Eduardo Montes stacked the kindling and lit a match to it. The flames began to spit softly as it caught. Then, standing he walked to his desk chair, sat down, and glanced at the 19th-century Breguet Souscription pocket watch ticking quietly on the blotter: 2:35 P.M.

Excellent, he thought. If Sylvio had called, then things were proceeding as planned.

Two blocks down from the well-maintained mansion were Samuel Taylor and Kelly Michaels. ''Nice place,'' Taylor said, craning his head back to look at the house.

''Must be a real shortage of Cuban art teachers.''

''What do you think?'' Taylor asked.

''I'm not sure. Pull over to the fence under those trees. I want to take a look.''

Taylor eased the Blazer forward to a spot next to the six-foot stone wall surrounding the property. Pulling onto the grass, he inched along until the front bumper touched the rock.

Reaching into the console, Michaels grabbed the spotting scope and opened his door. ''Down with the tyrants and evil gentry,'' he quoted, climbing out.

''A Michaelism?''

''Mao,'' he winked, closing the door. ''Tis the font of all we hold dear.''

Michaels moved to the front of the Blazer, stepped on the front bumper, and stood up, laying the scope on the top of the wall as he began to survey the grounds.

He was good, Taylor realized. Different, but good just the same. It was unfortunate that the wedge was embedded so deeply between them. He would probably make a hell of a friend.

As he looked through the scope, Kelly Michaels spotted that the grounds were wired—tightly: pressure-sensitive grid patterns backed up by infrared sensors. He looked at the house. Nothing. The garage. Two cars: the BMW and an old sports car.

He focused tighter on the rooms. Empty. Empty. *Montes*. He zoomed the lens back a bit. Left front of the house. He zoomed back farther. The roof. A chimney—smoking. He zoomed in tight. It was a study. Tighter. Montes sitting behind a desk. Doing what? Zoom out a bit. Nothing. Just sitting.

Above him, Michaels could hear the distant rumblings of thunder and was aware of the sky growing darker. It would be sleeting in a few minutes.

Eduardo Montes sat patiently, watching the fire as he waited for Sylvio's call.

Growing in intensity, the flames twirled, quivering before his eyes as the study was filled with the sweet scent of scorched bark. "Yasif," he sighed. Poor bastard.

Prior to the conversation of the Lincoln Memorial, he thought the Libyan-Soviet connection was all roses. Santana had told him otherwise. The revelations were remarkably astute, and Montes was glad he'd had the foresight to pass along the information.

As Santana explained, the Muslims were acutely sensitive to the Central Committee because they were impossible to control. They even refused to control themselves. Open warfare, assassination within their ranks, political throat-cuttings between those striving for power . . . even the Kremlin could not control the rivalries. The Muslims persisted in petty internecine warfare.

A United Kingdom of Islam? Santana had laughed at the suggestion. It was a joke—a joke which would find itself crushed when it approached the realm of possibility.

To the Kremlin, Santana had said, it was a matter of survival. A matter of economics. To meet financial commitments to a host of Soviet satellite nations, Moscow had been forced to sell oil reserves to offset the monies lost when oil prices plunged in 1986. More oil had to be sold to keep profits up.

Unfortunately, by 1990, the inbalance between price and production would reach a point where no amount of new drilling could keep pace without dipping into reserves. At that point, Moscow would withdraw support to the satellites in order to keep its own economic security intact.

Control of Middle Eastern hydrocarbons was critical to long-range Soviet planning. A United Kingdom of Islam was certainly not part of the strategy.

The Iranians? Libyans? Syrians? Of course they were being used. Why not? Their various terrorist "foreign policies" were not altogether distasteful to the KGB.

Moreover, the attacks gave Moscow the opportunity to cite terrorism as a cancer of Western societies while criticizing violence in the process. The fine line between condemnation and support, interrelated yet apart. The constant twisting of the propaganda machine.

The Americans were the real hypocrites, he decided. Always first to condemn terrorism of others, they, too, had set examples. Granted that the methods employed by Islamic guerrillas were brutal, they were less inhumane than the American bombing raids over North Vietnam. Or the Allied bombings of Dresden and the other German cities during the Second World War.

And what of Hiroshima? Of Nagasaki? By comparison, the entire Islamic world could not begin to equal the trail of destruction paved by the Americans. Even the targets—the cities. There had been no *military* significance attached to their selection; rather, the purpose of the carnage was an expressed intention to terrorize civilians and undermine morale.

As a Communist, Eduardo Montes could not ignore the pleasure he experienced at Washington's consternation with Peder Crandon's activities. The man had no specific target, but waged a general terrorizing of the British in the same manner as the American bombing raids.

It was a sweet justice, Montes decided, allowing himself the luxury of a small chuckle. A sardonic justice nurtured by the malevolence of immaculate loathing. *Que magnificencia!*

Suddenly his thoughts were interrupted by the ringing of the telephone on the corner of his desk.

"Yes," he answered. It was Sylvio. Eduardo Montes listened carefully, and when the Haitian finished, he hung up without responding. It was 3:30 P.M., and Sylvio already had everything in place. Always eager, Sylvio was a fine man. He was 30 minutes ahead of schedule. Montes would remember to give him a raise in salary.

Eduardo Montes picked up the receiver and tapped out the number to the Washington Hyatt Regency.

It was time to set the deception in motion, time to allow Yasif to write his sonnet of death. It was what Santana had wanted.

Chapter 47

WHEN THE TELEPHONE rang in the suite, Yasif jerked awake. He felt peculiar—anticipation, maybe. He ignored it and glanced at Catlin. She had also been awakened and was watching him curiously.

The phone rang a second time. Yasif grabbed for the receiver. "Yes," he answered.

"It is in place," Eduardo Montes told him.

"Everything as planned?" Yasif asked.

"As you instructed. You will find the vehicle in East Potomac Park. A U-Haul rental van. The package is in the rear."

Yasif was pleased. "Excellent, Eduardo," he smiled. "And the other?"

"Also in place. The location you indicated. It has been hidden in an abandoned basement—the Peyton Inn. He will be informed at eight P.M."

"Fine, Eduardo. Your rewards will come. I will see to it personally."

Hanging up the receiver, Yasif turned to Catlin. "It will be over within two hours," he told her. "Crandon will be arriving to pick up his weapons at five-thirty. I will be waiting for him."

"Do you want me to go with you?" she offered.

"No, it is something I must do alone. Do you know where East Potomac Park is? The cache is there," Yasif explained, realizing that she had heard only his side of the conversation. "Inside a rental truck."

"Do you need my car?"

Yasif shook his head. "No. I have one."

Walking to the dresser at the foot of the bed, Yasif picked up a Washington visitor's guide. Opening it to the District of Columbia, he passed it over to Catlin. "Show me this East Potomac Park."

Catlin put her finger on the spot. "Are you sure you don't need me?"

"Not this time," he said, kissing her on the forehead. "I shall be fine. Wait for me here." Yasif tore the map out of the magazine and shoved it into his coat pocket. A moment later, she was alone in the suite.

After waiting for a few minutes, assuring herself that he was not returning unexpectedly, Catlin walked to the bedside table and picked up the telephone.

What was it Yasif had said about the mirror being parallax?

He was wrong. Mirrors were also two-way.

"It's getting cold out there," Michaels said, climbing back inside the Blazer. "Give me some heat."

Turning on the ignition, Taylor flipped the heater fan on high. "What's the layout?"

"Tight," Michaels told him. "Real tight."

"Electronics?"

Michaels nodded. "He has a double-grid defensive matrix. Infrared. Pressure. Probably something else I didn't even see."

"Can you beat it?" Taylor asked.

"Probably," Michaels said, leaning over and putting his hands next to the warm-air vent. "I looked at the telephone lines. No external monitoring feed. I guess it's just local. Maybe it isn't even on. Problem is, we won't know unless it activates. Kinda risky. I mean, I'd hate for him to know we're coming."

"Any life?"

"Besides Montes?"

Taylor nodded. "Yeah, some old woman shuffling around. Nobody else. Montes is sitting in a study. Two cars . . . the BMW, some older foreign job."

"What do you think?"

Michaels shrugged. "Your guess is as good as mine. I don't see any point in running on him yet. He damned sure isn't going to help us, and Crandon definitely isn't in there. If you don't have anything else up your sleeve, I'd guess we'd better just wait for Montes to make the next move."

No, Taylor thought, *all sleeves were empty at the moment*. "Well, I guess we continue to sit," he said. "Take five before you get back on the wall."

Michaels cut his eyes over. "You're making me work for my money this time, aren't you?"

"If you get pneumonia, I'll have Uncle Sugar give you a week's worth of penicillin on the cuff."

"I'm allergic to penicillin," Michaels teased.

"Sounds like a personal problem," Taylor smiled, lighting a cigarette. "You've got four minutes now."

"And counting?"

"And counting," Taylor nodded.

"COMSEC two-five," the voice answered.

"This is Broussard," Catlin said into the receiver. "You get anything?"

"Wait one, Broussard."

Catlin was put on hold. A moment later, the voice returned. "That's affirmative, Broussard. One call. Approximately fourteen seconds time lapse. You need a date-time grouping?"

"No," Catlin answered. "Have the tape transcribed and send it to the Section . . . attention Taylor."

"You want the intercept to remain operational?"

Catlin thought about if for a moment. "Until further notice," she ordered. "Now I need a phone patch."

"Go ahead with your number, Broussard."

* * *

The four minutes were up. Just as Kelly Michaels began to climb reluctantly out of the Blazer, the truck was filled with the soft beeping of an incoming telephone call.

Reaching into the glove compartment, he pulled out the handset and passed it over to Taylor.

"Go ahead, COMSEC," Taylor answered.

"It's me," Catlin told him.

"Where are you?"

"In Yasif's suite."

Taylor was cautious. "I think we need to talk."

"I agree," Catlin said. "No time now though. Yasif is on his way to meet Crandon. He and Montes have worked a trap."

Taylor sat upright in his seat. "Is this righteous, Catlin?"

"Of course," she shot back. "What'd you think—I'd gone over? Get real. I'll take Leavenworth over Libya any day of the week."

Taylor didn't smile. "Where's this going down?"

"East Potomac Park. Five-thirty."

Taylor glanced at his watch; 4:05 P.M. "Okay," he said. "We're rolling. Hold on a second."

Pulling the Blazer into reverse, Taylor backed away from the wall and out onto the road. Then, straightening the wheels, he jerked the transmission into low and floored the accelerator.

"What else?" he asked Catlin as the truck shot forward, speeding past the entrance gates to Eduardo Montes's estate and back towards Washington.

"The goodies are in a rental truck."

Taylor made a note of it. "What about you?" he asked. "I want you out of there now."

"No," she answered. "Too soon. Something messes up at the park, and I'm the only one inside."

Taylor didn't like it. "Bullshit, Cat——"

"Sam," she interrupted. "It's all covered. When I left Kelly's room, I called COMSEC and had a wire placed on Yasif's telephone. We've got it all on tape—Montes, Yasif, the whole ball of wax.''

''So get out of there,'' he repeated, his voice louder.

''No,'' she told him. ''Like I said, something screws up, I'm still inside. Fire and ice, Sam . . . it's the only way to play it.''

The handset went dead in Taylor's ear. He handed it back to Michaels.

''I gather we've got a new card?'' Michaels asked, returning the telephone to the glove compartment.

''East Potomac Park,'' Taylor nodded. ''Five-thirty. Both Yasif and Crandon.''

''How do you want to work it?'' Michaels asked.

''Depends . . . have to check the layout first.''

''That's not what I meant,'' Michaels told him. ''I mean, do you still want Crandon alive?''

Taylor thought about Jennifer Bishop. ''No, Kelly, I don't.''

''Well, then, my fee has just doubled.''

Taylor shook his head. ''No, it hasn't,'' he said flatly. ''Crandon is going to be mine.''

Michaels arched an eyebrow. ''You sure you can still hack it?''

The question hung heavily in the air, but Taylor refused to respond. Directing his attention to the road, he began to whistle softly to himself.

''Some Enchanted Evening.''

Kelly Michaels thought it odd.

Chapter 48

PEDER CRANDON ORDERED his first scotch and continued to ignore the others in the restaurant. Purposely, he had arrived over an hour early for the meeting with Eduardo Montes. He needed time to observe, to reassure himself that the Cuban would not attempt to cross him. To get comfortable, to be able to maintain some measure of control over the negotiations.

The Broker was another one of those out-of-the-way places which seemed to open monthly in Washington's inner circle. Once an old hardware store, it had been converted into a quiet cafe boasting a small but enthusiastic clientele.

A single arched window illuminated the interior by directing outside lighting onto highly polished brick walls and mirrors. Dimly lit, a slatted ceiling added to the atmosphere by diffusing the reflections cast from brass lamps into a smooth infinity as they drowned themselves in the hand-waxed mahogany tables.

It was the darkness that Peder Crandon liked. And, considering the Cuban's choice of a meeting place, he predicted that Eduardo Montes would be the perfect host.

With the decision on the next target made, Peder Crandon looked forward to the professor's arrival. He was eager to receive the equipment, destroy the embassy, and flee the country. Already he could smell the cool mountain air of the Peruvian Andes.

It would be a good vacation.

The waiter returned and Peder Crandon took a sip of the

scotch, letting the liquid drip down the back of his throat. He wasn't being forced to leave America, nor was there any concern being captured. The fact was—Washington bored him.

He had a much higher calling. A duty to continue onward, to even more spectacular operations. The Bahamas, Mauritius, Australia, New Zealand. All those sniveling countries which recognized the whore Elizabeth as their chief of state.

The liquor was tasty; it gave him thought. Consummate ideas. Studies in power. Revelations. *Chop-knick, knick-chop.*

If the British were good, he projected, *then am I evil?*

Yes. I am the antithesis of their paltry morality. Amazing. Why couldn't they see it? It was the exquisite difference between good and evil.

A sip of scotch.

But the fact of evil, he decided, was itself the most powerful argument against the existence of God. For if God *were* all-powerful, then He would not permit evil's existence. No. But since evil did exist, then God could not be stronger. The vicar had been wrong all along.

A sip. Another. A gulp and the signaling of the waiter for a fresh drink. Munching ice—waiting.

Could there be another point of view? He thought about it. Yes, he decided. If evil existed, then God could not prevent it. In that case, the vicar was wrong again. For God could not be omnipotent. Or, if he *could* prevent it and declined, then he would not be benevolent. But then a Being who was neither omnipotent nor benevolent could not be God. For the vicar had used both terms in the definition of a divine entity.

Returning with Crandon's second scotch, the waiter placed it on the table and walked away.

Why yes, Crandon decided. He knew the answer *now*. It was the purpose of his own existence. He had become the true personification of evil, and, as such, he was not being stopped by God.

Taking a sip of the fresh drink, Peder Crandon allowed

himself a sly grin. Finally it was clear. He was more powerful than God.

In the shadow of the Capitol Dome, East Potomac Park was essentially a reclaimed and landscaped swampland bordering the Potomac River. A peaceful place, it was popular during warmer months; however, in late November, it was icy and deserted by the time Samuel Taylor slid the Blazer onto the access road.

It was getting dark, so he switched on the headlights. Darkness, with a snow flurry beginning. He glanced at his watch: 5:12 P.M. The weather and traffic slowed the drive from Maryland by fifteen minutes. He hoped they had enough time to set up before Crandon and Yasif arrived.

"See anything?" he asked Michaels.

"Dead-looking trees and ice," Michaels answered. "I kinda expect to see Doctor Zhivago to come riding by."

Stopping the Blazer, Taylor flipped the headlights on high beam. "There," he pointed through the windshield. "See the taillights?"

"Flick the brights again," Michaels told him, reaching to the floorboard and picking up his submachine gun.

Taylor pushed the column switcher three quick times. This time they both saw the reflectors winking in the distance.

"You ready?" he asked.

Michaels jacked a round into the Skorpion's breech. "Take it in easy."

Pulling the .45 from his waistband, Taylor placed it on the seat between his thighs, and they began to roll slowly toward the reflectors.

One hundred yards.

Fifty.

He stopped at 20. In the headlights, the words *U-Haul* were clearly visible—orange on a cream van door.

Parked in a tight cul-de-sac, the rental truck was sitting

parallel to three snow-covered concrete picnic tables less than 30 feet from the backdrop of the river's east bank.

"Suggestions?" he asked Michaels.

Skorpion at the ready, Michaels cracked his door ajar. "Deserted," he said. "Open. With the river behind, there's no place for Crandon to go." He looked around. "They've got it like a dope ripoff. My guess is that Yasif will wait for Crandon to get to the truck, then move in and pop him when he comes out."

"Yes," Taylor agreed. "With this weather, a scope would be useless. It'll have to be close."

Michaels nodded. "Which means we can ambush the shit out of them. I'll be ground hammer; you use the truck as the anvil." He pointed to Taylor's left. "You've got 4-wheel drive in this thing. You back it into that clump of shrubs over there, kill the lights and nobody will spot you if you can get in deep enough."

"You'll be behind?"

"Yeah," Michaels said. "Between the U-Haul and the riverbank. When our two boys get together, I'll run on 'em from the back; you block the front."

Taylor understood. Time was running, so anything fancier was out of the question. "Good as any," he told Michaels, reaching down and engaging the Blazer's 4-wheel drive and putting the truck into reverse.

"See you in the movies," Michaels said as he hopped out and slammed the door behind him.

Killing the lights, Taylor turned around and looking out the side window, began to back toward the underbrush, the Blazer jerking violently as its tires ate their way over the curb and into the muddy ice lining the pavement.

As Taylor pulled away, Michaels turned and sprinted toward the U-Haul. He had noticed a break in the trees behind the truck and planned to hide behind a low rise 15 yards from the swirling waters.

As he reached the truck, he ran to the left between the front bumper and a thick, gnarled oak tree. At exactly 5:16 P.M., his right foot broke a thin copper triggering wire activating the MV-5K pressure fuse, which in turn detonated the Soviet TM-46 antitank mine. As instructed, Sylvio had booby-trapped four sides and inside the truck so that ''instant detonation'' would be achieved.

Kelly Michaels felt no pain. Nor did he even realize he had tripped the wire. Running through the darkness, shielding his eyes from the blowing cold, he went from life to death without a thought, vaporized instantly in a blast of heat, concussion, and molten metal as the van blew up and became a spectacular plume of orange-blue whiteness.

Fifty yards away, Taylor's temple slammed against the steering wheel as the Blazer rocked with initial concussion. Groggy, eyes fixed with horror, he forced himself to look. There was nothing but twisted metal and flames.

He screamed, then caught himself. It was Manila again. The nightmare. Washington—a new nightmare. Car bombs. He began to groan. The nightmare returned as he began to slide into a charcoal void; he fought the images away, but they refused to die.

His brain flashing. Disjointed shadows. The beast again, nipping at the tendrils of his sanity. Manila-Washington. He began to cough. To sweat. More shadows. Candles. Burning cars. Flag-draped coffins floating on amber altars.

He couldn't stop the *mindburn*, so he forced himself to watch.

It was eyes. The accusing eyes of his wife. Then Michaels's eyes. Then the four eyes together. Fixed. Whispering hushed chants of indictment against him. His work. His trembling soul marched in half-time toward them. A private star chamber imploded in mind-throbbing violence.

Then it was dark. Sleep? Dream? Awake? He knew no difference.

Numbed by the concussion, Taylor began to pant. The beast returned to form, to grow, to develop into something more human. Taylor screamed in recognition.

He remembered them. It was his wife now. His wife and Kelly Michaels. Together they were changing the beast. It had become their friend. It welcomed them. Accepted them. Lifted them up toward a clear cobalt sky. It was time to move forward, they were telling Taylor, time to forget the past. Michaels begging her forgiveness, she giving it openly.

Then they were gone. Washed away in the crystalline light of absolute purity as the cleansing of Samuel Taylor's guilt became complete. It was over now, he realized as he slowly regained consciousness. His contrition had been consummated.

Rubbing his eyes, Taylor reached to the glove compartment and pulled out the telephone. For the first time, it was clear. Manila had been Michaels's fault, but he accepted the blame. Now the book was closed. It was a strange melancholy feeling.

"COMSEC two-five," a voice answered.

"Taylor," he breathed into the receiver. "I need a sweep team at East Potomac Park."

"Injuries?"

"One," Taylor said, "Deceased—a friendly."

"That's clear, Taylor. Sweep team en route."

Taking a deep breath, Taylor didn't respond. Tossing the telephone onto the passenger's seat, he pulled the Blazer into forward and began the twenty minute drive to the general's residence.

Brayden had to be told. Catlin was *his* person. Why had she set them up with the bomb? He was in anguish.

For the first time in thirty years, Samuel Taylor felt like quitting the circuit. *Gypsy war dancer?*

It seemed he'd forgotten the steps.

Chapter 49

PARKED SOME 200 yards away on the opposite bank of the river, Yasif watched the explosion in East Potomac Park with amusement.

It was always best to be sure, he reminded himself. Always best to test. Man, woman, it really made no difference what came from their mouths; it was their actions which proved to be the true measure of their loyalty. Catlin had failed the test. Now she would have to be eliminated.

Yasif drove onto the expressway and crossed the 14th Street Bridge, driving back to his hotel slowly. Besides Montes, she was the only one who knew the rendezvous and time. The explosion proved her collusion with the British or Americans.

The only item remaining was the meeting with Peder Crandon in Annapolis. He would kill the Irishman, and then Catlin Broussard.

Eduardo Montes was following instructions perfectly.

Pulling into the driveway of the Foxhall residence, Taylor saw the British embassy Cadillac near the front doors. Prescott. He guessed the general had already told him about the truck bomb.

Parking the Blazer a few feet from the limousine's rear bumper, he climbed out and walked toward the porch. The door was opened by the general before he reached it. "COMSEC advised me you ordered a sweep team?" Brayden said.

"East Potomac Park," Taylor explained. "We got turned around; Michaels bought it."

Walking into the foyer, the general closed the door, and Taylor found himself standing between the general and Prescott in the small holding area between the front door and the hall. Neither man made any effort to move farther into the house. Taylor predicted a short meeting.

"Sir Elliot," he said politely.

"Taylor," Prescott replied.

"I need an explanation, Sam," the general told him.

Taylor glanced at Prescott.

"Explain." Brayden made it an order.

Reluctant in the presence of the Englishman, Taylor did as he was told. Listening carefully, Thomas Brayden began to rock back and forth on his heels—a gesture, Taylor knew, which indicated that he was consciously attempting to control his temper in the face of Sir Elliot.

"So where do we go from here?" Brayden asked as Taylor finished talking.

"Find Catlin," Taylor said quickly. "Cut our losses."

Before commenting, the general looked at Prescott. "Well, we won't keep you any longer, Sir Elliot," he smiled rather thinly. "I know you have other meetings to attend."

Prescott took the hint. "Yes," he said, making an exaggerated show of checking his watch. "It's past six. I'm needed at the embassy to tidy up a few details prior to the prime minister's visit."

Brayden opened the door for him. "I will keep you advised."

As he stepped toward the door, Prescott looked directly at Taylor. "I don't have to tell you who will be held responsible if anything happens to upset the prime minister's plans." It was said with the sharkmouth smile. "I'll be in touch within the hour, Good evening, gentlemen."

As the Englishman walked out, Brayden closed the door and

looked at Taylor. ''Just what in the hell do I tell the president? I'm meeting with him tonight. I'm supposed to have some answers.''

''Tell him the truth,'' Taylor shrugged. ''Tell him we think Catlin's gone over. Ursula Brandt's dead. And Yasif is either hunting or not hunting Crandon himself. I don't know what to believe anymore, general.''

''What about Montes?'' Brayden asked.

''I don't know that, either,'' Taylor admitted. ''We pulled off him to go with the information Catlin gave me.''

''Do we need more people in on this?''

Taylor shook his head. ''Not enough time to get them pulled in and briefed. My gut feeling is that Crandon is going to try for the prime minister.''

The general stiffened. ''I've already covered that with Sir Elliot. He feels the Libyans would never sanction her assassination.''

''What do *you* think?'' Taylor asked.

''I agree. The connection with Yasif is simply too direct for it to be politically feasible. Their exposure is too certain.''

''But if what Catlin told me is correct, then why would Yasif be trying to stop Crandon himself? It stands to reason that he isn't under Yasif's control anymore.''

''But she set you and Michaels up in the park,'' the general reminded him. ''Why would she do that, then turn around and tell you the truth about Yasif's doings? That doesn't hold water.''

''Whatever passes under the bridge in the meantime, can we afford to assume that Crandon will not make an attempt on the prime minister? She's too attractive a target.''

Thomas Brayden sighed audibly. ''No, of course not. I'll notify the Secret Service White House Detail after I talk with the president. They can pass the word to the agents assigned to the prime minister.''

''I can handle that if you like,'' Taylor offered.

''No, that's all right. I'll be at the White House anyway. You just see if you can turn up anything else on Catlin. The way it looks, if we find her, we find Yasif. With Yasif comes Crandon. Get back to me at nine tonight—my meeting with the president will be over by eight-thirty.''

''Okay,'' Taylor nodded. ''Do you have a copy of the prime minister's itinerary?''

''I'll get one—just a minute.''

Turning around, Brayden walked down the hall to his study. He returned a few moments later, handing Taylor a piece of paper.

''Actually, we've had a bit of luck,'' he told Taylor. ''She's not going to overnight now.''

''What do you mean?''

''Originally, she was going to meet with the president, then go to New York and give a speech on international trade to the U.N. Then they had her scheduled to spend the night in the captain's cabin aboard the *Queen Elizabeth II* before flying back to London the following morning.''

''What changed her plans?'' Taylor asked.

''She has to address Parliament the first thing Wednesday morning. Prescott indicated that the Conservatives are anticipating all kinds of Socialist-Labour protests to arise out of her joint announcement with the President. The Tory whip feels he's going to need her personally to quash the protests about the STEALTH deployment.''

''The less she's here, the less chance Crandon will have to get to her,'' Taylor said, folding the itinerary and putting it in his jacket pocket. ''I'll be back at the section, general,'' he said wearily. ''I need a few minutes to work all this out in my mind so we don't make any more mistakes.''

Brayden agreed. ''I don't want any more nonsense, Sam. That little escapade at the park, while it wasn't your fault, was sloppy. Keep on this thing hard. I can't tell you what to do—you know your job too well for that. But let's catch Crandon. It's a team effort, Sam.''

As the general opened the door, Taylor stepped outside. ''Thanks for the pep talk, *coach,*'' Taylor said.

''It wasn't meant to be a pep talk, Sam,'' Brayden snapped back. ''I just don't want to be the one who allows the president of the United States to make an ass of himself in front of the British government. Understand?''

Sis-boom-bah, Taylor thought. ''I understand,'' he said, walking back to the Blazer. ''I'll check you later.''

A team effort, he thought, climbing in the truck and firing the engine. The only people who ever used that analogy were the bosses who never played on the field.

''Well, big surprise, *Herr General,*'' he whispered, dragging the Blazer into gear and tearing from the driveway. ''From here on in, this old circuit rider works alone.''

Chapter 50

"GOOD EVENING, MR. CRANDON."

The sound of his name interrupted Peder Crandon's thoughts. He found himself staring into the face of the dapper little Latino.

"Professor?"

"May I join you?" Eduardo Montes asked, sliding into a chair and staring into the terrorist's eyes. "Are you well, Peder?"

Self-conscious, Crandon was surprised by the question. "Well?" he repeated, slurring the word. "Yes. Why?"

"You're perspiring," Montes observed.

Reaching up, Crandon touched his forehead. It was damp. He averted his eyes. "I—it is too warm in here," he stammered, wiping his fingers quickly on a table napkin.

"I suppose." The professor saw no reason to press the subject. It was none of his concern. "Shall we get down to business?"

Crandon nodded. "You have the equipment? My chalice of blood."

Eduardo Montes leaned back in his chair and, placing his fingertips to his lips, examined the man across from him. Crandon was obviously mad. He had felt something was amiss when he first approached the table. Now he was sure.

Peder Crandon's eyes were ghostly, and the Irishman had a slight tic at the corner of the left eye. His palms were damp, and even in the restaurant's dim light, Montes could clearly see a thin sheen of perspiration on his face.

But it was more than nervousness, Montes realized, remembering to remain cautious. More than apprehension. When he had approached the table initially, Peder Crandon had been snickering to himself, muttering unintelligable phrases.

But waiting for a moment prior to announcing himself, he heard one fragmented sentence—*I am God*—followed by a new round of snickering. Eduardo Montes shuddered. If not for Santana's instructions, he would want none of this man.

"The equipment?" Crandon repeated.

"Of course." The professor forced a smile. "The equipment. It has been arranged. Now about our negotiations——"

Crandon glared at Montes, the tic vibrating. "Negotiations?" he repeated. "There are no negotiations. I buy, you sell. Do not attempt to direct *me,* professor. You are not worthy."

"Of course not," Montes said softly, attempting to placate him. "It is simply a matter of semantics."

Crandon stared blindly into his empty glass. "Where is my equipment?"

"In a safe place."

Eyes narrowing with unrestrained rage, Crandon leaned across the table. "Don't fuck with me, Cuban," he snarled, his voice low. "Never fuck with me. It is not permitted."

Madman, the professor thought, recoiling from the stench of his breath. Crandon was losing control. The anger was the pivotal point.

Like most psychopathic criminals, Montes decided, Peder Crandon was metastasizing his anger. It was not a good sign. A relatively isolated problem, such as the procurement of weapons, could spread, enveloping his mind to the point of losing all perspective. Then it would be impossible to predict his actions or control the aftermath.

Peder Crandon had to be calmed, if he were to execute Santana's plan.

"I have learned of your operations," Montes smiled. "I am fascinated by their expertise."

Crandon did not respond. Eyes fixed, he continued to stare at the Cuban.

"You are a genius," Montes added softly, looking for some measure of recognition to cross the Irishman's blank face.

Slowly, almost painfully, Peder Crandon thought to speak. "You wish to please me?" he asked.

"I wish to support you," Montes answered, raising his hands in a gesture of subservice. "To provide you with your needs."

A sardonic grin slid across Crandon's lips. "But you are," he whispered. "The embassy. It is worthy."

"Bold indeed," the professor nodded. "Perhaps the second-boldest target available."

Crandon was confused. The *second?* "You know of something bolder?" he asked. "Something more worthy of my attentions?"

"Infinitely more worthy," Montes smiled. "The British prime minister. It seems she will arrive here tomorrow morning."

Crandon began to snicker. "You are fucking with me again, Cuban."

"No, no," Montes whispered. "Never. I can tell you where."

"It is a secret?" Crandon asked.

"A special place," Montes answered.

The elimination of Margaret Thatcher would be a tremendous plum. The woman was well respected by other world leaders and astute politically. She could serve as the prime minister well into the next decade.

The strikes? If the British-American STEALTH plan were actually to become reality, the economy of Great Britain would begin to recover. In spite of the Central Committee's optimism, the British trade unions continued to flounder. Their value systems vacillated constantly as the less militant members found themselves torn between loyalties to the past and the problems of the future. With the STEALTH and its attendant $50 billion cash infusion into the economy, perhaps millions would see the strike unnecessary since they were finally finding work.

With the "Iron Lady" eliminated, Labour, along with the Socialists, could hold off the project until after the election— a time period when the strike could start as scheduled, with the election won by someone less committed than Margaret Thatcher.

The anti-Conservative elements could vote the STEALTH out of England forever. Sinister, but perhaps even more so was the effect stemming from Peder Crandon directly.

In his psychopathic state, if captured, any references to the Soviets could be denied categorically by the Kremlin. He was an Irish terrorist. Moreover, he was operating in the United States at the direction of the Libyans. If he lived, which is what Santana wanted, he would be the perfect scapegoat for Moscow's condemnation of the murder—a condemnation which would be shared by all the world nations. It would result in the severing by both Syria and Iran of their support of Libya, hopefully to the point of setting back the United Kingdom of Islam.

As for the American response? The president would allow Crandon to implicate the Libyans for no other reason than his traditional loathing of Libya. Crandon would be referred to as another "lone gunman" in the classic American rationale, and spend the rest of his life in some mental hospital, which was exactly where he belonged.

"Your money," Crandon said, interrupting his thoughts as he placed a plain white envelope on the table between them.

Eduardo Montes gently slid the envelope back to him. "Keep your money, Peder. It is not important."

Speaking in a low monotone, the professor relayed to Crandon what Santana wanted him to know. Nodding enthusiastically, Peder Crandon agreed to the plan.

* * *

"He didn't show," Yasif lied, walking back into his suite.

"I don't understand."

"Nor I. But there is a fallback location. Annapolis. I want you to come with me and drive."

Catlin's mind clicked. *Annapolis?* She'd have to get word to Taylor. "Why don't you get my car out of the garage? I'll meet you downstairs."

"No time," he said. "Crandon will be there by eight, and it's six-thirty now. I want to be there to make sure he doesn't come early and leave."

Damn, Catlin thought. "What makes you think he'll show this time?"

Reluctantly, Catlin followed Yasif downstairs. One minute to call COMSEC, she thought. Surely she could get away from him for sixty seconds.

Even Yasif had to use the restroom sometime.

Eduardo Montes replaced the receiver on the wall phone. Excellent, he thought. Santana was pleased. It was a masterstroke—carefully planned and brilliantly manipulated.

Clearly enjoying himself, he returned to the table. Crandon had left. Good. For that matter, he never wanted to see the Irishman again.

Signaling a waiter, the professor said, "May I see a menu, please?"

"Of course, sir."

As the waiter scurried off, Montes glanced at his watch: 6:15 P.M. Yasif would just about be leaving for Annapolis. It was unfortunate that he would not be able to observe his reunion with Crandon.

As the waiter returned with the menu, Eduardo Montes decided that it was going to be an interesting evening. Santana suggested that he take the 10:00 flight to Mexico City as a precaution. It precluded any thought of Montes's involvement with the night's activities. He didn't mind. He had always enjoyed Mexico anyway. It was where *mariposas* went in the winter.

He asked the waiter for a whiskey.

"Of course," the waiter nodded. "Anything in particular?"

"Yes," Eduardo Montes said. "Irish."

Chapter 51

"SORRY, TAYLOR." COMSEC advised. "No answer at that location."

"Thanks for trying," Taylor said, tossing the handset on the passenger's seat.

Nobody in Yasif's room. Where were they? Where was Catlin? Where was anybody?

The car ahead of him moved forward, and Taylor eased the Blazer up to the outside menu.

"Welcome to McDonald's," the speaker hissed. "May I take your order?"

A liter of Jack Daniel's and a jug of water, he thought. "Two fish sandwiches."

"Would you like french fries with those fish filets?"

"No," Taylor answered.

"How about some onion rings?"

Taylor thought about it. Ulcer said no. "I'll pass."

"How about a hot apple turnover?"

"No."

"Anything to drink with those fish sandwiches and that hot apple turnover?"

"I don't *want* a hot apple turnover?"

"Peach?"

Taylor was too tired to argue. "Peach is fine. And a large coffee. Cream, no sugar."

"Thank you, sir. I have two fish filets, one toasty hot peach turnover and a large coffee, cream, no sugar. Is that all, sir?"

Two out of three ain't bad, Taylor thought. "Good enough."

"Thank you, sir. Drive to the window, please."

Pulling the Blazer into gear, Taylor rolled forward. Waited. Paid a chubby Iranian cashier. Waited. And finally received his meal.

Driving a few feet from the window, he stopped and prepared the food to his liking. Opening both fish sandwiches, he took the actual filet of one and stacked in on the filet of the second. He discarded the first bun and took a bite. It burned the roof of his mouth.

Then he pulled out the coffee. There was no cream in the bag. He glanced back toward the serving window. Already another car had moved into the slot. "Shithead!" he muttered, deciding to drink it black.

Taking another bite of the fish, he allowed the Blazer to roll toward the street and stopped, taking a sip of the coffee. It, too, burned the roof of his mouth. "Shithead!" he repeated, turning right onto 14th Street, and, eating as he went, sped toward the Pentagon.

By the time Samuel Taylor arrived, the peach turnover, toasty hot as promised, had also burned the roof of his mouth as well as given him a regal case of indigestion.

He supposed it was appropriate. He still hadn't pegged Mario Lanza.

Driving her Toyota carefully, Catlin wheeled onto Route 50, speeding through the frigid night toward Annapolis for Yasif's confrontation with Peder Crandon.

But Yasif was acting peculiar, she thought, sneaking a look at the man occupying the passenger's seat next to her. Aloof. Detached, maybe.

Probably apprehensive, she decided, returning her attention to the icy road.

She glanced at the Toyota's digital clock: 7:05 P.M. If nothing held them up, they would be in Annapolis by 7:30. Perhaps she could get away long enough to contact Taylor and tell him about the meet.

"Weather's horrible," she said, trying to make conversation.

Yasif looked over at her. In the glow of the instrument panel, he looked almost sickly. Hollowed-out eyes and cheeks.

"The will of Allah," he answered.

Catlin glanced at him curiously. *Strange response,* she thought. Not like Yasif at all—at least the Yasif she normally dealt with.

She forced a grin. "Well I'm glad he gave us a heater."

The man felt the cold as he parked his car across from the Colin Fish Market and walked the two blocks to the Peyton Inn. Blowing on his hands to ward off the chill, he could hear foghorns in the distance clearly. Mournful cries warning ships of the sodden mists which always blanketed the city in winter. Moanings from a forgotten past.

The man liked Annapolis. The capitol of Maryland, it was a city steeped in history. An old town which, in 1783, served as both the ruling seat of the United States as well as the home of the Continental Congress. And even now, some two hundred years later, fine examples of 18th-century architecture and old Georgian homesteads remained preserved, lining the city's quaintly narrow brick streets.

Breathing deeply of the thick, salty air, it was as if he were walking back through time. It was illusion, he reminded himself. His visit was not for tourism—he had come to kill.

Finding the Peyton Inn, he slipped through the tavern's open door and entered the deserted building, the odor of mold assaulting his nostrils.

By summer the tavern would be remodeled and open to the public. Perhaps he would come back then with friends. They would enjoy the history, and he would remember this night.

Cautiously. Silently. The man located the stairs to the basement and eased down into the cellar. He waited, allowing his eyes to adjust to the dim light as he observed his surroundings.

In the corner, illuminated by gas street lamps seeping their rays between the rotted ceiling planks, he could see a faint outline of packing crates stacked neatly in the corner.

He smiled. The luminous stencil markings blinked at him.

He would not open them. It was not necessary—he already knew their contents.

The man checked his watch: 7:35 P.M. In less than a half hour, both Crandon and Yasif would arrive. Santana had been correct. It was a good plan. Only one obstacle stood between Peder Crandon and the assassination of Margaret Thatcher: Yasif. By 8:00 P.M. that obstruction would be eliminated.

Making his way to the corner of the cellar, the man opened a closet door. The screech of hinges filled the deserted room.

He entered the cubicle, sat down on a dirty wooden box, acutely aware of the filth soiling his expensive trousers. He made a mental note to have the pants cleaned.

Inch by inch, he pulled the pitted door closed, leaving a narrow gap to observe the entire basement. Opening a plain plastic briefcase, the man extracted an Israeli-made Uzi submachine pistol and screwed on its thick black silencer.

Checking the alignment, he snapped on a twenty-round magazine and cocked the weapon. He was ready. Only the wait remained.

In thirty minutes, his latest assignment would be finished.

Chapter 52

BACK IN HIS section office, Taylor slumped at the rolltop, tore open the 8″ × 10″ envelope, and took out a cassette and a small envelope.

At first he had no idea what the contents were; then he remembered Catlin's telling him about the wire on Yasif's suite phone. What had she told him? Something about Montes and Yasif? The whole ball of wax?

Tearing open the smaller envelope, he took out the paper and spread it on his desk. It was a transcript of the tape. Lighting a cigarette, he began to read:

INTERCEPT [045-SPS-9926-BROUSSARD]

091187-1532:17

01: Yes.

02: It is in place.

01: Everything as planned.

02: As you instructed. You will find the vehicle in east potomac park. A [unintelligible] van. The package is in the rear.

01: Excellent eduardo and the other?

02: Also in place. The location you indicated. It has been hidden in an abandoned basement. The peyton inn. He will be told eight p.m.

01: Fine eduardo your rewards will come. I will see to it personally.

02: As always as always.

091187-1532:38

[045-SPS-9926-BROUSSARD]

Considering the information, Taylor reread the transcript a second time. Then a third. Speaker One, he realized was obviously Yasif. So Two would be Montes. Taking a pencil, he wrote the names over the numbers and read the transcript again. It made a bit more sense.

The van in the park—Montes.

The other—Yasif.

Suddenly Taylor stopped reading. The *other?* What other? He dropped down a line and inserted the word *Yasif* for *you*.

Montes: Also in place. The location *Yasif* indicated. It has been hidden in an abandoned basement. The Peyton Inn. He will be told at 8:00 P.M.

He? Taylor thought. Who? Obviously Crandon—that's who. But why then the truck bomb if it wasn't for Crandon?

Taylor felt his blood run cold. Catlin. She had heard only Yasif's side of the conversation. Quickly, Taylor scanned the transcript again—this time, only Yasif's part of the dialogue.

"Shit!" he whispered. Catlin hadn't turned, she'd passed along what she had heard. But why the van in the first place? Taylor knew the answer as soon as he asked himself the question. To test whether she'd really gone over to Yasif's side. Crandon didn't even know about the van. He was going to be at the Peyton Inn at—he circled the time—8:00 P.M.

Taylor glanced at his watch; 7:40 P.M. Twenty minutes, he thought. The Peyton Inn. That's where Yasif and Crandon would be. Catlin? If Yasif hadn't killed her, then she'd be there, too.

"Bastards!" Taylor cursed, turning to his computer keyboard and querying PCAC for the location of the Peyton Inn. A moment later, the data began to spew across the screen, Taylor waiting as the computer indicated all the initial programming data which PCAC had stored for recall: Department of Interior . . . National Park Service . . . Historical Landmarks . . . The Peyton Inn, and, finally, the words *Annapolis, Maryland*.

Twisting in his chair, he grabbed the telephone and punched in the number of the Pentagon's staff duty officer and requested immediate call-up of one of the six passenger Bell helicopters which remained on standby for senior members of the joint chiefs' staffs. Five minutes away, the executive fleet was based at Washington's Fort McNair.

"Destination?" the officer asked, after verifying Taylor's RAINDANCER access clearance.

"Classified," Taylor said flatly. "I'll brief the pilots personally."

"That's clear, Mr. Taylor," the officer responded. "The JACOM bird is en route. You're cleared an immediate launch and fueled for a maximum range of one hundred and ninety nautical miles. Pad TANGO-four."

"Thank you, colonel." Hanging up the telephone, Taylor ran quickly out the section and to the stairs landing toward the helipad in the central courtyard of the Pentagon complex.

Puffing with the effort, he realized that if he were wrong about Catlin or Annapolis, the general would really have his ass.

"No guts, no glory," he said reaching the bottom floor. Besides, he wouldn't miss the Annapolis floor show for anything.

"What if he doesn't show?" Catlin asked.

Yasif ignored the question. Sitting in a window booth at the Market Dock Cafe, they were across the street and down the block from the Peyton Inn. Crandon had yet to make an appearance, but Yasif was prepared.

The fog was closing in, Yasif observed, watching the inn carefully through the cafe's frost-ringed window, gradually reaching the point where the antique street lamps were but milky blobs suspended in a cushion of haze.

Then Yasif tensed. It was Crandon.

"Wait here," he told Catlin, rising from the table and walking toward the cafe door.

As Catlin watched, Yasif walked past the window, heading toward the Peyton Inn. A second later, he had melted into the night.

Sliding from the booth, Catlin walked to the telephone and dialed the COMSEC operator.

"COMSEC two-five," a voice answered.

"This is Broussard. Is Taylor on the air?"

"Wait one, Broussard."

An instant later, the voice returned. "That's negative, Broussard. You wish to leave a message?"

"Do you know where he is?"

"Negative."

Catlin sighed. "Tell him it's going down in Annapolis. *Now.*"

"That's clear, Broussard. Copy Annapolis. We'll pass the message when Taylor checks in."

Digusted, Catlin hung up the telephone and walked back to the booth to wait for Yasif. Until Taylor and Michaels could get on the scene, there was really nothing else she could do. She had to keep playing the part.

Dressed in black, Peder Crandon slipped in and out of Yasif's vision like some fleeting ethereal shadow. Yasif shivered. It was a diabolic image, and he resisted a compelling urge to run forward and shoot Crandon in the back. But no, he thought, feeding his hatred. As he destroyed the malignancy of his creation, he wanted to watch Crandon's eyes.

Fading into the archway of a door, Yasif observed the terrorist. Footsteps muffled by the fog and damp, Peder Crandon moved to the doorway of the Peyton Inn, cast a cursory glance in each direction, then entered the building.

For a few strained seconds, Yasif continued to wait. Then quickly, silently, he padded across the street, poising at the entrance to the Peyton Inn. From inside, no sound emerged, and he felt his hatred peaking.

Conscious of the pulse racing in his brain and the weight of the Browning pistol in his right hand, he took a deep breath. Then he allowed himself to slip inside.

The helicopter exploded out of the night sky, its arrival heralded by a violent whipping of waterwind compressed forcibly by roaring turbines, thwacking rotors, and growling concussion spheres which tore at Samuel Taylor's face. It felt wonderfully invigorating. He loved it.

Shielding his eyes as much from the searchlight's blinding glare as the thin shards of rotor-slashed rain, Taylor climbed aboard and flopped down behind the pilot. "Annapolis," he shouted. "Don't spare the horses."

Nodding, the pilot tipped the angle of the blades and the helicopter rose. Clearing the top of the Pentagon, he dropped the nose, and they shot forward into space heading east across the District and toward Maryland.

Taylor felt an irrepressible twinge of excitement as he enjoyed the momentary loss of gravity. The pilot was an expert. Actually on the pad no longer than five seconds, he had kept the engines powered to maximum torque, holding the chopper down solely by a skillful manipulation of the rotary's tilt. Even now, Taylor realized, he was flying the helicopter at an almost 45 degree angle, nose down, allowing the blades to suck in airspeed prior to gaining altitude.

Taylor glanced at the pilot. As expected, he could clearly see the teeth of the man grinning behind the small microphone attached to his flight helmet. Taylor understood completely. Military chopper pilots were the same the world over. A unique breed, they liked nothing better then to tear through the sky, inches off the ground, and violate every safety rule known to twentieth-century man. Taylor trusted them implicitly.

"Having fun?" he shouted, leaning forward into the cockpit.

A pilot, a young, rugged-looking army captain, looked back over his right shoulder. "JACOM said we were tactical. Are we?"

Nodding his approval, Taylor slapped the pilot on the shoulder. "Sam Taylor."

"George Washington Bennett." The pilot completed the introduction.

"George Washington?" Taylor asked.

"Yeah," Bennett shouted over the turbines roar. "My folks were big fans of cherry trees." He flashed a broad grin with the joke. "Better hang on, Mr. Taylor."

Before Taylor could respond, Bennett pulled back on the cyclic control and the helicopter arched into the sky, slamming Taylor into his seat with a steady traction of centrifugal force.

Soon they reached maximum altitude, and, enclosed in a thick cocoon of fog, leveled off at 11,000 feet. Increasing the heat to the rear passenger area, George Washington Bennett ignored the danger of the night, and, flying on instruments, raced toward Annapolis.

For Taylor, the red glow of the chronometer branded itself directly on his optic nerve: 7:52 P.M.

He hoped they wouldn't be too late.

Crouching at the top of the stairs, Yasif listened. Below, he could hear a rodent-like scratching and knew Crandon had found the cache. It was time to move.

Cautiously, he began the descent into the cellar. One step. Another. Careful measurements of the distance between boards to ensure balance. He held his breath.

Peder Crandon sensed, rather than heard, someone behind him and knew he was not alone. Still he refused to move. Not trusting his perception, he thought it merely a flash of paranoia. A pulse of weakness.

Bending over, Yasif peered under the level of the basement roof. Crandon was leaning over an open wooden crate in the far corner of the room.

Incredible, Yasif thought. *The Irishman was giggling.*

Taking another step, Yasif raised the Browing in his right hand, steadying it with his left, and slowly bringing the weapon up until the terrorist's back filled his sights. Fingers slick with perspiration, he forced himself not to shoot.

"Crandon," he hissed, his voice echoing in the hollow cellar.

Freezing in place, Peder Crandon immediately recognized the voice of his old mentor.

"Hello, Yasif," he whispered, turning slowly to face the stairs.

"Why, Peder?" Yasif asked, allowing himself to wait a few moments longer.

"Why what?" Crandon taunted, a twisted smile appearing the corners of his mouth.

Choking with anger, Yasif held his composure. "Ursula."

Crandon laughed—a loud, mocking laugh which vibrated loosely, splashing off the cellar's brick and mortar walls. Then his eyes narrowed with loathing. "She was a whore," he spit. "An Arab whore. Your whore, Yasif."

Eyes glazed with a slushy release of fervor, Crandon lowered his voice. "Put your pathetic gun away," he whispered. "I will let you live. Give you life as you gave me mine and allow you to observe the fruits of your labors."

"You're insane!" Yasif tightened the pressure on the Browning's trigger.

Crandon laughed again.

"Tomorrow, Yasif. Tomorrow my act will be sovereign."

Walking slowly toward Yasif, Crandon raised his arms, palms up, in an open gesture of submission. "You have taught me,

Yasif,'' he whimpered. ''You sent me here. You allowed me to avenge father's death. Mother's.''

At the reference of his parents, Peder Crandon's tears flowing unchecked. ''You are my leader, Yasif.''

Falling to his knees, then stomach, Crandon began to crawl the last few yards toward the stairs. ''Tomorrow, Yasif. I will chop her tomorrow. For us. For you.''

Consumed by a preverse sense of horror, Yasif watched as Crandon curled himself into a fetal position, whining as he began to rub his face against the floor inches from Yasif's shoes.

For an instant, he felt pity for the man. But the moment passed swiftly. Lowering the pistol until the muzzle was but inches from the back of the Irishman's exposed neck, Yasif bent over.

''Whom will you chop, my son?'' he asked, barely breathing. ''How will you avenge me?''

Crandon attempted to answer. The effort produced only unintelligible sobs.

''Who, my son?'' he repeated, his voice soothing, reassuring.

His face buried in the floor's filth, Crandon's voice broke, tearing the words from his knotted soul. ''Thatcher,'' he screamed, sobbing openly.

''No, Peder,'' Yasif sighed, his finger tightening on the trigger. ''It is over now.''

''One minute,'' Bennett yelled to Taylor as he dropped the helicopter down, roaring over the United States Naval Academy. ''Pick your poison.''

''Shit!'' Taylor said, leaning over Bennett's shoulder and looking out the front cockpit glass. ''I can't see a damn thing in this fog.''

''Give me a second,'' Bennett snapped. Banking the helicopter sharply to the left, he plowed down, piercing the clouds.

"There," Taylor shouted, pointing to the mist-shrouded square forming the center of the town. "That's large enough."

"You got it," Bennett yelled over the throbbing engines. He had landed in tighter spots before, and in spite of the weather, could just barely make out the perimeter of the landing site. Flipping on his searchlight, he took a deep breath and held it.

As Bennett began his final approach, oblivious to the buildings and power lines surrounding the square, Taylor moved back to the passenger compartment, pulled out his .45 automatic and slid open the passenger door.

The rainwind beating at his skin, he stepped out on the skid and waited to jump.

Whether it was the sound of the approaching helicopter or some other deep-seated reluctance, he never knew, but for some reason, Yasif hesistated. He did not see the man who fired a burst of six rounds that tore into his body. Nor did he hear the discharge of the bullets. The only thing penetrating the consciousness of the Islamic diplomat was the steady metallic clicks of the firing mechanism as it ignited the 9-millimeter, hollow-point projectiles spitting from the UZI's muzzle.

Dropping the Browning, he fell to the floor. Yasif heard another sound—oddly familiar, yet not something normally experienced. Curious, he thought, his mind racing to place the rhythm. Then, slowly, the recognition began to grow in his brain. It was not a sound, it was a physical palpitation: the pressure of his arteries leaking their fluid into his lungs. For a blurred second, he thought to protest, then decided against it. The cool sensation was not all that unpleasurable. He would enjoy it a moment longer.

Peder Crandon knew exactly what was happening. Slapped back to reality by the gunfire, he grabbed Yasif's pistol, rolling over to face the short man coming from the closet. Eyes wide, they riveted to the stranger's UZI, still smoking in the cold, damp air.

"Get the equipment and get out," the man ordered.

Crandon was confused. Already he was putting the UZI into a briefcase. He giggled. The man was not a threat, he was a friend. A friend sent by the professor to ensure that everything went according to plan.

"Who are you?" he asked.

The man walked over and jerking Crandon by the shoulder, shoved him in the direction of the crates.

"*Shavki,*" he growled, insulting the terrorist in Russian slang. "We take the rear door. Get what you need and follow me out."

Peder Crandon did not argue. Scrambling over to the cache, he selected the materials he needed. Then, in silence, he followed the man up the stairs.

Fred Jarvis had been in the Annapolis Police Department for nine years . . . nine boring years.

Sitting in the lobby of the old Cranston Hotel, he popped another Gelusil into his mouth, and, for the umpteenth time, resolved to avoid the greasy chili dogs served at the Market Dock Cafe. Even if they were half-price for law-enforcement officers, he was sure any savings he realized were spent on the huge quantities of antacids he consumed after every meal.

"Definitely not worth it," he breathed, enjoying a particuarly satisfactory belch. "Definitely not worth the——"

The sound of the approaching helicopter interrupted Fred Jarvis's resolution. *Impossible,* he thought. *Nobody could be stupid enough to be flying in such lousy weather.*

As usual, Fred Jarvis would be wrong.

Gathering his considerable girth together, he slid off the wide, soft couch and waddled to the hotel's front door to investigate. Searchlight flashing through the darkness, it *was* a helicopter. Even worse, he decided. It was *landing*.

Groaning at the thought of having to do something policewise, he left the hotel and shuffled reluctantly the 15 yards to the square.

Samuel Taylor was off the skid as soon as Bennett flared the chopper in. Jumping from the helicopter two feet above the ground, he landed in a crouch, pistol at the ready.

"Freeze!" Fred Jarvis shouted, aiming his service revolver alternately between Taylor and the helicopter.

"Federal officers," Taylor yelled, ignoring the revolver and sprinting over to the portly policeman. "Where's the Peyton Inn?"

Jarvis was distraught. All of this was unauthorized. The helicopter. The landing. Especially this bulldoggish man with the .45 automatic. "Now wait a——"

"The Peyton Inn," Taylor repeated, lowering his voice an octave. "Where is it?"

Feeling another squirt of acid shooting into his stomach, Fred Jarvis pointed his pistol in a general direction behind him. "Uh . . . over there."

"I'll follow you," Taylor said, grabbing the officer's arm and urging him in the direction of the tavern.

Unable to figure a way not to, Jarvis shrugged his shoulders and led the way.

As they reached the door to the inn, Taylor turned to Jarvis. "Wait here," he ordered. "Nobody comes in unless I say so."

The officer didn't protest. Although he didn't exactly know what was going on, he really didn't care. The whole situation was much too elaborate for his rather meager aspirations. "Let me know if you need any backup," he responded, glad to be left outside.

Forcing himself not to smile, Taylor raised the automatic up, flipped off its thumb safety, and glanced over at the policeman. "Appreciate it," he said, realizing he was showboating. "It's always a pleasure to work with a professional."

Watching Taylor disappear into the darkness of the inn, Fred Jarvis shuddered and tossed another Gelusil to the back of his throat. *Professional?* he thought. What a nice thing to say. The chief would be pleased.

* * *

Immediately squatting, Taylor moved away from the doorway and allowed his eyes to adjust to the lower light level.

He listened. Aside from the sound of the helicopter's turbines winding down, he could hear nothing. Cautiously, he slid deeper into the inn's damp interior.

Samuel Taylor did not feel fear. He knew Crandon's and Yasif's backgrounds and had compared them with his own. They fought by surprise, usually killing unarmed citizens or attacking from afar with bombs. In a face-to-face encounter, Taylor knew he would win.

Nonetheless, he was prudent enough not to allow himself to be lulled into a false sense of security by underestimating them. Yasif was shrewd, Crandon psychotic. Both were capable of drawing on unknown variables. *Perdidistos,* Taylor reminded himself. Fine-tuning his senses, he programmed his reflexes to kill.

Fifteen yards inside the door, he heard a sound. Then he heard it again, and the hair at the nape of his neck went erect. No, not the wind. Something human.

He inched forward.

Reaching the top of the stairs, he heard it again. Louder. Coming from the basement, he thought. Holding his breath, he listened. Barely audible, he could make out ragged breathing, sporadic coughs and soft chokings.

He knew the sound: a man drowning in his own blood.

Thrusting the .45 out in front of him, he pressed his back against the wall and began to descend the stairs. One . . . a pause . . . another . . . a check for trip wires . . . a step . . . a check . . . hunting . . . tracking . . . inching down. The smell assaulted his nostrils. Pungent scents of cordite, burned gunpowder, and smoke. He was too late.

One was gone, the other dying.

Quickly covering the last few steps, Taylor found the man on the cellar floor. Yasif. Twisting in agony, he was attempting to control his own bleeding.

Squatting down, Taylor rolled the man over, inspecting his body and counting wounds. He found three.

One bullet had entered Yasif's right thigh, passed through, and exited without hitting the bone. Another had glanced off the extreme edge of his left hip. It was not fatal.

It was the third round which was killing the man. After shattering his rib cage, the bullet remained lodged in his body, leaving a large sucking chest wound. Nothing could save him.

From above, Taylor could hear shouts.

"Get the hell out of my way!" Catlin was yelling.

"Nobody goes in," Jarvis responded.

"I'll have your ass, you fat slug! Now get out of my way."

"Let her in," Taylor yelled. "She's with me."

Seconds later he could hear the sound of feet running down the stairs as Catlin appeared at his side.

"Who is it?" she asked, kneeling down next to him.

"Yasif," Taylor said. "And he's got about a zero chance of making it through."

Taylor watched Catlin closely. She was showing no emotion whatsoever. "Michaels is dead," he told her softly.

Catlin looked over at him, then around the cellar. "Where?"

"East Potomac Park. The U-Haul was a setup. For us and you."

She looked back down at Yasif. "Bastard!"

Considering Catlin's response, Taylor knew she really didn't know Yasif had suspected her. He would have to explain it all to her sometime. "You know, Cat——"

Taylor's words were cut off by Yasif's fluttering eyelids and his attempt to speak. "Morning . . . Crandon . . . Thatcher." He vomited. A torrent of frothy oxygenated blood spewed from his mouth.

"Thatcher?" Catlin asked.

"Thatcher," Taylor confirmed, reaching over and grabbing

Yasif's shoulders. "What about Thatcher?" he shouted, shaking him violently.

"Easy Sam," Catlin cautioned. "You're gonna put him into shock."

"He's already in shock," Taylor snapped, jerking Yasif to a sitting position and shaking him harder. "What about Thatcher?"

Yasif coughed again, blood trailing from both his nostrils and mouth. "Tomorrow morning," he gasped. "Thatcher . . . That——" He lapsed into unconsciousness.

"Where?" Taylor screamed, slapping Yasif's face, attempting to jerk him back. "Talk to me, you sonofabitch. Where?"

But Yasif did not hear him. Choking in his own mucus, he had suffocated.

"You bastard," Taylor continued.

"Sam," Catlin grabbed his arms. "He's dead."

Taylor immediately let go and Yasif crumpled back on the floor. "I'm sorry, Catlin. Every time we get something—anything, it just slips through my fingers."

Disgusted with himself, Taylor stood and looked around the cellar. Noticing the open packing crate, he walked toward it.

"You think Crandon is going to assassinate Margaret Thatcher?"

"I've been thinking about it all day." Taylor knelt down next to the crate.

"But she's not even here."

"She will be, tomorrow morning."

"How does Crandon know that? I didn't even know it."

Who knows? Taylor thought. Montes? Maybe Mario? What about *valentine*—Prescott? He knew before anyone else.

"Shit!" Taylor said, pulling back the packaging material.

"What?" Catlin moved next to him.

"We've got trouble in River City."

Catlin knelt down at the side of the crate. "What——"

They both realized what they were looking at: the Soviet packing crate was unmistakable. It had contained a SAM 14

Strela launcher and four missiles. The launcher and two of the missiles were missing.

"Rockets," Catlin said.

"Heat seeking," Taylor said, shaking his head.

The Strela was the artillery of terror and the SAM 14, the most advanced surface-to-air missile in the Russian arsenal. Also known by the NATO code Grail, the weapon was used extensively by Kremlin-backed forces for shooting down high-performance aircraft.

Its track record was impressive.

In Lebanon, Syrian troops had used them against Israeli jets. In Chad, a number of French Mirage fighters had been destroyed by Libyan Strelas. And in the Persian Gulf wars, both Iran and Iraq exchanged daily Strela launchings to protect their respective territories from air attack.

Taylor groaned. Crandon would know this weapon intimately. Not only had the IRA deployed it against British helicopters in Northern Ireland, but it had been an Islamic weapon of choice in their terrorist wars against Israel. Yes, he predicted. The Irishman would be expertly trained in its deployment.

Lifting one of the missiles from its Styrofoam nest, Taylor mentally clicked off the Strela's specifications. Total weight of the launcher and two missiles: 60 pounds . . . extremely portable.

Effective range: 3,000 yards . . . excellent potential.

Target recommendations: both static and moving . . . broad application.

"Damn!" Taylor said. Accuracy aside, the warhead could penetrate over a foot of armor, explode, and destroy the target with the force of a large shell. Even worse, once fired, there was absolutely nothing conventional security personnel could do to prevent its overtaking the target.

Crandon would have to be stopped prior to firing.

Placing the missile back in its crate, Taylor stood next to Catlin. For a moment neither spoke, both continuing to stare at the half-empty box at their feet, both thinking.

''She flying in?'' Catlin asked, breaking the silence.

''Andrews,'' Taylor nodded.

''Then he'll try for her jet.''

''Or the choppers,'' Taylor added. ''Or the arrival points. Hell, he may even try for the White House.''

''You know her schedule?''

''Yeah.'' Taylor reached into his pocket and pulled out the itinerary. ''Why don't you get to a phone and get us a sweep team down here.'' He handed her the paper.

Catlin nodded. They both knew what had to be done. ''There's a little cafe off the square . . . the Market Dock. I'll wait for you there.''

Turning, Catlin walked slowly toward the stairs. ''Sam?''

''What?'' he answered, not looking back.

''I'm sorry about this. About Kelly.''

''You needn't be,'' he said, his voice low. ''What goes around comes around.''

''I know, but——''

Taylor silenced her with a wave of his hand. He didn't need any apologies or conversation. And as Catlin headed up the stairs, he began to search the basement. Trying to figure out Crandon's plan. Trying to put himself in the mind of the terrorist.

As much as he tried, he couldn't get one image out of his brain: that of a Strela missile and an aircraft destroyed in flight.

Catlin? He would chew her ass out later.

Now it was a matter of priorities.

Chapter 53

WITHIN THE HOUR, the entire town of Annapolis was alive with all manner of emergency vehicles. Lights flashing, their roof racks shimmered in brilliant displays of blues and red, reflecting off windows, the mirrored beams blended with the harsh white strobes of the waiting helicopter.

Catlin observed the panorama with fascination. Everybody wanted a piece of the action; it made them feel important.

Looking toward the door, Catlin saw Taylor heading toward her booth. ''Another coffee over here,'' he said to a waitress as he walked to the table and slid in.

''What a nightmare,'' he told Catlin, nodding toward the window. Through the glass they had an unobstructed view of the entire square as well as the entrance to the Peyton Inn.

''Sweep team get here?'' she asked.

''Finally,'' Taylor answered. ''Problem was that local fat cop called everybody he knew in the meantime. Just look at what he's caused out there.''

Taking a sip, Taylor nodded. ''And the state police and the county police.'' He smiled caustically. ''There are two captains from the naval academy over there poking around.''

He took another sip of the coffee. ''The press is going to have a field day with this one. Yasif being a diplomat, the fact that he was also Libyan is probably really going to be exploited by the reporters.''

"The bigger the crisis, the bigger the story," Catlin shrugged. "No doubt everyone will think the Israelis killed him."

Watching Catlin closely, Taylor didn't answer the question. "You really didn't like him, did you?"

"No," she said flatly. "I hated him."

"But you made——"

"Love?" she interrupted.

Taylor didn't move.

"I didn't make love with him, Sam. I fucked him to get close. That was what the general ordered. That's what I did. End of story."

Taylor didn't know what to say, so he said nothing. The cafe was filling rapidly with police, reporters nosing around for information. They bothered him.

"Why's the prime minister coming here tomorrow, anyway?" Catlin asked, her voice low as she changed the subject purposely.

"A joint announcement with the president."

"What about?"

For a moment, Taylor considered telling her about the STEALTH bomber plans. Then he decided against it. As far as he knew, the project was still classified, and, until made public, it was his responsibility to respect confidentiality.

"I can't tell you that yet. It's nothing to do with our deal."

Catlin understood and didn't press it. "What do we do?"

"Let me see the schedule," Taylor asked.

Reaching in her purse, Catlin took out the paper and handed it to Taylor. Unfolding it, he reread it.

0900 PM—arrive Andrews AFB via BA 001

0915 PM—depart Andrews AFB via USMC helicopter tail number N6644 [chase—N8264]

0935 PM—arrive South Lawn White House greeted by POTUS

0940 PM—POTUS private time

1200 PM—POTUS lunch [open press coverage]

1300 PM—POTUS joint press statement

1345 PM—depart South Lawn White House via USMC helicopter N6644 [chase—N8264]

1405 PM—arrive Andrews AFB

1415 PM—depart Andrews AFB via BA 001 en route London

"Five hours," Taylor whispered, thinking out loud. "In by nine and out by two-fifteen."

His mind clicking, he again tried to put himself in Crandon's head as he ran through some rapid mental computations.

"Considering the Strela's applications, he won't be able to get close enough to the Andrews arrival point or the White House to make the shot work—at least not effectively."

"What about the open press coverage?" Catlin suggested.

Taylor swung his eyes to her. "No. I doubt he'll be able to get into the White House with a SAM missile, Cat. Even the Secret Service should notice that."

Catlin ignored his sarcasm. "Then it has to be the plane."

"Yeah," Taylor agreed. "The plane or the choppers. My money goes on choppers."

"It's a lot more than just your money," Catlin reminded him.

Taylor didn't want to think about it. "I know. But the helicopters will be moving relatively slow and flying closer to the ground. They're an easier target than the jet."

He looked into Catlin's eyes. "Comments?"

"I don't know," she admitted. "You're the guns-and-butter expert. I'm just the computer whiz."

Taylor knew *that* was wrong. "No," he said. "It'll be the

choppers. That would also allow him some margin for error—assuming, of course, he wants to escape."

Standing, Taylor tossed a dollar bill on the table. "I've got to get back to the chopper. I need to talk to the pilot."

Sliding from the booth, Catlin followed Taylor into the square, waiting while Taylor finished his conversation with the helicopter pilot.

"You need a ride back?" he asked her.

"My car is here," she told him. "You want me to come in to the section?"

Taylor thought about it. "No reason," he told her, looking at his watch: 9:15 P.M. "I'm already fifteen minutes late for a meeting with the general."

"I can meet you at Foxhall," she offered.

"After this mess? No. He's going to drag my ass over the coals, and there's no point in you watching the bloodshed. I suffer much better without an audience."

Beside them, the turbines began to whine as the helicopter powered up in preparation for takeoff. "You know, Cat," Taylor said, raising his voice. "I'm going to reprimand you for going off on your own."

"I expect it," she said, her voice firm. "I had too much time invested in Yasif to let it slide like that. Besides, the general got what he wanted. Yasif's dead. Does it really make any difference how?"

Looking back toward the cluster of emergency vehicles parked at right angles to the Peyton Inn's door, Taylor realized that he might have done the same thing in her position. She was a gutsy woman, and he respected her for that. Nonetheless, they still didn't have Peder Crandon, and, in that context, Catlin had screwed up.

"It makes all the difference in the world," he told her. "We've got to——" Suddenly he caught himself. He'd almost completed the sentenced *work as a team*. Those words would never pass his lips. He swore against it for too many years.

"Got to what?" Catlin asked.

"Stop Crandon," he answered softly.

"You think we really can?"

Taylor thought of Jennifer Bishop. "Yes, Catlin. I know we will."

As the helicopter's rotors began to turn, Taylor climbed aboard, watching Catlin walk away. "In the morning," he called after her.

Covering her mouth, she yelled something back to him, but he couldn't make it out.

Moments later, the helicopter rose, and the town of Annapolis was lost behind its blanket of fog.

It had been a rough day, and the morning would be even rougher. But first he would identify Mario Lanza. If he didn't, he'd never be able to sleep.

Chapter 54

THE DRIVE HAD taken Peder Crandon sixty minutes, a time measurement now well beyond his limits of conception. Now an hour was little more than a millisecond inserted casually between infinity and eternity.

Annapolis was forgotten, lost in the helix of his memory. It was not important. For now the future was finally at hand. He smiled. Tomorrow he would alter the world. Tomorrow the whore would die.

"I grow restless, me lady. I grow restless for your death."

In spite of the cold, Peder Crandon drove with his window down, inviting the sting of the wind to whip his face. Adversity ignored. Pain to be suffered.

Lost in thought, Peder Crandon did not notice the vehicle following him from the time he took Loop 495 around Washington and exited south on Route 5 heading into Maryland.

Nor did he realize that the vehicle had been tailing him for almost twenty minutes. At that particular moment, Peder Crandon was an entity solely unto himself, suspended somewhere space, aloof from his surroundings.

Maryland State Trooper J. L. "Jimbo" Walker was very much aware of the surroundings. A one-man unit, he had been observing the dark blue TransAm in front of him for the last fifteen minutes. It wasn't because its driver was breaking the law. They were merely traveling the same stretch of deserted highway.

His police radio squawked. "Attention units sector nine David . . . "

Annapolis, Walker thought, wishing he were still assigned to the bay-front town instead of the mostly deserted Lexington Park region of the state. Reaching down, he twisted up the volume on the speaker.

". . . Unit two-oh-one advises a wanted-for-questioning. Repeat, wanted for questioning, white male, twenty-five to thirty years, five foot ten, one fifty, blond hair, dark clothing. Believed driving a dark late-model General Motors two door. Possibly Firebird or Camaro."

201, Walker thought. Intelligence unit. Probably another informant had turned them around and they wanted to scare him back in line.

Personally, Walker was glad he had selected to remain in uniformed patrol. "Leave the glory boys to their informants," he whispered. "And leave me the hell alone."

Slumping in his seat, he glanced at the clock on his dashboard: 9:35 P.M. "What the hell," he said. Nothing else to do in the hour-and-a-half until his shift ended. Might as well check out the TransAm. Might get lucky. You never knew when you would need something from the intelligence boys, and it was always best to have them owing a favor.

Depressing the accelerator in his cruiser, Walker easily closed the distance with the other car. Pulling up next to the TransAm's left side, he paralleled it while attempting to distinguish the driver's features.

"Pretty boy," he said, surprised. As much as he could tell from the TransAm's dash lights, the driver did kind of match the description from Annapolis. Damn sure enough a probable cause for a stop.

Easing his foot off the pedal, he allowed the cruiser to slide back, pulling in behind the TransAm and flipping on his blue emergency roof lights.

A twelve-year veteran of the state police, "Jimbo" Walker

knew the rules. Grabbing for his microphone, he attempted to call the dispatcher and give the identifying information on the TransAm just in case something went wrong.

"Twelve-George-six," he said, pressing the microphone to his lips.

The dispatcher did not respond to his unit number.

"Twelve-George-six," he repeated.

Still nothing.

Sounded like geese, he thought, listening. The only noise coming from the speaker was all the radio traffic in the Annapolis district. The dispatcher probably hadn't even heard his call over all that racket.

Screw it, he decided, tossing the microphone to the seat next to him. Even if pretty boy turned out to be the snitch, he was only wanted for questioning. A lightweight. From the way he looked, probably even a fag.

The blue lights flashing in the rearview mirror reflected into Peder Crandon's eyes. Twisting in his seat, he glanced at the side door mirror and pulled the TransAm to the far right edge of the lane.

As expected, the police cruiser held its position and he could clearly see the outline of only one head in the car. "Infidel," he whispered, reaching to the passenger's seat and pulling the Ingram closer.

As the TransAm slowed, pulling to the side of the road, Walker followed in tandem, stopping the cruiser ten feet from the Pontiac's rear bumper.

Grabbing a Kelvar clipboard, he adjusted his bulletproof vest and stepped from the squad car. Closing the cruiser's door, he unsnapped his holster by habit, but then, as usual, decided not to draw his revolver.

Peder Crandon did not move as Walker approached. Watching the trooper in his rearview mirror, he noted that the man's weapon was still holstered. He chuckled as he eased the machine pistol into his lap.

''Would you please step out of the vehicle,'' Walker shouted, stopping by the TransAm's left rear bumper.

Pretty Boy's speed stunned ''Jimbo'' Walker. In his mind, he saw only a series of tightly paced mosaics—the man, the submachine gun, and the staccato flashes from the muzzle spitting fire at him.

Peder Crandon had not bothered to aim. He didn't feel the officer worth the effort. Possessing the element of surprise, he fired his thirty-round magazine in the officer's direction. Considering the close range, he predicted a 10 percent hit ratio. He was wrong. He had underestimated. Eight of the Ingram's bullets had met center body mass.

The bulletproof vest stopped four of the rounds. And, as designed, the Kelvar clipboard deflected another two. But these were not the projectiles that killed J. L. ''Jimbo'' Walker. The two responsible entered his face within a quarter-inch of one another, simulatenously imploding his nose, upper lip, and left eye. Already dead at the moment of collapse, his service revolver remained in its holster.

It would be buried with him.

Peder Crandon did not remain at the scene, nor did he bother to walk back to the dead trooper. He had eleven miles to travel and was anxious to complete the journey.

The Maryland State Police? Just a minor inconvenience. Quickly pulling the TransAm back on the road, he deemed them unworthy of his time.

Police were peasants. He found them boring.

Flicking a match with his thumbnail, Samuel Taylor sat on the edge of his rolltop, staring at the carving of Saint Eloy as the General chastised him over the telephone.

''Uh huh,'' he muttered, lighting a Marlboro and wishing he hadn't bothered to call.

''I know that, general.''

''I'm aware of that, too.''

Finally he had had enough. "Look, general," he said. "Here's the deal. Yasif is dead. Crandon is running around with SAM missiles, and I think he's going for the prime minister. Now I don't know what you and Prescott are thinking, but I'm going with what I know. You have any problems with that?"

Thomas Brayden said it couldn't be done, but Taylor decided not to listen. It was the same old rhetoric. A waste of time.

Closing his eyes, Taylor wished he were somewhere else. The whole Crandon investigation was one of those situations where nobody wins. From his point of view, he was doing everything possible. But from the general's, and, by extension, Prescott's, Taylor was the star in a comedy of errors.

Screw them, Taylor decided. Regardless of what anyone else thought nobody could change one fact: he was the last chance left to stop Peder Crandon.

Taylor checked his watch: 10:05 P.M. Eleven hours. History would tell the tale.

"I've got another call coming in, general," he lied. "Let me get back to you."

"Yes, general."

"I'll do that, general."

"First thing in the morning." Taylor replaced the receiver and crushed out his cigarette. He left the section and walked down the hall to the joint chiefs' library. It was time to figure out who Mario Lanza was.

It was empty except for its supervisor, the eternal Miss McThorn. A spinster, she was a painfully thin woman who wore her fifty-year service pin like the *Croix de Guerre*. Taylor liked her.

"Evening, Miss Mac," he smiled. "Working overtime?"

Looking up from a card file, she saw Taylor and nodded.

Although she would never tell him, in the entire Pentagon, he was one of the handful of men she actually liked, and on holidays, he brought her chocolate covered cherries. They were her secret passion.

"And you, Mr. Taylor," she said in her gravelly voice. "Looking for a little light reading."

"Get in anything sexy lately?" he asked, beginning their usual bantering.

Miss McThorn furrowed her brow in mock seriousness. "What about this?" she said, lifting a document from her desk.

"What is it?"

Holding the manuscript at arm's length, she read the title. "NATO and the Warsaw Pact: Theories of Automated Force Planning Contingencies." Eyes twinkling mischievously, she looked up at Taylor. "I understand Meryl Streep is going to star in the movie version."

Taylor chuckled. "Well, I'll just wait for the movie," he said. "Meanwhile, what I really need is your guidance on something. I'm trying to identify someone I saw today. Latin type. I know I've seen him somewhere before, but I just can't place the face. He looks kinda like Mario Lanza."

Miss McThorn thought for a moment. "Military?"

"No."

"American?"

"Foreign, I'm sure. But someone who's been around the District."

"What about a diplomat?" she suggested.

Taylor's mind clicked. That was it. He'd seen the man's picture in the *Washington Post*—society section. "Yes, I guess I was thinking too hard about it. But that's where I remember seeing his photograph. A diplomatic reception. You have anything like that? Pictures? Bios?"

"I have something on everything," she said proudly. "Wait here."

As Miss McThorn stood from her chair and disappeared into the rear of the library, Taylor looked down at her desk. On its corner was a small, framed piece of calligraphy. Leaning over, he read it:

"Generals may come and go . . . Miss McThorn is constant."

Underneath the quote was the scrawled signature of Dwight D. Eisenhower, General, United States Army.

Taylor smiled. *Ain't it the truth,* he thought as she returned carrying two large books.

"Let's look here first," she said, placing the books on her desk.

Taylor read the title on the first. *Defense Intelligence Agency. Foreign Diplomatic Corps Source Book. 1986. Volume I.*

The second one was Volume II.

"If you can find his picture in these, I can run a cross-check on the name for deep background," she told him. "They are in alphabetical order by country, so just go through it page by page."

Opening the top book, he found *Afghanistan*, a page of pictures of those individuals who may have been granted diplomatic privilege by the U.S. State Department. It was like a high-school yearbook, he realized. A photograph, a name and a title. *Yes,* he thought. *This dog would hunt.*

For the next twenty minutes, Taylor patiently flipped page after page as he ran through the Latin countries:

Argentina . . . Bolivia . . . Brazil.

Chile . . . Colombia . . . Costa Rica.

He finished Volume I. Nothing. Beginning to think he was wrong about the *Washington Post* picture, he flipped open Volume II:

Mexico . . . Nicaragua . . . Paraguay.

Peru . . . The Philippines . . . Spain.

On Spain, he stopped. "Hello, Mario," he smiled.

"Find something?" Miss McThorn asked.

"Yes," Taylor said, showing her the photograph. "Antonio de las Marias. Say's here he's the protocol chief at the Spanish embassy."

"Humph," she breathed, leaning over and looking at the photograph. "He really *does* look like Mario Lanza. I wonder if he sings tenor. I'll get his bio and we'll soon know."

To Taylor it seemed as if she were back before she left.

"That didn't take long," he told her.

"I pride myself on organization, Mr. Taylor," she said, handing him a legal-size manila folder. "Here's his dossier."

Taylor flipped it open. On the first page was an abstract of the entire twenty-five-page file. The latest update was March 1984.

"Mind if I borrow this?" he asked.

She shook her head. "Reference material," she told him. "I can't let it out of the library." Then, she looked around the room conspiratorially. "Of course I can be bribed."

The cherries, Taylor thought. "The usual?" he asked.

She nodded.

"Plain brown wrapper?"

"*With* my file," she told him. "By tomorrow evening."

Taylor smiled. "I won't tell if you don't." He winked, turned and headed toward the library door.

Just before he walked out, Miss McThorn called after him. "Mr. Taylor?"

"Yes, Miss Mac?"

"He never took singing lessons. I peeked."

Taylor laughed. "That's okay, Miss Mac. I don't really like opera anyway."

"Neither do I, Mr. Taylor. Neither do I."

Waving good-bye, Taylor walked rapidly back to the section and sat down at his desk. Lighting a cigarette, he opened the dossier and began to read about Antonio de las Marias.

He was a career diplomat, Taylor decided, scanning the abstract. Previous assignments: United States—1983 to present. Great Britain—1970 to 1983.

Before 1970? Taylor read faster. Quick trips, it seemed. A year or two rotating between Madrid and any number of countries as a trade representative for the Spanish government:

1968—Czechoslovakia.

1965—Indonesia.

1962 to 1963—Great Britain, first tour there.

1956—Hungary.

1954—France, first foreign assignment.

Before 1954? Taylor flipped a page. He found what he wanted.

1950 to 1954—Third Foreign Secretary for the Office of Generalissimo Francisco Franco.

Turning another page, Taylor found a brief biographical sketch. *Interesting,* he thought. As a young man in the late 1930s, Antonio de las Marias had served as a liaison officer in the International Brigade—those non-Spanish, leftist intellectuals who fought in the Spanish Civil War in the years preceding World War II.

Placing the dossier on the desk, Taylor leaned back in his chair and rubbed his eyes. The International Brigade, he thought. If memory served correctly, there had been a number of Communists in the organization: French Communists, Moorish Communists, British Communists.

Suddenly the word "valentine" flashed in his mind. Of course, Kim Philby—the Kremlin's British agent. Philby had infiltrated the International Brigade—for that matter, while working undercover as a correspondent for the London General Press Agency, Philby had actually been decorated for bravery by Franco personally—the Red Cross of Military Merit for actions against the Spanish government.

Philby would have known Antonio de las Marias. It would have been impossible for them *not* to have met.

Getting excited by the information, Taylor grabbed the dossier and flipped back to the pages detailing de las Marias's previous assignments. The first British tour—1962 to 1963.

Then he went to the PCAC keyboard and requested the file for Philby, Kim. A moment of whirring and the screen danced with the name Philby, Harold Adrian Russell [Kim].

Complete name, Taylor thought, pressing the recall key and watching Philby's dossier abstract appear on the screen. He looked to the last entry. 1963—Philby defects to USSR.

Bingo, he smiled. Antonio de las Marias was in London during Philby's run to Moscow. But doing what? Controlling or being controlled?

Realizing he had stumbled onto something important, Taylor began to cross-reference de las Marias's other foreign assignment dates. In two minutes, PCAC had completed an initial composite analysis:

1954—French lose to Communists in Indochina.

1956—Soviets suppress anti-Communist revolution in Hungary.

1963—The Philby connection in Great Britain.

1965—The Communist coup attempt in Indonesia.

His mind swimming with disjointed thoughts, Samuel Taylor leaned back in his chair once again. No, there was no doubt in his mind. Antonio de las Marias was a Soviet intelligence agent. Probably he had been recruited personally by Philby well before the Second World War and had stayed in place without the knowledge of the Spanish government for all these years.

Sticking one of the wooden kitchen matches into his mouth, Taylor began to chew on it as he studied the computer screen.

But after Czechoslovakia, he wondered. Great Britain for thirteen years? Doing what? Penetration of British intelligence? What about Sir Elliot? A mole? *Valentine*. He could be going both ways. Check into it later. A level higher than Prescott could reach.

And what about now? Taylor thought. Antonio de las Marias had been in the United States since 1983. Back to the questions. Doing what? Controlling? Who? Eduardo Montes? Of course. How many others?

What about Crandon? Why would the Soviets be interested in a nut case? Reaching into his pocket, Taylor pulled out seven spent 9mm cartridge shells. Freshly fired, he had found the empty little brass trinkets in the cellar of the Peyton Inn after Catlin had left.

Lining them up on his desk like tin soldiers on parade, he knew that Crandon hadn't killed Yasif—the angles were all wrong. There had been a third person in the basement, someone who wanted Crandon to be able to complete his attack. But who?

Picking up one of the shells, he turned in his fingers, inspecting it. *Remmington*. Could have been bought anywhere. Fingerprints? No. It had been loaded into a magazine—a partial or a smear, at best. Not enough for anything.

Placing it back in line, Taylor pulled out a fresh Marlboro and lit it. If Montes supplied the missiles, then Montes would have known that Crandon would be in the basement. In that respect, it stood to reason that Montes also had had a part in Yasif's death. Stretching it, if Montes was working under de las Marias's instructions, and the Spaniard, perhaps through him, the Soviets were involved. But why would Moscow want Yasif dead? Russia and Libya were allies. It didn't make sense.

Full circle, Taylor thought. *Speculative at best. Still no solid answers.*

Could it be proved? No, at least not beyond a reasonable doubt. No, there would be no prosecution against Antonio de las Marias. The Spanish government would be informed, and he would be asked quietly to leave the country.

Eduardo Montes? Another story. Prosecution for weapons trafficking. Conspiracy. Probably any number of collateral charges.

But what about Sir Elliott? No real proof there either. That would be an English problem. Let the Brits wash their own dirty linen.

"Shadowmen," Taylor whispered. Wasn't that what Prescott called them? He'd inadvertently shone the spotlight on a whole new pack of them. Unfortunately, nothing could help the immediate problem: finding Peder Crandon before he killed again.

Taylor glanced at his watch: 11:02 P.M. He had to get home to get some sleep before morning.

He began to walk to his office door. Then he remembered something. The Secret Service should be notified about the missiles. That information had been developed since the general's White House meeting.

Moving back to his desk, Taylor picked up the telephone and punched the first four digits of the general's home number. Then he changed his mind. Brayden would only start a new round of negative comments, second-guessing, and team-playing bullshit. He decided to call the Secret Service himself. It would save time and effort all the way around.

Depressing the receiver button, he cleared the line and called COMSEC.

"Get me the Secret Service," he told the operator. "Intelligence Division."

A moment later the connection was made. "Secret Service. I.D." He spoke for three minutes; then Samuel Taylor was on his way home. *Shadowmen,* he thought, wishing he had never heard the term. It seemed as if they just kept coming.

Chapter 55

IN THE DARKNESS, Peder Crandon checked his watch: 11:22 P.M.

Fortunate, he thought. The hole was deeper than he'd originally thought. It was good. The air was getting even colder, and the rain beginning once again. At least the berm offered some protection from the wind. The water he could endure.

Reaching over, he caressed the Strela launcher. Cold. Smooth. As beautiful a weapon as it was wicked. Tomorrow the Strela would propel him toward immortality. Toward his destiny.

Rolling onto his back, Peder Crandon pulled the thick Antarctic-white tarpaulin around his shoulders and stared into the night sky. There was no moon, and the stars were hidden behind a boiling tapestry of wind-raced storm clouds.

The dawn would be overcast and the helicopter flying low. A hot little target on a cool, cool sky. He snuggled deeper into the tarp's warmth and fell asleep.

He was ready for the sun.

For a chopping at dawn.

''We're living in a world of make-believe,'' Catlin said as Taylor walked into his condominium. Finding her there was no surprise. She was still dressed in sweater and jeans, lying on his bed. ''I saw your car downstairs,'' he told her, moving to the kitchen.

''I didn't try to hide it.''

"I know." Reaching into a cabinet, Taylor pulled out a tumbler and poured in two fingers of Jack Daniel's, then opened the freezer and tossed in a handful of ice. "Want a drink?" he asked, walking to the sink to add water.

"I'll sip yours."

"I don't share," Taylor said. Reaching into the cabinet, he pulled out a second tumbler.

"You didn't answer me," Catlin said, as he made her a drink.

"About what?"

"The world of make-believe."

"It seems that way at times," he sighed, sitting down on the bed, handing her the drink. "You pick the lock?"

Catlin nodded. "I was a cat burglar in a previous life."

Taking a deep gulp of the liquor, he said, "I was upset. I really thought you'd gone over."

"Not a chance. I told Michaels to tell you Saint Eloy was calling me."

Taylor shrugged. "I guess I didn't understand. Still don't."

"Go for it," Catlin reminded him. "When we were starting this Crandon thing. You told me Saint Eloy would want me to go for it."

Taylor remembered. "Well Saint Eloy almost got you killed."

"I know," Catlin said softly. "I just can't believe Yasif set that trap at the park. He told me he was taking me to Libya. I'm stupid. I thought I had his confidence."

"It wasn't stupidity, Catlin," Taylor said. "You were too close. What had it been, a year? He had to make sure you were his person. I'd have done the same thing—maybe not a bomb, but something like that if I were bringing an agent in who'd been on the other side for any length of time. He'd have been a fool not to set up some kind of loyalty test."

Catlin took a sip of her drink. "I guess I just underestimated him."

"Like I said, you were too close."

"And Michaels is dead because of it," Catlin said glumly.

Taylor lit a cigarette. "Second place in a two-man race."

For a moment Catlin watched Taylor closely. He was showing no outward signs of emotion stemming from Kelly Michaels's death. She wondered what it was doing to him inside. She decided she had to know.

"Sam?"

"What?"

"If I ask you something, will you level with me?"

Taylor shrugged. "Depends on what it is."

"It's about Michaels. What was the problem between you two? There was friction from the beginning."

Taylor looked at her sharply. "It began a long time ago," he said, draining his drink, then walking to the kitchen for another. "It's not important anymore."

"I think it is."

From the kitchen, Taylor looked back at the bed. He could tell from her eyes she was serious, not just curious. He splashed two fingers of bourbon over the ice and decided that he might as well explain. He wanted someone to know the truth.

"I knew Kelly in Manila," he blurted out. "He was responsible for my wife's death."

Catlin realized she had struck a nerve. "Look, Sam. If this is going to hurt——"

"No," he interrupted. "Let me finish. I want to get all this out in the open and never talk about it again. Okay?"

Catlin nodded.

"Michaels was working for State security. You already know that. Well, he was in Manila for about six months. Same time I was. I'd just got married, and we invited Kelly to our house for dinner. We decided he needed a date to make it a foursome. My wife called her cousin. She and Michaels hit it off, and they started running around together."

Taking a sip of the new drink, Taylor walked back to the bed, sat down, and continued.

''Then I was called away on a job. To Samar, one of the out islands. While I was gone, Kelly decided to take my wife, the cousin, and a younger sister out for drinks. They went to a restaurant in the Panay district south of Manila. They drove. To make a long story short, Panay was ripe with insurgents. Michaels left the car on the street, got drunk, and wanted to stay late. The women wanted to get back to Manila. He gave them the keys. A car bomb killed all three of them. Michaels was only scratched. He told me he was sorry.''

It was a horrible story, Catlin thought. ''Sam,'' she whispered. ''I don't know what to say.''

''Don't say anything yet. There's more. When I got back, I had Michaels transferred out. It was either that or kill him myself. After he left, I began to blame myself for the whole thing. I had introduced Michaels, you know. It began to eat at me. It was all I could think about. The damned guilt.''

Looking over, Taylor stared directly into Catlin's eyes. ''I swore I'd never become involved with another woman until I could make Kelly Michaels pay for what he did.''

He took a drink. ''I never did, Catlin. Yasif did it for me.''

''I'm sorry, Sam.''

''Don't be,'' he sighed. ''It's all a moot point anyhow. The only thing I got out of all that guilt was impotence. Does that surprise you?''

''Yes,'' she lied. Now she understood his aloofness. The reason he never initiated anything. ''But it's all over now.''

Twisting around, Taylor sat up in the bed, his back against the headboard. ''The job's all I have, Catlin. And if I can't pull something out of the hat pretty soon, it doesn't look like I'll be around much longer.''

Finishing her own drink, Catlin said nothing. Within a few moments, she could hear the sound of Taylor's breathing. He had dozed off. Climbing from the bed, she went into the bathroom and shut the door.

But Samuel Taylor slept fitfully. Ten minutes later, the sound of the opening bathroom door jolted him awake. Eyes wide, he lay perfectly still, attempting to identify the noise.

"It's only me," Catlin said softly.

Holding his breath, Taylor jerked his head toward the voice. Silhouetted in the bathroom's back lighting, she was nude with the exception of a thin ribbon of ivory lace panties.

He couldn't think of any words.

Catlin understood. "As long as we're leveling, let's not have any other secrets between us anymore."

"I'm not sure I can handle this, Catlin."

"It won't show," she smiled warmly.

"You sure?"

"I want to be with you, Sam."

"Why?"

"Because you're you."

"I don't understand," he shrugged.

"I don't either," she whispered, walking closer to the bed. "I couldn't even admit it to myself until tonight. Until just a few minutes ago."

"So what do we do now?" Taylor asked.

"Turn a page. Start trusting again."

"Is that why you're doing this? Trust?"

Catlin shook her head. "No, Sam. I care about you. I think this could be all that's missing, that's all."

Taylor knew she was right. "You're a beautiful woman, Catlin. I never even thought of my being——"

"Don't lie to me, Taylor," she said, interrupting him. "Talk to me. Hold me. Let me comfort you."

He undressed slowly, wishing he were twenty years younger. "No promises, Catlin," he said pulling down the sheets and climbing into bed. "Too many of my pages have been burned. You need to know that up front."

Sliding in next to him, Catlin kissed him tenderly on the cheek. "No full court press, Sam. Just us." She ran her hand gently over his muscular body.

Feeling like a teen-ager, Taylor began to awkwardly go through the motions. He desperately wanted to make it work.

"Let's just slow-dance through it," she whispered in his ear, licking his face. "Slow-dance and make some sense out of it all."

Smelling her fresh-washed hair, he pulled her to him, squeezing her tightly. "I don't know if I can, Cat."

"Turn the page, Sam," she breathed, kissing his throat. "It's something we both have to do."

Samuel Taylor felt the stirrings of desire. Moving his hands to her waist, he slowly tugged the panties over the lush hips, thighs, calves, and ankles. He turned over, opening her beneath him, kissing the smooth taut skin of her stomach as his mouth trailed down further.

Her fragrance took his tongue, his throat and then his brain. A parole of long-repressed joy. A need to be fulfilled. It was exciting and prohibitive. Tasting. Caressing. Needing to possess her totally.

Arching her hips, Catlin ground into him. Hands pinioning his face between her parted thighs, her body became a steaming, insatiable entity unto itself.

Pushing, pulling, Catlin rocked into him, his hands guiding, coaxing, raising her up. His mouth becoming her center, her passion his soul.

Hands snaking around his neck, she rose to meet his abandon. Lashed by contractions, her total being ripened into a throbbing caldron.

From deep within, her release evolved, then radiated out in consummate posssesion. Arching, twisting, her body spiraled for a shuddering instant as she teetered on the brink. Then, yielding violently, she convulsed into a long spasm.

Pushing his love-streaked face away from her, Catlin looked into his eyes and saw his love. She experienced the unveiled intensity of his desire. Pulling him up, she kissed his lips, guiding him into her.

Locking her legs around his waist, she pumped with a fury equaling his frenzy, as if they were a human machine, each oiling the other with mutual precision. Only each other in the pleasure of pure, unblemished passion.

And then, as guilt evaporated and their bodies relaxed, they stayed in each other's arms. ''That's not a slow dance, Mr. Taylor!'' she laughed.

By 11:59 P.M. Taylor dreamed of shadowmen.

The Final Morning

At the right moment the right weapon must be employed. One stage is probing the opponent, a second is preparation, a third is assault.

Adolf Hitler
1943

Chapter 56

CURSING THE HOUR, Special Agent Scott Brody eased the car from his driveway and into the predawn darkness of suburban Alexandria, Virginia. A tall, almost pretty man, at thirty-nine, he still retained the blond good looks and physique developed during a youthful stint as a Southern California lifeguard. Only the tan had faded.

Little wonder, he thought dejectedly. It seemed as though every assignment of his seventeen-year career began in the dark and this morning was no exception.

The operant word, he decided, remained *bullshit*.

Assigned to the Washington Field Office of the United States Secret Service, he was to function as the security detail leader for Margaret Thatcher. Entering the expressway for the 40-minute drive to Andrews Air Force Base, he enumerated mentally the stops in the prime minister's itinerary. Hopefully, there would be no problems. The last thing he needed was for something out of the ordinary to happen.

Scott Brody had planned his career with the skill of a watchmaker and now, at last, it looked as though his reassignment to San Diego had been approved. He had paid his dues—two divorces worth—in the New York, to Cleveland, to Washington Field Office shuffle, and now all he cared about was retirement after a few more years of easy Southern California duty. The government owed him that much, at least.

Reaching under the dashboard, he grabbed the radio microphone to check in with the White House Command Post covering the prime minister's visit.

"Crown, Crown, Brody," he said softly.

There was a burst of static as the communications repeater transmitted the response. "Brody, Crown. Go ahead."

"Roger, Crown," he answered. "I'm en route Andrews. Any changes?"

"Brody, Crown. That's negative. Special Branch advises an on-time departure their location."

Clicking the transmit button twice to signal that their message was received, Brody replaced the microphone in its dashboard slot. Good, he thought. At least she was going to be on time. And, thank God, no motorcades. He definitely didn't feel up to any problems. He smiled. Yes, it was going to be an easy trip.

Wheeling his new Buick onto Loop 495, Scott Brody began thinking about the protective responsibilities he was inheriting. Granted, it was a never-ending job; nevertheless, it was also one he thoroughly enjoyed.

From his point of view, the problems of protecting world leaders from assassination, kidnapping, and other forms of violence were certainly nothing new. The only difference was that it had become increasingly more complex following the progress of civilization. Modern communications, transportation, and weapons technology in the hands of would-be assassins posed concerns for the protectors; but, Brody realized, the dagger which stabbed Caesar remained just as deadly as the rifle which killed John Kennedy. In both cases, the results were identical.

Brody exhaled. He couldn't remember who coined the phrase, but its jest was particularly appropriate: *Executive protection was hours of boredom punctuated by seconds of sheer terror.*

After John Hinckley, Jr., "Squeaky" Fromme, it was the perfect summation of his career so far; but if he had to do it all over again, he wouldn't change a thing. Life was too short not to enjoy, and besides, San Diego was only three months away.

Flipping off the headlights, he glanced at his watch: 6:55 A.M. The security briefing was scheduled for seven-thirty and it would be bad form to arrive late. Depressing the accelerator, the Buick surged forward, crossing the Maryland state line and speeding toward Andrews.

When it came to protection, Scott Brody was a martinet. He demanded perfection and expected nothing less from those agents assigned to him.

Nobody would screw up his transfer to San Diego.

He simply wouldn't allow it.

Shivering from the cold, Peder Crandon awoke as the first hint of dawn began its innocent glow on the horizon. Surprisingly, he actually slept through the entire night without the restlessness which had been plaguing him for weeks. He felt rested and filled with anticipation for the day's activities.

Taking a deep breath, he pulled back the tarpaulin, shattering a thin crust of frost. Carefully he surveyed the terrain surrounding his position.

To the south was the twelve-foot, chain-link fence forming the extreme northern perimeter of Andrews Air Force Base. It was exactly two miles away.

To his north was the treeline. He smiled. After firing the missiles, he would retreat the 30 yards to its cover, slipping easily into the shadows of its foliage. Once concealed, he would then change into the dark business suit supplied by the professor and wait for an opportunity to escape.

Peder Crandon realized that an incident of this magnitude—the assassination of the prime minister—would draw a minimum of two representatives from almost every agency in Washington to the crash site. Montes had predicted as much.

The FAA, CIA, FBI, Secret Service, State Department, Air Force, and who knew how many Brits would be tramping around conducting their own investigations. In the confusion, it would be a simple task to blend into the crowd and steal away.

Crandon picked up the small Motorola HT 44 radio sitting next to the Strela launcher. He flipped it on, heard a short burst of static, then the scratchy sound of conversation hissed from its speaker.

"Brody, Brody, Crown."

"Crown, Brody. Go ahead."

"Roger, Brody. Metropolitan Police advises a small crowd of demonstrators gathering in Lafayette Park. No problems at this time."

"That's clear, Crown. Keep me advised."

"Roger, Brody. Crown clear."

Crandon laughed. The Cuban had done well. With the radio he could monitor the Secret Service frequency and, in addition, know exactly what the prime minister was doing. He would also be privy to any suspicious alert or altered plans.

Now all he had to do was wait.

Draining the last of his coffee, Samuel Taylor heard sounds of an approaching helicopter. Catlin heard it as well. Coming from the bathroom wrapped only in a towel, she walked up to him in the kitchen, stood before him and said, "Your ride is here."

Taylor nodded. Since they'd awakened, he had avoided conversation as much as possible. The lovemaking had left him uncomfortable and somehow vulnerable. Catlin sensed it and gave him his space.

It was one of those things that just happened. There was nothing to say until they found out how it would affect their working relationship.

Catlin looked into his eyes. "Be careful, Sam." Involuntarily, she hugged him and released him.

"I'll see you at the section later," he told her, pulling on his jacket and inserting the .45 in a shoulder holster. The warmth of her gesture and his need to be wanted sent a glow through him.

Catlin watched as he walked to the closet and pulled out a

Remington 870 riot shotgun. With a 20″ barrel and magazine extension tube, the old trench gun could hold seven rounds. Maximum effective range: 40 yards—a spray of 27 pellets, each approximately .22 caliber. Taylor had *reappropriated* the weapon during the Vietnam War. It had one purpose; to kill and maim. He had used it before.

Checking the shotgun, he walked to the bedside table and pulled open the bottom drawer. It was crammed with ammunition. He selected two .45 pistol magazines, both loaded, and slipped them into his left jacket pocket. He grabbed a handful of the shotgun shells and placed them in the other pocket.

"I guess that's about it," he said, turning to Catlin.

"I guess," she whispered, averting her eyes.

"Hey," he told her as he pulled on a black L. L. Bean stocking cap. "It'll be fine. Come on, walk with me to the elevator."

Nodding glumly, Catlin, still wrapped in a towel, followed him out of the apartment and down the hall. Reaching the elevators, she turned and looked up into his face. "I feel I should be going with you."

Taylor grinned openly. "You know better than that," he said, caressing her cheek gently with an open hand. "This is what I get all the big bucks for. Besides, you're not dressed for it."

"I know." She kissed his palm. "Just take care of yourself."

The elevator doors opened and Taylor stepped inside. "I will," he said softly as the door slid closed. "See you in a couple of hours."

Pressing the button for the roof's mechanical room, Taylor thought about Catlin. It was like being in high school again. Strange feelings, somewhere between a crush and love. He wondered what she was feeling.

Reaching the roof, Taylor was surprised to find George Washington Bennett standing just on the other side of the opening elevator doors.

"Jesus, captain," he flinched. "You scared the hell out of me."

Bennett grinned, a flash of white against black. "I was just coming to get you."

"Well you found me." Returning his smile, Taylor noticed that Bennett was wearing an issue Beretta automatic. "Artillery?" he asked, noting the weapon.

"You never know," Bennett answered. "And you ain't seen nothing yet."

Following the pilot out of the mechanical room, Taylor immediately understood Bennett's remark.

Squatting ominously at the roof's edge was a helicopter—a different helicopter than the one used for the Annapolis trip. Bennett had exchanged his executive-configuration chopper for a gunship.

Taylor nodded his approval. "Nice touch."

"Yeh," Bennett agreed. "I think so. I borrowed it from a guy over at Fort Lee. I'm supposed to have it back by lunch."

Climbing aboard, Taylor realized that, stripped down, both the executive and the gunship were actually identical models—Sikorsky UH-60A Black Hawks—the replacement for the old Huey which had served so well in Indochina.

Notwithstanding, the differences were readily apparent.

Instead of a shiny green finish, the gunship was painted a flat black with no visible markings. Instead of plush executive seats, this one had only plain canvas slings. And instead of smooth sides, the gunship had twin pintle-mounted, M60D machine guns on either flank. Each 7.62 millimeter weapon was manned by a black-uniformed door gunner whose faces were hidden behind the mirrored visors attached to their flight helmets.

"Where's the copilot?" Taylor asked.

"I'm soloing it," Bennett drawled, climbing into the cockpit and flipping on the ignition trigger switch. "Figured you'd want to ride in the left front."

"Good thinking," Taylor said, squeezing forward between

the two command seats and buckling in on Bennett's left. Watching the young captain busy himself with the starting checklist, Taylor realized that the gunship would have looked more appropriate in some guerrilla war rather than flying around the nation's capitol. But appearances were not the reason for his concern.

In spite of the Black Hawk's firepower, they were still severely outgunned by the missiles. Breathing deeply, he decided not to share his reservations with George Washington Bennett.

"You're a good man, captain," he shouted over the whine of the turbines. "I like your style." Taylor meant it.

"Better safe than sorry," Bennett nodded. "Like I said, you never know."

Before Taylor could respond, Bennett tugged lightly on the cyclic control stick and they were airborne, sweeping out past the Capitol dome, over the eastern fork of the Potomac and rocketing into Maryland.

Ignoring the chill in the cockpit, Taylor sat in the copilot seat and, eyes fixed on the horizon, allowed the deep thwacking of the rotors to get him thinking of Peder Crandon, Eduardo Montes, and their little nest of shadowmen.

"*Tarde o temprano,*" he whispered, totally committed. Sooner or later . . . he'd get them all.

The earpiece squelched in Scott Brody's ear. "Brody, Brody, Crown."

"Crown, Brody. Go ahead," he answered into his sleeve microphone.

"Roger, Brody. FAA liaison advises an estimated arrival your location in forty minutes. Repeat. Four-zero minutes."

"Crown, Brody. That's clear. Copy four-zero."

Looking out over the tarmac at Andrews, Scott Brody studied the two waiting helicopters. Normally used to transport presidential parties on short trips, today the two Sikorsky HH-3Es had been placed at the disposal of the prime minister.

Beautiful aircraft, he thought walking in their direction. Even in the pale overcast morning they gleamed from the hours of waxing and pampering provided by the Marine Air Wing responsible for their maintenance.

Pride of the corps, he knew, moving closer to the helicopters' side and looking up. Painted a deep, dark green, both Sikorskys had the words *United States of America* emblazoned across their fuselage in a brilliant, stark white.

Image, Brody decided. Even to the most cynical observer, there was no doubt as to the power and prestige of the helicopter's passengers. The ultimate political perk.

"Crown, Crown, Brody," he said into the sleeve mike.

"Brody, Crown. Go ahead."

"Roger, Crown. Advise status on demonstration."

"Wait one." There was a short pause; then his earpiece squawked again. "Brody, Crown. Metropolitan Police advises Uniformed Division crowd now numbering approximately seventy. Repeat. Seven-zero. Under control and peaceful. No problems anticipated."

"Copy seven-zero, Crown. Time check?"

"Roger, Brody. ETA your location in approximately, uh . . . wait one. ETA now estimated in thirty minutes. Repeat. Three-zero minutes."

"That's clear, Crown. Copy three-zero."

Almost tenderly, Peder Crandon reached over and pulled the missile launcher closer to him. Rubbing his cheek on it, he whispered softly, reverently, to himself. "Thirty minutes, me lady."

"We've got clearance from Andrews," Bennett shouted over to Taylor. "But we've got to stay away from the NOTAMS vectors and VIP choppers at all times."

Shifting in his seat, Taylor leaned over toward the pilot. "What's our time frame?"

''On station in approximately''—Bennett checked the chronometer''—ten, maybe eleven minutes.'' He cut his eyes to Taylor. ''How do you want it handled?''

Staring out the cockpit window, Taylor answered quickly. ''Well, her jet will be approaching from the south, so let's start south of the main runway with a slow sweep outside the perimeter wire. Once she's on the ground, we can circle the fence on the outside and increase our radius until the choppers lift off.''

''What then?'' Bennett asked.

''Depends on what happens. We'll play it off the cuff.''

Nodding as he pressed the left directional control pedal, Bennett increased the torque and began his descent into Andrews' air space.

''By the way?'' he asked. ''What kind of heat is this dude supposed to be packing?''

''SAM 14s,'' Taylor said flatly. ''Two of them at least.''

Bennett took the news in stride. ''I guess we'll have to get him first.'' It was not a question.

Taylor didn't respond.

''Who's flying lead?'' Scott Brody asked.

''I am,'' answered the tall marine full colonel.

''I'm junior man,'' the freckled, almost chubby major answered good-naturedly.

Brody smiled. He had never know it to be any different.

''Okay, major,'' he said, turning to face the shorter officer. ''I want you to be ready to lift off immediately after everyone boards. You'll be carrying the newsies and the rest of the straphangers, so I expect they'll be dragging ass as usual.''

''Story of my life,'' the pilot nodded.

Brody agreed. ''Anyway, as soon as they get their collective butts in gear, I want you to get moving as soon as the colonel here lifts off with the prime minister. Remember we're on a tight schedule. The networks are televising the South Lawn arrival on a live West Coast feed.''

"I'll smile for the cameras," the major winked.

"Where are you riding?" the colonel asked.

"With the prime minister and you," Brody told him. "Save me a seat backing up to the cockpit.

"You got it," the colonel confirmed.

Brody grabbed for his microphone. "Crown, Crown, Brody."

"Brody, Crown. Go ahead."

"Give me an ETA."

"Roger, Brody. FAA advises an arrival your location in ten minutes. Repeat. One-zero minutes."

"Crown, Brody. That's clear. Copy one-zero."

Turning from the helicopters, Scott Brody began the short walk to the point where the aircraft would stop and the prime minister disembark.

He was glad everything was under control.

With cold precision, Peder Crandon lifted the twenty-pound Strela missile and mated it to the launcher. He was grinning. Although the missile itself was only slightly longer than four feet, it contained a three-stage solid-propellant-fuel rocket and a spin-activated firing device.

As he licked his lips in anticipation, the compact Motorola radio broke its static once again:

"Brody, Brody, Crown."

"Crown, Brody. Go ahead."

"Roger, Brody. Be advised aircraft on final approach."

"Crown, Brody. That's clear. Copy final."

Arming the weapon, Peder Crandon lay down, burrowing deeper into the soft earth and ensuring that the tarp camouflaged his position completely.

Trembling, he waited in silence.

"There she is," Bennett shouted above the noise, pointing to a speck on the southern horizon.

Jerking his head to the right, Taylor searched the sky. He saw it. Rapidly approaching in the distance was the British Airways Concorde containing the prime minister and her official party.

Looming larger, the aircraft's long needle-nose was already tilting downward as the slim white fuselage slowed in preparation for landing.

"Take it down low," Taylor yelled. "Let's sweep the approach pattern on the deck."

Slamming the cyclic control stick forward, Bennett responded immediately, diving the gunship within 20 feet of the snowslick ground. Icefields in motion.

The rotors beating concussions against his ears, Taylor twisted around and looked at the door gunners. Both were leaning far out on the skids, the blurring groundrun flashing cold reflections off their visors as they scanned the area for anything abnormal.

They saw nothing.

"Tower's ordering us away," Bennett shouted, his voice tight.

Taylor's mind clicked. If he was going for the Concorde, the missiles would already be in the air. They weren't.

"Okay," he yelled back. "Parallel the wire on the north end of the base. That's the direction the choppers will go when they move."

Nodding, Bennett dipped the cyclic to the left, banking the Black Hawk to the north. Face set in grim determination, his left hand tightened on the power control sleeve, steadily twisting up the power until the screaming turbines threatened to rip the rotors from their assembly.

"Gut it out, baby," he whispered to himself, twisting out even more torque. "It's gonna be our show now."

Heavily, like some lumbering dinosaur, the Concorde drifted, then touched down, its tires smoking as they grabbed the runaway.

"Crown, Crown, Brody."

"Brody, Crown. Go ahead."

"Roger, Crown. Signal an arrival. My location."

"That's a Roger, Brody. Copy an arrival at eight fifty-eight. We'll make the notifications."

"That's clear, Crown." Turning, Scott Brody walked the 20 yards to the arrival ramp being pushed toward the aircraft. After it was nudged gently into place, he climbed the stairs, waiting as the hatch slid open from the inside.

"Scott Brody, Secret Service," he said, offering his hand to the tall, well-dressed man who greeted him. "Welcome to Washington."

"Basil Chatsworth," the man replied, shaking his hand. "Security. I assume everything is in order?"

Turning, the two men began to descend the stairs; Brody explained the details as they walked.

"I think you'll find everything in order," he said. "You'll be riding in the lead helicopter with the prime minister and myself. Once we arrive at the White House, the prime minister will be greeted by the president and——"

"Agent Brody?" a voice interrupted him.

Reaching the bottom of the stairs, Brody could see a man charging up to him. "I'm Brody," he answered, Chatsworth close at his side.

"So sorry I'm late," the man puffed. "Elliot Prescott . . . Whitehall staff. Do you happen to know what helicopter I'm assigned to ride?"

"Yes, Mr. Prescott," he said, locating Sir Elliot's name. "You'll be on the first one with the prime minister."

Prescott thought for a moment. "If it's all the same to you, I'd much rather travel with the press."

Replacing the manifest in his pocket, Brody shrugged. "That's no problem, Mr. Prescott, but I suggest you board now. We lift off in five minutes."

"Thank you, Agent Brody," Sir Elliot smiled. Then he turned his attention to Chatsworth.

"Chatsworth," he nodded curtly.

"Sir Elliot," Chatsworth responded, his face impassive.

Fussing with his collar, Prescott left the two men, walking quickly toward the helicopters.

"What's his story?" Brody asked out of the corner of his mouth.

"Sir Elliot is a vain man," Chatsworth answered, a knowing smile crossing his face. "With the prime minister, he is a subordinate. With the press . . . a newsmaker. Shall we say, Sir Elliot savors the limelight?"

Brody understood. "Politicians," he mumbled softly as they walked toward the waiting Sikorskys. "Always out for number one."

"They're identical everywhere," Chatsworth added. "Cut from a uniquely self-centered mold."

"Exactly what the world needs," Brody smiled. "More political stars."

"Indeed," Chatsworth chuckled. "But look at it this way, Agent Brody. At least they keep our kind in work."

Thinking of San Diego, Scott Brody agreed. "I suppose they do, Mr. Chatsworth. I suppose they do."

"Anything?" Taylor shouted over the roar of the rotors.

"No," Bennett answered. "Not a damn thing. Just acres and acres of ice and snow."

"Well let's get some altitude," Taylor ordered. "Maybe a different angle will help."

Jerking back on the cyclic, Bennett pulled the gunship into a steep climb, finally leveling off at 400 feet and expanding their search radius.

Staring out the side window, Taylor attempted to put himself in Crandon's mind.

Soon, he thought. Something was going to happen soon. He could almost feel the Irishman's intensity.

Taylor's mind kept shifting the unknown factors.

Where? When? Passing, seconds felt like minutes. Minutes, hours.

* * *

Watching the official party file onto the lead helicopter, Scott Brody glanced over his shoulder toward the second Sikorsky. The press was milling around taking pictures and interviewing aides.

''Fucking newsies,'' he whispered reaching for his microphone. ''Crown, Crown, Brody.''

''Brody, Crown. Go ahead.''

''Roger, Crown. Be advised we have an imminent departure this location. Notify our next site.''

''Brody, Crown. Copy imminent departure. Crown clear.''

The young major stared at the temperature gauge of the chase Sikorsky with increasing concern. Already its needle was flickering into the danger range and the press was still straggling aboard.

Tensing, he realized once airborne, the manifold heat would dissipate; but it had to be soon. If not, he would have to reduce the torque he had been holding for takeofff.

Ugly, he thought. Then he wouldn't be able to lift off, and his ass would really be in a sling with the colonel.

Back to the field, he predicted sullenly, envisioning his career going down the drain.

''Bastards.''

The radio squawked once again:

''Crown, Crown, Brody.''

''Brody, Crown. Go ahead.''

''Roger, Crown. Be advised we have a wheels-up this location. Alert our next stop we are en route.''

''Brody, Crown. Copy your wheels-up at nine-eighteen. I'll make the notifications.''

Pulling off the white camouflage tarp, Peder Crandon blinked as the hazy sunlight flooded his eyes.

''Come to me bitch,'' he grimaced, bringing the launcher

up over the edge of his hole. "Behold the purity of my vengeance."

A crew chief slammed the passenger hatch closed.

"Finally," the major whispered, sighing with relief. The last of his troop was aboard. They could move. Quickly adjusting the collective pitch, he twisted the power control, waiting as the giant rotors slapped the air, sucking for life.

Suddenly, slowly, the ponderous helicopter began to roll, shuddering violently as it picked its way into the sky, racing to catch the lead ship already airborne.

Flipping a switch, the major retracted the wheels. Then, dropping the nose, he allowed the Sikorsky to gather air speed, maneuvering into his assigned slot trailing the Colonel. Finally, set, he relaxed at the controls and glanced out his side window.

"Piece of cake."

Flying in tandem, the two officers piloted the Sikorskys out over the northern perimeter of Andrews Air Force Base.

Continuing to increase their airspeed, the men were careful to maintain the prescribed 200 yards between their helicopters.

It was more than a regulation.

It was a margin for error.

"There," Bennett screamed. "By the tree line."

"God!" Taylor breathed, immediately seeing Crandon crouched on the far side of the Sikorskys. They were too late. He'd been there all the time.

Simultaneously his mind and mouth screamed, "Get him!"

Through sheer instinct, Bennett was already responding. Shoving the cyclic forward, he dove the gunship toward the terrorist, threading the Black Hawk 20 yards beneath and between the two larger Sikorskys.

"Stitch that bastard," he growled, activating the internal microphone with his left foot. "Now!" It was an order.

Following their pilot's command, the two door gunners opened fire, the thin phosphorus tracks of their bullets blistering the sky in long arcing tongues of white-hot metal.

Orangeburn, Taylor thought, ignoring the staccato bursts of the machine guns vibration as he climbed over the seat to the rear compartment, scrambling toward the open door.

Useless at this range, he gripped the shotgun tightly in his left hand and waited for them to close in.

Enraged, he gritted his teeth, ambivalent about the gunners not getting a hit and the need for that pleasure himself.

For Jennifer Bishop.

Taking a deep breath and holding it, Peder Crandon ignited the Strela.

For a millisecond, nothing happened.

Then a click and it was gone. Its route indicated by only a thinly plumed trail of blue white smoke.

He screamed his mother's name.

Chapter 57

THE YOUNG FRECKLE-faced major did not have time to prepare for death. He was destroyed instantly as the Strela's infrared heat-seeking guidance device impartially selected the chase Sikorsky because of its elevated manifold temperature.

Elliott Prescott did not know what was happening. He, too, was cremated instantly, along with twenty members of the press and four Secret Service agents.

In the prime minister's helicopter, neither Scott Brody nor Basil Chatsworth understood. Both security men were speechless as they watched the flaming wreckage of the chase ship plunging toward the earth. Only their pilot fully grasped the situation.

"Missile!" the colonel shouted, slamming the cyclic control forward, plummeting his helicopter down. "Hang on to your asses."

This was not the first time the marine colonel had come under fire. Frequently in Vietnam and later in Grenada, he had been forced to take evasive maneuvers.

SAM missiles. He had cut his teeth on them.

Ten feet off the ground, the colonel jerked back on the cyclic and buried his left foot in the directional control pedal. The Sikorsky responded sluggishly, at first, then, as he adjusted the pitch, the rotors caught heavier air and pulled the machine into a steep, bowel-twisting bank.

The tree line, he thought, glancing to the horizon. *Get to the tree line.*

Twisting the power control sleeve to its limits and stamping on the right control pedal, the colonel simultaneously heaved the cyclic stick to the right and forward. This time the increased airspeed immediately whipped the Sikorsky into a tight fast turn, slinging the helicopter toward the rapidly approaching trees.

"One minute more," he whispered, his mouth dry. Sixty seconds of luck, and they would be home free.

Refusing to blink, he squeezed the controls as he suffered privately. It was agony. The palpable blend of dread tempered with hope.

Biting his lip, he held his breath.

He had run this race before.

George Washington Bennett aimed his gunship directly at the terrorist.

Crandon laughed openly. Ignoring the tracers pocking the ground ice around him, he had already reloaded the launcher for his attempt at the remaining Sikorsky.

"My chalice, my chalice, my chalice," he screamed, his mind awash with twisted visions of charred flesh as he leaped out of his hole, preparing for the second shot.

"Chop-pence, chop-pence, chop-pence."

Watching Crandon from the Black Hawk's open door he shouted, "Let me out," as Bennett rocketed ten feet over the terrorist's head.

Completing the first strafing run, Bennett banked the gunship to a stall as he prepared to turn back and begin another.

"Hit it!" he yelled to Taylor as the Black Hawk reached the apex of arch, nearly stopping in the air.

Out on the skid, Taylor looked at the ground below. Fifteen feet and little forward movement—no worse than leaping off the top of a rolling moving van.

Gripping the trench gun tightly, he jumped to the frozen ground.

With Taylor out, Bennett whipped the tail of the gunship around, lowered its nose, and accelerated back toward Crandon.

Teeth bared in a fixed grimace, he activated the Black Hawk's intercom system, listening to the door gunners as they tore at the terrorist's position with long bursts of sustained fire.

One was praying. The other singing. Hail Marys blending in harmony with an off-key rendition of "Dixie." They were good men. Bennett hovered the gunship directly over Crandon's head and allowed the gunners to take him.

George Washington Bennett never got the chance.

Peder Crandon realized two things. First, the remaining Sikorsky was almost out of range and secondly, if he didn't do something, the gunship would thwart his escape plans.

Calmly, precisely, he turned and aimed the second Strela at the small helicopter.

Observing the terrorist through the thin Plexiglas windshield, George Washington Bennett had a thought. At that exact moment, he realized he was going to die.

Closing in on the terrorist he did not waiver; neither did the gunners. Even as the puff of smoke indicated the missile's launch, he continued to charge ahead, not even aware of the fear gnawing at his brain.

"You asshole," he hissed. "Rot in hell."

It was over a moment later.

Bursting in flames, the sky exploded directly over Samuel Taylor's left shoulder as the Black Hawk was destroyed.

"Shit!" he breathed, rolling away from the wreckage. Where was the bastard? He had to pinpoint Crandon's position before he could move.

He half-stood, pumped a shell into the shotgun, and fired a round in Crandon's general direction.

The boom of the trench gun was answered immediately by a long burst of automatic fire from Crandon's Ingram. *Good guess,* Taylor thought. Falling back into the slush, he scratched for cover as the bullets split the air around him.

Peder Crandon considered his options. He had to get to the tree line. His escape route. Firing another short burst toward Taylor, he stretched out flat and started a slow crawl across the thin patch of open ground to the shadows of the trees.

Watching, Taylor could clearly see where Crandon was heading, and he decided to outflank him. Crouching, he began to run, pumping the shotgun and firing a round toward Crandon every third time his left foot hit the ground. If he could reach the tree line first, Crandon would be isolated and in the open. Then he could kill him.

Samuel Taylor never made it to the trees.

Reloading the Ingram, Peder Crandon rose and began firing with one hand, while charging directly toward Taylor. One of the Ingram's bullets glanced off Taylor's left hip and spun him around.

Taylor twisted as he fell over and saw Crandon running directly at him.

Thirty yards. Twenty-five. Twenty. Pumping the last shell into the trench gun, Taylor fired without hesitation.

Click—nothing.

The shotgun was jammed. It had been hit by a stray Ingram round. Tossing it to the side, Taylor ignored the pain in his hip, jerked out the .45, and snapped off five rounds without aiming. At 12 yards, two hit. One low, at the juncture of the terrorist's thigh and groin. The other, one inch above the bottom tip of the sternum.

The .45's relatively slow moving 230-grain bullets had slammed into Peder Crandon's body with the one-two punch of a pneumatic jackhammer. Screaming, he was thrown back 8 yards and tossed to the ground like a punctured balloon.

No new Beretta 9 millimeter packed that kind of knockdown power, Taylor thought. He'd take the .45 any day of the week.

Pulling himself to his feet, Taylor limped over to Crandon.

He had two questions. He needed two answers before Crandon

could die. With the automatic stuck out in front of him. Taylor inched closer.

"Crandon," he hissed.

Eyes glazing, the Irishman looked up blankly, seemingly unable to comprehend as his blood pumped onto the snowy ground.

"Listen to me, Crandon."

"It is my chalice," Crandon answered, dipping his fingers in the blood and holding them before his eyes. "It is my chalice and my wine is warm."

Taylor ignored the rambling. "The coins?" he asked. "Why the coins?"

"Coins?" Crandon giggled. Tiny bloodcoughs at best. "Pence or chopping. Chopping or pence. Ursula told me so. I love my mother."

Staying five yards away, Taylor squatted down. "What do they mean? What do the pence pieces mean?"

Blood now dripping from his nose and the corners of his mouth, Crandon began to nod. "Ten pence a bullet. A bullet ten pence. My mother had bullets, ten pence apiece."

Then, quite unexpectedly, he began to sob openly. "I loved my mother. They chopped her with bullets. Ten pence for a bullet. Ten bullets for mother. They will pay. I will see."

Taylor understood. The ammunition used by the British to kill Crandon's mother cost ten pence a round. *God,* he thought. *If they only knew what they had started.*

Standing again, Taylor looked down on the Irishman. The man was hopelessly insane. "The basement?" he asked. "Who was in the basement? Who killed Yasif?"

Crandon, still crying softly, glanced up. "A friend," he whispered. Then, raising his head, he looked back beyond Taylor and smiled. "Here is my friend . . . he comes again . . . he will . . . "

At that moment, Peder Crandon's chest, neck and face exploded before Taylor's eyes, followed instantly by the delayed sound of the UZI ripping through the air.

Wheeling around to face the gunman, Taylor realized his suspicions had been correct. He was more angered than surprised.

"I was going to have you arrested later this morning," Taylor said coldly, aiming the .45 at Thomas Brayden's mouth.

Holding the UZI against Taylor's middle, the general smiled. "What gave it away?"

"I called the Secret Service last night. You never were at the White House. The president was at the Kennedy Center all evening, and the Secret Service hadn't heard a word about Crandon. You never went."

Brayden shrugged. "I had another engagement."

"But why you?" Taylor asked. "Surely de las Marias has other people who could do the job."

"He does," the general answered. "Unfortunately, none who could explain their presence at the scene if something went wrong."

Pistol still aimed at Brayden, Taylor began to circle to his right. "When did they recruit you, general? After Korea? When you were assigned to the military liaison mission in Madrid?"

Following Taylor with the UZI's muzzle, Thomas Brayden began to chuckle. "You've been doing your homework."

"What about Prescott? Your side?"

The general shook his head. "No," he said flatly. "Prescott was a British agent. A pathetic one, at that."

As Brayden talked, Taylor's mind clicked rapidly, trying to figure out a way to shoot the general without getting shot himself. At 10 yards, his .45 was no match for an UZI automatic. If he missed, it would be the last shot he would ever fire. Brayden would rip him apart. But what other choice did he have? He needed a distraction.

"You're the worst kind of scum," he taunted, hoping to rile the general into doing something stupid, leaving himself open.

Brayden shook his head calmly. "An interesting observation,

Taylor, but quite worthless. What with you and Crandon now out of the picture, I will write the report. Once in writing, my story becomes fact.''

A brief smile crossed the general's face. ''You should have taken the medical retirement, Sam. Now you'll never have the chance. Good-bye, Sam. Your services are no longer——''

''Taylor?'' a voice shouted from the tree line, ''You okay?''

Thomas Brayden whirled instinctively, firing the UZI in a wide arc toward the general direction of the voice.

Samuel Taylor did not hesitate. He fired three quick shots from his old Colt. The bullets found their marks in the general's stomach, chest, and face.

''Bastard!'' he whispered, watching Brayden's body slump to the ground.

''Taylor?'' the voice called again. ''Are you all right?''

''Over here,'' he called back, reloading the .45 in case any new shadowmen popped out from somewhere.

None did. A moment later, Catlin appeared, walking cautiously through the scrub brush as, in the distance, the sound of the rescue helicopters from Andrews began to beat across the open field.

''The general?'' Catlin asked, staring incredulously at Thomas Brayden's prostrate form.

''He was a Soviet agent,'' Taylor told her. ''He'd been one for over thirty years.''

Catlin was stunned by the news, but before she responded, she noticed Taylor's bleeding hip. ''You're bleeding, Sam,'' she said, running to his side.

''It missed the bone,'' he smiled weakly. ''But it hurts like hell.''

Suddenly they were washed with rotorwind as the first medivac chopper swooped down, blades popping as it flared to a landing.

''Let's get out of here,'' he told her, limping toward the helicopter. ''I want to get to Bethesda, get this thing taken care of, and get back to the section. We've got a lot of loose ends to tie up."

"But my car is over there on the highway," Catlin said.

"Forget the car," he told her, climbing aboard the helicopter, "I want you with me."

"What about this mess here?" Catlin said, climbing aboard and sitting next to him.

Taylor looked out on the field. Splashing through the slush, more emergency vehicle were racing toward the crash sites. And in the sky four other helicopters were already airborne. "Our job's finished here," he told her. "The rest is all paperwork and creative writing."

Sighing heavily, Taylor leaned forward and spoke to the pilot. "Where's the prime minister?" he asked.

"The White House," the man answered.

"Good," Taylor told him. "Get me to Bethesda."

As the medivac chopper powered up, lifting into the cold gray sky, Taylor surveyed the burning carnage below. *I'm sorry, Jennifer Bishop,* he thought. *This really wasn't your war.*

After a moment, he turned to Catlin. "You sure you still want to be part of all this?" he asked. "It gets kinda mixed up at times."

"You still want me in?"

Taylor arched an eyebrow. "I'm not sure," he teased. "What would Saint Eloy say?"

Catlin smiled warmly. "He'd say, 'Go for it.' "

They did.

Epilogue

We are but warriors for the working day. Our gayness and our guilt are all besmirched with rainy marching in the painful field.

William Shakespeare
1598

IN THE WEEKS after the assassination attempt, there was a groundswell of public speculation as to the cause of the 'copter crash. It became a problem which forced a White House response.

The president, with the advice and consent of the prime minister, effectively quashed all rumors indicating that the helicopter had been destroyed by a Soviet missile. In a nationally televised news conference, the president released the findings of a blue-ribbon panel which had investigated the "accident."

Chaired by the vice-president, experts on the panel from the United States and Great Britain testified under oath and agreed that, based upon their independent evaluations, the Sikorsky HH-3E exploded as a direct result of a ruptured copper valve in the fuel coolant system.

Two days after the president's address, a spokesman for Sikorsky Aircraft Corporation made a public announcement stating that the corporation would replace the entire coolant system on any HH-3E helicopter in service.

The spokesman made no attempt to refute the findings of the experts.

Three months after the incident, Sikorsky Aircraft submitted sealed bids to the Department of Defense for seventy additional HH-3Es which were earmarked for NATO service.

They were awarded the contract within twelve hours.

* * *

Samuel Taylor was immediately promoted to the position previously held by General Thomas Brayden, and Catlin to Taylor's old position.

Two weeks after assuming her new duties, Catlin activated the PCAC interactive processing system and began clandestine retrieval of raw intelligence data from the computer memories of several Middle Eastern governments.

The system functioned flawlessly.

The Islamic nations continued to squabble among themselves. However Libya, with Triad consent, struck back against the Israelis after being told by KGB representatives in Tripoli that Tel Aviv was responsible for Yasif's death. At the end of March, they truck-bombed the Israeli embassy in Rome. The final tally was twenty dead and thirty-seven injured.

The Israelis responded by assassinating Hadi al-Haffad, Yasif's replacement to the United Nations Mission.

And so it continued.

The Soviets maintained an unusually low profile regarding the entire Crandon matter. They neither claimed any knowledge of his activities, nor offered any observations on his death.

Antonio de las Marias never returned to Spain. The day following the Andrews Air Base tragedy, he disappeared, only to surface some six months later, living quietly at a palatial estate on a lovely stretch of Adriatic seacoast just south of Dubrovnik, Yugoslavia.

Defecting from Spain, he had been given political asylum by the Communist-controlled government.

Soviet intentions in Great Britain came to a grinding halt by the joint announcement regarding the building of the STEALTH bombers in England. People returned to work, the economy rebounded, and membership in the Conservative party reached an all-time high.

The strikes never took place.

The names Thomas Brayden and Peder Crandon were added to the passenger manifest for the Sikorsky helicopter destroyed by the missile.

Brayden was given a hero's burial at Arlington National Cemetery.

Crandon was cremated, his ashes dumped unceremoniously into the frigid waters of the Potomac River by an army corporal.

Kelly Michaels was also cremated. However, his ashes were personally carried to Bottle Key by Taylor and given to Mai Lei. True to his promise, Taylor attempted to help Mai Lei. She wanted American citizenship. She had it in two weeks. Samuel Taylor also offered Mai Lei a position in the section.

She said she would let him know.

The destruction of George Washington Bennett's gunship was listed officially as pilot error. Unofficially, rumors circulated that Bennett was a coward and had panicked when the Sikorsky crashed so close to his position. Within six months, Taylor would arrange for a silver star and an increase in rank for Bennett. It would help his family.

Because of the system, Special Agent Scott Brody was transferred to Detroit. He spent the remainder of his career at a desk interviewing mentally unstable people who wrote threatening letters to the White House.

He continued to dream of San Diego, and, with Detroit's weather being what it is, he watched his tan fade.

Basil Chatsworth returned to London with the prime minister, was promoted, and spent the remainder of his career advising the technicians who manufactured "specialized" equipment for British Intelligence.

He was able to provide considerable insight into the workings of the human mind.

Eduardo Montes never returned to Washington. He had no place to live. On the afternoon of the crash, federal authorities, armed with a warrant, seized his residence in the Maryland countryside, searched it, and arrested Sylvio.

A sizable cache of arms was found buried on the grounds. Sylvio was returned to Haiti and executed for previous crimes. The maid was retained for the new occupants.

By summer, with nobody to question the proceedings, the former residence of Eduardo Montes had been converted into a property of the United States Government. Specifically, the new home of the Special Projects Section.

Moving everything into the large mansion, Taylor and Catlin also lived there. They shared a bedroom.

To actually run and organize the day-to-day operations of the mansion, Taylor selected another person: Miss McThorn. At first, Miss McThorn objected to Taylor and Catlin's living arrangements, but it was resolved when Catlin brought her a case of chocolate-covered cherries. They became fast friends.

As for Montes's BMW, Catlin appropriated it for her own use. Taylor kept his Blazer, and McThorn took the antique sports car.

Eduardo Montes was not located during the first seven months. However, within a year, another RAINDANCER contingency would bring the Cuban and Taylor together again.

The location would be South America.

The *mariposa* had finally landed.

The details of the London Letter were never revealed.